The Promised Lie

The Unwritten Words I

ALSO BY CHRISTOPHER G. NUTTALL

The Mind's Eye

Bookworm series
Bookworm
Bookworm II: The Very Ugly Duckling
Bookworm III: The Best Laid Plans
Bookworm IV: Full Circle

DIZZY SPELLS SERIES
A LIFE LESS ORDINARY

Royal Sorceress series
The Royal Sorceress
The Great Game
Necropolis
Sons of Liberty

INVERSE SHADOWS UNIVERSE
SUFFICIENTLY ADVANCED TECHNOLOGY

The Promised Lie

The Unwritten Words I

Christopher G. Nuttall

Elsewhen Press

The Promised Lie
First published in Great Britain by Elsewhen Press, 2018
An imprint of Alnpete Limited

Elsewhen Press, PO Box 757, Dartford, Kent DA2 7TQ
www.elsewhen.press

British Library Cataloguing in Publication Data.
A catalogue record for this book is available from the British Library.
ISBN 978-1-911409-21-2 Print edition
ISBN 978-1-911409-31-1 eBook edition

Designed and formatted by Elsewhen Press

To my second son, John, who made his appearance
as this book was being drafted.

The Summer Isle
Cold Harbour
Northern Realm
The Narrows
Georgetown
Galdsworth Lands
Horsford Lands
Wild Mountains
Temple of Dusk
Allenstown
Racal's Bay
Summer Bay
Racal River
Wildlands
Oxley Lands
Andalusia
Havelock

Prologue

The valley was dark and cold and as silent as the grave.

Lord Havant of Hereford glanced from side to side, warily, as his guide led him further down the rocky path. He'd been warned, time and time again, that the forbidden lands were forbidden for a reason ... that they were dangerous, rather than places the Grand Sorcerers preferred to keep to themselves. Walking into the valley bothered him on a very primal level, even though his rudimentary magic sensed no threat. There was something about the cold seeping into his bones that urged him to flee.

He banished the feeling with an effort, drawing his cloak tighter around his body. He'd expended a great deal of effort on crossing the Wild Mountains – far too close to the Goldenrod Lands for comfort – to back out now, despite the sensation of danger that pervaded the dark air. Hark had told him, time and time again, that the ancient temple was the only place they could perform the rite and Havant believed him. The monk knew better than to lie to the heir to an earldom.

The shadows seemed to shimmer as they reached the bottom, revealing a strange building hidden within the darkness. He couldn't quite *see* it, as if there were a spell concealing its precise dimensions. All he could make out were impressions: strange towers, dark runes on the walls, stone statues positioned by the entrance ... and a faint light that seemed to come from everywhere and nowhere. His guide didn't hesitate. He walked past the statues and through the entrance as if he didn't have a care in the world. Havant knew himself to be a brave man – he'd led his brother's forces in war – but it took all of his courage to follow the guide into the building. The urge to flee was growing stronger and stronger all the time.

Inside, the building was empty, save for a single stone

altar. The light grew stronger, radiating out of the stone walls. Hark was standing on the other side of the chamber, his hood pulled back to reveal his long beard and stern features. His dark eyes flashed with a fanatical determination that made him seem a different man. Havant had to force himself to look back, evenly. He was the master outside the building. He could be the master inside, too.

"You have come," Hark said. His voice boomed in the shadows. "Did you bring the blood?"

"I did," Havant said.

He reached into his pocket and produced the tiny vial. It had been his sister, Queen Emetine, who'd obtained the blood. Her husband's guard had slipped, just once. Perhaps Emetine felt guilty for what she'd done, or for what she'd set in motion. But it didn't matter. Emetine had failed in the first duty of a queen and it was only a matter of time before her husband put her aside for someone younger, prettier and fertile. A childless royal marriage simply couldn't be allowed to last.

And then it will be just a matter of time until the civil war resumes, Havant thought. His family couldn't afford another round of strife. They'd worked hard to secure their position and he had no intention of losing it. *We have to strike first.*

Hark walked forward and took the vial, then snapped his fingers. Monks started to walk into the chamber, the shadows moving around them like living things ... as if the monks were themselves shadows. Their faces were hidden completely behind their cowls, lost in the darkness. They made no noise as they moved. Havant couldn't even hear them *breathing*. It was easy to believe, just for a moment, that they weren't truly human. Suddenly, all of the strange tales about the forbidden zone seemed terrifyingly believable.

"Ours is the gift of death," Hark said. His voice echoed in the chamber. "We offer it freely to those who wish it."

Another hooded figure stepped out of the shadows and walked towards the altar, then stopped and removed her robe. Havant stared, despite himself, as the robe pooled around her bare ankles. She was naked, old enough to wed yet untouched by life; her face both enchantingly sweet and strangely alien. There were no blisters on her body, no hints of a hard life on the farms. She showed no sign of feeling ashamed or vulnerable, even though most girls on the Summer Isle were raised to keep their clothes on at all times. The sense of wrongness grew stronger as the girl climbed onto the stone altar and lay on her back. Havant could feel ... *something* ... drifting in the air, a *presence* waiting to be born. The entire world seemed to be holding its breath.

"Death is our gift," Hark said.

He unstopped the vial and poured the blood onto the girl's chest. She didn't move, even when he dipped his crooked finger in the blood and used it to draw lines and runes on her body. Havant wondered, suddenly, if she'd been drugged or enchanted. There were plenty of spells and potions that would account for the girl's calm. And yet ...

"Mighty Dusk," Hark said. "We ask for Your blessing. We ask for Your gift. We ask for Your guidance as we work for Your day."

"Death is our gift," the monks said.

The sense of presence grew stronger. Havant watched, feeling almost as if he was floating outside his own body, as Hark withdrew a silver knife from his robes. Something told Havant that he should be alarmed, but ... he felt calm, utterly unmoved. And then Hark raised the knife up and held it above the girl's chest.

"Death is our gift," he said, once again.

He stabbed down, hard. The girl cried out, once. Blood splashed in all directions. The presence grew even stronger, pressing against the boundaries of reality ...

... And, four hundred miles away, King Edwin of the Summer Isle screamed and died.

Chapter One

"Well?"

Isabella ignored Big Richard's rather snappy demand as she concentrated on the village in the distance, reaching out with her senses. It was a small village, forty miles from the nearest town: fifteen hovels, a blacksmith's forge, a hedge-witch's home and very little else, all surrounded by patchwork fields. It should have been teeming with life – men working in the fields, women and children tending the animals – but it was deserted. She couldn't pick up a *hint* of life.

Big Richard snorted, rudely. "Performance issues?"

"No," Isabella said, tartly. She concentrated. There was *something*, right at the edge of her awareness. A sense of ... *something*. She couldn't put it into words. "There doesn't seem to be anyone in the village."

"Magicians," Big Richard sneered. "Always coming up with excuses for failure."

"There's no one within eyeshot, either," Little Jim pointed out. "Or can you see something the rest of us can't?"

Big Richard made a rude sound. Isabella looked at him, then his brother. It was hard to believe they were related, even though they had the same eyes. Big Richard was a short, but beefy man, so muscular that Isabella rather suspected he had some orc blood in him somewhere, carrying a massive axe slung over one shoulder. His brother, by contrast, was tall and slim. The only thing they had in common was red hair ... and a prejudice against magic-users. Big Richard hadn't made any bones about distrusting *anyone* who used magic, Isabella included. If Lord Robin hadn't insisted on Isabella joining the company, Big Richard would have tried to drive her away.

Which wouldn't have been easy, Isabella thought. The protective amulets Big Richard wore were effective, against hedge-witches. *She'd* been taught ways to get spells through basic protections, ways to curse someone who thought he was safe. *And yet, that would have probably cost me my job too.*

She rolled her eyes as the two men turned back towards the deserted village. She'd been with the company for six months and she knew, despite everything, that she'd been lucky. Female mercenaries were rare, even in troubled times. And while she had proven herself to Lord Robin, she was aware that too many of the other mercenaries distrusted her. They knew very little about her past.

And if they did know about my past, she reminded herself, *they'd distrust me even more.*

Very few people would have recognised her, even if they'd heard her name. Isabella was hardly a *common* name, but it wasn't *that* uncommon. Her close-cropped black hair, scarred face and form-fitting brown leathers – complete with a sword, a knife and a wand – were very different from the clothes she'd worn years ago, in another life. No one would draw a connection between her and the Isabella who'd left the Golden City, seven years ago. And that was how she wanted it to be.

Lord Robin cantered up and smiled at them. He was a handsome man, Isabella admitted privately, with short blond hair and shining armour. And he was a good leader, one strong enough to rule a band of mercenaries and yet smart enough to *listen* to their concerns. She had no idea if he truly was an aristocratic bastard or not – he was the only person who called himself a lord – but it hardly mattered. There were countless noblemen seeking real power now the Empire was gone.

"I can't sense anything," Isabella said. There was no point in telling him about the feeling at the back of her mind. If she couldn't pinpoint it, no one would take it seriously. "I think the village is deserted."

"Probably hiding from the taxman," Robin said. "King Romulus has been squeezing his peasants pretty hard over the last few months, hasn't he?"

He raised his voice. "Mount up!"

Isabella nodded as she scrambled up into her horse's saddle

and followed the others down the dusty road towards the village. The heat grew stronger, a grim reminder that everything – even the weather – was in flux these days, as if the final days had come. Her eyes narrowed as she glanced from side to side. Too many streams intended to water the fields had run dry, leaving the crops spoiled. Even the millpond looked painfully shallow. She wondered, sourly, if Robin was right. The villagers had plenty of reason to know that drought was not an acceptable excuse for not paying their taxes. Perhaps they'd decided to hide somewhere in the countryside rather than pay.

And a tax collector vanished out here, she reminded herself. *That's why Lord August hired us to investigate.*

She looked up as they approached the gate. The palisade wasn't anything more than a boundary marker – it wouldn't have stood up to a battering ram, let alone a spell – but there should have been someone on guard. Villagers tended to be suspicious of strangers, particularly ones who might be taxmen or recruiting sergeants. And yet ... they cantered through the open gate and into the village, heading straight for the headman's hut. The village was deserted, utterly deserted. Isabella felt her sense of unease growing stronger. Something was very definitely wrong.

"He should have come out to grovel by now," Mandan said. The archer was looking from side to side, his eyes worried. He had good instincts, for someone who didn't have any spark of magic. "Where *is* he?"

"Probably hiding all the comely lasses," Big Richard said. "Wouldn't it be a shame if one of them took a liking to us?"

Isabella silently contemplated the virtue of stealthily hexing his horse as she swung her legs over and dropped to the ground. Dust rose around her boots as she landed. Mandan was right, damn him. *Someone* should have come running by now, if only to plead for mercy or swear blind they didn't know what had happened to the taxman. Maybe the villagers *had* gone into hiding. Lord August wasn't known for his mercy. The village would be destroyed if they dared to lift a hand against him and his servants.

"Isabella, with me," Lord Robin ordered. "The rest of you, guard the horses and *wait*."

"Aye, sir," Little Jim said.

Isabella felt Big Richard's eyes on her as she followed Lord Robin up to the headman's hovel. It was a large hut, compared to the others, but tiny by her standards. She pushed her senses forward as Lord Robin opened the door and peered inside, yet she sensed nothing ... save for the strange *something*. It was there, right at the back of her mind ...

"Deserted," Lord Robin said.

Isabella entered the hovel and looked around, feeling old training and instincts coming to the fore. The headman's chair – a rickety construction that allowed him to look down on his fellows – sat in the centre of the otherwise barren room. She felt her eyes narrow as she pushed aside the curtain to peer into the kitchen, where the headman's wife would have cooked for her husband. It was large enough to suggest that the woman had probably also held court, inviting the other women to chat with her in the evenings. Shaking her head, Isabella scrambled up the ladder into the loft. There was enough bedding to suggest that the headman and his wife had had at least two children.

Perhaps more, she thought. *They would have shared bedding as soon as they were old enough to sleep away from their parents.*

She shuddered, despite herself. She'd slept in all sorts of places, since she'd left home, but she hated the thought of having no privacy, day in and day out. A slave pen would be kinder, she thought. And yet, none of the villagers would have known any better. The children would grow up, marry the girl or boy next door, then have children of their own. The headman's kids wouldn't be considered any better than anyone else's children. Her lips twitched in cold amusement. The village simply wasn't big enough to support an aristocracy.

And they'd probably hate the thought of marrying someone from the next village, she considered. Villages could be remarkably insular. *Even somewhere five miles away might be too far for them.*

Pushing the thought aside, she searched the upper floor. It was uncomfortably warm and stuffy, worse than anything in the Golden City. She hoped it got cooler at night. A handful of clothes – shirts and trousers, long dresses that had been patched so extensively that she doubted there was anything left of the original garment – were piled in one corner. No underwear, of course; underwear was a luxury. A set of smaller clothes – she guessed the children were somewhere between five and seven, judging by the sizes – and a handful of padded cloths. There wouldn't be anything saved for later, she knew. The villagers would pass clothes around when the original owner didn't need them.

But there was nothing to suggest what might have happened to the villagers. She took one last look around, feeling a flicker of sympathy for the headman's family, then walked back to the ladder and clambered down.

Lord Robin met her at the bottom. "Anything?"

"Deserted," Isabella said, curtly. "And nothing useful at all."

"It looks as though they left some time ago," Lord Robin said. "The food on the table wasn't abandoned today."

Isabella nodded as they walked back outside into the bright sunlight. It was hard to be sure, but Lord Robin was right. It didn't *look* as though the villagers had seen the mercenaries coming and fled in all directions. Come to think of it, it didn't look as though the villagers had planned their exodus either. They hadn't taken their clothes or tools, particularly the tools that would be hard to replace. It wasn't the Golden City. A decent axe might cost a villager more money than he earned in a decade.

"Richard, Jim, check out the north side of the village," Lord Robin ordered. "Isabella, go with them. If you find anything, call me at once."

Big Richard opened his mouth. "Sir ..."

"That's an order," Lord Robin said, sharply. "Do as you're told."

Isabella shrugged as the two men headed towards the north side of the village. She'd worked with people she hadn't liked – or hadn't liked her – before, although there was something deeply *personal* about Big Richard's dislike that bothered her. She was fairly sure she'd never seen him before. And she was certain he didn't know anything about her past. He would have told the entire company if he'd known the truth. Unless he thought he could blackmail her ...

Nah, she thought. *He's too dumb for blackmail.*

The hovels were empty, completely empty. They made their way from hut to hut, finding nothing but faint signs suggesting that the occupants had left in a hurry. Isabella kept a silent tally of everything they'd left behind, puzzling over just how much had been abandoned to the elements. Even if the villagers *were* hiding somewhere within the countryside, they should have come back to recover their tools. If worse came to worst, they could sell them to raise funds.

Big Richard spun around, drawing his axe. "I saw something move," he said. "I saw it!"

Isabella frowned. There was nothing ... nothing, save for the odd background sensation. And yet, Big Richard looked spooked. He was holding his axe at the ready, his eyes moving from side to side as if he expected an attack at any moment. Little Jim looked concerned too, his hand resting on the pommel of his sword. Isabella wasn't sure if he was worried about a mystery attacker, or his brother waving the axe around in a confined space.

"I can't sense anything," she said, slowly. And yet, she knew that might be completely meaningless. There were ways to hide from a magician's senses. "What did you see?"

"I saw ... I don't know what I saw," Big Richard said. "It was ... just *there*."

His piggy eyes narrowed. "And you can't sense *anything*?"

"Not really," Isabella said. And yet, *something* was nagging at the back of her mind. "Shall we go outside?"

The sunlight seemed brighter, somehow, as they stepped out of the hut. She looked around, noting the abandoned pigpen and chicken run. The villagers wouldn't have abandoned their animals, not when they needed the beasts for their own survival. And ... her eyes narrowed as something clicked in her mind. There was no life at all within the village. No birds sang in the trees, no insects buzzed through the air ... the village was dead.

"There's one more building to check," she said, nodding to the hedge-witch's hut. "And then we'll go back to the others."

The two men didn't make any rude remarks as they

followed her to the hut. They *were* spooked. Isabella paused as she reached the wooden door, reaching out – once again – with her senses. There should have been a locking spell or two on the door, perhaps a sneaky transfiguration spell on the knob. Hedge-witches lacked the formal training of sorcerers who went to the Peerless School, but that didn't stop them studying magic. Or sharing knowledge, despite the law. And yet ... there was no magic protecting the hut. If the door hadn't been covered in carved runes, she would have wondered if it *really* belonged to a hedge-witch or merely someone trying to compete with the headman.

"No protections," she mused. "I wonder ..."

She pushed the door open, gingerly. The interior was dark, too dark. She cast a light-spell, revealing a wooden table, a cauldron perched over a burnt-out fire and a shelf of potion ingredients. There didn't seem to be anything too exotic, let alone forbidden, within eyeshot, but that meant nothing. She knew from grim experience that anything forbidden, anything that would bring the Inquisitors down on the hedge-witch like Richard's axe, would be carefully hidden. And yet ...

Richard poked her, roughly. "What is that?"

Isabella bit down a sharp remark – she knew he expected her to show some reaction – and followed his pointing finger. A tree – a small tree – was growing in a wooden pot, its branches reaching up towards the ceiling. Her eyes narrowed as the background sensation grew stronger. The tree, whatever it was, wasn't just out of place. It was ... *wrong*.

"I don't know," she said. The back of her neck started to prickle. Every instinct she had told her to back away from the tree as quickly as possible. "I think ..."

"There's another one," Little John said, sharply. He jabbed a finger towards the rear of the building. "I ..."

Isabella forced herself to keep looking at the tree. It seemed to loom larger and larger, as if it was somehow more *real* than any of them. And then ... she thought, just for a second, that it had moved. Something was very wrong ...

She yelped as something snapped onto her right wrist. For a moment, she thought Richard had grabbed her ... and then she looked down. A tree branch had wrapped itself around her wrist, a tree branch that had grown out of the wooden walls. She reached for her magic, trying to cast a spell, only to have the magic flicker and snap out of existence. The branch tugged a second later, pulling her towards the wall. Both trees were growing now, turning into a nightmarish vision of tentacles reaching for the human intruders. A defensive spell? She'd never seen – or heard – of anything like it.

Another branch grabbed her left wrist, an instant before she could draw her sword. She tried to cast another spell, but the magic simply refused to form ... no, it faded almost as soon as she drew on it. The branches yanked her forward ...

Little Jim lashed out with his sword, cutting through both of the branches. The wood around Isabella's wrists went limp, falling to the ground. Isabella drew her sword as she looked desperately from side to side, trying to find a way out of the chamber. The door was gone, replaced by a writhing mass of tree branches that were growing at terrifying speed. She looked up, just in time to see more branches reaching down towards them.

Richard grabbed her shoulder. "Use magic," he shouted, as he swung his axe at the nearest branches. Pieces of wood flew in all directions, but the mass came on. "Get us out of here!"

"I can't," Isabella snapped back. Her magic seemed to have completely deserted her. She couldn't muster the power to cast even a simple spell. The light was already failing. "It isn't working."

"Fucking useless," Richard snarled at her. "I ..."

Little Jim pulled a bottle out of his back and splashed the contents on the nearest piece of wood. Isabella barely had a second to realise what he intended to do before he snapped a firelighter at it, setting the liquid on fire. Flames spread rapidly, burning through the wood at a terrifying speed. She heard something *scream* in her head, an instant before a pathway started to open to the outside world. Richard ran forward, swinging his axe with immense power. The branches parted, allowing him to flee.

"Go," Little Jim shouted. "I ..."

A branch stabbed him from behind. Isabella watched in horror as the branches *melded* with him, turning him into ...

into a monster. And then they reached for her. She turned and ran, waving her sword frantically as she evaded the swinging branches and threw herself into the open air. Behind her, something was roaring in anger ...

"Jim," Richard shouted. "Where is he?"

"Gone," Isabella shouted back. "Run!"

The entire village was coming to life, the wooden buildings turning into ... *things*. She ran towards the horses, hoping they could get out in time. Lord Robin and the others joined them a second later, swinging themselves into the saddles and running for the gate. The palisade was coming to life, *creepers* slowly reaching out towards the fleeing mercenaries. Isabella heard something laughing, in the back of her mind, as she dug in her spurs. They made it out with only seconds to spare.

"Well," Lord Robin said, once they had put some distance between themselves and the village. "We now know what happened to the villagers, don't we?"

Isabella nodded, slowly. Something ... something had moved into the village. And it had killed the villagers and their animals and the taxman ... she cursed under her breath. Seven years at the Peerless School and three more in the hardest training course known to mankind – and seven years of experience as a mercenary – and she *still* didn't have the faintest idea *what* that creature was. She'd never heard of anything like it ...

... And yet, there were *stories*. Whispers of *things* ... she hadn't believed what little she'd heard, but ...

"I'm not going back," Alexis said. The swordsman was trying to hide it, but it was clear that he was terrified. "Whatever that was, sir, I don't want to face it again."

"That's for Lord August to decide," Lord Robin said. "We carried out our mission. We'll go back to the inn and collect our wages."

And mourn our dead, Isabella thought, grimly. She'd have to write a report, although the gods alone knew who might be alive to read it. *What* was *that thing?*

Chapter Two

"This is an insult, father," Crown Prince Reginald of Andalusia said. He threw the parchments to the floor, contemptuously. "This is an insult to you, to me, to our entire lineage!"

He slammed his palms onto the table, hard. "He has the *nerve*, the insufferable *nerve*, to write to you and ask for your congratulations, even as he steals a *kingdom* from you!"

"A kingdom that was never part of my patrimony," King Romulus said. Unlike his son, he was calm and composed. "We have no historical claim to the Summer Isle."

"King Edwin swore a mighty oath that you would inherit his kingdom, if he failed to produce an heir," Reginald said. "And we paid in full for his oath."

He scowled at the map. King Edwin had needed help to regain his throne, after his enemies had driven him out of his capital and forced him to flee. King Romulus had provided it, at a price. Edwin had no heir, no one he *wanted* to inherit his kingdom. It had been easy for the weak king to offer his kingdom in pawn, in exchange for money and military supplies. And now Edwin was dead. Murdered, perhaps. The only thing that any of the reports actually *agreed* on was that King Edwin was dead.

"He made an agreement, Father," Reginald said. He leaned back in his chair, trying to copy his father's calm. "And we have to enforce it."

He felt a hot flush of impatience, mingled with annoyance that someone – anyone – had dared to challenge his father. King Romulus hadn't been *expecting* to actually have to *fight* for his kingdom – the Grand Sorcerers had frozen all conflict – but he'd held Andalusia together after the Golden City had fallen and the Empire had vanished. Reginald himself had led troops in combat, crushing rebels and intimidating foreigners. Andalusia was relatively stable these days, unlike some of the other kingdoms. The Summer Isle had been on the brink of civil war for as long as he could remember ...

King Edwin had given his *word*, damn it! The document was very clear. In the absence of a suitable heir, King Romulus would inherit the Summer Isle. It would be *good* for the Isle, no doubt. Andalusia's ruler – and his firstborn son – were hardly dependent on the snake pit of vipers King Edwin had called his nobility. Romulus could crush King Edwin's former vassals like bugs, if they displeased him. Reginald had led troops against two overmighty noblemen himself, over the last five years. Neither one had lived to regret defying their king.

His father tapped the map. "We do not *need* the Summer Isle."

"No, but we cannot afford to let people think that we are weak," Reginald pressed. "If we don't collect what we're owed, others will think they can cheat us too."

He took a breath. "Edwin was a *king*, Father," he added. "It would weaken *us* if we decided his word wasn't his bond."

King Romulus looked as though he had bitten into a lemon. Kings wielded absolute authority these days, now the Grand Sorcerers were gone. The Summer Isle had been Edwin's personal fiefdom, his lords drawing their power from their monarch. And yet, Edwin's corpse hadn't managed to cool before Earl Rufus Hereford had declared himself King Rufus I. Reginald had no idea how the earl had managed to convince the other two earls to go along with it – or at least stay out of his way – but it hardly mattered. The only thing that mattered was that Hereford had cheated King Romulus – and, by extension, Reginald himself – out of his due.

And if people start thinking that a king's word is worthless, he thought grimly, *our word will also be called into question.*

He studied his father for a long moment. King Romulus had aged over the last five years, as he'd fought to hold his kingdom together. His brown hair had started to turn grey, even though he was fitter and stronger than many of the young men in his court. Reginald knew it would be a long time before his father died, something that left him relieved and fearful in equal measure. What was the point of becoming king if one was crowned too late to have an impact on the kingdom? His father was a cautious man, but Reginald ... there were entire kingdoms to seize, if one had the power and inclination. He *wanted* to test himself against the other monarchs before it was too late.

Raising his eyes, he looked around the room. Lord William – his father's personal toady – refused to meet his eyes. Reginald scowled at him anyway, on general principles, then turned his attention to his own oldest sister. Sofia looked back at him, her dark eyes silently daring him to make a snide remark about how women shouldn't be involved in government. Reginald pitied the poor bastard who got married to her. Sofia's combination of iron-willed determination and religious fanaticism would make her a stubborn wife. If she'd been born a man ...

We would probably tear the kingdom apart after father died, Reginald thought. *Even as a woman, she's formidable. And she might be able to rule if I died.*

The thought made him scowl again. He knew his father was worried about having only one son – he had three daughters, but only one son – yet Reginald couldn't share the sentiment. Having too many sons was unsafe, particularly now. But then, as King Edwin had found out, having *no* sons was even worse. The man had been infertile. He hadn't even managed to sire a single bastard. Queen Emetine had been forced on Edwin – she was the sister of Earl Hereford, who'd now seized the throne – and she'd probably been her brother's spy in the king's bedchamber, but kings had mistresses. Even a bastard son could have been given the throne, if there was no legitimate child.

"You are correct to argue that we are owed the island," King Romulus said, calling his son's attention back to him. "But taking it will mean an extensive military operation ..."

"No, Father," Reginald said. "The other two earls will support our claim when we land troops."

"You *think* they'll support our claim," King Romulus said, flatly. "You will discover that noblemen have a habit of turning their coats, as long as a blade isn't kept pointed at their throat."

"Our troops will be the blade, Father," Reginald said. He'd

wiped out one aristocratic family – *pour encourager les autres* – and he had no compunction about doing it again. "I will cut their throats if they disobey."

"And they will fear a decline in their power," King Romulus added, as if Reginald hadn't spoken. "They are big fish in a small pond, Son. But what will they be if the Summer Isle is added to our kingdom?"

Reginald shrugged. "Those who join us will be rewarded," he said. "And those who don't will be exterminated."

His father studied him for a long moment. "You are determined, then?"

"The Isle is part of my patrimony," Reginald said. "We cannot just let it ... slip away."

"True," his father agreed.

Reginald grinned. He couldn't help himself. He'd done it! He'd talked his father into authorising the campaign. The Summer Isle would be his! He would rule as a noble lord, shaping the island as he pleased. And when his father died, Reginald's son would inherit the island as his personal demesne. It would be a good training ground to learn the skills one needed to be king.

"We cannot spare too many soldiers, though," his father said. "You will have to hire and pay mercenaries."

"I command the regiments," Reginald said, stiffly.

"Yes, but they are needed along the borders," his father countered. "How quickly could we recall them, if our ... *friends* ... decided it was time to adjust the boundary lines in their favour?"

Reginald nodded, crossly. The crystal ball network was gone. It would take days, perhaps weeks, to get a message from Andalusia to the Summer Isle, then longer to move the regiments to the ships and sail back to Havelock. By then, a mobile force could have crossed Andalusia's borders and made its way to the capital city. He might occupy the Summer Isle, only to lose Andalusia itself. His father was right. Only a handful of regiments could be spared for the invasion.

"I will hire mercenaries to make up the numbers," he said. There was no shortage of mercenaries in Andalusia. His father had often fretted over what to do with them, now that the kingdom was stable again. The mercenaries could easily cause trouble ... or go to work for a discontented nobleman. "And many of them can be given land on the Summer Isle."

"Assuming you win, Son," King Romulus said.

"I will win," Reginald promised. "I thank you, Father."

He rose, then bowed. He'd go straight to his rooms, then send out heralds. The call to war would echo across the land, summoning mercenaries and adventurers who wanted to fight under his banner. He'd have to send a formal demand for submission to Hereford, of course – protocol demanded that he gave the usurper a chance to think twice – but he'd make sure it was worded to discourage surrender. Beating the living daylights out of the former earl – he was damned if he was calling Hereford a *king* – would go a long way towards convincing the rest of the snake pit to bend the knee. Besides, Reginald *wanted* the war. It would be a new and exciting challenge.

"Be careful, Son," King Romulus said. "You will be a long way from help."

"I know, Father," Reginald said. "But I will survive."

***

Lord William had not grown up in the court – in the days before the Golden City had fallen – for nothing. He was adept at concealing his thoughts and feelings from his superiors, particularly his monarch. King Romulus was a hard man to love, at times, but he was an easy man to follow. His son had all of his father's determination and sheer bloody-minded stubbornness – William admitted that, in the privacy of his own head – yet he lacked the maturity King Romulus had developed over the years.

Reginald was charismatic, William conceded. The prince's blond good looks had set more than a few hearts aflutter around the court, including those of William's own daughters. It was a shame, in many ways, that Reginald was unlikely to be married off to anyone less than a princess. Becoming the young prince's father-in-law would have solidified William's position beyond challenge, as well as allowing him to act as a moderating influence on the future king. But it wasn't going to happen. William couldn't help worrying over what *would* happen when King Romulus died. Reginald was hardly likely to listen to *his* advice.

And sending him off on an adventure will either turn him into a challenger or disgrace him beyond salvation, he thought. *What is his father thinking?*

King Romulus looked up. "William," he said. "You will accompany my son."

William blinked. "Sire?"

"You are a colonel in one of the regiments," King Romulus reminded him. His voice was absent, as if his thoughts were elsewhere. "You will serve as its commanding officer, which will give you a seat on Reginald's council of war. I expect you to keep an eye on him."

"Yes, Your Majesty," William said. There was no other answer he could give. "I ... may I ask a question."

King Romulus inclined his head, graciously. "You may."

"Thank you, Your Majesty," William said. "I ... why are you allowing him to go?"

He took a breath. "The Summer Isle is a desolate wasteland, populated by barbarians," he reminded the king. "Their nobility is noble in blood only. The endless skirmishes with the Northern Realm cost their monarchy in blood and treasure. There is nothing to be gained from taking and holding the island."

"The Summer Isle does have potential," King Romulus countered. "And a powerful ruler might accomplish much, if he had the force to back up his words. And *Earl* Hereford could become a threat, particularly if we *do* go to war with our neighbours."

"They swore before the gods that they would respect the borders," Sofia said.

William felt a hot flash of irritation. What a ... what a *womanish* thing to say. No one who knew how the world actually *worked* would expect sworn oaths to keep Andalusia's neighbours from falling on her borders like ravening wolves if they scented weakness. It was proof, as if he'd needed any, that women should stay in their chambers and leave the hard work to the men. No wonder there were so few ruling queens. *Men* understood that weakness invited attack.

And if Reginald dies, he thought coldly, *whoever marries Sofia will rule through her.*

It wasn't a pleasant thought. There was no shortage of suitors for Sofia's hand – and those of her sisters – but her father would have to choose very carefully. Whoever won her hand might just win the kingdom too. And the wrong choice could prove disastrous.

King Romulus smiled. "There is a secondary concern," he added. "And I expect you – both of you – not to discuss it further."

William bowed his head, concealing his annoyance. He knew how to keep a secret – one didn't become a king's trusted confidant if one had loose lips – but women gossiped all the time. Sofia would probably share her father's secrets, the minute she was secluded with the other ladies of the court. And then they'd be all over the kingdom. He didn't understand why the king allowed Sofia to attend the meeting. She didn't have to worry her pretty little head with the hard realities of life.

"Reginald is twenty-four," King Romulus said, reflectively. "I was twenty-seven when my father died. It will not be long before Reginald starts agitating for more power for himself. His courtiers will nag him into pressuring me, even if *he* doesn't want to do it. And I am running out of tasks to keep him busy."

William nodded, slowly. The Crown Prince wanted – needed – to distribute patronage of his own if he wanted to bind his household to him. Land, titles, castles, even heiresses ... Reginald needed to grant them, yet he had little to grant. His father couldn't give Reginald too much without weakening his own position. And even if he gave Reginald the entire kingdom, it wouldn't be enough to satisfy the prince's courtiers. They were a demanding crowd.

"You think he can turn the Summer Isle into his own personal kingdom," he said, slowly.

"There are other concerns," King Romulus said. "Yes, my son can take and hold the island and parcel out the land to his supporters. But it will not be long before he starts wanting power – real power – for himself. Wielding it over the Summer Isle will keep him from trying to take it from me."

"He would not," Sofia said.

William felt cold. The Crown Prince would be King, when his father died, but until then ... all his power came from his father. Reginald outranked everyone else, yet he had less power than a duke, a lord or even a baron. His father could overrule him at any moment. King Romulus was right. Sooner or later, Prince Reginald would want *real* power. And the only way to get *that* was to overthrow his father. And that meant ...

"You want to keep him distracted, Sire," he said.

"I want him to succeed," King Romulus said. He looked down at the map, one finger tracing out the Summer Isle's borders. "I never really expected to inherit the Summer Isle. I gave Edwin help because I wanted a stable kingdom on the other side of the channel, not a realm constantly blighted with civil war. But now ..."

He stroked his beard. "Reginald is right to say we have to claim what we are due," he added, slowly. "We cannot allow such a precedent to stand. But I also want Reginald to be occupied for a while, ruling a land that will allow him to satisfy his supporters without turning him into a threat to the throne. And I *don't* want him to get into trouble."

"Yes, Your Majesty," William said.

"Go with him," King Romulus ordered, curtly. "Be the voice of caution on his council. And inform me as quickly as possible if he is likely to overstep himself. The Summer Isle is not *small*. Hereford has plenty of space to trade for time, if he wishes. My son's natural impatience will urge him to make mistakes."

"He is a good soldier, Father," Sofia said.

"Yes," King Romulus agreed. "But he is also too young to be a good strategist. He will seek battles for the sake of seeking battles, rather than choosing his fights with one eye firmly fixed on his goal. And there are times when declining battle may be the smarter choice."

At the risk of being called a coward, William thought. *And that is one word that could never be attached to the Crown Prince.*

"Watch my son," King Romulus said. "And be there for him."

William rose and bowed, first to the king and then to his daughter. He didn't want to go – he certainly didn't want to walk away from the centre of power, let alone go to the Summer Isle – but he knew he had no choice. King Romulus wouldn't thank him for *refusing* to go. He just hoped he'd be able to get back before the king found a new advisor. Prince Reginald had never bothered to conceal his dislike of William and the other old men on the king's council. William had no illusions about his ability to moderate the prince's behaviour. It was non-existent. The prince would probably banish William from the council as soon as they landed on the Summer Isle.

I have no choice, he reminded himself. *I have to go.*

Chapter Three

"My brother is dead," Big Richard thundered. He sat at the front of the bar, swilling a tankard of beer. A barmaid sat on his lap, looking thoroughly uncomfortable as his fingers played with her shirt. "Let us drink to his honour!"

Isabella rolled her eyes as she nursed her beer. It had been two days since Little Jim's death, two days since they'd made their way to the town and reported to Lord August ... two days since Big Richard had started a wake for his dead brother. He was going to regret it soon, she was sure. The hangover was going to be a nightmare. And the discovery that he'd spent all of his money on the wake would be worse.

She leaned back in her chair and surveyed the inn. Dozens of people were crammed into the room: drinking, talking and vomiting on the earthen floor. The barmaids moved from table to table, pouring out cheap beer and cheaper wine while doing their best to evade pinches, gropes and worse. A handful of whores were doing a roaring trade at the rear, taking their customers upstairs for a quickie before leading them back down again and finding the next customer. She'd been in worse places, she knew, but there was something about the bar that offended her. And yet ...

It is more honest than the Golden City, she told herself, as the band started to play a mournful tune. A number of couples stood up to dance, moving in a manner that suggested they were well on their way to outright drunkenness. The beer was flowing freely, thanks to Richard. It was astonishing just how many people were prepared to mourn Little Jim, in exchange for free beer. *No one here tries to hide what they are.*

She took a sip of her beer, grimacing at the taste. The gods alone knew what the brewer had put in his vats, apart from hops. Perhaps the beer was so cheap just to make sure the drinkers didn't complain about the flavour. Or to get them drunk so quickly that they didn't notice. The nasty part of her mind insisted that the pallid liquid should have been poured back into the horse. Her spells had told her that it wasn't poisonous, but drinking more than a pint or two would probably pickle her liver anyway.

A crash echoed through the room as a fight broke out, a dozen drinkers throwing punches at each other with staggering force. The barmaids hurried to the rear, trying to get out of the way, as more and more drinkers joined in the brawl. Isabella hurriedly readied a spell, just in case she needed to defend herself. The melee was already getting out of hand. She couldn't help thinking, as a chair flew across the room and smashed against the far wall, that brawls broke out every hour or so. There were too many lowlifes crammed into too small a space.

And more mercenaries than normal, she thought. Lord August had always kept a stable of mercenaries, but now ... now there seemed to be hundreds of mercenaries in the town. Lord Robin had insisted that he smelt opportunity, just waiting for them to find it. Isabella wasn't so sure. *Lord August could be plotting a strike against the throne.*

She sighed at the thought. Andalusia was hardly the most developed country in the world, but it had weathered the collapse of the civilised world far better than some of the other nations. King Romulus had done a good job, somehow. It was an impressive feat for someone who'd been little more than a puppet king five years ago, with the court wizard pulling the strings. Perhaps he'd had contingency plans all along. Or perhaps he'd been planning a rebellion.

And if Lord August wants to rise up against his king, she thought, *we might find ourselves caught in the middle.*

She took another sip of her beer, feeling down. Mercenaries were not popular. Even spellbound slaves – or soldiers – were more popular than men who fought for money, men who'd change sides as soon as someone offered a better deal. Noblemen despised them, priests denounced them, commoners hated and feared them. It was hard to escape the feeling that, as King Romulus tightened his control over the kingdom, the company would soon have no work at all. Mercenaries were dangerous in peacetime, after all. King Romulus might intend to dispose of them as soon as possible. Perhaps it was time to go elsewhere.

And if Lord Robin doesn't want to leave, I can go myself, she considered. It wasn't as if she didn't have marketable skills. She knew enough magic to make herself useful. *Or even go travelling ...*

It was a pleasant thought. It was rare for a woman to travel alone, particularly in such troubled times, but she'd never had any problems disguising herself as a man. Or finding a male companion, for that matter. She could join a merchant's team or even wander from place to place like a travelling preacher. There were plenty of places she'd never visited, even after she'd left the Golden City. She could even go home ...

She clamped down on that thought, hard. There was no way she *wanted* to go home, not after everything she'd done. And even if she did ... no two rumours from the far-distant Golden City agreed, but it was clear there *had* been some form of catastrophe. The Grand Sorcerers were dead, the Empire was gone, the puppet kingdoms were asserting themselves ... she didn't think she really wanted to know what had happened. All that mattered was that she was alone in the world.

The brawl came to an end, as quickly as it had started. A handful of men carried the wounded or unconscious bodies outside, dumping them by the drunkard's trough and leaving them for the City Guard. They'd spend a day and a night in the stocks, if they didn't recover by curfew. Or if they didn't have the cash to bribe the guardsmen. It wouldn't take much, not in her experience. Guardsmen were underpaid and underappreciated. A handful of silver would be more than enough to convince them to look the other way.

Isabella rolled her eyes as Big Richard called for more booze. He'd already drunk enough to float a ship ... she wasn't even sure he'd managed to sleep over the last two days. She'd known he was strong, but this ... she winced in sympathy as Big Richard's hands slipped under the barmaid's shirt. The barmaids knew that unwanted male attention was part of the job – Isabella wouldn't have been surprised to discover that the barmaids were also whores –

but she doubted any of them were *happy* with it. Whores tended to live short and unpleasant lives, no matter how hard they worked. The pimps would take their earnings and send them straight back to work. There was no shortage of replacements for when they finally died. The pimps had no trouble finding women who had to whore or starve.

Big Richard belched. The crowd laughed, even as the barmaid recoiled from the stench. Big Richard had obviously never been taught to brush his teeth. Isabella knew her personal hygiene had suffered since she'd left the Golden City, but at least she didn't smell like a cesspit. And then Big Richard's fingers reached the barmaid's breast and pinched, hard. She screamed in pain and tried to get away.

Isabella tensed as Big Richard howled in rage, one hand shoving the barmaid into the counter. She yelped in pain, trying to get away an instant before he caught and twisted her arm behind her back. He was going to kill her ... Isabella rose before she quite realised what she was going to do. Lord Robin would be furious if Big Richard killed someone, even a whore. It might get the company kicked out of the town ...

"Let go of her," she snapped, as she walked towards the counter. "Now."

Big Richard glared at her through unsteady piggish eyes. He was sodden with booze, she realised, swaying backwards and forwards as if he wasn't in complete control of himself. She hoped he'd have the sense to listen to her, to remember what Lord Robin had said. The rest of the company wouldn't thank him – or her – if they were kicked out of the town. A bad reputation would make it harder to find work elsewhere.

The barmaid tried to pull away. Big Richard yanked her arm, hard. Isabella heard it break, an instant before the barmaid screamed in pain. A break like that wouldn't be easy to heal, not without magic. Big Richard had just crippled her. He let go, allowing the barmaid to scurry off into the backroom. Her arm was twisted at an unnatural angle.

"You killed my brother," Big Richard growled. He lifted one of his protective amulets, as if he believed its mere presence would send her reeling back. "You killed ..."

Isabella winced. Little Jim had died saving her life. She

owed it to Little Jim not to kill his brother. But she had her limits. She had no idea why Big Richard hated magic-users so much, but that didn't give him the right to speak to her like that. He was so drunk he probably didn't have the slightest idea what he was actually doing. No matter how much he detested her, he was normally careful not to annoy his boss.

"My brother is dead because of you," Big Richard said. He bunched his fists. "You should have died instead ..."

He threw a punch. Isabella darted backwards, allowing training to take over. He missed her, but kept coming anyway. She heard the crowd shouting and cheering – and placing bets – as she threw a jab at his eyes. Magic crackled along her fingertips, demanding that she unleash it, but she held it back. No one would respect her if she froze him in his tracks or turned him into a toad. She had to win through force.

"Detestable whore," Big Richard swore at her. He moved with surprising speed for such a drunk man. "You ..."

Isabella grunted in pain as he caught her wrist, pulling her towards him. She pressed her fingers together, then thrust them into his eye. He howled, snapping her arm back with terrifying strength. Isabella gritted her teeth – he'd nearly pulled her arm out of the socket – and brought up her knee as hard as she could. He laughed as her knee struck an armoured codpiece, hidden below his trousers. He'd protected his groin against attacks.

He yanked her forward, again. Isabella twisted, bringing her hand down hard on his wrist and striking his pressure points. His hand snapped free as he cursed out loud; she darted backwards, hoping the pain would be enough to convince him to think twice. Her shoulder was hurting, badly enough to slow her down. She muttered a healing cantrip under her breath as she looked up at him. The raw hatred in his eyes startled her. It was deeply personal.

"Get the bitch," someone shouted. Others took up the cry, cheering one or both of them as they placed newer bets. "Kill her!"

Isabella braced herself as Big Richard gathered himself. She knew a dozen spells that would probably break through his protections, but using them ... she cursed under her breath. Even if she beat him physically, he'd never forgive her. Everyone would mock him for being thrashed by a woman. And using spells would ...

He lunged forward. Isabella dodged to the side, trying to get a punch through his wavering fists. But he was practically made of solid muscle. She slammed a fist into his jaw, only to see him shrug the blow off and keep coming. His arm swung at her wildly, nearly striking her head. She ducked back, trying to think of a way to end the fight without killing him or smashing his reputation. A single blow from him would probably be enough to knock her out and end the fight. She didn't want to *think* about what he'd do to her unconscious body.

She evaded a second blow, then tried to drive a stab at his other eye. This time, he lunged forward and crashed into her with breathtaking force. She fell backwards, her head striking the floor hard enough to make her see stars. Big Richard shoved her down, pushing one hand into her chest while drawing back the other to put her lights out. Isabella reached for her magic, hastily. She wasn't going to let him beat her into unconsciousness. She'd be lying there, completely at his mercy. And it was all too clear that he'd probably have his fun, then slit her throat ...

"Hold," a sharp voice said.

Isabella twisted her head as Big Richard froze. Lord Robin was standing there, looking furious. She wondered who'd gone to fetch him, dragging him out of his meeting with a potential client ... she silently thanked the tattletale, even though she knew she'd never be able to say it in person. He'd probably saved a life. She just wasn't sure which of them had been saved.

"Get up," Lord Robin snapped.

Big Richard rolled off Isabella and stood, carefully not looking at her as he lumbered to his feet. Isabella followed, silently grateful that no one had tried to help her up. It wasn't easy commanding respect as a female mercenary, even though the fight had – technically – been a draw. She wanted – she needed – to be treated as one of the boys. If they started thinking of her as a weak and feeble woman ...

"I told you *not* to start any fights," Lord Robin said. "Do you have an excuse for this behaviour?"

"No, sir," Big Richard said. Drunk or not, he was still smart enough not to annoy Lord Robin. "None."

Lord Robin's eyes moved to Isabella. "None, sir," she said. Telling the truth wouldn't help, not when they *had* been ordered to behave. Besides, *she* couldn't afford to sound like a tattletale either. "We have no excuse."

"I see," Lord Robin said.

He raised his hand. Isabella winced, inwardly, as he slapped Big Richard across the face, the sound echoing in the silent chamber. The crowd was silent. Isabella gritted her teeth, then forced herself to stand still as he slapped her too. Her cheekbones exploded in pain, stars flittering across her eyes. She'd never experienced such discipline in the Golden City. But then, Lord Robin didn't have an entire society backing him up either. He had to be the alpha dog if he wanted to stay in command. And that meant showing them that he was the strongest person in the room.

"Richard, go lie down until you've slept it off," Lord Robin ordered. His tone made it very clear that he knew he wouldn't be disobeyed. "Isabella, with me."

He turned and walked out of the room. Isabella walked after him, feeling countless eyes following her until she closed the door. She'd given a good account of herself, she knew, but she'd come very close to losing. And she'd reached for her magic ... her fingers reached up to stroke her cheek, silently casting another cantrip. If Lord Robin noticed her using magic, he gave no sign.

I'll have to find the barmaid, she told herself. She wasn't a druid, but she knew enough about healing magic to save the poor girl's arm. *And then warn her to stay well away from Big Richard until we're on our way out of here.*

"We have a new job," Lord Robin said, as they walked up the stairs. "And you have a visitor."

Isabella blinked. "*I* have a visitor?"

"Yes," Lord Robin said. "He asked for you personally. By name."

"Oh," Isabella said. "And who is he?"

"He said his name was Smyth," Lord Robin said. "I

suspect it isn't his real name."

Isabella had to fight down a giggle. Smyth was a joke ... a *Golden City* joke. The name was assumed by someone who wanted to remain anonymous, even though it was often blindingly obvious that the disguise wasn't fooling anyone. Anyone who used the name wanted privacy and was prepared to pay for it. And that meant ... what? Someone from the Golden City? Or someone who was familiar with the city? It wasn't as if the city had been *that* exclusive before the fall. Countless magicians, noblemen and merchants had spent time in the Golden City.

She forced herself to think. One of her old clients? It was possible, she supposed, although they were a long way from the last place she'd worked. Or someone else ... she shook her head. None of her former lovers had any way to track her down. Besides, she'd made it clear to them that the relationship wouldn't last. Did someone know who she was? She doubted it, but ... it was possible.

Lord Robin stopped outside an unmarked wooden door. "I'll be holding a formal meeting tomorrow, in the bar," he said. "Be there."

"Yes, sir," Isabella said.

"And see if you can find a hangover cure," Lord Robin added. "I want everyone to be ready to listen."

"As you wish," Isabella said. She didn't really want to find something to help Big Richard get over his headache – if he had enough brain cells to have headaches – but she wasn't being given a choice. "I'll go looking after I meet with ... Smyth."

She knocked, then pushed open the door. The room was larger than she'd expected, illuminated by a single ball of glowing magic. And sitting in a rough chair was the last face she'd expected to see ...

"Alden?"

Her brother looked up. "Come on in," he said. "We have much to discuss."

Chapter Four

Isabella had to fight to keep her legs from buckling.

Alden hadn't changed much, as far as she could tell. He'd been fifteen years old when she'd been born and they'd never really been close. Alden had been the kind of person who'd never truly been young, parroting their father instead of developing a mind of his own. He hadn't been a *bad* elder brother – not compared to some of the assholes she'd met since leaving the Golden City – but he hadn't been a very good one either. He'd acted more like a parent than an older brother, bossing her around practically since she'd learnt to walk. The only point she could see in his favour was that he'd supported her, once, when their father had threatened her with a fate worse than death.

She sat down and studied him, using the pause to get her thoughts under control. Alden looked more like their father than ever, his greying hair tied back in a long ponytail that made him look ready to cast spells at a moment's notice. He wore a black shirt and trousers rather than magician's robes, but the wand at his belt spoilt the illusion that he was a wealthy merchant rather than heir to a magical family. And his face ... Isabella shivered as she met his eyes. They were the eyes of a man who had seen terrible things.

Her heart was beating in her chest, thumping so loudly that she was surprised he couldn't hear the sound. She calmed herself as best as she could. Alden ... Alden shouldn't have been able to find her, not after she'd been disowned. She should have been cut right out of the family magic, her blood wiped from the family tree. How the hell had he found her? Even if he'd heard of an *Isabella* in Andalusia, he shouldn't have connected her to the youngest daughter of House Majuro. Her name wasn't *that* uncommon.

"Isabella," Alden said. He *sounded* just like their father too. "I ..."

He stopped, just for a moment. A shiver ran down Isabella's spine. She'd never seen Alden be anything less than completely certain of himself, even when he knew he was on unsteady ground. No, he'd often acted *more* confident when he wasn't completely sure of himself. A show of complete confidence, their father had often said, could make up for problems, if done properly. Isabella hated to admit it, but the old bastard had been right.

"Isabella," Alden repeated. "Right now, you and I are the last of House Majuro."

Isabella stared at him. Her mouth dropped open as she struggled to comprehend what she'd been told. They were the last ...? They couldn't be the last. She'd had six siblings, counting Alden. House Majuro had more than enough children – and cousins – to keep going, even after the patriarch died. Her thoughts caught up with her a second later. Their father was dead?

She found her voice. "Our father ... our father is dead?"

"Yes," Alden said. "And so are our siblings."

Isabella barely heard him. Alay Majuro was dead? The old man had been a nightmare, ruthlessly pushing his children into careers and occupations he felt would benefit the family ... and to hell with whatever they wanted for themselves. He'd told Isabella that she was going to be an Inquisitor, ordering her to study advanced magic and beating her whenever her marks slipped too low. She'd fought back as best she could, but it hadn't been until she'd managed to get herself kicked out of the training course that she'd been formally disowned and told to leave. It had been something of a relief. And yet ...

She felt her heart twist. The old man had meant well, hadn't he? The family was their heart and soul. Except he'd broken all of them ...

And now he's dead, she thought. She didn't know how she felt. She'd loved it when he'd praised her achievements, even as she'd hated the punishments for not living up to his expectations. Aldan hadn't been helpful, either. Her oldest brother should have spoken up for her, but instead ... he'd said nothing. *Father is dead and I ...*

She looked up. "What happened?"

"What happened?" Aldan stared down at the empty table. "What happened was a nightmare."

Isabella listened, torn between disbelief and horror, as Alden stumbled through an explanation. The death of the Grand Sorcerer was no surprise – the old man had been ailing for years, even before she'd left the Golden City – but everything else? An Emperor? An Empress? A godlike entity from the depths of history ... she wouldn't have believed it, if the Empire hadn't fallen. The gods alone knew how many magicians had died in the Golden City. It was clear that none of the court wizards had returned to their puppet kingdoms.

"There aren't many survivors," Alden finished. "Most of the Great Houses are gone, Isabella, or badly weakened. The Inquisition no longer exists, to all intents and purposes. There are only five or six Inquisitors left ... you might be one of the handful of outsiders with the training. And the Empire is gone too."

He shook his head. "Didn't you hear *any* of this?"

"Just rumours," Isabella said. She hadn't wanted to know, not really. She'd been disowned and that was the end of the matter. "Did father ... I thought father disowned me."

"I talked him into not disowning you completely," Alden said. "But he was very clear that you would not be allowed to reclaim your place until after his death. I just ... I just don't think he expected the rest of his children to die."

"No," Isabella said. She put a hard block on her emotions. She'd loved her siblings, even though they'd fought like cats and dogs when they were younger. She would have to mourn them properly, later. "So what's happening now? And why are you here?"

Alden sighed. "We don't have the influence we had five years ago," he said. "The Golden City is effectively gone. We still have the Peerless School and we're taking students from all over the world, but ... it's only a matter of time before rival schools get underway. And then ... frankly, the only thing that keeps the Golden City from being overrun is the threat of defences buried within the mountains. We are trying to keep ourselves neutral, Isabella, but that isn't going to last."

"I imagine not," Isabella said. Sooner or later, a king would see advantage in keeping the Peerless School and Great Library to himself. There were secrets buried within the vaults, secrets that should never be allowed to see the light of day. But if Alden was telling the truth, there was no way the school's former defenders could keep those secrets to themselves indefinitely. "So ... why are you here?"

"Your friend, Lord Robin, has been hired by the Crown Prince," Alden said. He looked pained for a moment. "Please tell me you're not sleeping with him."

Isabella felt a flicker of annoyance. "The Crown Prince? I'm not sleeping with the Crown Prince."

Alden gave her a long-suffering look at her deliberate misunderstanding. "Lord Robin," he said, tartly. "Are you sleeping with him?"

"No," Isabella said. She was tempted to wind him up, as she'd done when she'd been a little girl, but ... she was old enough to know better. Besides, she didn't think he had time to waste being overprotective. "He's my boss. I don't sleep with my boss."

"Good," Alden said. "Is he *really* a lord?"

"He claims to be," Isabella said, curtly. "Are you going to get to the point sometime in this century?"

Alden's eyes narrowed in a manner she remembered all too well from her childhood. She forced herself to look back evenly. She was no longer a little girl and he was no longer her know-it-all older brother. If he wanted something from her, he could damn well do her the courtesy of treating her like an adult. Besides, if she hadn't been disowned permanently, he had certain obligations towards her.

"The Crown Prince believes that Andalusia has a right to the Summer Isle," Alden said, finally. He gave her a tight little smile. "Unfortunately, the denizens of the Summer Isle disagree. One of their noblemen has declared himself a king and dared Andalusia to do something about it. The Crown Prince intends to pick up the gauntlet and *do* something about it."

"I see," Isabella said. A war ... there would be plenty of work for mercenaries in a full-scale war. "And what does this have to do with us?"

"There have been odd ... *rumours* coming out of the Summer Isle," Alden said. "It was never considered very important, Isabella, and most of the old intelligence networks rarely paid it any real attention. Quite a few of the agents we had in place are gone now, it seems. But the stories are worrying."

Isabella met his eyes. "*What* stories?"

"Impossible magics," Alden said. "Strange creatures. Weird ... encounters. People vanishing. Magic ... behaving oddly."

"We saw something weird two days ago," Isabella said. She briefly explained what they'd seen in the village. "I still don't know what it was."

"Me neither," Alden said. "And you say it sucked out your magic?"

"None of my spells responded properly," Isabella confirmed. "I couldn't shape the magic before it faded and vanished."

Alden considered it for a long moment. "There have always been odd stories on the fringes of civilisation, as you know, but these stories ... Isabella, we have to know what's going on."

Isabella nodded, slowly. She rarely paid any attention to rumours. The more outrageous a rumour, the more likely that the truth was buried beneath a mountain of nonsense. If, of course, there *was* any truth to the rumour. There were hundreds of old biddies in the Golden City who'd produced more bullshit than a herd of bulls. No ... there had *been* hundreds of old biddies. The Golden City was no longer the centre of the known world. If Alden was correct, it was nothing more than a backwater – or a prize to be won.

She sighed. She wouldn't have believed the rumours, if she hadn't seen the ... whatever she'd seen. She'd read about all kinds of magics that *might* have produced some of the effects, but ... none of them would have produced the whole. And most of them couldn't have hidden from her senses either. Whatever they'd encountered had been something *new*. Once upon a time, that would have fascinated her. Now ... now, she was scared.

"All right," she said. "You have to know what's going on.

What do you want *me* to do about it?"

She met his eyes. "Even if I wasn't disowned, even if my blood is still connected to the family, coming this far from the Golden City must have taken weeks," she added. "I assume you haven't come just to give me the news."

"No," Alden said. "Lord Robin has been hired by the Crown Prince. I want you to go with them when they cross the channel. And ... once you're there, I want you to investigate the stories. If there's any truth to them, we need to know."

"I see," Isabella said. "And how much are you going to pay?"

Alden blinked. "Pay?"

"I'm a mercenary," Isabella said. She took a certain savage glee in being able to shock him, even now. He hadn't looked so flabbergasted when Isabella had been caught in bed with one of her fellow trainees. "I need to be paid."

"You're my sister," Alden said. "You ..."

Isabella fought down a rising tide of red anger. "Don't even *think* of going there," she snarled. "You ... father kicked me out, remember? You were there when he disowned me."

She cut him off before he could say a word. "You didn't stop him from giving me the boot, did you? You never got in touch with me, did you? Not until you *needed* me. What do I care about the family? It's ..."

"It's not about the family," Alden said. There was a hint of guilt in his voice. "It's about finding out what's going on."

"And why," Isabella demanded, "should I *care* about what's going on?"

"Whatever is happening," Alden said, "needs to be investigated. The Golden City ..."

"The Golden City is a ruin," Isabella said. "And the Grand Sorcerers are dead!"

Alden took a long breath. "What do you want?"

Isabella hesitated. She'd often told herself that she'd demand a high price, when her father finally realised his mistake and called her back home. But ... she'd never expected the old bastard to die. He'd been a powerful sorcerer, one of the strongest magicians in the Golden City.

He should have lived longer. The magic in his bloodline should have kept him alive for over a century. But now he was gone.

She felt a sob catch in her throat. Her other brothers were gone. They'd been closer to her than her sisters, but ... they were gone. And her sisters were gone too. She'd never imagined losing everyone but Alden. She'd never imagined that the whole family – and civilised society – could die. The Empire had seemed utterly indestructible. It was terrifying to realise just how quickly it had fallen apart. Andalusia was one of the most powerful kingdoms in the region, but it was tiny compared to the immensity the Grand Sorcerers had ruled.

"I don't know," she said. "I just ... don't know."

Alden reached out and touched her hand, gently. Isabella nearly jerked away before relaxing into the contact. It wasn't one he'd offered her very often, not when he'd spent far too long pretending to be their father. And yet ...

"You can come home, if you like," Alden said. "Or ... there are places for you, if you want."

Isabella snorted, rudely. It wasn't as if she'd be welcome in the Golden City, even now. Or ... the city *was* ruined, after all. Maybe she would be welcome. Or ...

"My share of the inheritance," she said, finally. "And ... and enough money to keep me going for a while."

"That can be arranged," Alden said. His lips quirked. "You do realise that most of the inheritance is gone?"

"You give me half of what's left, save for what's entailed," Isabella said. Alden *was* the eldest son. The entailed property would go straight to him, now their father was dead. It was a point of law. "And you send the money out here."

Alden took a long breath. "And afterwards, will you come home?"

"You told me that home no longer exists," Isabella said, sharply. She felt another odd pang of grief. The family mansion in the Golden City had been a hard place to grow up, but the estates in the countryside had been fun. She'd loved running in the fields and playing in the gardens more than she cared to admit. "What is there to come home *to*?"

"We are trying to rebuild magic," Alden said. "You have

training we can use."

"I know," Isabella said, softly. Oddly, she felt better about knowing he did have an ulterior motive. She would have been suspicious if he'd professed brotherly love for her. "I'll consider it, after we return from the Summer Isle."

Alden rose. "I thank you," he said, formally. He produced a sheet of parchment from his trouser pocket and held it out to her. "I have established a number of contacts at King Romulus's court. You can send a message to me through them."

"Which will still take weeks to reach you," Isabella said. She'd grown far too used to the crystal ball network. "Is there any way to speed letters up?"

"Not any longer," Alden said. "And even if we could, the kings wouldn't let us."

Isabella looked down. *How the mighty fall ...*

She rose. "I ... thank you for coming," she said. She wasn't sure how she felt, but ... she knew she should say something. "And ... I hope we'll see each other again, soon."

"I have rooms at the bank," Alden said. "You are welcome to join me."

He paused. "And you probably should get married," he added. "Right now, I'm unmarried too."

Isabella's eyebrows shot up. She'd always assumed their father would have found Alden a bride, eventually. There would come a time when Alden would shuffle off the marriage market anyway, unless he wanted a vast age difference between him and his wife. And their father would have wanted grandchildren ...

"I haven't had the time," Alden said. "And even if I wanted to, I don't have a bride."

Because the family is no longer what it was, Isabella thought. Once, Alden would have been sure of a girl from the very highest levels of magical society. She'd known parents who would cheerfully rid themselves of an unwanted son-in-law just so their daughter could marry into House Majuro. But now ... Alden was nowhere near so important. *And who'd want to marry him without a vast dowry?*

"I'm sorry," she said. She didn't think any of the friends she'd known at school would have wanted him, not without the promise of powerful children. "I ..."

She closed her eyes in pain. Too many of the friends she'd known – and the enemies who'd hexed her and been hexed in return – would be dead. She wasn't sure she wanted to know what had happened to them. The boring girls who'd only talked of marriage, the boys who'd bragged of adventure ... where were they? Dead now, perhaps. So few had left the Golden City ...

"It's not a problem," Alden said. "Just ... think about it, please."

Isabella snorted. "No one would want to marry me," she said. "And to hell with anyone who says differently."

Chapter Five

It had been years – literally – since Isabella had spoken a prayer for the dead.

She sat in the centre of her room – dark, cramped, smelly and thoroughly disgusting – and placed a candle on the floor, lighting it with a single spell. It wasn't a traditional candle, but she doubted her family were in any state to care. They were one with the household gods now, if tradition was to be believed ... unless they'd earned eternal damnation instead. She found it hard to decide where her father would have gone, after his death. He'd been a hard man, but he hadn't been *evil*.

The flame flickered as air blew through the room. Isabella sucked in her breath, then began the prayer. It was five years too late, but it hardly mattered. She hadn't *known* about their deaths until Alden had told her. She'd always assumed that her father and his children had survived whatever had destroyed the Golden City. She certainly hadn't felt their deaths ... although, as she'd been disowned, that was probably meaningless. Or had *been* probably meaningless. Alden *had* told her she could go home, if she wished.

Home doesn't exist anymore, she thought, as she concentrated on the flickering light. The flame seemed to grow brighter as she muttered the prayer, repeating it for each of the dead. *I am still alone.*

She shook her head, mournfully. She'd never dared put down roots, not since she'd left the Golden City. It had seemed easier to keep herself to herself, joining mercenary bands or private guardsmen for a few months and then moving on when she started feeling too comfortable. It just hadn't been *safe* to relax, she'd thought. There'd been no reason to believe that anyone was after her, but ... she sighed, shaking her head again. She'd always been given to wanderlust.

Father's influence, she told herself. *He always wanted me to stick to one thing.*

She finished the prayer, then reached out and snuffed out the candlelight. The room went dark, completely dark. There were no chinks of light from the outside world ... she smiled, wryly, as she realised the room genuinely *was* sealed. She hadn't expected so much, when she'd requested a private room. But then, there was no need to bed down with the rest of the company. It wasn't as if they were marching to war.

Some people claimed to see visions of the dead, shortly after speaking the prayer. Isabella waited, but saw nothing. Her father and siblings were already gone to the next world, she guessed. Alden would have cremated their bodies, if they'd ever been found. There was too great a chance of a powerful magician rising again – as a soulless lich – or their blood and bones being used for dark rituals. Their bodies had to be destroyed and the ashes scattered over the estate.

She closed her eyes for a long moment, recalling her father. He'd shaped her more than he'd wished, she thought. She had all of his stubbornness and magical talent ... too much stubbornness to accept his plans for her, too much talent to be simply ignored or married off at the first opportunity. Their fights ... by all the gods, their fights! She'd loved him, in her way, but she'd also wanted to strike out on her own. Her disownment had seemed a blessing in disguise. It wasn't as if she'd had any trouble earning money after she'd been kicked out with nothing but the clothes on her back.

Father probably considered that a huge concession, she thought, sourly. *Technically, a disowned daughter can't take anything from the family ... even clothes.*

She concentrated, reaching out in hopes of feeling her father's presence. But there was nothing ... nothing but the faint sense of background magic. She took a long breath, then opened her eyes. The darkness ebbed and flowed around her as she picked up the candle and lit it again, then removed her boots and walked to the bed. Lord Robin wanted an early morning meeting, after all. He was probably going to regret it. Big Richard was *definitely* going to regret it.

He'll have one hell of a hangover, she thought,

vindictively. Thankfully, she'd managed to find and heal the barmaid before her father took the poor girl to the nearest sawbones. A magic-less healer couldn't have done anything for her, save perhaps for amputating the broken arm. Big Richard deserved to suffer. *And it serves the bastard right.*

She lay down on the bed, muttering a couple of spells to keep bugs away. Sleeping in her clothes was uncomfortable, but she was damned if she was sleeping naked on the bed. The gods alone knew how many people had slept on it, over the last few years. She rather doubted it had been cleaned, either. Spells or no spells, she was probably going to be itchy tomorrow. It was a shame there were no washtubs in the inn ...

Closing her eyes, she concentrated on meditating. Her father was dead ... her *family* was dead, save for her least-liked brother. The irony irked her more than she cared to admit. If any of the others had asked her home, she might have agreed. But Alden ... she sighed as a wave of tiredness threatened to overcome her. They'd always got along better when there was some distance between them. And ...

She opened her eyes. She'd slept and now ... she sat upright, casting a light-spell as she swung her legs over the side of the bed. It was early morning, but she could hear people moving in the streets outside. Commoners never got to sleep into the later hours, not when there was too much to do. She stepped into the washroom, splashed a little water on her face and then headed through the door. A handful of guests were already making their way down to the dining room. Breakfast would be waiting for them.

Lord Robin greeted her with a wave as she stepped into the room. He looked disgustingly fresh and cheerful as she shuffled over to sit at his table, even though she was *sure* he'd gone to bed later than her. But then, he'd always put more effort into his appearance than *she'd* ever done. If she hadn't known he'd had a string of mistresses, she would have wondered if he was more interested in men than woman. But then, Big Richard and quite a few others had accused *her* of being strikingly masculine.

The barmaid bustled over. "What can I get you?"

Isabella made a face. The inn's food wasn't very good,

although there was plenty of it. She didn't really want to eat, but ... she knew she had to keep up her strength. She ordered food and drink, then sat back to wait. The barmaid returned with surprising speed, carrying a platter of eggs, sausages and a single goblet of wine. She wanted coffee, but there was none to be had. These days, with trade routes lying in ruins, no one – not even the rich – could find coffee for love or money.

"Very suspicious looking sausages," Lord Robin said. "What do you think they are?"

Isabella shrugged as she cast a spell, making sure the food was safe to eat. She didn't want to *know* what sort of meat had gone into the sausages. Pork or lamb or ... something far less savoury. Commoners would eat anything, even rat. Whoever had minced the meat to create sausages had flavoured it heavily, probably to disguise the original taste. Perhaps it was horse. There was a knackery just down the street.

She met his eyes. "What did Alden say to you?"

"Alden? Smyth?"

Isabella mentally kicked herself. "His name is Alden," she said, crossly. Perhaps, just perhaps, Lord Robin would draw a line between Alden Majuro and Isabella Majuro. Or perhaps not. The Golden City was a long way away. *And* House Majuro was no longer the power it had been. "What did he say to you?"

"Very little," Lord Robin said. "He just said he wanted to talk to you."

He cocked his head. "Was it something I should know about?"

"I don't know," Isabella said. "But I'll tell you when I find out."

They finished the meal in silence, then headed down to the private meeting room. Robin nodded to one of the chairs, inviting her to sit, then hurried to find the others. Isabella felt a flicker of sympathy for the men, even though some of them had been more than a little unwelcoming. Robin expected them to attend, hangovers or no hangovers. She concentrated on casting privacy spells as the door opened, admitting the remainder of the company. Big Richard didn't look at her as he slunk into the room, one hand half-covering his eyes. The drink had finally caught up with him.

And I was supposed to find him a hangover cure, Isabella remembered. *Oops.*

Lord Robin returned, locking and bolting the door as soon as he'd counted heads. "Isabella, please make this room secure," he said. "Everyone else, sit down and take a glass of water."

Big Richard didn't make any snide remarks as Isabella finished casting the privacy spells. He must be *really* hungover, she decided. Or perhaps he was ill. She checked the wards carefully, layering them in place to deter any spying magicians. It was hard to imagine any of the remaining magic-users bothering to spy on Lord Robin and his mercenary company, but it never hurt to take precautions. Besides, *Alden* had visited them. If someone knew who he was, they might pay more attention to the company.

"Done," she said. "The room is as private as I can make it."

"Very good," Lord Robin said. He strode to the end of the table and sat down. "We have a new contract. Crown Prince Reginald is building an army – and we're invited."

A rustle of excitement ran around the table. Isabella looked from face to face, noting who seemed pleased and who seemed concerned. A contract from the Crown Prince would be sure to pay well – aristocrats knew better than to try to cheat their mercenaries – but being part of a larger force would cause problems. Sharing out the loot would be harder if there were more grasping hands. And the Crown Prince would probably count his mercenaries as expendable...

Lord Robin ran through the same explanation she'd heard from Alden, although with a few new details. The Crown Prince, it seemed, was building a *vast* army. There was at least a vague possibility that the prince intended to wage war on his father, rather than the Summer Isle. But he'd also put out a call for shipping as well as mercenaries, inviting sailors to join his invasion force. It certainly *looked* as though he intended to cross the channel as soon as possible. The longer he delayed, the harder it would be to unseat King Rufus and claim his kingdom.

"We will be serving as scouts and special operatives," Lord Robin finished. "On one hand, we'll be paid very well; on the other, we'll be carrying out some very dangerous missions."

He smiled, rather thinly. "If any of you want to back out now, say so."

Isabella shrugged to herself. Alden had made it clear that *something* was happening on the Summer Isle. She had to go there. The others ... she smiled, inwardly, at the flurry of chatter. Lord Robin's core group – seven mercenaries, including herself – would probably follow wherever he led. It was a small band, but they'd worked together for months. A larger force would be harder to control.

"I want to go," Big Richard said. He rubbed his forehead, roughly. "Anyone want to back out?"

Isabella ignored his challenging stare. The mercenary code demanded that each mercenary be offered a chance to back out, before the formal contract was signed. No one would hold it against someone who left now, but later ... a mercenary who fled would be regarded as a deserter. And it would be harder to flee on the Summer Isle. She'd never been there, but she suspected a stranger would stick out like a sore thumb. Mercenaries who were cut off from the rest of the group were often brutally murdered by the locals, when they were caught. It wasn't as if *they* were protected by the honour code.

Nor are soldiers, not really, she reminded herself. *The locals have plenty of reason to fear and detest soldiers too.*

She pushed the thought aside as Lord Robin issued orders. They'd be departing within the hour, riding straight for Humber. The port city wasn't too far from Havelock, if Isabella recalled the map correctly, but it *was* closer to the Summer Isle. And far enough from Havelock that King Romulus couldn't supervise his son. She wondered if that should bother her, then decided it probably didn't matter. The world had changed, five years ago. If a prince wanted to overthrow his father ... who cared?

Everyone who gets caught up in the civil war, she thought, crossly. *And the victor, who will have to make some hard choices after the fighting is over.*

"I'll have the innkeeper pack us some lunch," Lord Robin said, rising. "We *should* be able to make it to Humber before dark."

"If we ride hard," Dolman said. The swordsman didn't look convinced. "We don't want to get to the town gates after dark."

"We should be fine," Lord Robin said. "And if we have to sleep in the open air ... well, it won't be the first time."

"We could just climb the walls," Big Richard suggested. "It might be fun."

"It might also get us beheaded," Isabella countered. Townsfolk took a dim view of people climbing their walls at the best of times. Now, with an army and fleet assembling in the town, she suspected that any intruders would be taken for spies. "Better to sleep outside than risk death."

"Coward," Big Richard said. "We've sneaked into towns before."

"There's no *need* to sneak into Humber," Isabella snapped. "I ..."

Lord Robin slapped the table, hard. "If we get there after the gates close, we will wait," he said. "I do want to get there quickly, but there's no point in breaking into the city."

He nodded to the door. "Isabella, stay here. Everyone else, grab your stuff and meet me at the stables, twenty minutes from now."

Isabella silently dismantled the privacy spells as the rest of the company headed out of the door. It wasn't as if they had much to grab, in any case. Their bags should already be packed. *Her* bag was sitting on her bed, just waiting for her. She hoped a maid hadn't tried to move it. The protective spells she used to keep her bag safe would give a maid a thoroughly unpleasant surprise, if she touched the bag without permission.

"The Crown Prince has also put out a call for magicians," Lord Robin told her. "I was planning to make it clear that you were attached to my company."

"I see," Isabella said. Two of the pieces fell into place. "But you're also planning to use me as a way to gain influence."

Robin didn't bother to deny it. "A chance to enter the

prince's personal household is not to be denied," he said, seriously. "And it could be good for you too."

Isabella nodded, slowly. There *was* a shortage of magicians in Andalusia – and the Summer Isle as well, she assumed. It was quite possible that *she* was the most powerful sorcerer in the kingdom. Hedge-witches had their uses, but they lacked the training she'd been given at the Peerless School. She couldn't blame the Crown Prince for wanting magicians to join his invasion force. He might face significant problems if his enemy had more magic-users than he did.

And Robin would have a chance to build up a power base for himself, she thought. *Not a bad opportunity for a landless bastard son.*

"Tell him, then," she said. "But don't tell him *too* much about me."

"As you wish," Robin said. He winked at her. "You *do* realise the Crown Prince is unmarried."

Isabella barked a harsh laugh. "I don't think he'd be interested in me," she said. The hell of it was that wasn't true. If the Crown Prince knew her bloodline, he'd have excellent reason to court her. "And you know that, don't you?"

She walked through the door and back up the stairs to her room, where she collected her bag and headed down to the stables. Big Richard was standing in the bar, kissing and fondling a very enthusiastic whore. Isabella wondered, cynically, just how much he'd paid her as she made her way out to the stables. Big Richard would be in real trouble if he was late. Lord Robin *did* have a good reason to want to reach Humber quickly. How else could he make himself useful to the Crown Prince?

And he's going to use me to do it, Isabella thought. She felt a flicker of annoyance. Being close to the Crown Prince might be useful, particularly if the rumours were more than just lies, but ... at least she wasn't posing as a kept woman. *That* would be worse. Pretending to be stupid had always got on her nerves. *It's worse than making love to some fat oaf.*

Somewhat to her surprise, Big Richard joined the group an instant before Lord Robin arrived, carrying a bag of food.

Isabella took her share and stowed it in her saddlebags, then clambered up and into the saddle as the stable doors opened. Her horse whinnied in delight – being confined to the stable couldn't have been fun, even if there were mares in the nearby chambers – and started to move forward. Isabella let Lord Robin take the lead as they cantered out onto the road and headed west.

We'll be riding all day, she thought, sourly. *But as long as we get there on time, it will be worth it.*

Chapter Six

Humber was not, in Crown Prince Reginald's frank estimation, a particularly important city. It was too close to Havelock to have its own identity, yet too far from the capital to be absorbed into its teeming masses. The port facilities were good, but successive monarchs had worked hard to ensure that Havelock – not Humber – handled the vast majority of the shipping trade. Only fishing – and trading missions to the Summer Isles – had kept Humber afloat. It wasn't something that had seemed likely to change.

But it *had* changed, Reginald told himself, as he stood on the tower and peered west. The Summer Isle was visible, barely. The Summer Channel was relatively narrow, as seas went, but it was treacherous as a demon from the darkest hells. Storms blew up out of nowhere, the sailors had warned; the tides and currents were dangerously unpredictable, changing seemingly at random. The body of water between Andalusia and the Summer Isle was hard to navigate, even for experienced sailors. Crossing the waters was not going to be pleasant.

He lowered his gaze, looking towards the port. It *thrummed* with activity as sailors struggled to prepare the fleet for departure. Reginald had hired nearly every ship in Humber that could make the crossing, along with a number of merchant ships whose captains had been looking for a sure thing. There were fifty-seven ships in the fleet, each one capable of carrying hundreds of soldiers. Disembarking the men – and their equipment – was going to be a hassle, but it was one he could surmount. And ... he turned his head, spotting the army and mercenary camps. Thousands of men had been coming in over the last two days, either as individuals or mercenary bands ... his sergeants were organising them now, preparing the men for departure. It was a logistics headache, but they could handle it. They knew that a mistake now might cost everything on the other side of the channel.

And the mercenaries also know to behave themselves, Reginald thought. *I taught them that lesson already.*

He gritted his teeth. He'd already had two men hanged for rape and a third for theft. It was hard to blame the mercenaries for wanting to entertain themselves while they waited to board the ships, but there were limits. There was no shortage of whores, after all. And besides, the last thing he needed was the city fathers finding excuses to slow down work. The fleet had to depart before summer slowly turned into winter or it would never depart at all. Reginald wasn't deterred by the thought of launching the invasion the following year, but ... it would give the usurper too much time to establish himself. A delayed invasion would be very costly indeed.

The door opened behind him. Reginald turned, just in time to see Equerry Caen step onto the battlements. He was a handsome youth, a year or so younger than Reginald himself. They'd grown up together, sharing their lessons as they inched towards adulthood. And yet ... Reginald felt a flicker of shame as he remembered how Caen had always been punished for Reginald's misdeeds. The tutors knew better than to strike the prince. It had been his father, eventually, who'd taken him to task for allowing his friend to get into trouble.

"Your Highness," Caen said. "The council of war is waiting for you."

Reginald felt a hot flush of excitement. It was hardly the first time he'd called a council of war – he'd also attended his father's councils as a growing youth – but this one was special. This was no border skirmish or campaign against rebellious noblemen. This was a war ...

"Then let us go greet them," he said, turning to the door. "We have much to discuss."

Humber Castle was old. It had been in poor condition until recently, when King Romulus had ordered the seneschal to prepare the building for a possible war. The castle was dark and draughty – and it stank like a privy – but at least it was defendable. Reginald wasn't sure who his father envisaged attacking Humber, although he understood the older man's paranoia. A foe who took Humber would be within striking distance of Havelock itself. He smiled to himself as he led his friend down the stairs to the council chamber. The Summer Isle was in the best place to mount an invasion, but it would never have the chance. He'd see to that.

He stepped into the chamber and watched as the council of war rose to meet him. They were a diverse crowd, including – his lips twitched in disapproval – his father's watchdog. Lord William looked as if he wanted to be somewhere – anywhere – else. Reginald heartily agreed that the wretched man should be somewhere else, but he knew his father would be annoyed if Reginald banished Lord William. It would have to wait until they crossed the channel, whereupon a role could be found for the older man that would keep him out of the way.

"Be seated," he ordered, as he sat down at the head of the table. He had no time for the pomp and ceremony that surrounded his father. "We have much to discuss."

He allowed his eyes to roam the chamber. His three Captain-Generals – Captain-General Gars, Captain-General Stuart, Captain-General Jones – looked eager to depart, even though they knew there was still much work to do. They'd been his constant companions since he'd first lifted a sword, alternately serving him and pressing for promotions for themselves. He didn't really blame them – they needed to establish themselves before it got too late – but it was frustrating at times. His father had given Reginald much, yet he hadn't given Reginald anything he could use to bind the men to him permanently. Gars, in particular, wanted to marry well. But Reginald didn't have the power to offer him the heiress he needed to make a mark on the court.

Behind them, Sergeant Ruthven was a short man with a fierce temper. He was the man who'd taught Reginald how to command, years ago. Reginald had admired him, right from the moment they'd first met; he had nothing but boundless admiration for the older man and ensured that he stayed with his prince. Common-born or not, Ruthven deserved to rise high. Reginald had every intention of making sure the man got an heiress of his own, when the time came. Ruthven deserved nothing less than the best. And, behind him, was Academic Milhous. He was out of place – he was a scholar, not a nobleman or soldier – but he was the greatest living expert on the Summer Isle. Reginald had insisted on bringing him when he'd discovered just how little was actually *known* about the island.

"Well," Reginald said, calmly. "Gars, where do we stand?"

Captain-General Gars leaned forward. Reginald had appointed him the Master of Foot, knowing that Gars had the experience to handle so many troops in battle. It was annoying to realise that Gars had more experience than Reginald himself, but it was just something that had to be tolerated. Reginald's father had been leery of letting Reginald *too* close to the front lines. The death of his only son would be an utter disaster.

"We have roughly five thousand men – soldiers and mercenaries – assembled now," Gars said, without bothering to consult his papers. "Assuming others continue to flow into Humber as predicted, Your Highness, we will be looking at around twelve thousand men – infantry, archers, horsemen – by the time we depart. I've started intensive training already in the fields outside the walls. So far, save for a few minor disciplinary problems, we haven't had any real issues."

"That will change, Your Highness," Captain-General Jones said, in his raspy voice. He hadn't been a healthy child and, even now, he was weaker than his peers. He'd gone into logistics because he could barely ride a horse, let alone swing a blade. "Feeding five thousand men is a nightmare. I dread to imagine what feeding twelve thousand will be like."

"I'm sure you will rise to the challenge," Reginald said. He liked Jones, even though most of their peers considered Jones a weakling. No one could fight a war without a solid understanding of logistics. "Where do we stand on supplies?"

"We are buying up everything in the area," Jones informed him. "But we have also driven prices up ..."

"Then set the prices," Gars snapped.

"Then shopkeepers will hoard food rather than sell it," Jones pointed out, tartly. "We cannot induce them to sell by setting prices."

Reginald held up a hand. "Can you feed the army?"

"Barely," Jones said. "We should be able to get enough supplies for the first month over with the army, but ... it isn't going to be easy."

"The Summer Isle is rich," Milhous said. "Can we not live off the land?"

"They may burn the fields to keep us from taking the grain," Jones said. "It has been done before."

Reginald nodded. He'd led the campaign against Baron Gaunt, a campaign that had come far too close to failure. The man had withdrawn most of his men into his castle, then burnt the lands for miles around. Reginald had been forced to storm the castle – a very costly endeavour – rather than swallow his pride and withdraw. Even now, two years later, the lands hadn't fully recovered. Far too many of the peasants had fled.

"We can solve all these problems," he said. "Shipping?"

"We should have enough ships to transport most of the army," Jones said. "But not every sailor wants to serve under your banner."

"Traitors," Gars muttered.

"Then offer them higher rewards," Reginald said. "Now ... our plan."

He nodded to Milhous. "Tell us about the Summer Isle."

Milhous cleared his throat. "Very little is known about the Summer Isle's past," he said. "However, it is clear that the island was settled from Andalusia two thousand years ago and so we have a valid claim..."

Reginald laughed. "I'm not interested in claims rooted so far in the past," he said, bluntly. If nothing else, treating that claim as valid would open up a thousand other claims that couldn't possibly be verified. "Tell us about it now."

Milhous reddened. "Politically, the Summer Isle is divided into three states," he said. "The Summer Isle proper is flanked by the Wildlands – untamed mountainous lands dominated by savages – and the Northern Realm, a marginally more civilised country inhabited by barbaric brutes. Both countries pledge homage to the Summer Isle, but practically speaking they're both independent."

"That will have to change," Reginald said.

"King Edwin's noblemen are a powerful lot," Milhous added. "He couldn't keep them under control and so ..."

Reginald tapped the map. "And your thoughts?"

Milhous looked as if he wanted to say something cutting, but didn't quite dare. "There are only three cities of real importance," he said, carefully. "Racal's Bay, Allenstown and Georgetown. I believe we will have to claim all three of them to secure the island."

"As well as miles upon miles of towns, villages, farms and untamed countryside," Gars said.

"Quite," Reginald agreed. He pointed to the map. "We need a port. Accordingly, we will land near Racal's Bay and move at once to take the city. Once secured, we will bring in the rest of the army and then march on Allenstown, the capital. The usurper will have to challenge us at some point, if only to keep us from taking the capital and forcing him to flee back to his own lands."

"Which are quite some distance from Allenstown," Jones pointed out.

"He will have to challenge us," Reginald said. "He wants to be a king. If he looks weak, his supporters will start to see us as the *real* power in the land and slip away. And if he leaves Racal's Bay in our hands, we can just keep bringing in men and supplies until we can overwhelm him."

He smiled, rather coolly. There had been no point in trying to disguise the invasion preparations, not when they could have only one conceivable goal. Reginald would be astonished if the usurper didn't already know what was coming. Instead, he'd sent the usurper a message, ordering him to submit and pay homage ... or die. And he'd worded the message very carefully. No nobleman would submit to it, not unless a sword was held to his throat. There would be no peace. And no peace meant that Reginald could take the Summer Isle at will.

"We will accept surrenders and homage, of course," he added. "But we will make it clear that we will not tolerate backsliding. I am not King Edwin and I have no intention of allowing my sworn liegemen to change their minds."

He allowed himself a moment of sympathy for King

Edwin. The poor man had never had the force to impose his will on his subjects. He'd been bullied into accepting a queen who couldn't or wouldn't give him children, something that had ensured his line would end with him. Reginald couldn't imagine being so weak. His father had always been strong enough to keep the barons in line, even in the chaos that had spread across the land after the Golden City had fallen. Reginald had banged heads together for his father himself.

"Those who submit will be watched carefully," he told them. "And those who refuse to submit will be crushed."

Milhous took a breath. "There were – there *are* – three earls," he said. "The usurper, formerly Earl Hereford. His family were, perhaps, the most powerful people on the Summer Isle, powerful enough to make the king their servant. They were certainly able to prevent him from putting his queen, Emetine Hereford, aside. Then we have Earl Goldenrod, who is probably fairly close to Hereford in power, and Earl Oxley. Oxley is the weakest of the three, which may make him amenable to diplomacy."

Reginald shrugged. Oxley *might* bargain or he might not. Either way, Reginald would make sure he held the whip hand. Weakest of the three or not, Oxley would still be powerful within his own lands. It would be best to ensure that all negotiations were conducted from a position of strength.

Gars leaned forward. "What will the other two earls do, when we land?"

"I think they'll wait and see who comes out on top," Milhous said. "Neither of them will welcome our arrival, but I can't imagine that either of them are pleased with Hereford declaring himself king. From their point of view, the ideal outcome would be a battle that leaves Hereford grossly weakened, allowing them a chance to strike to re-establish the balance of power. Or even a stalemate that gives them a chance to come to favourable terms with us."

"Which isn't going to happen," Reginald said. His father had had problems with overmighty nobles, even though he'd been far stronger than King Edwin. Reginald had no intention of allowing that problem to persist into his reign.

"And they have to know it."

"They may not," Milhous pointed out.

Reginald rather doubted it. Andalusia was the Summer Isle's closest neighbour – and the country that had provided men and materials to King Edwin, when he'd sought to retake his throne. Anyone with half a brain – and he assumed the usurper had a working brain – would keep an eye on his neighbour, just to determine which way the neighbouring monarch was likely to jump. The Summer Isle's nobility would have seen what Reginald and his father had done to their rebellious aristocrats, and trembled. It was unlikely that any of them would bare their throats for the blade.

Good, he thought. *I can take their lands and distribute them at will.*

"We may have to improvise, at times, once we arrive on the Summer Isle," he said. "But for the moment ... I want to be ready to leave in two weeks."

Jones frowned. "It may be doable," he said. "However, supplies may run short."

"We don't have much time," Reginald reminded him. "How long until the autumn winds start howling down the channel?"

Gars made a face. "I *hate* sailing."

Reginald nodded in wry agreement. He understood soldiering, from marching in formation to advancing to attack the enemy. He'd done all of it and more. But sailing ... he disliked sailing. He hated feeling helpless on a wooden ship as the wind started to blow, threatening to tip them over or drive them onto the shore. And he'd have to take orders from sailors. He knew, all too well, that he *didn't* understand sailing.

Lord William didn't look any happier. Reginald allowed himself a tight smile. Perhaps Lord William would remain below decks for the voyage. It wasn't as if it would take that long to cross the channel. He'd already rounded up sailors who knew the route into the Summer Bay and made them pick out possible landing sites near Racal's Bay. Who knew? Maybe Lord William would be so ill he'd have to be sent straight back home.

"Now," he said. "About the ..."

There was a tap on the door. Reginald looked up and barked a command. His staff knew not to interrupt him, unless it was truly urgent. Whoever had disturbed them must have a very good reason.

One of his staffers entered the room and bowed. "Your Highness," he said. "You asked to be notified when a sorcerer entered the city. One has just arrived."

"Very good," Reginald said. His call for magicians hadn't attracted many magic-users. It was a serious concern, if only because he had no idea how many magicians were waiting for him on the Summer Isle. "Was he invited to the castle?"

"*She*, Your Highness," the staffer said. "And yes ... she's currently travelling with a group of mercenaries."

"Then ask them to wait for me," Reginald said. He nodded to his council as he rose. "We'll meet again tomorrow evening. Dismissed."

Chapter Seven

Isabella could smell Humber hours before the city came into view, a stench of rotting fish mingled with the sour taste of far too many humans living in close proximity. Her stomach churned as they cantered down the road, racing the sun as it slowly dipped below the distant horizon. Sleeping outside was hardly a problem, particularly as the city's walls seemed to be surrounded by tents and makeshift barracks, but it wouldn't please Lord Robin. He'd want to get inside the walls before night fell and the gates were closed.

Her body ached as they finally rode up to the gates. She'd been sitting in the saddle too long; far too long. She hadn't ached so badly since she'd entered her training program, when her instructors – sadistic bastards to a man – had routinely beaten the crap out of her just to prove she didn't know as much as she thought she knew. But she had to admit that their beatings had served a purpose, unlike the long-distance ride. She rather doubted that being a day late would cause *too* many problems for Lord Robin.

The guards on the gate were alert, holding their swords and spears at the ready as the company came to a halt. Isabella thought she could see archers, half-hidden behind the arrow slits on the guardhouse. She didn't really blame the Crown Prince for being paranoid, not with so many strangers surrounding the city. Mercenaries weren't the most disciplined troops in the world – even regular soldiers could run riot from time to time – and the Crown Prince would want to nip any problems in the bud.

She watched Lord Robin speaking to the guard, turning her head from side to side to check out her fellow mercenaries. Big Richard looked disgustingly alert, for someone who'd had a hangover only eleven hours ago; he eyed her with his piggy eyes, then made a show of looking away. The others didn't look any better than she felt. They all needed hot baths and a long rest, but she doubted they'd get either. The mercenary camp probably didn't have anything beyond the basics.

Which means we'll be crapping into a pit, she thought, sourly.

She made a face. It wasn't going to be pleasant, not even slightly. There would be no shortage of camp women and inexpensive whores, but *someone* would try it on, as sure as eggs were eggs. She readied a handful of really nasty spells, ones that would teach any would-be rapist a permanent lesson. No one would complain if she castrated a rapist and then dumped him in the cesspit.

Lord Robin raised his voice. "We're being invited to the castle," he said. "Isabella, you're with me. Dolman, take the others to the camp and find a spot to set up our tents. I'll find you when we're finished."

Isabella frowned. "What did you tell them?"

"The truth," Robin said. "You're a sorceress and I'm an experienced war leader."

He pushed his horse forward, through the gate. Isabella followed, feeling a trickle of fear as they passed under the liquid channels. The guards would have boiling oil up there, waiting for someone to try to force their way into the city. She'd never liked walking under the channels, even though she knew it was safe. Her imagination kept suggesting that someone was about to pour the oil onto her head.

The smell grew stronger inside the city. Isabella muttered a spell under her breath, trying to dampen the stench a little. Humber was small and large at the same time, a complex network of stone houses leading down the hillside to the docks. Hundreds of guardsmen patrolled the streets, eying the mercenaries warily. There were only a few civilians – all of them male – in sight. Isabella guessed, as Robin led her up the road to the castle, that there had already been a string of incidents. The three men hanging from scaffolds, clearly visible as they approached the castle gate, were silent proof that the Crown Prince was determined to keep a firm grip on his men. Isabella nodded in approval. One had to be firm when dealing with mercenaries. Given an inch, they'd take a mile.

Someone must have sent a runner to the castle, as a fresh-faced young man was waiting for them just outside the massive stone building. He bowed politely to Lord Robin, then motioned a pair of stable boys to take the horses while he escorted their riders inside. Isabella clambered down, cursing her aching body under her breath. For once, Lord Robin looked just as worn. They'd been in the saddle for *far* too long.

"Thank you for coming," the man said. He looked from Lord Robin to Isabella and then back again. "Do you want to freshen up before you meet the Crown Prince?"

"Yes, please," Lord Robin said. "We are not particularly clean."

"Please follow me," the young man said. "I'll show you to the washroom."

Isabella followed him through the castle, looking around with interest. It had clearly been allowed to fall into disrepair over the years, although teams of workmen were hastily patching holes in the defences. She had no way to be sure, but she rather suspected that whoever held the castle had a mansion in town. The interior was cold and smelly, the mud-stained floors charred and pitted ... it was hardly suitable for a lord and lady. It didn't strike her as particularly defendable, either. The townsfolk had built their homes far too close to the castle's walls.

It must have been different, back in the day, she thought. *But the absence of any real threat made the owners lazy.*

The washroom was communal, unsurprisingly. Isabella made use of the facilities, then took a basin of water and washed her face and hands. There was no point in trying to change. She didn't have a spare set of clothes with her – she'd left them in her saddlebags – and anything the castle could provide would probably be unsuitable. She wasn't wearing a dress and she doubted the castle's seamstresses had bothered to sew leathers designed for wearers with breasts. The gods knew she'd had to have *hers* specially sewn years ago.

Lord Robin coughed. "You look a mess."

Isabella scowled. "So do you."

She rubbed her legs as Lord Robin headed for the door,

then followed him. She was going to be stiff tomorrow, no matter what spells she used. And she couldn't show weakness in front of the men, any more than she could wear a dress. If they started to think of her as a weak and foolish female, it would only be a matter of time before one of them did something stupid, even though she'd fought and bled beside them. She didn't want to have to kill one of the mercenaries to make a point.

The man led them up a narrow flight of stairs – narrow enough to make it hard for someone like Big Richard to get up without trapping himself – and into a small sitting room. A fire roared in the fireplace, but it still felt cold. Isabella looked around with interest, noting the empty bookshelves and places on the stone wall that had clearly been designed to take a painting or two. She'd been right, she decided. Whoever owned the castle had moved out long ago.

A door opened, revealing the Crown Prince, followed by a middle-aged man who had a sour expression on his face. Isabella didn't know the Crown Prince by sight, of course – all the paintings she'd seen were insanely muscular, to the point she doubted the poor man could *walk* – but no one else would wear a golden breastplate, marked with the double-eagle insignia of his family. Personally, she thought the golden armour was a little *too* striking, but it did distract attention from his face.

Lord Robin bowed, politely. "Your Highness."

Isabella followed suit, ignoring the sniff of disapproval from the sour-faced man. She was a sorceress, not some brainless beauty from a lineage so pure that there was more than a hint of incest hidden somewhere in the family tree. It was important that the Crown Prince saw her as a person, rather than a tool. Or someone to be married off, for that matter. She'd had too much of that from her family already.

She studied the Crown Prince with interest, aware that he was studying her back. He was tall and handsome, his face unmarred by scars ... his reputation as a soldier was either exaggerated, then, or understated. His frame wasn't anything like as muscular as his portraits, unsurprisingly, but it was clear that he *was* a very strong man. He didn't move like an untried one, either. Someone had given him some decent training, which had then been refined by experience. His blond hair was a little too long for her liking – she'd been brought up to expect men to cut their hair short – but otherwise ... he was a handsome man. And not too handsome to be true ...

"Your Highness," she said.

"Lady Sorceress," the Crown Prince said. He studied her with frank interest. "How powerful are you?"

"I studied at the Peerless School," Isabella said, flatly. "And I graduated with high marks."

The sour-faced man sniffed. "They all say that."

Isabella didn't hesitate. She lifted her hand and cast a spell. There was a brilliant flash of green light, followed by utter silence. The sour-faced man was gone. In his place, a large warty toad was sitting on the ground, blinking in confusion. The Crown Prince let out a peal of laughter. Isabella couldn't help feeling a flicker of admiration. There was no fear in his eyes, even after seeing her use magic. Most men were terrified when they came face-to-face with a witch.

"Impressive," the Crown Prince said. "And how long will he stay a ... a frog?"

It was a toad, not a frog, but Isabella kept that thought to herself. "How long would you *like* him to stay a frog?"

The toad let out a croaking sound. No one handled their first transformation particularly well, even if they were transformed into an animal instead of an inanimate object. The sour-faced man had to be panicking, wondering if he was stuck that way for the rest of his life. It wouldn't last long, if she left the curse alone, but with a few minor changes she could prolong the transformation indefinitely.

"Unfortunately, Lord William is meant to be helping me," the Crown Prince said. "Turn him back, please."

Isabella hesitated, just for a second. There was an edge in the Crown Prince's voice that annoyed her, even though she understood. He wanted – he needed – to test her willingness to obey orders as well as cast spells. And yet ... she wasn't working for him just yet, was she?

She released the spell. The man – Lord William – appeared in a flash of green light. He was trembling, shaking from head to toe. No doubt it was his *first* transformation. Outside the Peerless School and other magical communities, it wasn't *that* uncommon. The shock alone must have terrified him. He opened his mouth, as if he wanted to shout and scream, then closed it again. He was too scared to say a word.

"A vast improvement, no doubt," the Crown Prince said, dryly. "Are you willing to work for me?"

"I work for Lord Robin," Isabella said. The title sounded empty in her voice. Whoever had fathered Lord Robin hadn't left him anything he could use to establish himself. "But I'm sure we can come to some arrangement."

***

Reginald was torn, if he were forced to be honest with himself, between an urge to giggle inanely and a desperate desire to run. He was a soldier, but he knew – all too well – that he couldn't fight magic. The girl in front of him – the young woman, really – could turn him into a frog with a snap of her fingers ... or worse, if she wished. There was no shortage of stories about kings and princes who'd been turned into slaves by magic, all spread – he was sure – to ensure that no monarch defied his court wizard.

He studied the sorceress, trying to see ... he wasn't sure *what* he was trying to see. She didn't *look* like any sorceress he'd ever seen. She wore a set of mercenary leathers over a dark green shirt and pair of trousers. Her clothes were designed to hide the shape of her body, he realised slowly. The swell of her breasts were almost completely concealed behind the leathers. He would have taken her for a man if he hadn't known she was a woman.

Her face was feminine, he noted, although her close-cropped dark hair made her look like a slightly effeminate man. No Adam's apple, of course. She carried a nasty scar on her right cheek, as well as a bruise that looked to be fading slowly. And she was tall. The taller the magician, the stronger the magic. Or so he'd been told. Too many of his lessons in magic had been mindless generalities rather than anything useful. She was nothing like a woman of the court, yet ... she was attractive ...

He pushed that thought down, hard. His father had given him a handful of magical protections, amulets that had been passed down the generations, but they weren't perfect. The court wizards – damn them – had made *that* clear. And if he pressed her, he might end up a frog too. No one would follow him after they'd seen him turned into a frog. It would be the end of his authority.

"I need someone to provide magical support," he said. "And I also need someone to serve as liaison between the mercenaries and me. Lord Robin and his men will be welcome to serve in that role."

The woman glanced at her companion. *That* was interesting. It was hard to be sure, of course, but Reginald was fairly sure that Lord Robin – *Lord* Robin – was no magician. And that meant that she respected him enough to follow his lead. They didn't orientate on each other like lovers, which suggested they probably weren't sleeping together, but ... Reginald shrugged. It wasn't as though Lord Robin ran a troop of regular soldiers. A mercenary captain could hire whoever he wanted.

"That would be suitable, for the moment," Lord Robin said. "However, we were hired to serve as scouts."

"Rest assured, you'll have your chance," Reginald told him. He looked at the woman. "I have a handful of magic-users in camp and some more on the way. Will you supervise them?"

"If that is what you want," the sorceress said. "Although we do have to discuss payment."

"Of course," Reginald said. He smiled, thinly. "If we win, lands on the Summer Isle."

They haggled backwards and forwards for a long moment. Reginald found himself enjoying it, even though Lord Robin was clearly an experienced negotiator. He'd be loyal too, Reginald thought, as long as he was being paid. The promise of lands of his own – even lands on the Summer Isle – would be enough, at least for the moment. A natural-born son – and Reginald made a mental note to look up who'd fathered Lord Robin – would be set up for life.

And being part of my household would put him at the top, when I take the throne, Reginald thought. He had no particular objection to working with a bastard. No doubt Lord William would complain, when he got over the shock of being a frog. But Reginald found it hard to care. *As long as Robin remains loyal, I'll support him.*

He cocked his head when the haggling finally came to an end. "Do you know *anything* about magic on the Summer Isle?"

The woman's face went blank, just for a moment. "Very little," she said, finally. "I know of no magicians who came from the island. If there are magic-users over there, they're keeping themselves well-hidden."

Reginald frowned. She knew something. Or at least she *thought* she knew something. But what?

"We'll find out soon," he said. "My equerry will arrange rooms for you in the castle. You'll both be invited to my councils, starting tomorrow."

"I have to see to my men," Lord Robin said. "But afterwards, I will be at your disposal."

"Very good," Reginald said. "I thank you."

He watched the odd couple leave, then turned to Lord William. "I trust that wasn't *too* terrifying?"

Lord William was still shaking. "That ... that ..."

Reginald hid a smile. Giving Lord Robin – and his sorceress – a job had many advantages, not least that it would annoy the older man. It wasn't the one he'd tell his father, if King Romulus asked, but it was definitely the one he'd keep foremost in his own mind. And besides, he'd be able to hold the whole frog episode over Lord William's head for the rest of his life.

"I'm sure she'll work out fine," he said. "Just think of how quickly meetings will go if she does that to *everyone*."

"She'll feed you love potion," Lord William managed. "Or something worse."

"I don't think she'd need to bother," Reginald said. "And besides, we need her."

"We don't need *him*, Your Highness," Lord William said. He sounded steadier now. "Why did you give him the liaison job?"

A dozen answers ran through Reginald's mind. "Because we need someone who can speak to mercenaries as one of their own," he said, simply. It was a good reason. It just wasn't the *only* one. "And because Gars has too much work to do."

And because I don't want Gars getting too chummy with the mercenaries, he added, silently. He trusted Gars. But, at the same time, he didn't want to put temptation in his way. Too many princes and kings had died because they'd trusted the wrong man. *And the more my clients depend upon me, the harder it will be for them to betray me.*

Chapter Eight

"Your Majesty," Lord Havant said, as he stepped into the private audience chamber. His brother was seated on the throne. "You called for me."

"I did indeed," King Rufus Hereford said. He smiled in welcome. "Please, take a seat. Emetine will be along in a moment."

Havant smiled back, even though he knew that far too many noblemen – and commoners – would be outraged at the thought of allowing a mere *woman* a chance to address the king. A woman was meant to do as she was told, first by her father and then by her husband; she was not supposed to have a life or interests of her own. And yet, Emetine had been part of the Hereford Family's bid for power ever since their father had died. She had a different perspective on life.

And no one thinks a mere woman can be dangerous, Havant thought. No one had connected Emetine to King Edwin's death, not yet. It hadn't occurred to them that she might have taken a sample of her husband's blood and sneaked it out of the castle. *They didn't even think to search her bags when she left to visit her family.*

He sat down, smiling to himself. The long game of power wasn't over yet – there was still the threat from Andalusia – but the family was closer than ever before to absolute power. Havant and his brother would have happily backed a nephew, if King Edwin had actually managed to sire a child, yet ... Edwin had been infertile. Or impotent. Or simply unwilling to take the risk of siring a child on Emetine Hereford. Who knew *what* her brothers might have done after there was a legitimate heir, one too young to wield power in his own right?

Emetine entered and curtseyed to the king, then took the other chair. She was the youngest of the three siblings, at twenty-seven, but she looked older. Sleeping next to King

Edwin had aged his sister, Havant considered, even though the king had barely touched her. Her widow's blacks – her dress the same colour as her hair – made her look like a crow. And yet, there was a glimmer of amusement in her eyes. As the queen, she'd had almost no power; as the younger sister of Rufus and Havant, she wielded genuine power and influence. And she was still young enough to marry again.

"Goldenrod is stalling," Rufus said, without preamble. The siblings didn't need titles, not amongst themselves. They'd grown up together in the shadow of their father, struggling to escape his notice. "He hasn't given us any actual *answer*, so far, but that's an answer in its own right."

"He isn't convinced you'll stay king," Emetine said, flatly.

Havant nodded in agreement. The combination of the Crown Lands and the Hereford Lands made King Rufus the most powerful man on the Summer Isle, but it would take time for him to translate that advantage into real power. Earl Goldenrod – and Earl Oxley – had time to forge a counter-alliance or, if they thought they couldn't win in the long-term, sell out for the best terms they could get. Earl Goldenrod wouldn't allow his daughter to marry Rufus until he believed it was in his own best interest.

"What about Oxley's daughters?" He asked. "One of them might be a better choice."

"The oldest girl is too old to have children," Emetine said, curtly. There was a hint of resentment in her voice. She was the daughter of one of the most powerful men on the isle and sister to another, but she'd failed in the first duty of a wife. It would be hard to marry her off to someone else, whatever the short-term advantages. "The middle girl is already married. And the youngest girl is too young."

"A betrothal might help stabilise the situation," Havant pointed out. "It would certainly bind Oxley to us."

"It would also push Goldenrod into opposition," Rufus said. "And a betrothal is not a marriage."

Havant nodded. A betrothal could be broken at any time. Earl Oxley would use the promised marriage for leverage, using the threat of breaking the agreement to force Rufus and his family to comply. And besides, Goldenrod would see it as a threat. The alliance of Hereford, Oxley and the Crown

Lands would be more than enough to bring him to heel and he knew it. He'd strike before Rufus could mass the force to destroy him utterly.

"And we have the threat from the north to worry about," Rufus added. "Goldenrod may be talking to the Cold King."

"Treason," Havant said, dryly. It wasn't as if *they* hadn't talked to the Cold King, once upon a time. The ruler of the Northern Realm had every interest in keeping the Summer Isle divided into a morass of feuding noblemen. And who could blame him? The last time the south had invaded the north, they'd marched all the way to Cold Harbour and burnt it to the ground. "I assume we have no actual *proof*?"

Rufus snorted. "Would it matter?"

He tapped his armrest, firmly. "The north appears to be planning a large-scale raid into our lands," he told them. "The *family* lands."

"I don't like the timing," Emetine said. "How long will it be until Prince Reginald sets sail?"

"If he ever does," Rufus said. "Getting a large army across the channel will be an utter nightmare."

Havant frowned. He'd hoped that King Romulus would accept Rufus's ascension to the throne as a done deal. It wasn't as if King Edwin had any *right* to promise his kingdom to King Romulus. And besides, Andalusia had border troubles of its own. But it looked as though Prince Reginald was *serious* about invading the Summer Isle. He was certainly wasting a great deal of money if all he wanted to do was posture threateningly before coming to terms with the Summer Isle's new monarch.

And yet ... Havant had sailed the waters around the Summer Isle. He knew, all too well, that the weather could change in an instant, that a fleet of proud ships might find itself scattered to the four winds. Even getting *one* ship across the channel was a nightmare, particularly if the crew wasn't experienced. The currents and tides were enough to dishearten the stoutest of sailors. Prince Reginald would be gambling the fortunes of his entire house if he *really* wanted to invade the Summer Isle.

But Emetine was right. The timing *was* suspicious. A threat from the north, one aimed at the Hereford Lands, could not be ignored.   And yet, a threat from the south was developing at the same time. It was possible that it was a coincidence, he supposed, but it struck him as unlikely. There was no such thing as a coincidence when games of power were being played.

"Prince Reginald *has* nailed his colours to the mast," Rufus said. "You *did* read the ultimatum, didn't you?"

Emetine made a face. "He *was* very rude, wasn't he?"

Havant nodded.   King Edwin, for all his faults, would never have spoken to one of his noblemen in such a manner. The Summer Isle's noblemen were prideful. To be spoken to as if they were naughty children – or serfs – would have been utterly unacceptable. King Edwin would have been unseated – again – if he'd allowed his contempt to show so openly. None of his aristocrats would have stood for it. And no one would expect *Rufus* to bend the knee after receiving such an ultimatum. He couldn't. It would make him look weak in front of his vassals.

"I don't think he expected you to surrender," Emetine said. "I think he *wants* a fight."

"Perhaps," Havant agreed. His sister had always been the most *perceptive* of the three. She was certainly better at diplomacy than either of her brothers. It was just a shame that her husband had never appreciated her. "He's certainly made it impossible to come to terms."

He closed his eyes for a long moment, contemplating the situation. Prince Reginald *could* have demanded that Rufus pay homage to King Romulus, in exchange for ruling the Summer Isle. None of the siblings would have liked it, but the mere act of performing homage would have committed King Romulus to upholding Rufus's grip on the throne. It would certainly have allowed them to secure their gains and prepare for the inevitable next round.   Instead, Prince Reginald had demanded complete submission. Emetine was right. Prince Reginald was spoiling for a fight.

Rufus cleared his throat. "We cannot allow the threat to our ancestral lands to go unanswered," he said. "If we lose our power base ..."

He didn't need to finish. The siblings knew, all too well, what would happen if the Hereford Lands were devastated.

Their power base would be gravely weakened, their clients would seek protection elsewhere, their serfs would rebel ... it could not be tolerated. King Edwin hadn't managed to wield effective power because he hadn't been able to build up an army without provoking a renewed civil war. King Rufus could not afford to be weakened in the same way. He lacked even the paper-thin legitimacy that had kept King Edwin on a powerless throne.

"We shall act fast," Rufus said. "Havant and I will take two-thirds of the army to the Narrows, where we'll establish new defence lines. If the Cold King really does want a fight, we'll give him one. Smashing his army will set off another round of civil wars in the north."

Havant smiled, nastily. The northern aristocracy made the southern noblemen look like sweet little kittens. If the Cold King took a beating, it wouldn't be long before someone rose up against him or stuck a knife in his back. The north was littered with the bodies of kings – or would-be kings – who'd lost power ... and their lives, shortly afterwards. Rufus was right, he admitted coolly. A vigorous response to the threat might be enough to stop it in its tracks.

And marching a powerful army so close to the Goldenrod Lands might be enough to convince Earl Goldenrod to join us, he thought. *Or at least to agree to a truce long enough to keep Prince Reginald out.*

"Emetine will remain here, in charge," Rufus added. "And I'll dispatch a small force to Racal's Bay. If Prince Reginald really does intend to land an army, there is nowhere else he can go."

"Except Georgetown," Emetine said.

Rufus shook his head. "The logistics would be an utter nightmare," he said. "And he couldn't claim the kingdom until he held Allenstown."

"Unless he plans to devastate our lands," Havant said.

"We'll have our army nearby," Rufus said. "But really, if he wants to land an army, it's going to be tough enough landing at Racal's Bay."

Havant nodded, slowly. He couldn't disagree with his brother's logic. No one in their right mind would try to sail a fleet to Georgetown. And yet, he had a bad feeling about the whole affair. The timing was really – really – bad.

"I could go to Racal's Bay," he said. "What if I went there ...?"

"I need you with the army," Rufus said. "What happens if I die?"

Havant frowned. Rufus was right. *Someone* would have to take command – immediately – if the king was killed, and Havant *was* his brother's heir. Emetine couldn't take command of an army. The senior officers would see her as a prize to be won, or seized, instead of a potential commander. But whoever they sent to Racal's Bay had better be both competent and trustworthy. He was grimly aware that Prince Reginald could offer plenty of money to anyone willing to switch sides. The Prince would certainly need locals to help govern the Summer Isle after the fighting was over.

Assuming he wins, Havant thought. *If he loses, anyone who switched sides too soon will be in deep shit.*

"I'll leave Lord Francis here, with you," Rufus said, to Emetine. "I assume your ladies will be able to provide sufficient chaperonage?"

Havant rolled his eyes. Lord Francis wasn't interested in *women*. He was more interested in men. It wasn't frowned upon, not amongst the nobility, but Emetine would still need a chaperone. Lord Francis might overcome his disdain for the female form long enough to force Emetine into marriage, if her brothers were killed. Whoever married the king's sister – and the former king's wife – would have a very strong claim to both the throne and the family's lands.

And if that happens, he might be the best person to rule, Havant conceded. *At least Prince Reginald or Earl Goldenrod won't take the throne without a fight.*

"We'll depart tomorrow, once the army is ready," Rufus said. "If we force-march, we should reach the Narrows within a week."

Havant made a face. The army was not going to be in a good state by the time it reached its destination. They'd planned to construct a proper road network, once they'd consolidated power, but ... but they'd just have to make do with the muddy tracks they had. King Edwin had managed to build a handful of roads, yet he'd run into stiff opposition when he'd tried to extend them northwards. None of the aristocrats wanted the king to be able to move forces around the kingdom at will.

In hindsight, that might have been a mistake, Havant thought. *The roads would have been a double-edged sword for Edwin, during the last civil war.*

"I'll speak to Lord Francis later today," Emetine said. "And we'll work on preparing the city for war."

"Very good," Rufus said. He smiled, rather thinly. "Just don't do *too* good a job of it."

Emetine made a show of rolling her eyes. Havant understood. As a woman, Emetine couldn't take and hold power – let alone wield it – for herself. And, as an unmarried woman, she couldn't even pass power to her husband. He had no doubt that Emetine had found the restrictions maddening, when she'd been younger. She'd certainly always revelled in the chance to wield even a scrap of power. If she'd been a man, she would have been fearsomely ambitious. Havant certainly wouldn't have turned his back on her.

But she can keep the city safe for us, with Lord Francis's help, he told himself. Noblemen wouldn't take orders from women, no matter how nobly born. They'd choose to pretend that Lord Francis was in charge. *And if things go wrong, Lord Francis will be a convenient scapegoat.*

He rose, bowed to his brother and sister, then strode out of the chamber. A pair of guards in royal livery nodded to him as he left, careful not to bow so deeply they couldn't grab their weapons. There were noblemen who would make a fuss over not being shown the proper respect from the guardsmen, but Havant knew better. A king had to be guarded against all threats, physical as well as magical. It was just a shame that they didn't have anything like enough magicians to provide a proper set of magical defences.

But we have something better, he told himself as he walked down the stairs. *Don't we?*

King Edwin had been a devotee of Primus, one of the greater gods in the pantheon. He'd even installed a private temple in Allenstown Castle, evicting all the other priests from the building without even bothering to make sure they were installed safely somewhere else. It had been one of the reasons the priesthood had supported Rufus when he'd claimed the throne. Now, the temple had been put to a far greater use.

Havant looked around with interest as he walked into the chamber. The towering statue of Primus – which had borne more than a passing resemblance to King Edwin – was gone, replaced by a simple stone altar. Hark and his monks had scrubbed the walls clean, then carved incomprehensible runes into the stone. Four of the monks were kneeling in front of the altar, the remainder standing by the walls. The sense of ... *promise* ... was almost overpowering.

"Your Highness," Hark said. Havant tried not to jump. Hark was standing right beside him, yet ... he hadn't heard the man approach. Rufus would have laughed at Havant's lack of awareness. An assassin didn't have to get so close to stick a knife in him. "We trust you are pleased?"

"Indeed," Havant said. Hark had kept his promises – and more. The death of King Edwin had allowed Rufus to claim the throne. "And are you pleased?"

"The brethren are already preaching in the streets," Hark said. The Red Monks had demanded the right to proselytise openly, in exchange for their assistance. Havant had no idea why the Golden City had banned the Red Monks – and had even tried to wipe them out – but he didn't care. Power was power, after all. "Many are flocking to our temples, shunning false gods and worshipping ours."

Havant shrugged. Who *cared* what the common folk believed? As long as they were respectful, and worked hard, it didn't *matter* what they believed. And he didn't care what the priests thought, either. King Edwin had been a fool to allow them as much independence as he had. It wasn't a mistake Rufus intended to repeat. The Red Monks would be tolerated as long as they behaved themselves.

"Very good," he said. "But we may soon have to fight to keep our throne."

Hark leaned forward. "Our Lord is with us, Your Highness," he said. He gestured to the altar. "We cannot lose."

"Let us hope that you are right," Havant said. He'd been in

enough battles to know that anything could happen, even when one side appeared to have a decisive advantage. "Your prayers would be welcome."

"Our Lord is with us." Hark's eyes gleamed with fanaticism. "We will not lose."

Chapter Nine

Prince Reginald, Lord William admitted sourly, was a *very* energetic young man.

William had expected that it would take the prince *weeks*, if not months, to put together a fleet and an army, particularly if the latter was nearly two-thirds mercenaries. Instead, the prince had somehow managed to force the mercenaries to work together and assemble a fleet in just under two weeks. They would be in trouble if the Summer Isle managed to put together a defensive fleet of its own, Prince Reginald had cheerfully admitted, but that was unlikely. It was more likely that the weather would force them to turn back if one of the channel gales blew up during the crossing.

Two weeks, William thought. *It took him two weeks to put together a force capable of challenging his father.*

It wasn't a pleasant thought. William had no illusions about just how much Prince Reginald disliked him. He'd known that even before the wretched sorceress had turned ... had turned him into a frog. The whole experience was nothing more than a jarring series of impressions, each one sharp and utterly unrelenting, haunting his dreams while he slept. It was sheer luck that no one knew what had happened, save for the handful of people who'd been in the room when the bitch had cast the spell. But William knew that wouldn't last. And once the story got out, his reputation would sink faster than a rock in water. *Everyone* would be laughing at him.

He paced to the window and peered towards the docks. It was dawn, the first glimmers of light flickering over the distant horizon. They would be boarding soon, boarding and heading out to sea ... and then, setting sail for the Summer Isle. William had done his best to slow the headlong rush to war, pointing out the importance of logistics, but Prince Reginald had been determined to move as fast as possible.

And he had a point, William conceded. The usurper – Reginald had threatened to whip anyone who called Rufus Hereford a *king* – could not be allowed more time to dig in and prepare for war.

And besides, the longer we delay, the more dangerous the crossing, William reminded himself. *The Summer Isle is practically inaccessible in winter.*

He looked down at his hands, trying to hide the shaking. It had taken everything he had to keep the rest of the council from noticing that his confidence had taken a nasty blow. He knew – of course he knew – that there were better swordsmen than himself. He'd never been the finest blade in King Romulus's nobility, even as a young man. But magic? The sorceress had snapped her fingers and turned him into a frog. It ... it wasn't fair. How was one meant to defend against magic? He didn't even have a protective amulet he could wear to keep himself safe!

And the prince thought it was funny, William thought. Dull resentment burned within his breast. Prince Reginald and the sorceress – Isabella, if that was her real name – had spent too much time together, over the last two weeks. It worried him, more than he cared to admit. A sorceress was *de facto* the social equal of a high-ranking noblewoman – no one would dare to suggest otherwise – and would make a worthy mate for a king. *What happens if she marries him?*

He tried to tell himself, firmly, that he was being paranoid. King Romulus would be unlikely to agree, if his son wanted to marry a sorceress with a questionable background. William had set his patronage network of spies to work, trying to ferret out her secrets, but they'd found almost nothing dating back longer than six months. Isabella had appeared out of nowhere, to all intents and purposes, and gone to work for Lord Robin, the *so-called* Lord Robin. She was a trained sorceress, obviously, but there was little else for his agents to find.

And Reginald may have to marry someone on the Summer Isle, William thought. He'd done his research. Emetine Hereford was available, but so was Roxanne Goldenrod. And Earl Oxley had two daughters ... any of the four might make suitable brides, if the prince wanted to secure his conquests. *He might not be interested in a sorceress.*

He shivered, helplessly. The court wizard was dead – and so were far too many other magicians. William didn't know which of the stories to believe. The Golden City couldn't have been destroyed by a god, surely? And yet, it was clear that very few magicians were left alive. A powerful sorceress might just be able to carve out a kingdom for herself – or her husband – if she wished. It was an unnatural thought, yet ... it haunted him. And even so, he couldn't report it to his master. King Romulus would ask questions, time and time again, and then laugh when the truth came out. William had been reduced to a frog ...

There was a tap on the door. "Come!"

He turned as the door opened, allowing Equerry Caen to step into the room, closing the door behind him. William fought to keep his expression under tight control. He'd always disliked the young man, even though he understood the value of a decent whipping boy. Someone had to take the blame, after all, and it sure as hell wouldn't be the king or his son. There were times when William wondered if *he* was King Romulus's whipping boy, in fact if not in name. He might take the blame for something one day ...

"My Lord," Caen said. His voice was polite, but there was a hint of amusement behind the words. Caen had watched him being reduced to a frog, after all. "The Prince wishes you to be informed that we will embark in thirty minutes."

William nodded, curtly. The rank and file were already onboard, of course, cooped up below decks while their social superiors enjoyed what few entertainments Humber could provide. It would have been easy to ride to Havelock – the capital wasn't *that* far away – but Prince Reginald had refused to allow his councillors to leave Humber. William suspected it was nothing more than spite. It wasn't as if Reginald bothered to pay attention to anything William said.

"I'll be on my way shortly," he said. "Inform the Prince that I will attend to him onboard ship."

Caen bowed. "As My Lordship pleases."

William glared, feeling a hot flash of pure loathing. Caen's voice had that hint of amusement, again. If something happened to his patron – if something happened to the *prince*

– William would make sure that Caen's fall from grace would lead him straight to the gallows. It wasn't as if Sofia's husband – whoever he turned out to be – would have any interest in keeping Caen. William would make Caen pay ...

He pushed the thought to the back of his mind as Caen withdrew. William would go with the prince, of course. It was his duty. And who knew? Perhaps he could find evidence that the prince was planning to turn on his father. And who knew where *that* might lead?

His hands trembled, again. He ignored them.

***

"The prince really has done a good job," Isabella said, as the company walked towards the flagship. "This is amazing."

Lord Robin grinned. "And we're being paid very well too," he said. "Even if we lose ..."

"Good," Big Richard grunted. "I don't want land or property."

"You never know," Dolman said. The swordsman smirked. "Some poor noblewoman whose husband was killed during the fighting might *just* want you for her man. Or she might be *given* to you, as a reward for your services. And then you'll be defending her property for the rest of your life."

"And milking it," Mandan put in. "You'll be calling yourself *Lord* Richard."

Big Richard glared at them. "And is that likely to happen?"

"Anything can happen," Isabella said, although privately she rather suspected that no self-respecting noblewoman would want Big Richard anywhere near her. "How many men have made themselves kings in the last five years?"

She smiled to herself. Prince Reginald had promised vast tracts of land – or heiresses with vast tracts of land – to knights, soldiers and mercenaries who proved themselves brave and loyal men. The only problem, of course, was that they'd have to win the war before they could claim their land – and, worse, do it in a manner that ensured the original owners didn't have time to switch sides. Prince Reginald wasn't foolish enough to seize land and property from men who'd chosen to support him. No one would take his word seriously again.

And handing out land and heiresses will keep his men bound to him, she thought. *And in a decade or two no one will care how the land was acquired.*

"We have to take the land first," Lord Robin said. "Let's not get *too* far ahead of ourselves."

Isabella nodded in agreement as they reached the massive ship. It wasn't the biggest vessel she'd seen, but it was definitely the largest in the fleet. Dozens of sailors were swarming over the rigging, checking and rechecking everything before the prince and his councillors arrived. Isabella wasn't sure if the councillors *should* be sharing the same ship, but she had to admit it made a certain kind of sense. Prince Reginald couldn't take the risk of one of his subordinates going on to win the Summer Isle, then declaring independence from Andalusia.

What a snake pit, she thought, wryly. *It's just like home.*

She walked up the gangplank and onto the deck. The ship moved slightly, very slightly, below her feet. It would be worse on the open waters, she reminded herself. She wished, all of a sudden, that she'd learnt how to fly. There were spells that would allow her to breathe water, if necessary, but she'd never liked them. And they had dangerous long-term effects.

A sailor met them at the top of the gangplank. "Your cabins have been prepared, My Lords," he said. His eyes skimmed over Isabella without quite seeing her. "I'm afraid you'll have to double up."

"That is quite understandable," Lord Robin said. "Will we be ready to depart on time?"

"The tide is still coming in," the sailor said. "We should be ready to depart in an hour, if everyone is onboard."

Isabella nodded to herself as the sailor led them towards the nearest hatch. Prince Reginald struck her as being smart enough to understand that no mortal, not even a powerful magician, could command the tides. He and his councillors would be onboard ship at the right time, she was sure. She took a breath, then regretted it instantly as the sailor opened the hatch. A foul smell wafted out.

You've been in worse places, she told herself, firmly. *And you've slept in them too.*

"Partner up," Robin ordered, once the sailor showed them the cabins. "Isabella, you're with me."

The sailor looked as if he wanted to say something, but – thankfully – he had the sense to keep his mouth shut. Isabella smirked at him, making him flinch. It wasn't the first time she'd been mistaken for a man, thanks to her leathers. But everyone knew a sorceress called Isabella had joined the fleet. Thankfully, *most* people would presumably believe that the sorceress would be staying close to the prince.

Which isn't something I'd want to do, she thought, as she stepped into the cabin. *I need to be able to move freely.*

She felt a flicker of dismay as she looked around the cabin. It was tiny, the beds so small that she couldn't help wondering if they'd been designed for children. She was smaller than Lord Robin and *she'd* have trouble sleeping comfortably. It was going to be worse for him. But she supposed it beat sleeping on the deck or in the holds. The infantrymen below decks would be having a very unpleasant time.

I've slept in worse places, she reminded herself, again. She dropped her bag on the bed, then muttered a protective charm. *And I don't have to stay in the cabin.*

Lord Robin grunted in dismay. "How long is this voyage meant to take again?"

"Depends on the weather," Isabella said. "Optimistically, one day; pessimistically, six days ... or forever."

She groaned as she saw the chamberpot under the bed. It wasn't going to be a very pleasant trip, even assuming good weather. And if they encountered bad weather ...

"It's worth the risk," Lord Robin said. "Think of the rewards!"

Isabella shrugged. Lord Robin and Big Richard might get lands, if they wished, but it would be harder for Prince Reginald to give *her* lands. Unless, of course, she married an heir instead of an heiress. And even then ... she shook her head. She didn't want lands. But what *did* she want? She wasn't sure herself.

Look around the island and find out if there's any truth to the rumours, she told herself, firmly. *And worry about the future when it comes.*

***

"Your Highness," Lord William said. "The last of the soldiers have embarked."

Reginald nodded, curtly. William had been in a snit over the last few days, although it hadn't been enough to keep him from sitting on the council and making a nuisance of himself. Damn the man ... it wasn't as though he contributed anything *useful*. The risks he whined about? There were always risks in war. Reginald knew that as well as anyone else. He could do everything right and still lose.

"Very good," he said, as he looked around the deck. The rest of his council were already below decks, hopefully catching up with their sleep. "Admiral Tanoan, are we ready to depart?"

"The tide is in," Tanoan said. He was a gruff man with decades of experience sailing the waters around Andalusia, liked and respected by the entire waterfront community. Reginald had made Tanoan an admiral as soon as he'd joined the fleet. "We can depart on your command."

"Then let us depart," Reginald said.

Tanoan turned and hurried away, barking indecipherable commands to his men. The sailors went to work, releasing the ship from the docks and hoisting sail. Reginald watched, feeling a thrill of admiration for the sailors as the ship got under way. He was sailing for the first time in his life.

He lifted his eyes, picking out Humber Castle. It looked imposing from a distance, even though he knew it wasn't anything like as defendable as he might have wished. He was going to have to do something about that, sooner or later. He'd informed his father of the risks, but Humber was very low on his father's list of priorities. The small city simply wasn't very important, not compared to Havelock.

The boat lurched, a shudder running through the wood as she inched between the harbour walls. Waves started to slap against the hull, now they were past the breakwater. Reginald felt a flicker of fear, mingled with excitement.

He'd never been allowed to go sailing before – it was one of the few things his father had flatly forbidden – and now ... now he was excited and nervous. He understood battlefields, but ships ...? A single accident could drown him as easily as any of the men in the hold.

"Your Highness," William said. "With your permission, I think I would like to go below."

Reginald eyed him, mischievously. William was looking pale ... was he seasick? Reginald weighed the irritation of William's presence against the possibility of making William very uncomfortable, then decided it wasn't worth the bother. He dismissed the older man with a nod and turned his attention back to the receding shoreline. Small boys were clearly visible on the rocks, fishing or scooping up small crabs to supplement their diet. One of them made a rude sign towards the departing ships, clearly confident that none of their crews would recognise him. Reginald smiled and waved at the little scamp, then dismissed the matter with a shake of his head.

He wasn't too surprised, to be honest. Humber had appreciated the money he'd brought into the city, but the city fathers hadn't enjoyed the bar fights or violence on the streets. And even though he'd made a show of punishing soldiers or mercenaries who took advantage of the civilians, he knew there were limits to their gratitude. They couldn't decide if they welcomed the prospect of more trade with the Summer Isle or feared what would happen if their city became more important.

The wind blew stronger. He took one last look at the city, then turned to peer forward. The Summer Isle was clearly visible in the distance, shadowed cliffs mocking him with their impassable walls. A handful of smugglers had told him that it was possible to disembark men under the cliffs and climb up, but not – alas – an entire army. They had no choice. They had to land near Racal's Bay.

A cold gust of wind brushed against him as he clasped his hands behind his back, watching the fleet as it slowly moved further into the channel. It was an impressive sight, for all that he knew it had weaknesses. A lone sorcerer – or sorceress – could wreak havoc with a handful of fireballs.

And if the usurper had had the time to put a fleet of his own on the waves ...

But he didn't have time, Reginald told himself. The Summer Isle had never been a major naval power. Even now, King Edwin hadn't had time to start a construction program before his untimely death. *And the Summer Isle is ripe for the taking.*

He smiled, again, as the winds blew stronger. The future was waiting for him ...

... And it looked bright and full of promise.

Chapter Ten

"This is supposed to be Summer Bay," Prince Reginald shouted.

Isabella barely heard him over the rolling thunder. The skies had opened seven minutes ago, rain lashing down on the fleet while lightning flashed high overhead. Summer Bay was sheltered, according to the sailors, but if that was true she dreaded to think what it would be like to face a storm in the open sea. The ship was heaving so violently that it made her want to throw herself overboard before the inevitable happened and the ship was overturned.

She caught hold of the railing as the ship lurched again, peering into the distance. Dark grey clouds, pregnant with heavy rain, dominated the horizon. Visibility was almost zero. In the half-light, she could barely make out a couple of other ships, half-hidden in the gloom. They might be *supposed* to be in the mouth of Summer Bay, but for all she knew they were hundreds of miles in the wrong direction. She gritted her teeth as the ship rocked, again. The wind was buffeting them savagely.

The prince looked in his element, even though his hair was wet and his clothes were soaked, clinging tightly to his skin. He laughed as water dripped down his face, looking into the storm as if he was daring it to defy him. Isabella wasn't sure if she should admire his determination or roll her eyes at his stupidity. The storm wouldn't care if Prince Reginald screamed his defiance into the wind or not. But then, she'd noted that young men were often prone to dramatic gestures. The Crown Prince had to look good as well as *be* good.

Lightning flashed, again. Thunder echoed over the bay a second later, so hard on the lightning's heels that the storm *had* to be directly overhead. Isabella shook her head as the prince laughed again, feeling water dripping down her shirt and into her trousers. She'd be drenched to the bone if she stayed outside, yet ... she wanted to stay through the height of the storm. It wasn't something she'd ever done before.

The boat rocked, time and time again. Isabella kept a tight grip on the railings, hoping that Lord Robin and the others were alright. Big Richard had been the only one to avoid seasickness, although the others had got better fairly quickly. She'd be glad when the voyage was over, even though she knew the fighting would begin as soon as they landed on the Summer Isle. Two days of sailing had cured her of any desire she might have had to go to sea permanently. She didn't envy the handful of cabin boys clinging to wet ropes as they hurried about their duties.

Her lips twitched. Unless she missed her guess, two of the cabin boys were actually cabin *girls*. It wasn't something a man would notice, not unless he had his nose rubbed in it, but the signs were there if one bothered to look. She was tempted to talk to them, although she knew it might merely draw unwelcome attention in their direction. The girls could pass for boys as long as no one had a reason to look too closely.

Lightning flashed, once again. This time, it was several seconds before the thunder roared through the air. Isabella allowed herself a smile as the gloom slowly began to lift, more and more ships becoming visible in the distance. Sailors whooped and hollered, sending up prayers to the gods of the sea for having spared them a cold and watery grave. Isabella wasn't so sure. There was still plenty of time for the gods to condemn the sailors – and soldiers – instead.

"Land HO," the lookout called. "LAND HO!"

Reginald turned to her. "Look," he said, pointing into the distance. "I see land!"

Isabella followed his gaze. He was right. A faint patch of land could be seen in the distance, barely visible in the haze. And that meant ... the navigators hadn't been wrong after all. The fleet had entered the mouth of Summer Bay.

"Get changed," Reginald urged. "I'll be calling a meeting in twenty minutes."

"I can use a spell to dry myself," Isabella said. The rain was slowly coming to an end. She smiled at him, then looked into the distance. The land was coming closer.

"What about you?"

Reginald shrugged. "I'll change before we land," he said. "Shall we go?"

***

Reginald had been warned, time and time again, that the weather in the channel could change very quickly, but he hadn't really appreciated what he'd been told until he'd actually made the crossing himself. Two days of sunshine and rainstorms had left him questioning the wisdom of invading the Summer Isle, even though the voyage was finally coming to a conclusion. The sunlight beaming down on them, making it hard to believe that it had been raining twenty minutes ago, might vanish at any moment.

"We're going to land here," he said, pointing to the map. He'd taken over the captain's cabin and turned it into a war room. "Two miles to the north of Racal's Bay."

"Very good, Your Highness," Gars said. The Captain-General sounded weak. He hadn't enjoyed the voyage any more than anyone else. "When can we land?"

"We can start disembarking the first wave in an hour, more or less," Admiral Tanoan said. "But unloading the rest of the fleet will take time."

"We need to take Racal's Bay," Reginald said. The plan they'd worked out was good, but two-thirds of his soldiers were in no condition to fight. "Captain-General Stuart, I want pickets fanning out in all directions – make sure all approaches to Racal's Bay are covered. If they decide to meet us on the beaches, I want to know about it. Captain-General Gars, assemble the healthy men and prepare to meet an offensive."

"Yes, Your Highness," Gars said. He sounded better, now that there was a prospect of fighting in the very near future. "And Racal's Bay itself?"

"We'll proceed against the city as soon as our forces are assembled," Reginald said. He hoped they wouldn't have to lay siege to the city. He'd brought siege engines along, but unloading them without a harbour was going to be damn near impossible. And storming the city without them would be costly. "I want pickets thrown across the roads westwards, while preparing the regiments to move in for the kill."

"Yes, Your Highness," Stuart said.

"We'll send a formal demand for surrender as soon as we're in position to attack," Reginald continued. "If they accept, well and good. We'll keep the mercenaries out of the city as long as they cooperate. And if they don't ..."

He shrugged, expressively. Taking the harbours intact was the first priority, but afterwards ... if the city fathers chose to resist, he'd make their city pay. He wasn't particularly bloodthirsty, but storming and sacking Racal's Bay would convince other city fathers to surrender on demand. It wouldn't be the first time he'd committed an atrocity to make sure he didn't have to commit any others in future.

"You have your orders," he said, once they'd gone through the handful of other contingency plans. "Shall we begin?"

He walked back onto the deck. Racal's Bay was clearly visible in the distance, faint plumes of smoke reaching into the sky. It wouldn't be long before the fleet was spotted, if it hadn't already been seen by a passing fisherman. Summer Bay was supposed to be teeming with fish. One of the fishermen might have abandoned his nets and sailed straight home to alert his superiors. Not that it mattered, he reminded himself firmly. He'd planned on the assumption that they wouldn't have the advantage of surprise.

Which only leaves us with one question, he thought. *What's waiting for us in Racal's Bay?*

He sighed, inwardly, as the shoreline came closer and closer. He'd done everything in his power to gather intelligence, but very little *trustworthy* information had made it back over the channel. Racal's Bay would have a City Guard, of course, yet what *else* would it have? A militia? An army camp? Or would the usurper have massed his entire force to greet Reginald on the beaches? If everything had gone according to plan, the Cold King would already have started *his* advance ...

Reginald dismissed the thought, irritated. There was no way of overseeing so many things at once, not now the crystal ball network was gone. He'd find out when he landed and then adapt his plans to deal with whatever he found. It was unlikely the usurper would gamble everything on a single engagement. And if he did ... Reginald would welcome the battle. His men were hardened veterans. How many battles had the usurper's men fought in the last ten years?

The land came closer. He peered forward, scanning the beach. A handful of hovels were clearly visible, just out of reach of the tides; fishing and rowing boats rested by the walls, turned upside down to defeat the rain. There was no sign of anyone visible, suggesting that the occupants had seen the fleet approaching and scarpered. Reginald didn't really blame them. Soldiers and mercenaries had a reputation for looting, raping and murdering when they were on the warpath. The peasants were probably getting out of the way before it was too late.

But a shame we can't ask them for local knowledge, he thought. *We'll just have to see who we capture once we start exploring inland.*

"Drop anchor!" the captain shouted.

Reginald blinked in surprise. They weren't going to get any closer? He kicked himself a moment later. Getting closer would run the risk of running aground, when the tide retreated from the shoreline. Or simply hitting a sandbank below the waves. He doubted the defenders had had time to hide any unpleasant surprises under the water – they could hardly have predicted precisely where the defenders were going to land – but they might not need to bother. The sailors had told him, with grim conviction, that the beaches were almost as treacherous as the waters.

He heard someone walking towards him and turned. Gars stood there, one arm raised to block the sunlight.

"Your Highness," Gars said. "The first soldiers are moving now."

Reginald nodded, turning to watch as the ships launched dozens of small rowing boats, each one crammed with soldiers. They looked keen to get back on solid land, even if there *was* a reasonable chance of being killed in the next few hours. He didn't blame them, either. He'd gone down to the holds once, just to make sure he showed himself to the men, and the stench of piss and shit and vomit had been enough to drive him back out. He'd been on battlefields, with carrion crows swooping to peck at the dead, that had smelt less noxious. The men were probably in the mood to kill someone.

"I'll take the next boat," he said, once the beach was secure. A handful of protesting horses were being shipped now, their riders keeping them under tight control. The cavalry would start picketing the landing zone as soon as they were on the beach, half of them heading out to watch the approaches while the other half went straight to Racal's Bay. "I need to get on the beach myself."

Gars looked as if he wanted to object, but said nothing as Reginald walked to the ladder and clambered down to the boat. The soldiers raised a muted cheer, much to Reginald's private amusement. Some of them looked as if they wanted to be sick still, even though they were heading for land. He pretended not to hear a couple of men being sick as the boat was rowed rapidly towards the shore. No one would thank him for taking notice of it.

The boat grounded, hard enough to shake him. He put one hand on the side and jumped overboard, splashing into the knee-deep water. It was bitterly cold, but he ignored the temperature as he waded through the water and up onto the land. The sand felt unstable beneath his feet, but he welcomed it anyway. It was land! He turned to look at the fleet, more and more boats plying backwards and forwards as the army was rapidly disembarked. It wouldn't be long before he could start an advance on Racal's Bay.

Sergeant Ruthven saluted Reginald as he approached. "Sir," he said. "The pickets are heading out, as per orders. So far, we have seen no sign of any enemy presence."

"That will change," Reginald said. He lifted his head, peering into the distance. The land towards Racal's Bay looked like fallow fields, as far as he could tell. A handful of sheep were contentedly munching the grass. They'd be lucky to survive the day when his men had had nothing to eat for two days but hardtack and salt beef. "Assemble the regiments in the field – keep men back if they're too unwell to fight, then combine the able-bodied into smaller regiments if necessary."

"Sir."

Reginald looked around. "And set up the war tent in the field," he added. "Remind the senior officers that I expect them to share the hardships of their men. Their tents are not to be erected until we have everyone under cover."

"Yes, sir."

"Good," Reginald said. Lord William would hate it – the wretched man was too old for soldiering – but the younger officers would understand. And if they didn't ... they could do as they were told anyway. Men would fight for money, but they'd die for a superior who genuinely cared about them. "And inform me the moment the pickets are in place. I'll have to write a formal note to the defenders."

He looked back at the fleet and frowned. A couple of smaller ships had come close, alarmingly close. Men were jumping off the decks and swimming to shore, holding their bags over their heads. Were the ships in trouble? Or were they merely obeying his orders to get the ships unloaded as fast as possible? There was no way to know.

The captains know what they're doing, he thought. It was clear that not all of the ships had made it to Summer Bay. He hoped that meant they'd been blown off their course, instead of being sunk by the gale. Hopefully, anyone who'd lost their way would head to Summer Bay as quickly as possible. *Let them handle it while you do your job.*

Turning back to the field, he peered south towards Racal's Bay. The locals would know, now, that the fleet had landed. And how would they respond?

We'll find out, he thought, feeling a thrill of anticipation. There would be a battle soon. He could feel it in his water. *And then we'll claim this land for ourselves.*

***

Isabella kept one hand on her sword and the other on her wand as she splashed ashore, trying not to stumble and fall into the water. Countless soldiers had churned up the sand to the point where it was impossible to tell just where she was putting her feet. She heard curses behind her as a couple of men slipped, one landing face-first in the drink. His comrades laughed like loons as they helped their friend up and pushed him towards the shore.

"Hotter than I expected," Lord Robin said, behind her. He was holding his sword, looking around as if he expected invisible enemies to materialise at any moment. "And perhaps not as elegant as I expected, either."

Isabella frowned as she followed his gaze. The hovels didn't look very nice, but they were some distance from the nearest farms. There were plenty of people who tried to make a living catching fish and selling it, people who had to live close to the sea. She headed after Lord Robin as he walked towards the nearest hovel, putting his boot into the door when it refused to open. The stench of unwashed humans drifted out.

It still smells better than the boat, she thought, as she peered inside. *But then, a latrine would smell better than the boat.*

Her eyes adjusted, slowly, to the dim light. The hovel was larger than she'd expected, but still smaller than her bedroom in the Golden City. A collection of blankets in one corner suggested that the inhabitants had huddled together for warmth. A pot sat on a stove, perched over a bed of damp ashes, which suggested that whoever had been cooking had put the fire out in a hurry, then fled the beach. Lord Robin glanced into the pot, then made a disgusted face. Isabella didn't want to know what the occupant had been cooking. Fish, probably. A peasant in such a place wouldn't be allowed to eat anything larger than a rabbit.

"They fled," Lord Robin said. "I ..."

Equerry Caen ran up. "The Prince requests your presence," he said. "He's in the war tent."

"We're on our way," Lord Robin said.

Isabella frowned to herself as they left the pitiful hovel and strode over to the hastily-erected war tent. A handful of mercenaries were already searching the other shacks, looking for women or loot. Isabella doubted they'd find anything worth the effort. The huts might shelter a handful of men from the rain, but little else.

Prince Reginald was studying a map as they entered. "We spotted some enemy horsemen," he said, his finger tracing out a line on the map. Someone had added a handful of markers, showing where the pickets were meant to be. "They retreated as soon as we challenged them."

"So they're well-trained," Lord Robin said. "Most cavalrymen would at least try to slow you down a little, whatever they were ordered to do."

The prince nodded in agreement. "I can only assume they were given very strong orders to report back as soon as they made contact."

Lord Robin studied the map for a long moment. "I assume they headed towards Racal's Bay?"

"Yes," Prince Reginald said. He sounded pleased, rather than discontented. "They know we're here."

Chapter Eleven

"They got here so quickly!"

Sir Garston gritted his teeth and did his best to ignore Councillor Wade's whining. If it was up to him, Racal's Bay's city fathers – the elderly men who ran the city – would be put in the stocks and pelted with rancid tomatoes. Wade was the smartest of the councillors and he was an utter fool. Given the chance, he'd turn his coat faster than a whore could lift her skirts.

"Yes, they did," he said. It *was* a shock. He'd assumed – the *king* had assumed – that it would take longer for Prince Reginald to assemble and dispatch an army. It said worrying things about Prince Reginald's general competence that he'd managed to land troops on the Summer Isle before Garston had managed to complete his preparations. "And we have to deal with it."

"Our Lord is with us," the Red Monk said. "We will not fall."

Garston concealed his annoyance with an effort. He'd never had time for organised religion, beyond regular sacrifices to the God of Battles. The Red Monks were just another bunch of tame priests, promising everything to their followers and giving nothing. But the king had insisted that he install one of the sinister bastards on his staff ... no doubt as payment for services rendered. The man had done nothing, as far as Garston could tell. His face was so thoroughly hidden behind his robes that there was no way to tell if there was *one* monk or a multitude. But at least the Red Monk wasn't as annoying as the councillors.

Perhaps the king will let me execute the councillors, if we win, he thought. The Summer Isle didn't need a bunch of treacherous morons running its second-largest city. *And then we can put the city under a more practical regime.*

He studied the map, cursing under his breath. Prince

Reginald had landed a vast number of troops *before* Garston's pickets had located the landing site. If Garston had had more men under his command, he would have marched on the landing site at once and tried to push the invaders back into the sea, but he barely had enough troops to hold Racal's Bay. And *that* depended on the city's guardsmen – and militia – remaining loyal. Racal's Bay had switched sides before and would do so again, if the alternative was worse. The city fathers would only stay loyal for as long as a blade was held against their throats.

"You can't fight them in the city," Wade insisted. "I suggest ..."

Garston ignored the rest of his wittering. The hell of it was that Wade had a point. Racal's Bay wasn't particularly well defended, even in these troubled times. The walls were strong, in theory, but any experienced commander would have no difficulty getting men over the stone and into the city. And then ... half the city was made of wood, for crying out loud! If Prince Reginald wanted to burn the city to the ground, he'd just have to start shooting flaming arrows over the walls until the fires spread out of control.

An officer stuck his head into the room. "Sir, a messenger has arrived, under flag of truce," he said. "We're holding him in the gatehouse."

"Blindfold him, then escort him up here," Garston ordered. Using messengers as spies was an old ruse, one that had been rediscovered in the last few years. Letting the bastard see how paltry the defences really were would only encourage Prince Reginald to demand stiffer terms. "And make sure he stays away from the troops."

"We should not talk with the enemy," the Red Monk said. "He ..."

"Might be offering us terms we can accept," Wade said, quickly. The councillors had lodged official protests about the Red Monks preaching in the streets, protests Garston had simply ignored. "We should not be so quick to dismiss their words."

Garston ignored the byplay and waited until a young man – his eyes hidden behind a makeshift blindfold – was escorted into the room. It was impossible to be sure, but the young man – still a boy, in many ways – held himself like an aristocrat. A junior nobleman, then, someone seeking glory and lands beside his prince. He wouldn't be someone too important, Garston reminded himself. Killing a messenger was a declaration of total war, but it had been known to happen. Sometimes, it had even been the accident it had been claimed to be.

"I am Sir Garston," he said, once the blindfold was removed. It was unlikely the messenger had ever heard of him. The Summer Isle's peerage had waxed and waned over the last few years as round after round of civil war claimed hundreds of lives. "What do you have to tell me?"

The young man straightened. "I am Caen, Equerry to Crown Prince Reginald, rightful heir to the thrones of Andalusia and the Summer Isle. He calls on you to surrender Racal's Bay to him without further delay. Your officers and men will be treated fairly, as laid down in the books of war, and the population of Racal's Bay will be protected by my lord."

Wade made a coughing sound. Garston ignored him.

"I assume there's an *or else* attached to this," he said, calmly. "What *is* it?"

"If you refuse to surrender, you will be treated as rebels against your rightful lord," Caen informed him. "The consequences will be ... unfortunate."

Garston glared. *Unfortunate.* The city would be sacked; men would be killed, women would be raped, children would be brutally slaughtered ... by the time Prince Reginald called a halt, Racal's Bay would be devastated. And his men ... if they were treated as rebels, they'd be executed on the spot. Prince Reginald hadn't even bothered to offer to accept turncoats. It wasn't a good sign. Garston's future looked very short and unpleasant indeed.

"King Rufus is our rightful lord," the Red Monk said. "We will not surrender ..."

Wade choked. "But the city ..."

"You have one hour to decide," Caen informed them. "If you refuse to accept these terms, or if you decide not to let me return to my lines, there will be no further negotiation."

"You will be returned," Garston said, shortly. An hour ...

Prince Reginald clearly wasn't in a position to attack, not yet. A lot could happen in an hour. "You will have our answer before the hour runs out."

He nodded to the guards, ordering them to escort Caen back to his master, then turned to the other two. Wade would want to surrender, of course. Racal's Bay would be devastated by the fighting. Who knew? It might push the freemen to demand a *new* set of city fathers. If, of course, the invaders allowed their new subjects that much freedom. A population seized by war could be treated as nothing more than serfs and Wade knew it. But Garston ... he had no future, not if he surrendered. King Rufus would order his execution when he returned to Allenstown.

And Prince Reginald clearly isn't interested in making a deal with me, he thought. *That* didn't bode well for the future. Garston was minor nobility, only raised up after the last round of civil war, but he was far from incompetent. Prince Reginald probably intended to parcel out land to his supporters. And *that* meant that he had to remove the current owners. *I don't have a future at all.*

"We must agree to his terms," Wade said. "I ..."

"This is treason," the Red Monk snapped. "This city must be held for King Rufus!"

"The city *can't* be held," Wade said. "And I will not allow ..."

"Enough," Garston said. "We will fight."

He rang his bell. Two messengers hurried into the room and snapped to attention.

"You are to ride straight to Allenstown," he ordered. Prince Reginald would have pickets blocking the roads, he was sure, but the invaders lacked any kind of local knowledge. "You are to inform Lord Francis that the enemy has landed – and that we intend to fight. He must dispatch reinforcements immediately."

"Yes, My Lord."

The timing was unfortunate, he conceded ruefully. King Rufus and his army had set off to the Narrows, if the last report was accurate. It would take days – if not weeks – for messengers to reach them, then yet *more* days for the army to march to Racal's Bay. By then, Prince Reginald would be well on his way to Allenstown. He might even have a chance to lay siege to the city before King Rufus arrived.

"Tell your sailors to start destroying the docks," he added, addressing Wade. "We can destroy most of the facilities before time runs out."

Wade paled. "We *need* those docks."

"The kingdom *doesn't* need those docks," Garston said. "And it certainly *doesn't* need them in enemy hands."

He summoned his subordinates. There wasn't much time to prepare. They'd just have to make the best possible use of it. And then ...

We won't see another sunrise, he thought, morbidly. He felt a flicker of pity for his wife and son, who would soon be at the mercy of their legal guardian. Thankfully, a wife and underage son could not be held responsible for his failure. His wife might be married off to the king's choice, but she wouldn't be killed. *All we can do is fight to the last.*

***

Reginald kept one eye on the hourglass as he paced the war tent, watching his subordinates update the map while he waited for time to run out. Everything was going perfectly, if the map was to be believed, although he knew from bitter experience that it could be treacherously deceptive. A unit on the map – everything from a lone picket to a regiment of soldiers – could be out of place or destroyed and he wouldn't know about it until someone brought a report back to the tent. It was frustrating, in many ways. The map seemed to offer the promise of moving his forces around like pieces on a chessboard, but it was just an illusion. There was no way he could manage every detail of a battle.

Caen stepped into the tent, looking relieved. Reginald allowed himself a moment of relief, too. Sending a messenger had been risky, even though very few would take the risk of harming or killing someone under a flag of truce. Doing so would put them completely beyond the pale. No one would complain if Reginald chose to slaughter the defenders to the last man in response.

"They promised an answer before time runs out," Caen informed him. "And then they sent me back."

Reginald glanced at the hourglass. Thirty minutes to go.

He would have preferred to push them a little harder, but he needed time to get his army into place. Thankfully, the troops were recovering fast, now they were on solid ground. He dreaded to think of what would have happened if they'd been caught on the beaches.

"With me," he said.

He strode out of the tent, Caen following like an over-eager puppy. The advance elements had established an observation station on a nearby hill, allowing them to peer down into the city. Reginald walked up the hill, nodded politely to the picket troops and then took a telescope for himself. Racal's Bay looked formidable, from the outside, but he was experienced enough to see its weaknesses. Clearly, the occupants had never believed they would come under attack.

Odd, he thought. *The Summer Isle has been fighting civil wars for the last five years.*

He swept the telescope over the city. A single wall, the battlements manned by soldiers; a gatehouse, dominating the sole road in and out of the city; a castle that barely deserved the name ... it didn't look very strong. The stone houses at the centre of the city would make good strongpoints, if the enemy had the troops to hold them, but the wooden houses on the outskirts would be nothing more than firetraps. The wretched idiots had allowed the citizens to build their homes on *both* sides of the walls! Reginald would have summarily demoted – or executed – anyone stupid enough to allow that during wartime. The defenders should have broken down the hovels for scrap years ago.

Pushing the thought aside, he glanced at Caen. "Did you see anything from the inside?"

"They had me blindfolded," Caen said. "I think they took me to the castle, but I don't know."

Reginald nodded. A *smart* defender would have made sure to walk Caen around the block a few times, just to confuse him. It was an acceptable ruse, all the more so as messengers were normally also spies. The defenders *might* be in the castle, but given how poorly it had been designed it was quite possible that they were elsewhere. He shrugged, dismissing the thought. Racal's Bay couldn't hold out for long.

He heard the sound of hooves and turned to see a

messenger riding up. "Your Highness," the rider said. "Captain-General Gars sends his compliments, Sir, and wishes to inform you that no enemy envoy has crossed the line."

Reginald frowned. The enemy commander *had* to know he couldn't hold out indefinitely, not when his city was so poorly defended. And there were no troops in range to come to their aid. Reginald's pickets would give him more than ample warning if *that* changed ... he glanced at the sun, silently estimating the time, then shrugged. He'd given them more than enough chances to surrender.

"My compliments to Captain-General Gars," he said. "Inform him that if the enemy fail to surrender by the time the hourglass runs out, he is to launch the attack without further delay."

"Yes, Your Highness."

Reginald grinned as the messenger turned and rode away. "Shall we go closer?"

"You shouldn't put yourself in too much danger, Your Highness," Caen said. "Your father wouldn't thank me if you died here."

"No," Reginald agreed. "But I can't afford to skulk at the back, either."

***

"Not a particularly well-defended town," Lord Robin observed. "What do you think?"

Isabella shrugged. She could see a dozen ways to sneak into Racal's Bay – without magic – that would have a very good chance of avoiding detection. She was mildly surprised Prince Reginald hadn't started sending infiltrators over the walls already, although she supposed he thought he didn't need them. The attack was scheduled to begin in less than twenty minutes, after all. Anyone who made it over the walls would run the risk of being cut down by their own side.

"We won't have any problem getting close to the walls," Dolman said. The swordsman looked eager for battle. "Are you sure you can knock them down?"

"Yes," Isabella said, flatly. It was impossible to be entirely sure, of course, but she hadn't sensed any magical defences woven into the walls. There weren't even the basic runes designed to make it harder for attackers to scramble up into the battlements. "I can put a hole in the wall."

"If you're sure you can do it without harming yourself," Lord Robin said. "I don't want to have to carry you back to the tent."

Isabella scowled at him. "I can do it."

"Remember to duck, afterwards," Alexis said. "They'll be firing arrows at you."

"Or don't duck," Big Richard muttered.

Isabella resisted – again – the urge to turn him into a frog. Or a pig ... not that anyone would notice any difference. He was already halfway to being a pig ... she pushed the thought out of her head as she gathered her magic, shaping the spell piece by piece. Failure would be embarrassing, particularly when Prince Reginald had asked her – personally – if she could cast the spell. She didn't want to fail in front of the entire army.

She listened, grimly, as Lord Robin spoke to some of his officers. Prince Reginald had put him in command of the first echelons, a decidedly mixed blessing. He was a mercenary and could speak to the other mercenaries on even terms, but the first echelons always took the worst of the casualties. Isabella didn't really blame Prince Reginald for classing the mercenaries as expendable – she understood his reasoning – yet it grated on her. She didn't consider *herself* expendable.

"We'll punch through the walls, with or without the spell, then open a breach," Lord Robin said. "And then we can rage into the town."

"And loot," Big Richard said.

"Battle first, loot later," Isabella reminded him. She'd seen battles lost because one side had stopped to loot before actually *winning* the battle, giving their opponents time to catch their breath and return to the fray. "We have to win."

Big Richard shot her an annoyed look, but said nothing. Isabella sighed. Maybe he'd take an arrow to the throat and shut up. Or something. It was hard to feel anything but annoyance when he kept sniping at her. She couldn't help wishing that it had been Big Richard, instead of Little Jim, who'd died in Andalusia ...

The trumpets blared. Isabella tensed. The city hadn't surrendered, then. She cursed their leaders under her breath ... didn't they know it was hopeless? Racal's Bay was isolated, completely cut off from the rest of the kingdom. No one would have blamed them for surrendering on terms. Prince Reginald had even offered them surprisingly *good* terms.

Lord Robin took a breath. "Here we go," he said. "Isabella?"

Isabella nodded, stepping forward as she gathered her magic. Flickers of light danced over her hand, as if she was on fire. And then she jabbed her hand towards the walls, casting the spell ...

The ground shook, violently. The wall exploded into a towering mass of flame. Debris flew in all directions.

"Go," Lord Robin ordered. He raised his voice. "No mercy!"

Chapter Twelve

"Sorcery," Wade gasped.

Sir Garston nodded in grim agreement. He hadn't expected the walls to hold for long – he was painfully aware that he didn't have the manpower to hold them indefinitely – but he'd hoped they'd last longer than a few seconds. The spell – he could see the damned sorcerer who'd cast it – had blasted a hole right through the wall. His men were hesitating too, damn them. He didn't think that *any* of them had seen battlefield sorcery before.

"Order the archers to take out that sorcerer," he snapped. "And then move the reserves into position to seal the hole."

"We should surrender now," Wade said, as the messengers hurried to carry out Garston's orders. "The walls are *gone*."

Garston waved to the guards, then jabbed a finger at Wade. "Take him to the dungeons," he ordered. "And then put the rest of the city fathers in the cells too."

He ignored Wade's shouting as he turned back to the peephole. The archers were firing, but it didn't *look* as though they'd hit their target. The enemy archers were returning fire, snapping off crossbow bolts at every target of opportunity. Wade was right, he conceded sourly. The city *was* undefendable. But it didn't really matter. All that mattered was killing as many of the enemy soldiers as possible before the final, inevitable end.

"We have sent word to our brethren," the Red Monk said. "The king will be informed."

Garston shrugged. It didn't matter either. By the time the king heard about the invasion force, it would be too late for Racal's Bay. There was no chance of escape for any of them. He just hoped that making a final bloody stand, with no hope of doing anything but delaying the enemy, would be enough to save his reputation. His son wouldn't grow up thinking his father had been a coward.

"Good," he said. "Now ... the battle."

***

Isabella sagged to her knees the moment she released the spell. She barely felt the first arrow whistling through the air, missing her head by mere inches. It was hard, so hard, to feel alarm. A moment later, a band of shield-bearers surrounded her, holding their shields in place to block the flurry of arrows. She didn't even notice them for a long moment. She hadn't been so drained since basic training, years ago.

But I haven't tried to cast such a spell for years either, she thought, numbly. The ground felt soft under her knees. She was tempted to lie down and close her eyes. Only the certainty that she'd be lucky if she was *only* robbed kept her eyes open. *I should have tested it first, before we set sail.*

The sound of battle raged around her as she drew on her reserves, slowly channelling energy back into her body. She could hear people shouting and screaming, some calling for their mothers as their lives ebbed away. She'd seen too many battlefields in her life to harbour any illusions about the aftermath. The wounded would envy the dead, if they survived. Far too many of them wouldn't last long enough to be tended by the army's sawbones.

A final arrow slammed into the shield, then silence fell. Isabella hoped that was a good sign. Prince Reginald had trained his archers to snipe at enemy archers, but she knew from experience that hitting an archer wasn't easy. They tended to be careful about showing themselves until they were ready to fire, forcing counter-archers to spot the target, take aim and fire before the archer ducked again. She'd even been told that only a third of arrows fired into a city ever found a target.

She turned as she heard men running towards her. Prince Reginald was funnelling a second regiment into the city, trying to secure what remained of the walls before pushing towards the castle and ending the fight. A handful of cavalry followed the troops, either keeping them in line or trying to draw fire from the archers. Isabella doubted the prince would risk sending horsemen into the city itself. Cavalrymen were convinced of their own superiority, but all of their advantages were wiped out in a city. They'd be cut down in their hundreds if they tried to crash through the streets ...

A horseman stopped beside her and looked down. Isabella looked up and blinked in surprise. "Prince Reginald?"

The prince smiled. "Madam Sorceress," he said. "Would you care for a ride?"

Isabella hastily cast a deflection ward. Prince Reginald was insane. Coming out in the open ... he had to be out of his mind. And yet, she couldn't help a flicker of admiration. She'd met too many noblemen who shied away from anything resembling danger. Prince Reginald might not have joined the charge at the walls, but he was sharing *some* of the risks. An enemy archer might *just* take a shot at him ...

And then his superiors might hang him, Isabella thought, wryly. *Killing aristocrats ... the very idea.*

She smiled at him. "Shouldn't you be out of harm's way, Your Highness?"

"I have to be in position to take command quickly, if necessary," Prince Reginald said. "And to accept surrender, if they finally offer it."

Isabella winced. The defenders might well have lost their last chance to offer surrender. Troops were in the streets now, troops fired by bloodlust and a burning urge to loot, rape and slaughter their way through the city. Reginald was liked and respected by his men, but even *he* might be unable to prevent a bloody slaughter. And he might not *want* to prevent a bloody slaughter. He'd offered reasonable terms and had them thrown back in his face.

"You cast a powerful spell," Prince Reginald said. "Can you do it again?"

"Not for a while," Isabella said. She'd expended more of her reserves than she cared to admit. She made a mental note to practice as soon as she had a quiet moment. "Do you need me to?"

"I hope not," Prince Reginald said. "But you never know."

***

Big Richard kept his head down as he jumped through the debris and ran into the city. A young man wearing a helmet that was clearly designed for a larger man popped up, out of nowhere; Big Richard cut him down in passing, concentrating on finding the way deeper into the city. More and more mercenaries were following him, plunging into fortified houses or tossing firebrands into wooden hovels as they advanced. The defenders seemed to be utterly disorganised.

A heavy object flew past him and smashed against the ground. He looked up, just in time to see another object being hurled out of a second-story window. Jumping forward, he slammed his axe into the wooden door, smashing it to flinders. A man came at him with a carving knife, waving it frantically in front of him. Richard knocked it aside effortlessly, then sliced out with his axe, cutting the man in half. He didn't bother to watch the body fall to the ground. Instead, he ran to the stairs and hurled himself upwards. Pieces of debris flew down at him, but he ignored them. An elderly woman screamed as he reached the top of the stairs, shouting orders in a language he didn't recognise. A younger woman stared at him in horror.

"Shut up, Grandmother," Richard growled. The old biddy was too old and ugly to be interesting – or useful. He silenced her with one blow of his axe, then turned to the younger girl. Lord Robin would be pissed if he wasted time entertaining himself when he should be firing, but Richard's blood was up and it was hard to care. "Come here."

The woman stared at him, aware – all too aware – of what he had in mind. She looked vaguely foreign, compared to the girls he'd seen in Andalusia. Perhaps that was what Summer Islander women looked like ... not ugly, although she wore her years poorly, but different. The parts would still fit, though. He'd seen enough women from all over the continent to know that was true.

"I won't kill you," he said, allowing impatience to colour his voice. He had to move quickly or Lord Robin would *know* he'd been playing games. "Come here."

The woman took one last desperate look at him, then turned and hurled herself out of the open window. Richard swore. He would have left the girl alive, afterwards. Probably. It wasn't as if anyone would have cared enough to punish him. Prince Reginald couldn't start hanging mercenaries unless he wanted mass desertions. But instead ... he shrugged – there would be other women – and headed back to the stairs. There didn't look to be anything worth looting in the house. No doubt the occupants had hidden their valuables while waiting for the end.

I'll have to come back and search, later, he thought. There would be a chance to loot, whatever Prince Reginald said. No one would dare to stop an occupying army from taking whatever it wanted. *Or maybe there will be richer pickings further in.*

Grinning, he rejoined his fellows. More and more soldiers were swarming into the city, half heading towards the docks while the other half were marching up towards the ancient castle, chaos following in their wake. Resistance seemed to be fading, now the attackers were firmly entrenched. A handful were already looting, he noted. Idiots. Doing it so openly would only draw attention from their superiors, who'd either put a stop to it or demand a share of the profits. It was much smarter to do any looting well away from prying eyes.

Lord Robin waved to him. "Get the squad assembled for an attack on the castle," he ordered, bluntly. "And hurry!"

"Yes, sir," Richard said.

He felt his smile grow wider as he barked orders, forming up the squad. Assaulting the castle would be bloody, but castles were *full* of loot. There would be no shortage of small items – or cash – that could be stuck in one's pocket and carried out, then sold later to the merchants who followed armies all over the countryside. And then ... who knew? There might be a noblewoman inside the castle, a noblewoman in need of a protector ...

This is going to be a very good war, he thought.

***

"Captain-General Gars reports that the docks have been secured," the messenger said. He was panting heavily as he gabbled out his message. He'd run all the way to Reginald's forward command post, right by the walls. "The dockworkers were ordered to burn the boats and destroy the facilities, but ... they refused to carry the orders out."

"Good for them," Reginald said. "Order him to make sure

that the dockworkers and their families are protected, from our troops as well as the enemy."

"Yes, Your Highness."

The messenger turned and hurried away. Reginald allowed himself a tight smile. He had no illusions – he knew the dockyard workers hadn't saved the docks for *him* – but that didn't mean he wasn't going to reward them. The docks wouldn't be easy to destroy, he'd been assured, yet even slight damage would impose unacceptable delays. And the boats ... capturing the boats was an unexpected bonus. He'd always assumed the defenders would have time to burn the boats before they could be stopped.

He turned to look at the burning city. Fires were spreading rapidly, mainly through the poorer parts of town. No one had time to fight the flames, not when the attackers were forcing their way to the castle. The defenders really hadn't thought through the battle, had they? He wanted the docks, not the rest of the city. He'd burn it to the ground if there was no other choice.

Another messenger ran up to him. "Your Highness, the advance body is in position to assault the castle," he said. "Lord Robin reports that he needs reinforcements."

The sorceress smiled. "He's a good man."

"He'll have his reinforcements," Reginald said. "Order him to demand the castle's surrender while he waits."

He rubbed his forehead in irritation. The defenders *had* to realise they were beaten now ... surely. Some of his troops were already running wild, looting and raping even though the castle hadn't been taken. He'd have problems reassuming control before the madness had run its course, if the troops got completely out of hand. He'd issued orders to destroy all alcohol stockpiles within the city, as soon as they were discovered, but that wouldn't keep the troops from drinking heavily. Very few people on the Summer Isle drank water. They simply didn't trust it.

And then I'll have to make an example of some of my men, he thought, crossly. It wasn't something he wanted to do. Men responded well to a firm commander, but they disliked tyrants. *Why aren't they surrendering?*

***

"My Lord," the messenger said. "They want us to surrender."

Garston made a face. The battle hadn't lasted long – it felt like forever, but he knew it was less than an hour – and yet the enemy had practically won. Their advance forces had reached the docks, then secured all the streets leading down to the waterfront; other forces, more intent on their final target, were already surrounding the castle. Garston knew it was just a matter of time before the enemy made their move.

"Our Lord is with us," the Red Monk said. "We will not lose."

Garston felt a hot flash of anger. "We cannot fight any longer," he said. The enemy sorcerer tipped the balance squarely in their favour. He could make the enemy bleed, if they tried to storm the castle, but the sorcerer could put a hole through his strongest defences. And then everyone in the castle would be put to the sword. "The time has come to ask for terms."

He sighed. The rules of war and honour allowed him to surrender, now that the situation was hopeless, but he'd already rejected an offer of surrender. Prince Reginald had no obligation to offer him anything, not even his life. Garston could only hope that the prince would prefer to end the battle, rather than endure heavy casualties by storming the castle.

But I'll take the blame, he thought. *My men won't be punished for my crimes.*

He felt an odd flicker of hope as he rang the bell for a messenger. He'd fought, despite knowing there was no hope of victory. No one could deny he'd tried, even though he'd lost in the end. King Rufus couldn't claim otherwise, no matter how much he might want to lash out at Garston's family. His honour would remain intact. It wasn't much, but it was all he had.

"No," the Red Monk said.

"Yes," Garston said. He was *tired* of the shadowy figure. "We will ..."

The Red Monk drew back his hood. Garston looked ... and saw ... *something*. His mind refused to grasp what he was seeing. It was big, so big ... his thoughts splintered, an instant before he felt *something* clutch at his heart. He opened his mouth, an instant before his knees buckled. The world turned grey ...

He was dead before he hit the ground.

***

"They're not surrendering, Your Highness," the messenger said. "The messenger we sent into the castle has not returned."

Reginald clenched his fists. Harming or killing – even imprisoning – a messenger? It was a breach of convention, a slap in the face of the gods of battle themselves. The defenders were mad! Their castle wasn't designed to sustain a long siege. He could storm it ... he *would* storm it. There was no way he was going to leave it dominating the city while he brought in more supplies from home.

And I can't let them defy me, either, he thought. *I cannot let others believe that they can break the conventions without reprisal.*

He closed his eyes for a long moment. "Inform Lord Robin that he is to storm the castle," he said, coldly. "Anyone with a weapon in hand is to be killed. Anyone without a weapon is to be captured and bound, held in the dungeons until I can tend to them personally. And if the enemy commander is still alive, I want him."

"Yes, Your Highness."

I'll kill the bastard, Reginald promised himself, as the messenger ran back into the city. *And it won't be an easy passing.*

The sorceress – Isabella, he reminded himself – looked at him. "Are you going to sack the city?"

"Not if it can be avoided," Reginald said. He'd have to find out *precisely* who'd decided the city wouldn't surrender. In his experience, city councillors were quick to surrender when the situation became hopeless. "We need the docks to bring in supplies."

"Good," Isabella said.

***

The first man over the ramparts was cut down by an enemy

soldier. Big Richard threw himself over the body and lunged at the defender, cutting him down effortlessly. Three more defenders came at him and he sliced them apart, laughing like a madman as he cleared the battlements. Lord Robin had told him not to kill anyone who wasn't carrying a weapon, but who cared? Anything could be a weapon with a little imagination.

He reached the stairwell and threw himself inwards, followed by a handful of others. The castle's interior was a mystery, but if it followed the conventional pattern the enemy commanders would be on the very highest levels. The man who captured them could be sure of a reward ...

He stopped suddenly, feeling a prickling running down the back of his neck. Something was wrong, but what? He hefted his axe, looking from side to side. His instincts insisted that he was missing something, yet ... he could see nothing. The torch-lit corridors were empty. And yet, his instincts were sounding the alarm.

Nothing, he thought, as the sensation slowly faded. It wasn't important. It had never been important. *I was imagining it.*

Shaking his head, he returned to the slaughter.

Chapter Thirteen

Racal's Bay was a blackened mess.

Prince Reginald rode his horse slowly down the main street, keeping a wary eye out for trouble. The locals – those who hadn't fled or been slaughtered – were remaining indoors, keeping well out of the occupiers' way. Some of them would emerge, in the hours to come, to discover that their city was no longer theirs, others would try to remain in hiding until the occupation was over. Reginald didn't really blame them. He'd stamped down on trouble with an iron fist, but there had still been hundreds of incidents between the occupied and the occupiers.

He shook his head slowly as the horse picked its way through the debris. Dozens of buildings had been scorched by the flames, a handful effectively destroyed even though the stone frame remained intact. Others – wooden houses – had been reduced to blackened rubble, when they hadn't been hastily torn down and turned into makeshift barricades. He felt a moment's pity for the city's population, many of whom were now condemned to spend the winter without shelter. But it had been the fault of their masters. Racal's Bay should have surrendered the moment he cut the city off from all hope of relief.

Dead bodies lay everywhere: men, women and children. A number looked to have been stripped of everything valuable, from weapons and armour to clothes and money. Soldiers and mercenaries were practical, above all else. A dead man couldn't wear his armour any longer. Why *shouldn't* it be taken from the corpse and put to use somewhere else? He made a mental note to ensure that the bodies were cleared away before they started to smell. Dead bodies spread disease.

They'll have to be cremated and the ashes dumped in a mass grave, he thought. It had been years since the last necromantic plague, but that had been bad enough to convince the Empire – and everyone else – that dead bodies were better off burnt. *And the survivors won't have time to mourn their dead.*

He jumped off the horse as they reached the castle, his bodyguards fanning out around him even though the entire area had been cleared of civilians. Reginald felt a flicker of annoyance, mingled with the grim awareness that the guards were necessary. Who *knew* who might be planning to strike at the prince when he was vulnerable? And what would happen after his death?

Lord Robin stood at the gate. He saluted as Reginald approached, then smiled. "Your Highness."

"Lord Robin," Reginald acknowledged. "The castle is secure?"

"We have searched the building from top to bottom," Lord Robin assured him. "The building is as secure as we can make it."

Reginald nodded, curtly. "And prisoners?"

"We took forty-seven prisoners, nine of whom claim to be city fathers," Lord Robin said, wryly. "They were apparently arrested by their former commander, Sir Garston. The remainder are mainly castle staff, with a handful of women."

Reginald frowned. "And Sir Garston?"

Lord Robin frowned. "Dead," he said. "We found his body when we broke into his chambers."

"Suicide?" Reginald asked. He'd heard of men who'd killed their commanders when they *didn't* want to waste their lives in a glorious last stand, but no one had tried to surrender even after the castle had been stormed. "What killed him?"

"I don't know," Lord Robin said. "There's no visible cause of death. Magic, perhaps. I was hoping Isabella could take a look at the body."

"See to it," Reginald said. "But right now, show me to the audience chamber."

The interior of the castle was odd, he decided as he followed Lord Robin through a maze of corridors. It looked, very much, as though the designer couldn't decide if he was building a mansion or a defendable castle. Some parts of the building were strikingly luxurious, comparable to King

Romulus's private hunting lodge; some parts were rough and crude, the muddy floor covered with hay. Perhaps the castle had simply been out of service for a long time. It would hardly be the first castle to have been neglected during the long centuries of peace.

And the kings of the island wouldn't want Racal's Bay to be able to defend itself too effectively, he thought, cynically. *This is the gateway to the rest of the world, after all.*

The audience chamber was definitely one of the more luxurious parts of the castle. A large throne dominated the room, resting on a carpeted floor. There were no other chairs in the chamber, as far as Reginald could tell. He wondered, wryly, if Sir Garston had forced the city fathers to stand or kneel in front of him. Sitting before a king was a gross breach of etiquette, but the rules weren't so strict for lesser nobility.

He tested the throne carefully, then sat down. "Bring the chief amongst the city fathers to me," he ordered the guards. "And then assemble my council."

The throne was surprisingly comfortable. He found it slightly disconcerting. He'd sat on his father's throne more than once, and *that* had been an unpleasant experience. His father had told him, when he'd asked, that a throne was *never* comfortable. A king who wasn't constantly aware of the dangers threatening his position was a king on the verge of losing everything. His father clearly hadn't seen *this* throne. Reginald wondered, as the guards escorted an elderly man into the audience chamber, if he should send the captured throne to his father. King Romulus would appreciate the joke.

"Your Majesty," the city father said, throwing himself to his knees. "I ..."

"The *correct* form of address is *Your Highness*," Reginald corrected, firmly. He wasn't going to allow the city father to flatter him, not after he'd lost far too many men taking the wretched city. "To whom do I have the honour of speaking?"

"Wade, Your Highness," the man said. "Wade, Son of ..."

Reginald cut him off. "Your city is mine now," he said. "Do you understand?"

"Yes, Your Highness," Wade said. "We wanted to surrender, but Sir Garston insisted on fighting and ..."

"So I am told," Reginald said. It might very well be true. "If you cooperate with me, I will spare your lives and those of your fellows. If you refuse to cooperate with me, or sabotage my endeavours in any way, you will be executed and your families enslaved. There will be no further warnings. Do you understand?"

Wade looked down. "Yes."

"*Yes, Your Highness,*" Reginald snapped. He refused to feel guilt over bullying an older man. City fathers were shifty fellows in his experience, more interested in milking their cities than defending them. They didn't even have the decency to stay bribed. "Here are the rules."

He stared down at Wade, speaking clearly and precisely. "First, I want all weapons handed in to my forces at once. If there are trained soldiers, guardsmen or mercenaries, they are to report themselves to my people. Second, my troops will patrol the streets. Their orders are to be obeyed, without hesitation. Anyone who gives them trouble will regret it. Third, I will be using the docks to bring supplies into the Summer Isle from Andalusia. The city will be responsible for paying the dockyard workers and sailors for their services. Fourth, and finally, any attempt to interfere with my operations will be severely punished."

There was a long pause. "Once I am seated on the throne, we will reassess your city's position in the kingdom. If you are deemed to have cooperated, you will be granted a charter akin to cities on the mainland. You will have a certain degree of internal autonomy, as long as you honour your obligations to your rightful king. If you are deemed to have *not* cooperated, I will install a Royal Governor and the council will be disbanded."

He saw the pain on Wade's face and smiled, coldly. The city fathers would have no choice but to cooperate. A Royal Governor, even a fairly benevolent one, would be disastrous for the city's long-term future. And yet, they had to know that their independence was about to be severely limited. Reginald could hardly allow them to put a stranglehold on trade between the Summer Isle and Andalusia. In the very long term, it might be worth establishing other trading cities along the coastline. It would certainly make it harder for Racal's Bay to hamper the crown.

"I understand," Wade said. He took a breath. "But ... but what about the safety of my people?"

"They will be safe, as long as they cooperate," Reginald said. "They are *my* vassals now."

He ignored the stricken look on the elderly man's face. His people had been freemen, technically speaking. They certainly hadn't been *serfs*. Now ... now, they were Reginald's possessions. They had no rights, beyond those he chose to grant them. He could make whatever use of them he wished. And if they weren't *useful*, he would *make* them useful.

"The guards will escort you out," he said. "I expect you to communicate the rules to the rest of the city. And may the gods have mercy on you if you betray me."

He watched the guards half-dragging the old man out, then leaned back in his chair. It had been a good day, all things considered. They'd landed, fought their first battle ... and won. It had been more painful than he'd expected – any sane opponent would have surrendered once he'd taken stock of the forces facing him – but the victory would be good for his army. Their morale would go through the roof.

But we can't afford to stay here too long, he thought, as Gars and the rest of the council entered the room. *The real battle is still to come.*

***

Big Richard looked displeased at being put on guard duty, Isabella noted, as she followed Lord Robin to the war room. He was shifting from side to side like a little boy who needed to relieve himself. The nasty part of her mind insisted that he was fretting over missing the chance to do a little looting, even though Prince Reginald had already told his men that they couldn't loot. Or maybe he was just bored.

"No one has entered this room," he said, as he opened the door for them. "And there are no other ways into the room."

Unless there's a secret passageway, Isabella thought. She'd never seen a castle that didn't have a handful of secret passages and hidden chambers, all buried behind magic or simple misdirection. Her father's mansion had been riddled with secret passages. *And a hidden way out of the war room would be very useful indeed.*

She motioned for Lord Robin to stay behind her as she stepped into the room, recalling skills she'd hadn't used since she'd been kicked out of the Watchtower. A single body – Garston, she assumed – was lying on the stone floor. The expression on his face suggested he'd died in agony. She reached out with her senses and frowned. There was no residual magic, as far as she could tell, but there was ... something, right at the edge of her awareness. Her frown deepened as she tried to narrow it down. The sensation reminded her of the abandoned village ...

Stepping forward, she looked around the room. It was surprisingly simple; stone walls, broken only by arrow slits; a large map of the island hanging from one wall; a solid wooden table, covered with smaller maps ... all illuminated by oil lanterns. The walls looked to be solid. There certainly didn't *seem* to be any secret passageways. No magic lights, as far as she could tell ... no magic at all. And yet, the strange sensation was still there.

"He might not have been alone," she said, slowly. "Do we know who was with him?"

"I don't think we took many of his staff alive," Lord Robin said. "They fought to the last."

Isabella rolled her eyes as she knelt down next to the corpse and started to cut its shirt free. Garston had been healthy enough, she noted; he wasn't as muscular as Lord Robin, let alone Big Richard, but he wasn't a weakling either. There was certainly no hint that his heart was on the verge of stopping ... she knew spells that could do that, easily, yet she couldn't pick up even a trace of magic. She cast a handful of charms that were meant to detect poisons, but drew a blank. There was nothing. Garston hadn't been poisoned, any more than he'd been knifed in the back. His heart had simply ... stopped.

Big Richard snorted. "Should we leave you alone with the body?"

Isabella bit down a very nasty reply. There were stories –

foul stories – about sorceresses reanimating corpses for sexual pleasure, but none of the stories were remotely true. Anyone with the power – and the complete lack of morals – required to actually *do* it would have plenty of options that *didn't* involve digging for a dead body. Assuming, of course, they could *find* a dead body in reasonable condition. They'd be lucky if they found anything more than a pile of ashes.

"I can't find any trace of what actually killed him," she said, reluctantly. It looked like a heart attack, but none of her spells were turning up any of the warning signs. It seemed to have come out of nowhere. "And yet, he shouldn't have died."

"Perhaps it was an odd form of suicide," Lord Robin said. "He sentenced his men to death, didn't he?"

Isabella shrugged and rose. There were options, she supposed, but none of them quite made sense. A long-distance curse would have left traces ... unless there had been time for the magic to dispel. And yet, there *hadn't* been time. She would have believed it was suicide if she'd been able to find something – anything – that pointed towards how it had actually been *done*.

"We should speak to the survivors," she said, slowly. Garston's staff might be dead, but not *everyone* in the castle had been killed. "See if they know anything."

"They were cowering in the lower levels," Big Richard growled. "I bet they know nothing."

Isabella shrugged. Servants ... aristocrats tended to dismiss servants as nothing more than tools, even though they were human beings. They were just part of the furniture. And yet, they were living beings ... *thinking* beings. It was quite possible that one of the servants had seen *something* that might point the finger at how Garston had died. Or committed suicide ...

She reached out with her senses, again. The strange sensation was still there, nagging at her mind. An odd form of magic – Alden's words echoed through her head – or a figment of her imagination? She was tired, more tired than she cared to admit. It *was* possible she was imagining it. No matter what she tried, she just couldn't zero it down.

"Come on," she said. "Let's go talk to the staff."

"Stay on guard," Lord Robin ordered Big Richard. "I'll send someone to relieve you shortly."

"The body will have to be burnt," Isabella said, as they walked down the stairs. "We could try cutting it open, but I doubt we'll find anything useful."

Lord Robin nodded. "It's spooky," he said. "He doesn't look like someone who was going to keel over at any moment."

Yeah, Isabella thought. *Did someone kill him? And, if so, how?*

They entered the lower levels and looked around. A handful of prisoners were seated on the floor, their hands bound behind their backs. They were trying not to look at the guards, who were leering at the bound women. Isabella looked from face to face, trying to determine who would be the most helpful. The castle's staff would probably not have been encouraged to wander. A cook would be little help, but ... her eyes focused on a terrified-looking maid and she smiled. Maybe, just maybe, they'd struck gold.

"Come with me," she ordered. "Now."

She helped the maid to her feet, even though the girl shrank away from her. Isabella would have smiled, if the situation hadn't been so serious. The maid had clearly mistaken her for a man ... presumably, she thought that the two *men* had bad intentions. She might have been right too, if someone else had come to inspect the prisoners first. A maid wouldn't be allowed to resist if one of her lords and masters decided he wanted to have some fun.

Assholes, Isabella thought.

The maid stared nervously at them as they escorted her into a private room. Isabella weighed up the situation, then freed the maid's hands. It wasn't much – she could have taken the maid with one hand behind her back – but it was *something*.

"Tell me this," she said, as the maid rubbed her wrists. "Did you attend upon Sir Garston?"

The maid nodded, jumpily. "Yes, My Lord."

"My Lady," Isabella corrected, absently. She smiled as the maid stared at her in complete disbelief. "Who was with him in the War Room?"

"I ..."

Isabella leaned forward. "Sir Garston is dead," she said, gently. "And whatever you tell us will be very useful."

The maid looked down at the floor. Gently, very gently, Isabella wove a spell to encourage the poor girl to talk freely. It wasn't fair, or right, but she didn't have time for a long interrogation. And she didn't want the girl subjected to torture, if Prince Reginald got it into his head that she was hiding something ...

"The city fathers," the maid said. She was shaking, very slightly. "And ... and a Red Monk."

"A Red Monk," Isabella repeated. "What is a Red Monk?"

"A ... a creepy person," the maid said. She sounded as if she was caught between two compulsions, one forcing her to talk and the other insisting that she had to keep her mouth shut. "He ... he was strange. He ..."

Isabella exchanged puzzled glances with Lord Robin as the maid's voice faded away. A Red Monk? She knew what a monk was – a man who devoted himself to a single god, to the point where he refused to even *talk* to unbelievers – but a Red Monk? She'd never heard of anything like it.

She spoke, very quietly. "A Red Monk ...?"

"I don't know," Lord Robin said. "But I think we'd better find out."

Chapter Fourteen

The Narrows were a desolate nightmare.

Havant stood outside the tent and peered into the darkening twilight. There was little to be found but scrubland that had no effective use, beyond allowing a handful of sheep to wander and graze at will. The pickets hadn't reported any sign of the enemy army, let alone reports of attacks within the Hereford or Goldenrod Lands. It was starting to look as though they'd wasted their time.

Not that it was a complete waste of time, Havant told himself. *We managed to impose our will on some of the king's least trustworthy vassals.*

He smiled, humourlessly. They'd force-marched to the Narrows, but they'd still had time to visit a number of noblemen and reassure them that the crown had no desire to interfere with their age-old prerogatives, while making it clear that the crown *did* have the power to crush them if they misbehaved. The noblemen who lived in the gulf between the Hereford or Goldenrod Lands were trimmers, switching sides whenever it seemed that one or other of the earls had a decisive advantage. Now, with Rufus on the throne and the Hereford Lands linked to the Crown Lands, Hereford had a major advantage. The noblemen had had no choice but to bend the knee to their new king.

As long as we stay in power, Havant thought. *If we lose power, the knives will come out.*

His lips quirked at the thought. The northern noblemen were a treacherous lot. Backstabbing was practically their hobby. He ought to know. He was one of them, after all: born and raised in the north. Simply getting along with his siblings – and the rest of his extended family – was a minor miracle in its own right. Normally, younger brothers were killed or driven away before they had a chance to murder their elders and take their power for themselves. But working together meant greater rewards for all.

Something rustled behind him. He turned to see Hark, his face half-hidden in his cloak. "Hark."

"Your Highness," the Red Monk said. He bowed, slightly. "I come with tragic news."

Havant's eyes narrowed. "What?"

"Prince Reginald has landed near Racal's Bay," Hark said, shortly. His voice was utterly toneless. "Sir Garston has fallen and the city has been put to fire and sword."

Havant stared. "When?"

"Today," Hark said.

Havant shook his head in disbelief. There was no way a horseman – even one of the famed steeds of legend – could reach them in less than a couple of days. King Edwin's attempts to set up a relay network – with fresh horses every twenty or so miles – had failed, simply because the noblemen *liked* knowing that it took time for the king to hear of their misdeeds, let alone do something about them. And yet, the Red Monks had strange powers. It never crossed his mind to doubt them.

He forced himself to think. His most pessimistic estimates of how long it would take Prince Reginald to assemble, train and launch an invasion force had clearly been far too optimistic. In hindsight ... it was possible that the Cold King had merely been posturing, hoping to draw King Rufus's army out of position. And if that had been the goal, he had succeeded admirably. Without the Red Monks, it would have taken *days* for a messenger to reach the army.

"I have to speak to my brother," he said, curtly. "What else do you know?"

"My brethren have hidden," Hark told him. "They have to remain out of sight."

Havant felt a flicker of bitter frustration. "Ask them to gather intelligence, if they can," he said. "We need to know everything."

"We will try," Hark said.

"Good," Havant snapped. He strode towards his brother's tent. Thankfully, Rufus had decided to go to bed early, rather than hold one of his wild parties. There was too great a chance of a sneak attack in the middle of the night. "We may need you to send messages to Allenstown."

"As you wish," Hark said.

Havant frowned, then stepped into the tent. His brother was sleeping next to a naked woman, one of his latest conquests. Havant rolled his eyes, then cleared his throat loudly. Rufus sat up, one hand reaching for the dagger he kept under his bed. Beside him, the woman squeaked loudly and grabbed for the blanket, lifting it up to cover her bare breasts. Under other circumstances, Havant would have enjoyed the sight. The woman was a noblewoman, not a filthy whore. But he didn't have time.

"Get out," he snapped.

The blonde woman gave him a nasty look, then wrapped the blanket around herself and headed for the flap. Not a particularly *bright* woman then, Havant decided, as she scurried into the night. Certainly not if she'd already opened her legs for the king, without waiting for a marriage contract. She might be hoping for a baby, in the fond belief that Rufus would marry her if she got pregnant, but that was unlikely. Rufus didn't need to marry her to legitimise the child. And the king's wife would be chosen for political advantage, not lust.

"This had better be important," Rufus growled. He sat upright, returning the dagger to its sheath. "Do you know how long it took me to get her into bed?"

"Not very long at all," Havant said, dryly. There was something about being the heir to an earldom – and later a king – that made a man absolutely irresistible to women. Even King Edwin, milksop though he'd been, had had a string of mistresses. A royal mistress would gain favour, influence and, if she played her cards well, power. "We have a problem."

Rufus glared. "What problem?"

"Prince Reginald has landed," Havant said. "And Racal's Bay has fallen."

"... Shit," Rufus said. The king stood and reached for his robes. "When did he land?"

"Today, apparently," Havant said. "The Red Monks just informed me."

"And Sir Garston?" Rufus pulled his robe over his head,

then buckled his belt. "What of him?"

"Dead," Havant said. "The city may well have been destroyed."

"A blessing in disguise," Rufus muttered.

Havant shrugged. Racal's Bay was – had been, perhaps – the most independent-minded city on the Summer Isle. It had bent the knee to the monarchy, but it had preserved a great deal of its independence ... even after round upon round of civil war. The city fathers had been very reluctant to pay more than the bare minimum of tax. Having the city destroyed – or at least severely damaged – wasn't entirely displeasing, but in the long term it would have a major effect on the island's economy. And he rather doubted that the *docks* had been destroyed.

Worst case, Prince Reginald captured the docks and fishing fleets intact, he told himself. *He can bring in his army at will, if he holds the docks, and feed it too.*

Rufus stuck his head out of the tent and bellowed for a messenger. When the young boy arrived, Rufus ordered him to find the senior officers and order them to assemble in the war tent. Havant couldn't help feeling a flicker of pity for the poor boy. Senior officers didn't like being woken unless the camp was under attack, he knew from bitter experience, and they might take their anger out on the messenger. But then, the child *was* the son of a powerful nobleman. Perhaps they'd think twice before slapping the boy.

"They can't possibly have expected us to hear of the invasion so fast," Rufus said. He reached for his sword and buckled it to his belt, then headed for the flap. "How long would it take a messenger to reach us?"

"Two days, at least," Havant said. Rufus was right. Any messenger sent from Racal's Bay wouldn't know *precisely* where to go. Finding the army would be a nightmare. Sending a messenger to Allenstown, then sending *another* messenger to the army would add at least another couple of days. "Prince Reginald won't expect us to react so quickly."

"No," Rufus agreed. He stepped out into the darkness, his bodyguards appearing out of the gloom and surrounding him. "He won't."

Havant followed his brother through the camp and into the

war tent, noting just how many men were moving around. The guards had been awake, naturally, but most of the others should have been asleep. Word would be spreading, of course. And not all of Rufus's vassals could be trusted. Havant wouldn't have cared to bet that a messenger *hadn't* left the camp to speed to the Goldenrod Lands. Earl Goldenrod might not believe the reports at first – he knew nothing about the Red Monks – but it wouldn't take him long to realise that the army was heading south. Who knew what he'd do then?

Rufus marched into the tent and bellowed for wine, then peered down at the map on the wooden table. It was the finest map the draftsmen could produce, although Havant knew from bitter experience that it wasn't particularly accurate. A *smart* commander knew better than to rely on maps to get a feel for the terrain. The Empire's mapmakers had never turned their attention to the Summer Isle, for better or worse. And no one else quite matched their skill at drawing maps.

Not that we complained at the time, Havant recalled. *We didn't want the Golden City to think we could pay more in tax.*

"We have been informed that the enemy has landed in Racal's Bay," Rufus said, once his officers had been assembled. The servants moved around the tent, handing out glasses of wine. "We must move at once to confront the threat."

Havant nodded, more to show that he was supporting his brother rather than anything else. Besides, he didn't really disagree with Rufus. They couldn't allow Prince Reginald to remain where he was, let alone start marching towards Allenstown. Losing the capital would shatter their grip on the island. Havant had no doubt of it. Too many of their loyal supporters would start thinking of ways to switch sides before it was too late.

Rufus traced out a line on the map. "We will force-march to Alcidine," he said. "That will put us between Racal's Bay and Allenstown, allowing us to either block an enemy advance or link up with Lord Francis and mount an offensive of our own. If Prince Reginald refuses our challenge, we will advance on Racal's Bay and push him back into the sea."

A risky operation, Havant thought. No professional soldier regarded the idea of a pitched battle without concern. The civil war had been a collection of minor skirmishes with big impacts, not battles on an awesome scale. *But we don't have a choice.*

He kept his face expressionless as he studied the map. Deliberately or otherwise, Prince Reginald had lured King Rufus into a position where all of his choices were bad. If the king refused to attack Racal's Bay, Reginald would have all the time in the world to consolidate his position, bring in reinforcements and eventually go on the offensive. But if the king attacked, he would be risking everything on a single engagement. And delay wasn't an option either. The weaker Rufus looked, the more likely someone would switch sides at the worst possible time.

Which means we can't wait for the autumn storms to block passage to Andalusia, Havant told himself. No one in their right mind would try to cross the channel in autumn. Ideally, the defenders could wait for the storms, then attack ... knowing the invaders couldn't call on reinforcements from the mainland. *But we don't have time to wait.*

He looked up, allowing his gaze to move from face to face. Some of the senior officers were loyal, insofar as that term meant anything on the Summer Isle. Others had switched sides, bringing enough of a dowry with them to convince the king to overlook their past indiscretions. They couldn't be trusted, not if the battle went badly. They'd bend the knee to Prince Reginald if they thought he was the stronger party.

"We will awaken the troops one hour before sunrise," Rufus said. "They are to be fed, then readied for a forced march at sunrise. Our baggage train is to be left behind, guarded by a single regiment. They can bring it south as quickly as possible."

Havant smiled at the shock echoing round the tent. Abandoning the baggage train was a colossal risk, even though the pickets hadn't picked up any signs of enemy activity. It would be a tempting target for everyone from Earl Goldenrod to rebels lurking in the mountain caves. And losing it would be bad. Perhaps not completely disastrous, as long as they retained control of Allenstown, but bad. Merely capturing the army's supplies would turn a rebel force into a very real threat.

"We have no choice," Rufus said. "I want to reach Alcidine before the enemy hears of our coming."

He paused, daring his officers to object. None of them said a word. They were all experienced enough to understand the dangers of leaving the baggage train behind ... and, more importantly, the risks of arguing with the king in public. Even *Havant* couldn't disagree with his brother publicly. The king was always right, even when he was wrong.

At least he listens to me in private, Havant thought. The officers would understand that, naturally. They could bring their concerns to the king's brother, who would take them to the king. *And wouldn't they be shocked to know he listens to Emetine too?*

"We'll send two messengers back to Allenstown," Rufus said. "After that, the gates are to be closed and guarded. *No one* is to send a message out of the camp – or the army, when we start marching. Is that understood?"

Havant nodded with the others, although he had a feeling it was already too late. Rumours would have swept through the camp by now, ranging from reasonably accurate stories to tales that no one would believe unless they were thoroughly drunk. The king would have to make an announcement shortly, just to keep the rumours from getting out of control. But it might well be too late to keep messengers from reaching Earl Goldenrod.

As long as he waits to see who comes out ahead, we should be fine, Havant thought. *But who knows what will happen if he decides to play kingmaker?*

It wasn't a pleasant thought. In theory, King Rufus could draw on the extensive resources of the Summer Isle to build an army and push the invaders back into the sea. In practice, those extensive resources simply didn't exist. Getting the nobility – even the loyalists – to work together was like herding cats, only worse. And if Earl Goldenrod decided to join Prince Reginald now, before Reginald had a chance to take Allenstown and declare himself king, he'd be in an excellent position to extract a steep price for his aid.

Reginald was unmarried, if Havant recalled correctly. Earl Goldenrod could request a royal marriage in return for his support.

Or he could just keep playing both sides, Havant told himself, sourly. *And as long as he times it right, he can get away with it too.*

He headed for the flap when Rufus dismissed the meeting. He'd have to speak to his subordinates, then make preparations for the march. And then ... he shook his head. He wasn't going to get any sleep tonight, clearly. Maybe a quick nap once the orders had been issued ... no, it wasn't likely to happen. Thankfully, he was still young and strong and experienced enough to cope. The older men would have real problems.

Good, he thought, savagely. *It might take their minds off betraying us.*

Hark met him outside his tent. His face seemed oddly hidden in the darkness, as if Havant's eyes were slipping over his features without quite taking them in. He had to concentrate just to look at the monk. It wasn't easy.

"It went well?" Hark asked. "They believed you?"

"We will be marching out at sunrise," Havant said. No one had questioned the information, not openly. "Thank you for informing us."

"You are most welcome," Hark said. "You have allowed us to spread the word."

"Yes," Havant said. He shrugged, dismissively. Who *cared* what the lower orders believed? "Do you have any other words of advice?"

Hark bowed. "I have spent many hours communing with Our Lord," he said. "It would be wise for you to be very careful. The coming battle is a turning point."

Havant looked up, sharply. "Can you see the future?"

"Only in the most general terms," Hark said. "But the coming battle is indeed a turning point."

Havant rolled his eyes. Fortune-tellers and soothsayers had been banned, right across the Empire. Anyone who claimed to be able to tell the future was burnt at the stake ... something the cynical part of his mind thought they really should have been able to see coming. The Inquisition had hunted them ruthlessly, even though it had always struck him as thoroughly pointless. They spoke in such vague terms that it was impossible to pin them down. There was no such thing as a *specific* prophecy.

And yet, the Red Monks did have strange powers ...

"I will heed your words," he said. He had never been particularly religious, but there was nothing to be gained by insulting the monks. Besides, religion existed – at least in part – to keep the commoners under control. "And I will be careful."

"Very good," Hark said. "We thank you."

He bowed, then glided off into the distance. Havant watched him go, feeling tired and worn, then stepped into the tent. He had work to do.

And Reginald has no way of knowing that we know, he told himself. *He won't expect us to start marching for at least two days.*

Chapter Fifteen

Racal's Bay felt on edge, Isabella decided as she walked down the cobbled streets. Soldiers patrolled the streets, their weapons clearly visible; press-ganged men were working in groups, picking up dead bodies and dumping them in carts for transfer to the mass grave outside the city. There were almost no women on the streets, even though it was mid-morning. The handful of women she saw were escorted by their menfolk, who looked jumpy. Isabella didn't really blame them. The mercenaries had been moved to camps outside the city – and the city's whores were doing a roaring trade – but the streets weren't safe.

She kept a wary eye on her surroundings, watching for potential threats. Lord Robin had offered to come with her – or detail a couple of bodyguards to accompany her – but Isabella had declined. If she ran into something she couldn't handle, she doubted anyone would be able to help. And besides, just in case she encountered something that should be reported to Alden, she'd prefer to make the report *before* telling the others.

Unless it poses an immediate threat, she told herself firmly, as she turned onto the street of the gods. *We might not have time to send a message to the Golden City.*

The street of the gods looked surprisingly intact, although the temples appeared to be deserted. There was one in every city, a small collection of temples gathered together to allow the faithful to worship freely. She recognised a couple of the gods, but others were unknown to her. *That* wasn't too surprising, she decided. The Summer Isle hadn't exactly been isolated, but there had been very little cultural bleed between the island and the mainland. None of the familiar temples looked very big.

But that means there might be hundreds of worshippers, she thought. Cults were frowned upon, but there was no way to keep people from worshipping in their homes. *Where are they?*

She walked up the street, glancing from side to side. The priests should have been outside, calling the faithful to prayer, but there was no sign of them. Perhaps Prince Reginald had ordered them to remain indoors, just to keep a troublesome priest from causing a riot. A crowd of worshippers could easily become a mob, with the right impetus. And then the mob would either be allowed to run riot or be brutally slaughtered. Neither one would be good, in the long run. The temples would have to be watched carefully as Prince Reginald tightened his grip on the city.

The Temple of Dusk – home of the Red Monks – squatted at one end of the street. It was a simple building, little more than a blocky stone mass, yet there was something about it that bothered her. The walls made it look old and new at the same time, as if the stone had aged overnight. She reached out with her senses and frowned. There was nothing inside the temple, as far as she could tell. Nothing at all, not even the faint sense of background magic that had been with her since birth. It was a void.

She cast a detection spell and aimed it towards the temple. The spell reported nothing ... it didn't even register any magic clinging to the runes that someone had carved into the stone. Isabella inched closer and inspected them, one by one. She was very familiar with runes – her father had beaten them into her, literally – but these were new. As far as she could tell, they weren't magic at all. And yet ... she reached out, holding her finger above the carvings. It felt as if something was watching her, waiting to pounce.

Gritting her teeth, she stepped up to the door and pushed it open with her sword. No magic snapped at her, yet the sense of *threat* was suddenly overpowering. The interior of the building was dark, completely dark. She cast a light-spell, half-expecting it to fail. Instead, the flickering light lit up a barren interior. Isabella frowned, puzzled. If the building hadn't felt so *off* to her, she would have wondered if she'd gone to the wrong place.

She'd seen many temples in her life, from the grand temples in the Golden City to small kirks in tiny villages.

They had all been extensively decorated, their walls covered in gold and silver ... even the poorest kirks had been decorated by their worshippers. But the Temple of Dusk was bare. The walls and floor were plain stone, unmarred by paintings or runes; there were no windows, no lights ... she wondered, absently, just how the worshippers were expected to *see*. The only object within the chamber was a plain stone altar, placed in the centre of the room. It was nothing more than a block of carved stone. She couldn't even see any runes carved into the stone.

Isabella stepped forward warily, holding her sword at the ready. Something was in the room with her. Her instincts were screaming in alarm. And yet, she could see nothing. Or sense nothing. The room was a gaping void, empty of everything. She knew how to look for an invisible person, with or without magic, yet ... there was nothing. The chamber was completely silent. Ice ran down her spine as she approached the altar. Something was very wrong. She touched the stone gingerly and ...

The impressions slammed into her mind. *Death*. Death and pain and suffering and ... above it, someone laughing. *Something* laughing. A vast strata of unlimited power, reaching out in directions beyond her comprehension; despair, defeat, death ... death ... death. She tried to pull back as the sensations grew stronger, cackling howling in her ears, but her legs refused to move. The torrent of thoughts and feelings poured through her brain, then snapped out of existence. She fell backwards ...

... And landed, hard, on the stone floor. Her sword clattered to the ground beside her.

For a long moment, she just sat there. She'd been under mental attack before – her training had included resistance to mind control spells – but the altar ... whatever had been lurking under the altar had been something else. She wasn't even sure she'd been the *target*, as if she'd been caught up in someone else's mind. And yet ... it was hard, very hard, to muster the strength to stand up. She was suddenly *very* glad she hadn't brought anyone with her.

She forced herself, inch by inch, to stand up, then reach for the sword. Her instructors would have been furious if they'd seen her drop the weapon. She'd been lucky not to land on her own blade! And yet ... she inspected it, carefully, before returning the sword to her belt. It was hard to escape the sense that the blade had come very close to snapping. She made a mental note to have it checked when she returned to the castle. Taking a brittle blade into a fight was a good way to wind up dead.

The altar stood in the centre of the chamber, utterly unmoving. Isabella glared at it, then reached out with her senses again. There was nothing, beyond the faint hint of ... *something*, right at the edge of her mind. She gritted her teeth in annoyance. She'd often felt strange sensations in temples, particularly as she'd grown into her magic, but this was something different. Something *wrong*. And yet, she couldn't put her finger on it. Magicians never talked about the magic in temples. Students were discouraged from asking questions.

And yet ... she recalled odd stories, whispered in the night. There were cults that practiced old rites, rites that were partly magic ... rites that led to *dark* magic. They didn't know what they were doing, if the rumours were to be believed, but that didn't keep them from being dangerous. Isabella wracked her mind, yet she couldn't remember anything else. The Inquisition would have known, if anyone did, but she'd never taken the oaths. She'd been kicked out long before completing her training.

The Red Monks are dangerous, she thought, as she surveyed the rest of the chamber. *What are they doing?*

She'd never heard of a god called Dusk. That didn't mean anything in itself, but combined with the odd sensations – and the reports of odd magic – it suggested that the Red Monks were up to something dangerous. And yet ... what? She looked around for any clues she might have missed, then headed for the door. The entire building would have to be sealed off, then destroyed. Except she wasn't sure that it *could* be destroyed. The gods alone knew what would happen if the temple was smashed to the ground.

She winced as she headed back to the door and stepped into the bright sunlight. It wasn't uncommon for magic to weave itself into a temple, particularly when a handful of untrained magicians were among the congregation. The uncontrolled magic could be very dangerous to unbelievers, although trained magicians had no trouble countering it if necessary. But here ... it felt different. It felt *wrong*. The last thing she wanted was to accidentally trigger another Blight. An entire district in the Golden City had been rendered uninhabitable after some idiot had started fiddling with dark sorcery.

The cool air outside felt *normal*, even though the stench of battle and death still hung in the air. She took a deep breath, enjoying the sensation. And yet ... now that she was outside the temple, it was harder to understand why she'd been so concerned. It felt like a dream, a waking dream. She wanted to look away ...

No, she told herself, sharply.

She clenched her fists, driving her fingernails into her palms and biting her lip until she drew blood. The pain helped her to focus. There was *something* in the air, all right. Something subtly inducing her to forget everything she'd sensed inside the temple. It was powerful and yet ... she ground her teeth in frustration. She knew how to resist and counter most compulsion spells – she knew how to turn them back onto their caster – but this one didn't seem to *have* a caster. And she couldn't sense the compulsion directly. She could only sense the effect it was having on her. It was hard, so hard, to *remember*.

Ice ran down her spine, again, as she reached for her notebook and pencil. *Something* was plucking away at her thoughts, making it harder to concentrate. She knew, although she wasn't sure *how* she knew, that the effect would only get worse as she moved away from the temple. And yet, it was hard to write it down. She had to bite her lip, again and again, just to focus long enough to write a short note to herself. Even so ...

Whatever they're doing is very dangerous, she thought, as she finished writing a reminder to herself. *But what are they doing?*

She took a long breath. Thankfully, the spell – whatever it was – didn't seem to be focused on her. She'd seen forgetfulness spells that urged their victims to destroy anything that might remind them of the past, without ever being quite aware of what they were doing. The ... magic ... seemed to be more like an aversion charm, rather than a direct attack. But she'd never heard of an aversion charm that literally reached into someone's head and removed their memories. Or even kept the victim from remembering something. It was beyond known magic.

Taking one last look at the temple, she turned and walked down the street. The sensation seemed to grow stronger for a second, then snapped out of existence as if someone had simply cancelled the spell. She looked down at her notebook, frowning as she realised how faint the memories had become. They were urgent – she *knew* they were urgent – and yet it was hard to work up any sense of *urgency*. It felt like something she'd put off, and put off, until it was suddenly unimportant.

Damn them, she thought. The question ran through her mind, time and time again. *What are they doing?*

It chilled her to the bone. She'd had the finest magical education money could buy – and then undergone one of the most rigorous training courses known to mankind – and she still felt as helpless as a powerless mundane would in the face of a hedge-witch. She had faced stronger magicians in her time, from older students to her instructors, but none of them had scared her as much as the unknown. They, at least, were predictable. She'd known what they could do to her. The unknown was far more terrifying.

No wonder Big Richard is so scared of magicians, she thought. *We're not people he can fight with his axe.*

She knew she should go straight back to the castle – and perhaps organise a hunt for whoever had worshipped in the temple – but it was hard to resist the urge to wander the streets and brood. Prince Reginald might listen to her or he might not. It wasn't as if she had proof of anything beyond strange sensations she couldn't put into words. She certainly wasn't going to risk taking *him* to the Temple of Dusk. *Alden* would listen to her, she was sure, but Alden was in Andalusia. Unless, of course, he'd already headed home. It wasn't as if he'd bothered to send her a copy of his itinerary.

The streets felt louder, somehow, as she made her way towards the docks. Prince Reginald had forced the city fathers to pay the dockyard workers double their normal salary, if they worked day and night to unload the ships. Isabella rather suspected that the workers would be cheering Prince Reginald, even if the rest of the city hated him. The promise of more work in the future – when regular trade between the Summer Isle and Andalusia was established – would be enough to keep them happy. And the city fathers might find themselves out of a job.

And they can't even raise taxes without sparking off a riot, she thought, wryly. *And the prince might simply veto anything standing between him and his supplies.*

Isabella stopped, sharply, as she heard someone – it sounded like a young woman – starting to cry. Her hand dropped to the pommel of her sword as the sound grew louder, accompanied by male laughter and loud whistles. She tensed – it could be a trap – and then started to follow the sound into an alleyway. The houses seemed to have been built at random, turning the alleys into a maze. Dirt and grime lay everywhere. She kept moving, keeping a wary eye open for ambushers. The alleys would be the perfect place for an ambush.

She rounded a corner and froze. A young woman was standing in the centre of the alley, her breasts exposed and her fingers working on her skirt. Tears ran down her cheeks as she swayed through a seductive dance. Three soldiers were watching her with hungry eyes, drinking heavily; a fourth was holding a blade against an older man's throat, forcing the young woman to strip. Her father, Isabella guessed. She felt a hot flash of pure rage. How *dare* they?

"Stop this at once," she snapped. The soldiers looked up at her, alarmed. "Now!"

The fourth soldier casually slit the older man's throat, then smirked at Isabella as the girl screamed and fell to her knees. Isabella cursed him – and herself – as she readied her magic. Of *course* they weren't going to stop. Prince Reginald had already hanged a number of men for rape. The rapists had no choice, but to fight. Killing her was their only hope of avoiding the noose and they knew it.

Not that it matters, she thought, savagely. Magic boiled through her, dancing around her fingertips. *They won't live long enough to be hanged.*

She lashed out at the murderer, slamming a blast of raw magic into him. His body flew backwards and slammed into a wall with a sickening crunch. Isabella sensed, more than heard, a number of his bones shattering under the force. The other soldiers froze, then threw themselves at her. They had no choice. And yet, it was futile. Isabella struck them with her magic, ripping them apart. Blood flew everywhere, covering the walls. The remains of three bodies crashed to the ground.

The girl screamed, again. "Father!"

"I'm sorry," Isabella said, gruffly. The magic receded, slowly. She didn't feel any pity for the would-be rapists. There were whores in the camp, if they'd had the patience to wait for the end of their shift. No doubt they'd found a stash of booze and got drunk. "He's dead."

She checked the body, just in case, but it was pointless. The older man's throat had been cut open. Even powerful magic couldn't heal such a wound before it was too late, let alone bring the victim back from the dead. None of the stories of resurrection magic had ever been substantiated.

"You killed them," the girl said. She fumbled her way back into her shirt. "You ..."

"Yeah," Isabella said. She reminded herself, sharply, that the girl had been on the verge of being raped. She couldn't be blamed for hysteria. "I'll walk you home."

She took one last look at the dead bodies, then took the girl's arm and led her down the alleyway. No one would question her, not when she was a powerful sorceress *and* reporting directly to Prince Reginald. And besides, the men had disobeyed orders. If she hadn't killed them, they'd have been executed without trial anyway. They'd known the rules.

And we have too many other problems to worry about, she thought, as they reached the main road. She waved to a sergeant, gave him a brief explanation, then led the girl onwards. *What are the Red Monks doing?*

Chapter Sixteen

"So you decided to kill four of my men," Gars said. "You didn't think to report them ..."

"I stopped them from committing rape," Isabella snapped back. "Would you have preferred me to just walk away?"

Reginald held up a hand before the argument could end in tears – or transformations. "I informed all soldiers that they were to treat the population with respect," he said. It was unfortunate that the would-be rapists hadn't survived long enough to be hanged, but he wasn't going to shed any tears over their deaths. "We do not need to alienate the workers."

Lord William made a rude sound. "They're your serfs," he said, with a sneer. "They will work for you."

"And most serfs are lazy assholes who won't do more than the bare minimum," Captain-General Jones said. "Freemen are far harder workers, My Lord, but they won't work so hard if they think their daughters will be raped."

"She probably asked for it," Lord William said. "She ..."

Isabella leaned forward. "By somehow inducing them to hold a sword to her father's throat?"

William flinched. "I ..."

"Enough." Reginald slapped the table. "The matter is now closed."

He took a moment to let his words sink in. "What did you find in the Temple of Dusk?"

Isabella looked, for the first time since he'd met her, slightly unsure of herself. It didn't suit her.

"I'm not sure," she admitted. She looked down at the notebook in her hand. "There was a ... *sensation* ... of *something* there, but I don't know what. It wasn't magic, Your Highness, not as we know it. It was something else."

William frowned. "Could you be *less* specific if you tried?"

"There were ... *forces* ... in there that I was unable to

identify," Isabella snapped. She sounded as though she was reaching the end of her tether. "There were ..." she shook her head in frustration "... effects of a kind I have never seen before. I nearly forgot everything I saw when I walked out of the building, everything. I am trained to resist all such spells, *Your Lordship*, and yet they nearly got me. Even now, just *thinking* about it is hard."

She made a visible attempt to calm down. "I spoke to a handful of people who visited the temple before we arrived. None of them were able to tell me what happened after they entered the building, not even in vague terms. They weren't even able to tell me when the temple was *founded*. Even the city fathers didn't know!"

Reginald frowned. It was rare, very rare, for a city to refuse permission to build a temple, particularly if there were enough worshippers to make trouble, but surely they'd know when the temple was built! Or who used it. Or ... it made no sense. He was hardly the kind of person to outlaw worship of a particular god, but the stories worried him. Magic was displeasing enough, to a soldier. The thought of something *beyond* magic was worse.

Gars cleared his throat. "There have always been stories of miracles in temples."

"Yes," Isabella said. "And most of them have magical explanations. This was different."

Academic Milhous leaned forward. "Even a cripple suddenly being able to walk?"

Isabella nodded, shortly. "An untrained magician who prayed would be feeding magic into the building," she said. "Another who prayed for a miracle might unwittingly direct that magic into a spell, *working* the miracle. It isn't impossible to use magic to help a cripple to walk, Academic. It's just expensive and difficult."

"This seems ... blasphemous," Captain-General Stuart said, darkly. "I *saw* a blind girl suddenly being able to see."

"And it has a natural explanation," Isabella said. "There are plenty of spells that can repair a blinded eye. Every *miracle* I've ever heard of, My Lord, is more a case of something being mended, rather than being built from scratch. The magic already had a pattern to follow. It just needed the impetus."

She paused. "What I sensed in that temple was something different," she said. "I don't know what it was. But I do know it is dangerous."

Reginald took a long breath. He understood military matters. But magic? And religion? It worried him. He certainly didn't know how to fight it.

"We will be wary," he said, firmly. He'd sealed off the temple. Perhaps they'd find someone who could give them answers. So far, none of the Red Monks had been found, but it was unlikely they'd managed to leave the city. "But we do have to decide on our next move."

He tapped the map, meaningfully. "How long until we have landed the first wave of supplies?"

"The first wave should be disembarked by tomorrow, assuming the workers don't decide to strike," Jones said. "It will be two or three more days before the *second* wave is disembarked."

Which includes most of the siege engines, Reginald thought. *Taking Allenstown without them will be a nightmare.*

He leaned forward. "We already have pickets heading out to cover all of the possible approaches," he said. "Once the first wave is disembarked, I intend to march east to Allenstown. We *should* be able to surround the city before the usurper hears of our arrival."

"Yes, My Lord," Gars said.

Reginald allowed himself a tight smile. Fortune – that most fickle of gods – had favoured him beyond his wildest dreams. The Cold King hadn't launched an invasion, as far as he knew, but the usurper had taken his army northwards anyway. By Reginald's most pessimistic estimate, it would be at least another day or two before the usurper even knew the invasion had begun. And then it would take at least three to four days to march south. By then, Reginald might well have taken Allenstown for himself.

Lord William coughed. "Should we not wait for a response to our messengers?"

"There's no time," Reginald said. It would be at least two days before the messenger he'd sent reached Earl Oxley – and five or six days before the *other* messenger reached Earl

Goldenrod.   He doubted either of the earls would immediately march to support him – or the usurper. It was far more likely that they'd sit on their hands and wait for a clear winner to emerge. "The chance to capture Allenstown cannot be allowed to slip away."

He studied the map, carefully. Trying to hold Racal's Bay against a determined attack would be risky, even though he had more and better troops than the late Sir Garston. Reginald's offensive had smashed the defences flat, after all. Rebuilding – and then improving – them would take more time than Reginald had. He couldn't take the risk of being trapped against the sea. No, he had to take the offensive. The usurper could not be allowed to seize the initiative.

"Prepare the troops to march out in two days," he ordered. "And make sure they're ready for anything."

There was another reason to continue the offensive, he knew. Soldiers got restless in barracks – and that went double for mercenaries. Staying in Racal's Bay would eventually lead to more and more trouble between the troops and the locals, no matter how many men he flogged for insubordination. Better to have the troops in the field than venting their frustration on the civilians.

"I shall see to it personally," Gars said. "I assume there has been no response from Allenstown?"

Reginald shrugged. Lord Francis – another stranger raised to the peerage by the usurper – probably knew about the invasion already. It was hard to believe the usurper had left *much* authority in Lord Francis's hands, but any local commander would have the freedom to take limited action without waiting for orders. And yet, what would Lord Francis *do*? Take whatever forces he could muster and march on Racal's Bay? Or dig in at Allenstown and force Reginald to come to him?

"He won't have received our surrender demand yet," Reginald said. He'd happily recognise Lord Francis's title – and allow him to keep his lands – if he surrendered at once, but somehow he doubted it. No one would be left as *de facto* regent – and rear commander – if he wasn't trusted. "We will assume that he won't surrender."

"Of course, Your Highness," Gars said.

Reginald looked around the table. "Are there any other matters of concern?"

"Merely the voyage back home," Lord William said. "I believe the autumn storms are on their way."

Reginald shrugged. The sailors *had* made it clear that only an idiot – or someone tired of life – would try to cross the channel during the storms, but it was hardly a problem. They'd have won – or lost – by then. He could winter on the Summer Isle and return to the mainland in the spring, if necessary. He'd certainly not been *planning* to return home for several years.

"We will have enough supplies by then to win," he said, dismissively. He frowned. He'd hoped to leave Lord William in command of Racal's Bay, but it was clear that the job required someone with a working brain. He made a mental note to choose someone later and leaned forward. "If you have any other concerns, bring them to me before we resume our march. Until then ... I'll see you all for dinner in the Great Hall. Dismissed."

He met Isabella's eyes. "Please remain behind."

Isabella nodded, sharing a glance with Lord Robin. Reginald leaned back in his chair as his councillors slowly departed the room, keeping his thoughts to himself. He had every intention of luring Isabella into his household and it was clear that Lord Robin knew it. Why not? A sorceress who worked directly for him would be one hell of an ace in the hole. Isabella had already proven she could be more than merely *useful*. And there was something about her – she was so different from the sheltered court girls – that he found appealing.

He waited for the last councillor to leave the room, then looked at Isabella. "Can you make this room private?"

Isabella waved her hand in the air. "Done."

Reginald frowned, inwardly. There was no way to tell if it *was* done. And yet ... he sat upright, dismissing the thought. He had to trust her. She'd had plenty of opportunity to turn on him if she'd wished. Her face, oddly puckish, betrayed none of her feelings. He couldn't help wondering just what she'd gone through, before winding up in his service. She was just so *different*.

She has power, he reminded himself. *And so many other women do not.*

It was an odd insight. Reginald had power, and he would have more when he succeeded his father, but his sister would never wield power in her own right. She could give the kingdom to her husband, yet she could never rule for herself. It wouldn't be long before their father picked a husband for her, someone who needed closer ties to the royal family. Sofia was a princess, yet she was powerless. Her life didn't belong to her. Ruling Queens had been rare, before the Empire's collapse. Now, he knew of only one Ruling Queen who'd managed to retain power.

But Isabella? She had power and she was willing to use it. She didn't need to flirt with him, she didn't need to influence him ... she didn't even need to pretend to *like* him. It made her ... *different.*

He leaned forward. "How dangerous *are* the Red Monks?"

"I wish I knew," Isabella said. The frustration in her voice was all too clear. "I'd understand another sorcerer, Your Highness, but the Red Monks are something ... *strange.*"

Reginald nodded, slowly. "Can they have disguised their magic in some way?"

"... Not *easily*," Isabella said. "The mere act of camouflaging their magic would be quite revealing. Anyone who had the power to do ... to do what I saw wouldn't have to hide."

"They could just have devised new spells," Reginald said.

Isabella's eyes flashed with sudden anger. "You might as well start talking out of your arse," she snapped. "It's simply not possible."

"I've met a lot of men who talked out of their arses," Reginald said, lightly. "Aren't there spells to make it happen?"

"Yeah," Isabella said. She looked down at the table, then back up at him. "Your Highness ... what I sensed is impossible, by all known magical law. It wasn't ... it wasn't understandable. I could take a normal spell apart to see how it was put together, then rewrite it on the fly. This ... I'm not even sure it *is* magic. And yet, something is happening. I don't know how to put it into words."

Reginald met her eyes. "Do you think we should continue?"

Isabella blinked. "You're asking *me*?"

"Yes," Reginald said. He was surprised at himself. It was hard enough to ask for advice from his trusted councillors, even though his father had drummed it into his head – time and time again – that disagreement, expressed in private, was not treachery. Being told *no* wasn't easy to hear. He was a prince, after all. But ... he needed to trust her. And he wanted her to trust him. "What do you think?"

"I don't know," Isabella said. She sounded honestly perplexed. "Whatever the Red Monks are doing is dangerous. It has to be stopped. And yet ... I don't know *what* we might encounter. This isn't conventional magic."

Reginald scowled. *That* wasn't an answer. It was *his* choice, in the end, that would determine if the army marched west or returned to the ships and sailed east, but he would have appreciated her advice. And yet, he understood her dilemma all too well. The fog of war – not knowing where one's own troops were, let alone not knowing where the enemy was lurking – was bad enough at the best of times. Now, facing unknown powers, it was impossible to even *guess* at what was lying in wait.

Caution dictates withdrawal, he thought. *But we cannot fall back now.*

He sighed. Retreating after losing a battle was one thing. Everyone would understand. But retreating from a shadow? From vague reports that could mean anything? He'd be the laughing stock of the northern kingdoms. His father didn't have another son, so there was no way he could be written out of the line of succession, but ... it would be hard to stamp his authority on the land, once he became king. The barons would see him as a coward. The hell of it was that they might well be right.

"We proceed," he said. "And we will tear down the temple before we leave."

"Just leave it sealed off," Isabella said. "You have no idea what will happen if you destroy it."

"As you wish," Reginald said. "But we *must* take one of those monks alive."

***

The house was practically identical to every other house on the street, Big Richard noted, as they marched towards the building. A wooden front door, a pair of windows ... *glass* windows ... it was small, compared to some of the other buildings Richard had seen, but whoever owned it had to be rich. Glass was a luxury. He had no idea if the owner was actually guilty of hiding a runaway nobleman or not, but it didn't matter. Guilty or innocent, his house was about to be turned upside down. There would be plenty of opportunities for some private looting.

He smirked at the rest of his squad, then lifted his foot and kicked the door hard enough to smash the lock. The squad rushed inside, clubs at the ready. An older woman gasped when she saw them, lifting a ladle as if she intended to use it as a weapon. The squad grabbed her, shoving her towards the wall. Richard saw a younger woman sitting on the floor and yanked her to her feet, taking advantage of the opportunity to grope her breasts. They felt full, suggesting she was a mother. He looked around and saw a baby lying in a crib. The little brat looked as though he was about to cry.

"Stand against the wall," he snarled. "Where are the others?"

The women gibbered in fear. The baby started to howl. Richard snorted and hurried up the stairs, axe at the ready. There was nothing upstairs, save for a pair of bedrooms ... he felt a flicker of disappointment as he realised there weren't rich pickings after all. And yet ... his instincts insisted that there was *something* to be found. He looked around and ...

... Something moved, behind him. He spun around. A hooded figure was standing there, wrapped in a red cowl that hid his features. Even his hands were hidden behind long red gloves. Richard grinned, raising his axe. He had no idea how he'd managed to miss the cloaked man, but it didn't matter. Prince Reginald had offered a large reward for anyone who managed to capture a Red Monk. Richard would make sure he got all the credit. And then ...

The Red Monk reached for his cowl and pulled it back. Richard raised his axe, too late. The face was ... the face ... *things* were moving under the cowl. His mind refused to grasp what his eyes were seeing. The world blurred, spinning around him. Someone was speaking to him, but he couldn't make out the words. And yet, they sounded important. He tried to listen carefully ...

His eyes snapped open. He was alone. He'd always been alone ... hadn't he? And yet, he couldn't escape the sense that *something* had happened. He looked around, warily, but nothing moved. There wasn't even anything worth stealing in eyeshot.

Shaking his head, he headed back down the stairs. He'd probably imagined it. He was tired and jumpy ... it wouldn't be the first time he'd jumped at shadows. Perhaps it had been a spell ... perhaps one of the women was a witch ... he felt a surge of pure hatred, so intense that he almost cried out. Magic-users ... he *hated* magic users. They couldn't be trusted.

Something moved at the corner of his eye, but he ignored it. It was just his imagination.

Right?

Chapter Seventeen

"I'm leaving you in command here," Reginald said. Captain-General Jones looked torn between pleasure and fear. "You know what to do?"

"Yes, Your Highness," Jones said. "Open the shipping lanes to Andalusia, then bring in as much as possible before the autumn storms."

Reginald nodded as he took one last look at the audience chamber. Jones was the best choice to hold the city, even though it meant that Reginald wouldn't have his services during the advance to Allenstown. Jones was enough of a pragmatist to work with the locals, rather than treat them as serfs. He'd already started forging ties with the city fathers. By the time the campaign was over, the city fathers would be in no position to switch sides. Their own people – enjoying a boom as the city started to trade with Humber and Havelock – wouldn't let them. It would keep the slimy bastards loyal.

"I'll leave you a small garrison," he said. "Make sure you work on the defences. I don't want to come back and discover I've lost the city."

"Yes, Your Highness," Jones said.

He knows what to do, Reginald reminded himself. Master of Food or not, no one became a Captain-General without a considerable amount of military experience. Logistics was boring, but vital. He wouldn't trust anyone who *didn't* have genuine experience to handle it. The officers who *didn't* know what they were doing screwed things up for the fighting men. *I have to trust him.*

They exchanged salutes, then Reginald turned and walked down to the courtyard. The castle staff knelt as he passed, a handful of men and women who'd either been allowed to resume their posts or had simply been hired from the city's population. Reginald would have preferred to bring in his own servants, at least until the war was over, but he couldn't afford to waste shipping on servants rather than soldiers and mercenaries. The locals *should* know better than to cause trouble, he hoped. It wasn't as if the usurper was close enough to take advantage of an uprising.

And he would probably slaughter the rebels afterwards, Reginald thought, with grim amusement. Kings and princes disliked commoner rebels, even if the rebellion was in their favour. *Rebellion is habit-forming.*

His bodyguard waited for him in the courtyard, their weapons at the ready. Reginald nodded to Isabella – he'd insisted on the sorceress staying close to him – and then clambered into the saddle. The horse looked ready to gallop, after a handful of days cooped up in the stables. Reginald felt a flicker of guilt. He'd been taught to take care of his weapons and horses – everything else could be done by the servants – but he hadn't had time. Someone else had to handle everything.

"Open the gates," he ordered.

The horse surged forward with the others, cantering through the gate and onto the cobbled streets. A handful of commoners – mainly merchants – could be seen on the streets, although almost all of them were men. Reginald reminded himself, again, that it would take time for Racal's Bay to recover from the invasion. Jones knew to keep the troops under tight control, but it would be a long time before any of the locals felt they could relax. A single mistake might be enough to get them killed.

He glanced back at the city as the small group headed towards the gates. The remains of the barricades had been cleared away, while teams of repairmen were already working on the walls. Jones probably didn't have time to make Racal's Bay impregnable, Reginald considered, but he could certainly stop an enemy troop from simply riding into the city and taking control. Unless, of course, the city rose in rebellion as soon as the enemy appeared on the horizon. It was another good reason to treat the city gently, but firmly.

They cantered through the outer gates – or what remained of them – and out onto a muddy road. Reginald scowled in annoyance. It clearly hadn't been a very good road at the best of times, before civil unrest and the passage of part of his army had turned it into a slippery nightmare. King Edwin had *talked* about building a proper road network, apparently, but very little had actually been done. Reginald silently revised his estimates of how long it would take to reach Allenstown, upwards. His men weren't going to be deterred by a little mud, but it would slow them down. Maybe King Edwin had calculated that the bad roads would make it harder for his enemies to send troops south.

And let's hope he was right, Reginald thought, as they caught up with Captain-General Gars and his men. *The usurper might well know we're here now.*

"Your Highness," Gars said. He raised a hand in brief salute as Reginald came up alongside him. More elaborate welcomes were forbidden during marches and combat. "The army is on the move."

Reginald nodded. Hundreds of soldiers and mercenaries were visible, marching westwards; hundreds more were out of sight, spread out across the countryside and watching for potential threats. The locals were probably already running for cover, hiding their daughters and whatever paltry food supplies they had before a horde of soldiers descended on their lands like ravening locusts. It was clear – his lips thinned in disgust as he surveyed the muddy fields – that modern farming techniques had never made it to the Summer Isle. They would have to be introduced, once the war was over. The Summer Isle would probably never be a major food exporter – the weather was too unpleasant – but it should definitely be able to support a bigger population. And a bigger population meant a larger army and tax base.

A problem for my sons, he thought. He smiled at the thought. It would soon be time for him to marry, although he knew he probably wouldn't get to choose his bride. King Romulus had been considering the matter for years. *They will learn to rule here, while I rule the homeland.*

"The pickets have reported no sign of enemy contact," Gars informed him. "The enemy doesn't appear to be watching us."

Reginald shrugged. There were plenty of hills between Racal's Bay and Allenstown. And Lord Francis *knew* the army was on its way. There would be enemy pickets on those hills, watching for Reginald's forces. Reginald would bet his crown on it. They probably wouldn't be seen – the enemy troops would know the land far better than his men – but they would be there. It was unlikely that he could be assured of complete surprise.

"Keep the river between us and the enemy," he said. The River Racal wasn't entirely impassable – although it had already swollen and burst its banks after the last set of rainstorms – but the enemy would have trouble getting an army across the waters. "And make sure the pickets stay on alert."

He settled back into the saddle as the sky darkened. It was going to be a long march, made worse by the rain and the mud. But at least they were on the way to Allenstown. And – if he was correct – he'd have an excellent chance of capturing the city before the usurper could respond to his invasion. And then ...

I'll hold all the cards, he thought. *The usurper will not be able to stand against me.*

***

Isabella was quite familiar with unpleasant weather conditions. She'd trained near the Watchtower, where the weather could swing from hot to cold at terrifying speed; she'd travelled to sandy deserts and icy mountains, where she'd alternatively sweated like a pig or frozen solid. And yet, there was something strikingly morbid about the Summer Isle's weather. The dismally dark skies opened regularly, discharging rain onto the marching troops; rain trickled into her collar and down her leathers, pooling in her pants and making her feel cold and uncomfortable. She kept her discomfort to herself, knowing she was one of the lucky ones. The marching troops didn't even have the comfort of a horse.

The army advanced in fits and starts, half the troops pausing to rest – and snatch what sleep they could under what little shelter they could find – while the other half advanced forward, weapons at the ready. Small farms and villages were discovered and searched for food and drink; the inhabitants, perhaps wisely, had fled to the hills the moment they'd seen the army approaching. The officers did what they could to ensure that the stolen food was evenly distributed – and that rations were handed out regularly – but it was hard to escape the sense of grim despondency that was falling over the army.

She found it hard to believe, despite herself, that the Summer Isle was really worth invading, let alone holding. None of the farms they'd seen had struck her as particularly prosperous, not compared to the estates her family had held near the Golden City. But then, the local gentry would probably take everything the farmers grew, save for the bare minimum they needed to feed themselves and seed the fields for the next year. It was hard to believe that *anyone* could be less enlightened than Isabella's father, yet she'd met too many aristocrats who regarded peasants as dumb animals. The Summer Isle didn't even have any middling classes, outside the cities.

Her horse squelched through the mud. Up ahead, a cart had overturned, scattering its contents into the gloom. A troop of soldiers were struggling to right it; she considered using her magic to help, but she knew they'd resent her assistance. Besides, she needed to conserve power as much as possible. It wouldn't be long before there was a battle. She'd need to fight to survive, if nothing else ...

Lord Robin rode up beside her. He looked like a drowned rat – he'd discarded his armour for a shirt and a set of leathers – but somehow he still managed to look good. Isabella resisted the urge to roll her eyes at the thought. She'd been told that leaders were *meant* to look good, even in the worst circumstances, but it had always struck her as nonsensical. A struggling man was more likely to resent someone above him than be struck dumb by admiration. She didn't want to know what *she* looked like.

As long as I don't look like a woman, she thought.

"Wonderful land," Lord Robin said. He smiled at her, rain dripping off his helmet and splashing onto the horse. "Lots of potential here."

Isabella gave him a sharp look. "I think we're being underpaid."

"Hardly," Lord Robin said. "We put the boot on the neck

of a few aristocrats – and kill those who refuse to submit – and then start making changes. A regular pattern of taxation with fixed rates will encourage the peasants to grow more ... ending serfdom itself will make the land more productive ..."

Isabella listened as he chatted on, talking about what he'd do with his estate ... once he'd taken it from its previous owner, of course. She doubted it would be *that* easy to get his hands on the land. King Rufus the usurper was marked for death, of course, but he had a brother who might bend the knee to Prince Reginald. And if he did, would he be allowed to retain his lands in exchange for loyalty? Isabella could easily imagine most – perhaps all – of the local nobility switching sides, once the usurper was dead. Where would the land come from *then*?

Reginald will have to balance the demands of his mercenaries – and his inner circle – with the rights of his new supporters, she thought. *And that won't be easy.*

She frowned as the gloom seemed to darken. It felt as though night was falling already, even though she knew it was early afternoon. Her sense of time wasn't *that* bad. Big Richard and the others were out there somewhere, but she couldn't see them. She supposed she should be thankful for small mercies, even though Big Richard wasn't the sort of person *she'd* send on delicate missions. Unless someone *wanted* a disaster ...

"There must be magic here," Lord Robin said. "Have you thought about setting up a school?"

Isabella gave him a surprised look. She'd never even considered it. And yet ... it wasn't something *she'd* do, but other magicians might well be glad of the chance to set up their own schools. There had been quite a bit of muted resentment about the Peerless School's monopoly on magical education even before the Golden City had fallen. Now ...

That's Alden's problem, she thought.

"I haven't heard of any famous magicians who came from the Summer Isle," she said, instead. "The gentry probably killed any commoners with hints of magic, instead of sending them to be trained. And if they had magic themselves, they kept it well hidden."

She shrugged. An aristocratic child with magic would

probably have been taken away, once upon a time. Court Wizards disliked the thought of aristocrats with magic. And the aristocrats probably wouldn't complain too. A magical child with aristocratic blood – *known* aristocratic blood – would screw up precedence beyond repair.

"We'll be at Allenstown soon," Lord Robin said. "After you ..."

He broke off, peering into the distance. One of the pickets was galloping towards them, hollering for attention. Isabella felt her blood run cold. The only reason for one of the pickets to return now, ahead of time, was enemy contact. She looked at Lord Robin, who looked back. His face was grim.

"Well," he said. "Shall we win a kingdom for the prince?"

***

There wasn't *much* to Alcidine, beyond a large stone bridge that had somehow survived decades of rainfall, flooding and round after round of civil unrest. A handful of stone houses, several more wooden hovels that looked as if a single gust of wind would be enough to flatten them ... and a lone temple, empty and abandoned. The town's only real value lay as a crossing point, the only place where troops could cross the river without having to ford the waters or swim. It was no surprise to Havant that the population had vanished long before the army had arrived. The inhabitants had already heard of the invasion.

And they know they're on the route to Allenstown, Havant thought, as he studied the map on the table. His brother had taken one of the abandoned houses and turned it into a headquarters. *They've already seen too many battles ...*

"We beat them, barely," King Rufus said. His finger traced lines of the map as scout after scout reported to their king. "The invaders are already on the march, but we reached Alcidine first."

Havant nodded. They'd been lucky, for a certain value of *luck*. Holding Alcidine would keep the enemy from crossing the river and attacking Allenstown on both sides, but it also limited Reginald's options down to one. The invaders had no choice. They *had* to attack the defences, such as they were.

And Alcidine had almost *no* defences.

"They'll be on us as soon as the downpour stops," Rufus added. "We dare not assume they'll wait for morning."

"They may even risk fighting at night," Havant agreed. Very few professional soldiers would risk fighting after dark, but Prince Reginald *had* to force the issue as quickly as possible. He couldn't afford to give King Rufus time to dig in. Nor, for that matter, could he take the risk of Lord Francis sending reinforcements from Allenstown. "We must expect a savage assault."

He peered through the window. The skies were lightening, slightly. It wouldn't be long before the rain stopped. And then ...

King Rufus nodded. "This is what I want you to do," he said, addressing his officers. "First, I want ..."

Havant listened as his brother issued orders. Rufus was clearly relishing the challenge, even though he knew it was risky. A pitched battle was *always* risky, particularly as they didn't have any idea how many men were advancing on Alcidine. The intelligence reports ranged from a few hundred men, which was absurdly tiny, to estimates in the high millions. Havant had even seen one report which confidently stated that the entire male population of Andalusia had invaded the Summer Isle. He hoped it was just a miscommunication, somewhere along the communications line. If someone really was stupid enough to think that ten million men were marching on Allenstown ...

He shook his head in wry amusement. *Even if Prince Reginald could raise, command and support an army of ten million, he'd never be able to get it over the channel.*

"You have your orders," King Rufus said, once he'd finished. Outside, the rainfall was slowly coming to an end. "Let's move."

Havant nodded and headed for the door. He'd command the reserve, ready to take advantage of a gap in the enemy lines – or, more likely, to plug a gap in the king's defences. It wasn't a particularly glamorous post, but it was vital. *And* it had to go to someone the king trusted completely.

Hark met him outside. He wore his cowl, but the red cloth looked dry, despite the droplets still falling from the sky.

He'd claimed that his god protected him from the rain, the last time Havant had asked. It was hard not to envy the monk. Havant's own clothes were drenched and there was no time to change. He hadn't even had time to warm himself by a fire.

"The enemy approaches," Hark said. "But we are with you."

"Good," Havant said, sarcastically. The monks had strange powers, but the coming battle would be decided by the sword. "Stay back. You don't want to be harmed."

"Our Lord protects us," Hark said. "And he will protect you too, if you open your heart and soul to him."

Havant frowned. "We will discuss it later," he said. He'd expected Hark to try to convert him at some point – it would be a coup for the monks – but he didn't have time. "Right now, we have a battle to win."

Chapter Eighteen

"That's most of their army, Your Highness," Gars said. He tapped the enemy position on the map. "They must have force-marched all the way from the Narrows."

Reginald nodded, crossly, as he paced the tent. The usurper had stolen a march on him – he admitted that to himself, even though it was something he could never share with anyone else – and he didn't quite understand how it had happened. There was no way the usurper could have heard of the invasion in time to reverse course and force-march to Alcidine, not if he'd been guarding the Narrows. Perhaps, just perhaps, he'd already been on his way back to Allenstown ...

He shook his head. In hindsight, he should have set out for Allenstown himself earlier, instead of taking a couple of days to regroup, but there was nothing to be gained by pointless woolgathering. No magic could change the past. He'd just have to cope with the consequences of his own mistake. And besides, it wasn't entirely a disaster. He'd known he would have to smash the enemy army sooner rather than later.

"We attack," he said, turning to the table. There really was no other alternative. And there weren't many options for tactical cunning, either. "Gars, deploy the first ranks of the army for a frontal assault. We want to hit them before they have a chance to build formidable defences."

Or night falls, he added, silently. He'd considered withdrawing long enough to ensure a good night's rest for most of his men, then attacking in the morning, but that would give the enemy time to get organised. They'd send raiders to hit his camp in the darkness, he knew. It was what he would have done. *We have to win this battle quickly.*

"Stuart, deploy the archers to provide cover," he added. "And then ready the cavalry to go on the offensive and tear their lines open."

He studied the map for a long moment. They'd been in a race, it seemed ... thankfully, the enemy hadn't had time to move their supplies across the Racal or it would have made matters a little more tricky. The enemy would be doing that now, at a guess, unless they'd somehow managed to summon troops from the south. He had to move fast.

"Detach raiders to hit the rear of the enemy positions," he added. "And then ..."

His fingers traced out a line on the map. "I want a regiment to ford the river here, then strike at the southern side of the bridge. They cannot be allowed to retreat south."

He looked at Caen. "You'll take command of that operation."

Caen bowed. "Your Highness."

"Very good," Reginald said.

He dismissed the council and took a moment to centre himself. The prospect of battle was thrilling, despite the risks. He was experienced enough to minimise them as much as possible. Hopefully, the enemy position would come apart when they realised their line of retreat had been cut. The usurper would have a hard core of loyalist troops, but the remainder would probably start thinking about their futures in a post-usurper world. And if it didn't, they'd still be trapped in Alcidine and running out of supplies. He was pretty sure they couldn't have brought most of their baggage train with them.

It might be worth trying to hunt it down, he thought. A baggage train large enough to support an entire army would be easy to find, if he dispatched cavalrymen on a search and destroy mission. But that would have to wait. Right now, he had bigger problems. *We have a usurper to kill. And a kingdom to win.*

He allowed himself a smile as he buckled on his sword, then headed for the flap. One way or another, it would all be over soon.

***

"Are you ready?"

Isabella nodded to Lord Robin as she peered into the lightening gloom. She'd gathered as much of her magic as she could, but Prince Reginald hadn't given her a definite target. There wasn't really a target to see, in any case. Alcidine – and the usurper's army – was somewhere in the mist, but it was completely hidden. She couldn't help wondering, as she reached out with her senses, if the mist was *natural*. It did odd things to her mind.

"Yeah," she said, when it became clear that he was waiting for a spoken answer. "I'm ready."

She looked down towards the massing troops. Prince Reginald was there, moving from squad to squad and speaking a few words of encouragement to each. It was one of the touches, Isabella had been told, that marked a good leader from a bad one, although it wasn't one she'd ever taken seriously. Prince Reginald wouldn't be joining the charge against the enemy positions, nor would he be in real danger if he was captured. The worst that would happen to him was being forced to surrender his claim to the Summer Isle, then being ransomed back to his father.

Unless he gets unlucky, she thought. In his armour, Prince Reginald could easily pass for just another officer. He might be struck down in passing, his death unnoticed until after the fighting was over. *And who knows what will happen then?*

It was a morbid thought, so she concentrated on it for a long moment. The army might come apart at the seams, if only because Prince Reginald had no clear successor. Some of the mercenaries might go to the usurper, others might cut loose and head home ... she had a vision of them trying to find a ship back to the mainland, only to discover they were trapped on the Summer Isle. It wasn't a pleasant prospect. Commoners disliked soldiers, but they *really* detested mercenaries. They might find themselves torn to shreds and fed to the pigs if they seemed vulnerable.

The remainder of the mists parted suddenly, revealing a small town by the riverside. Isabella leaned forward, eagerly. Alcidine was smaller than the maps had made it seem, barely a handful of buildings surrounding the northern end of the bridge. The enemy army was clearly visible, digging trenches and readying itself for war. It looked far bigger than the town it was defending.

Prince Reginald walked up. Isabella hastily cast a

protective ward. The enemy archers might *just* recognise the prince – or someone who seemed to be in command – and take a shot at him. She wouldn't care to bet that they'd miss, either. Archers could be terrifyingly effective if they had a clear shot at a target. A bolt through the head would be lethal. And even a minor wound could turn nasty, killing the victim in screaming agony. She'd seen men die like that, begging for their mothers as their lives slipped away. It hadn't been a pleasant sight.

"They're preparing to hold the town," Prince Reginald said. "But we're not going to give them time."

He raised his arm, then brought it down hard. The trumpets blared. Isabella heard the sound of archers lifting their crossbows, then launching arrows into the air. They might not *hit* anything, but a rain of arrows would force the enemy to take cover. In the meantime, who knew what could happen?

They might charge us, she thought. *But they'd be better keeping their strength in reserve.*

***

"They're firing arrows, Your Highness," the scout said.

King Rufus allowed himself a tight nod. It was a common tactic. And an entirely workable one. His men would be forced to duck, while the enemy troops advanced. It was a shame, really, they hadn't had more time to prepare the battlefield. A few thousand caltrops would have made life *much* more interesting for the enemy soldiers. It helped that the enemy had no choice but to attack.

"Order our archers to return fire," he ordered. The enemy troops would *have* to come out into the open, if they wanted to attack. And they'd be badly hurt by the arrows. "Tell the outer lines to prepare to repel attack."

***

Big Richard hefted his axe, grunting in approval as he tested its weight. They'd been offered swords and suits of armour, but he'd declined both. An axe was a good weapon, in the right hands. It always terrified the poor bastards who had to face it. And he'd never trusted armour. An arrow – or a spell – could punch through even the strongest armour. He'd seen knights blasted off their horses by crossbow bolts.

He glanced up towards Lord Robin, feeling a wave of sheer hatred for the woman standing next to him. She was a sorceress and sorceresses couldn't be trusted ... he'd never liked magic-users, but the hatred he felt for her was all-consuming. She'd killed his brother, she'd lured him into a trap ... she'd intended to do worse to Richard, but he hadn't given her the chance. And yet, it was only a matter of time. His feelings were so strong that, sometimes, they just didn't seem real.

Lord Robin will not forgive me if I kill her, he thought. He respected Lord Robin. The man was a strong leader, one who was firm and fair. *And yet ...*

Lord Robin is enchanted, something whispered at the back of his mind. *He cannot think for himself ...*

The whistle blew, again. Big Richard jumped up with the others, howling as they ran towards the enemy positions. Arrows hissed over their heads, flying backwards and forwards in search of a target. A man next to him was hit in the throat and tumbled forward, but Richard barely noticed. The bloodlust was rising in him, the urge to lash out with his axe and kill, kill, kill ...

He howled louder as the enemy lines rose up in front of him. They were skimpy, even compared to Racal's Bay. The enemy bastards simply hadn't had *time* to fortify the tiny town. Richard laughed at the thought, then swung his axe and cut an enemy soldier in two. Blood splashed around his feet as a second man jabbed at him with a sword, followed by a third. Conscripts, part of his mind guessed. They hadn't been trained in how to use their weapons properly. Allowing him into axe-range had been a dreadful mistake.

"Die," he shouted, as he struck out with his axe. "Die!"

The second man crumpled as he jabbed the pointed end of the axe into his eye, the third man ducking backwards in horror. Richard thrust onwards, slicing off the man's sword arm. He lifted his other hand in surrender, but Richard ignored it and beheaded him. There was no point in trying to take prisoners who obviously wouldn't fetch a good ransom. Besides, the man – a boy, really – had been a fool. What sort of idiot brought a sword to an axe-fight?

He grinned, savagely, then hurried forward and rejoined the others. The enemy had put their expendable troops on the outer edge of the defences, of course. Now, their inner lines were already mounting a counterattack. He prepared himself to meet it, blood dripping from his axe as more arrows hissed overhead. The enemy *might* push them back out of the trenches, but they'd pay a high price ...

We'll earn our pay tonight, he thought. *And then it will be time to settle accounts with the sorceress.*

***

An arrow struck an invisible barrier and shattered, the pieces falling to the ground. Reginald shot Isabella an appreciative look, then turned his attention back to the battle. The enemy lines were wavering, but the enemy were already feeding their reserves into the trenches. In a couple of places, they were even firing arrows into their own trenches. It was the only thing they could do to keep them from getting overrun.

He waved to a messenger. "Inform Gars that he is to concentrate his efforts on the eastern trenches," he said. They *had* to get through the lines before night fell. "They look to be the weakest."

The messenger nodded and hurried off. Reginald swept his telescope across the battlefield, trying to gauge the usurper's thinking. He'd be in there somewhere, planning his counterattack. Unless he'd already fled ... Reginald considered it hopefully, then decided it was unlikely. Deserting a battlefield before the battle was clearly lost would destroy his chances of holding on to the crown. Even if he tried, retreat would be difficult.

He sucked in his breath as the noise grew louder. Gars was feeding more and more men into the eastern trenches, as per orders. The enemy line was buckling, yet ... he frowned, considering the possibilities. Would the usurper withdraw forces from the other trenches to repel the attack? Or would he try to pull back into the town? Even getting a number of troops across the river would make life harder for Reginald. It was one of the reasons he'd launched the attack almost at once.

Another messenger ran up to him. "Sir ... the river has been successfully forded!"

"Very good," Reginald said.

He leaned forward eagerly, resisting the urge to scan the southern riverbank for Caen and his troops. Caen hadn't been able to cross *too* close to Alcidine or the enemy would have seen him, but ... but how long would it take to get his forces into position to hit the rear end of the bridge? And how would the enemy react? *Reginald* would have made sure to get a picket force onto the south side, even if he'd kept the majority of his force on the north. How long would it be until the usurper realised that his line of retreat wasn't secure any longer?

It will take as long as it takes, he reminded himself, firmly. Some things had to be left to chance, no matter what he did. *Caen knows what he's doing. And all I can do is wait.*

***

Rufus allowed himself a moment of cold pleasure as the eastern lines solidified again, despite the number of men hurling themselves against his defences. Using his weaker – and somewhat untrustworthy – troops on the outer edge of the defences had paid off in more ways than one. They'd slowed the enemy down, which was more than he'd expected, but their deaths had also weakened some of his nobility. They wouldn't be able to cause so much trouble in the long run. And none of them had been able to refuse his command to serve.

The assholes themselves may be dead, he felt, with a flicker of cold satisfaction. He'd taken pains to put the treacherous noblemen he disliked most in the front lines – or as close to them as possible. *And even if they're not, they will have no way to oppose me.*

He smiled, even as he barked orders to funnel more men into the trenches. The family had believed since time out of mind that *they* could turn the Summer Isle into a major kingdom in its own right. It had everything it needed to be great, save for a powerful and unquestioned ruler. King Edwin had been weak, the nobility torn apart by fratricidal conflicts ... Rufus's father, just like the rest of them, had seen his children as nothing more than pawns in the endless game of thrones. But his children had had different ideas. Together, they were far greater than the sum of their parts.

The enemy attack was losing steam, he thought. There were limits to what men could do, even fighting for a cause. The constant slaughter – the constant rebuffs – were crippling their morale, making it harder for them to fight. And all he really had to do was hold out until dark.

And then we can launch an attack at night, he told himself. The enemy didn't know the lands, but Rufus's men did. *And then we will win.*

***

Fife held himself still, aiming the bow with extreme care. There was a man standing by one of the stone houses, briefly appearing to survey the battlefield before snapping his head out of sight again. An enemy commander, perhaps. Messengers did seem to be going to him and then heading out again. Fife had left them alone. He wanted a bigger target.

The man appeared again, warily. Two messengers were approaching, shouting and waving urgently. Fife had no idea what they were talking about, but it didn't matter. It was an opportunity. He sighted, then fired. The arrow snapped into the air ...

***

"Sire!"

Rufus gritted his teeth. He knew it was bad news. "What?"

"An enemy force has attacked the southern side of the bridge," the messenger said. He looked as if he expected to be executed on the spot. "They've punched through the pickets and taken the far end."

"Shit," Rufus swore.

He forced himself to think as the messenger abased himself. It wasn't a complete disaster. If the enemy had a large army on the southern side, it would get torn to ribbons when it tried to cross; if they didn't, all they could do was block his troops from crossing the river. It wasn't a complete disaster, but it was a major headache. And if the troops thought their line of retreat had been cut, they might panic. His defence line might come apart at the seams.

"Get up," he snapped at the cowering messenger. He had no qualms about executing men for failure – and then selling their widows and lands to the highest bidder – but killing messengers was stupid. Even his father, a brutal and cruel man in many ways, hadn't killed men for bringing him bad news. "Tell the reserves to ..."

He stopped, some instinct making him look around. Time itself seemed to be slowing to a crawl, as if the world itself was fading away ...

... And then the arrow struck his forehead.

King Rufus crumpled to the ground and died.

Chapter Nineteen

"The King is dead!"

Havant swallowed, hard, as word echoed through the rear. The king was dead ... the king couldn't be dead! His brother could *not* be dead. But panic was already spreading through the lines. It wouldn't be long before some of the more treacherous noblemen decided to switch sides. They wouldn't even be betraying the kingdom! Their oaths to King Rufus had died with him.

A messenger ran up to him. "Sir, the enemy is resuming the attack!"

"Obviously," Havant snapped.

He gritted his teeth. Prince Reginald might not *know* what had happened, but the sudden chaos was unmistakable. It was a perfect opportunity to anyone who wanted to win the battle before someone else assumed control. And, with his forces on the far side of the river ready to cross, it was all too likely that he'd win before Havant could take command. Hell, far too many noblemen would refuse to recognise Havant until he was crowned in Allenstown ...

"Order the reserves to retreat and head north," he ordered, grimly. "The remainder of the army is to hold as long as possible, then head north themselves. We will rendezvous at" – he took a moment to think – "Montrose."

"An inspired choice," Hark said, calmly.

Havant bit down a number of icy remarks. The battle was lost. Worse, the *kingdom* might well be lost too. The core army could be reformed, given time, but many of Rufus's former vassals might switch sides now that he was dead. Even if they didn't, they might not stay with Havant for long. They'd want to extract as many concessions as possible while their nominal king was in no position to argue.

And Prince Reginald now has an open road to Allenstown, he thought. Getting the army reformed in time to save

Allenstown might be impossible. *The city may not be able to hold out for long.*

He summoned a handful of messengers and issued orders, then called for his horse. There was nothing to be gained from pretending that the battle wasn't over. All he could do was preserve as much as possible, either to continue the war or sell out for the best terms he could get. And yet, after everything the family had done, he knew it was unlikely that Prince Reginald would let them keep their power. Their wings would very definitely be clipped. It was certainly unlikely that Reginald would agree to marry Emetine!

Shaking his head, he climbed onto the horse and joined the retreat. Behind him, he heard the sound of fighting growing louder. The enemy had *definitely* scented weakness, then. It wouldn't be long before they mopped up the remaining troops, secured the town and opened the way to Allenstown. And then ... he sighed. It was in the hands of the gods now.

Hark walked beside him, keeping easy pace with the horse. Havant wondered, sourly, why the Red Monks hadn't done more during the battle. They'd done enough to convince him that they *could* work miracles, yet ... he shook his head. He would have to have a *proper* chat with Hark, once they reached Montrose. Now, all they could do was retreat.

And hope they don't harass us as we run, he thought. *They could finish us off if they press the offensive.*

***

Reginald had seen his first battlefield – the remnants of a brief clash with peasant rebels – when he'd been ten. He'd seen many more battlefields since, from a clash between two armies to a castle being stormed, but there was something about *this* battlefield that wore at him. Hundreds of bodies, most hacked to pieces, lay in piles on the ground, all concentrated over the trenches. The buildings beyond were blackened ruins, torn apart by his men when they stormed the town. It looked as though the tiny town – Alcidine was really nothing more than a village – would never rise again.

"That's the usurper," Caen said. He pointed to a single body, an arrow sticking out of its forehead. "The prisoners were quick to point him out to us."

Reginald nodded, slowly. The usurper wore plain armour – a sign of an experienced soldier – but it was clear that he was nobility. Nobles were normally taller and fitter than the average commoner, if only because they ate better. His face was clean, unscarred by pox; his hands bore the telltale signs of a sword, rather than a plough. It was hard to be sure, but Reginald would have guessed the body was in its late thirties. Rufus Hereford had been thirty-seven.

And now he's dead, he thought, wryly. It was a shame he didn't know which archer to promote. There was no hope of collecting a ransom for a dead body, unless the usurper's relatives wanted to pay to give his ashes a proper burial, but there hadn't been much hope of a ransom either. Reginald could not have left the man alive. *The kingdom is mine.*

He looked up at Caen. "How many prisoners did we take?"

"Seventeen noblemen of various ranks, all Hereford clients," Caen informed him. "And around five hundred soldiers. Some of the latter have asked to switch sides."

"I'm sure they have," Reginald grunted. He had no particular objection to absorbing defeated enemy troops into his army – most of them were little better than mercenaries, loyal only to their paymaster – but it was well to be careful. "The common soldiers can be held for a week, then released. They won't be a problem without leaders. The sergeants and suchlike are to be held indefinitely, unless they're willing to join us."

"Yes, Your Highness," Caen said. "I should add that the noblemen are all extremely eager to kiss your arse."

"They must be desperate," Reginald said. He smiled, despite himself. If the usurper was dead, his clients would need a new patron. "Have them taken to the camp, held in separate tents, and interrogated. I want to know what, if anything, they can do for us."

And they were taken in war, he thought, grimly. *We can confiscate their lands and they know it. They'll do everything in their power to seem useful.*

Stuart hurried up, his bodyguards trailing behind. "Your Highness," he said. "The enemy is still retreating northwards. Their rearguard" – his lips twisted, unpleasantly – "was alarmingly effective."

Reginald nodded, feeling a flicker of sour admiration for whoever had taken command of the enemy force. Retreating from a battle was difficult enough at the best of times, all the more so when subordinate commanders were suddenly dangerously untrustworthy. Reginald had no doubt that some of the surviving noblemen would make contact with him soon enough, offering troops and money in exchange for a place in the new kingdom. Whoever was in command of what remained of the enemy force was in a very tight spot.

A shame we didn't manage to cut off their retreat completely, he thought. By the time he'd realised what was happening, it was already too late. *And we don't have time to chase them now.*

"Bring up the remainder of our supplies, then throw out a line of pickets," he ordered, instead. "We'll make camp here, then resume our advance in the morning. I want to get to Allenstown before the enemy has a chance to regroup."

"Your Highness," Stuart said.

He smiled, suddenly. "Do you think this was the decisive battle?"

Reginald shrugged. The Summer Isle's laws insisted that the prospective king had to be acclaimed by the Gathering – an assembly of noblemen – before being crowned as king, but anyone with any real understanding of power knew that *force* was all that mattered. He'd smashed a chunk of the enemy army, then captured or scattered all that was left of it. It was unlikely anyone would dare to block him openly, no matter what happened.

And if we're lucky, the chaos caused by the death of the false king will make it impossible for them to stop us just walking into Allenstown, he thought. *And then we will be too strong to ignore.*

"We will see," he said. "But if they don't manage to rebuild their forces, we win."

***

"Hail, Your Majesty," Hark said, as Havant entered the house. "Hail, King Havant!"

Havant scowled. It had taken all the charm he possessed to convince most of his commanders to hail him as king, even though he'd been his brother's heir. And *those* commanders were supposed to be loyalists, their families clients of long standing. It would be harder to keep some of the more *distant* clients – and fair-weather friends – from slipping away once they heard the news. The army had taken one hell of a beating. Worse, it *knew* it had taken one hell of a beating.

He stomped over to the table and poured himself a glass of wine. The merchant who owned the house – and had surrendered it to the king at swordpoint – hadn't been a particularly rich man, but he'd known his wines. Perhaps he'd spent more time than he should aping his betters, Havant considered. There had certainly been more than a little defiance in his tone before the guards had taken him and his family away. He clearly hadn't realised that Havant was in no mood for anything but absolute submission.

"My brother is dead," he said, taking a sip of the wine. "Why did that happen?"

"Your brother refused to open his heart to Our Lord," Hark said. "And so he was outside Our Lord's protection."

Havant swung around, one hand dropping to the sword at his belt. "Are you saying you could have *saved* him?"

"Our *Lord* could have saved him," Hark said. His hood hid his features in darkness. "But he chose not to open his heart."

"And if he had, he would have lived?" Havant leaned forward, wondering – suddenly – just what he would see if he looked into the darkness. Hark was the only monk who didn't keep his face completely covered at all times. "Or would you make excuses for your failure, like all the other priests ..."

Hark lifted one white finger. "Our Lord does not fail," he said. "Or did he not kill your brother-in-law for you?"

"You needed a sample of his blood to kill him," Havant snapped.

"There is always a price," Hark said. "And sometimes that price is measured in the willingness to do whatever it takes to gain Our Lord's favour."

He leaned forward. The shadows seemed to darken.

"Open your heart to Our Lord," he urged. "And Our Lord

will help you."

Havant couldn't tear his eyes away from the darkness. And yet, he knew – on some instinctive level – that he didn't want to know *what* hid under the darkness. He'd been told, from birth, that priests were better kept at arm's length. They were useful to keep the peasants quiet and obedient – and fire the soldiers when they went to war – but they could not be allowed real power. Indeed, Rufus had insisted that *Havant* talk to the Red Monks because the head of the family could not be seen making an alliance with a single religion.

And yet, he *knew* the Red Monks had power. And yet ...

He wanted to close his eyes and think, but his eyelids seemed frozen open. He couldn't even blink. There were *things* moving in the darkness, *things* so strange that they didn't seem to be quite real. And yet, they were realer than real. Part of him wanted to turn and flee, to run north to the family lands and prepare for a fight; the rest of him knew there was power here, power just waiting for him ... if he paid the price.

They wanted to be recognised as a sanctioned religion, when they approached us, he thought, numbly. *What will they want now?*

But what choice did he have? Prince Reginald wouldn't let him live. It was unlikely he'd let *Emetine* live. Rufus was already dead ... and *none* of them had had children. Havant's closest relative, apart from his sister, was a third cousin. His father had made sure of that, eliminating everyone who might pose a threat to *his* children. The Hereford line would end with him.

He took a long breath. "What do you want me to do?"

Hark made no sound, but he must have sent *some* kind of message. The door opened, revealing two Red Monks – their faces hidden behind their cowls – and a struggling girl, held between them. Someone had torn off her clothes, then drawn eerie tattoos on her skin with blood. The girl looked at him, then started to scream. One of the monks slapped her on the head, then dropped her on the floor. The girl kept struggling until the monk leaned down, as if he was going to kiss her. And then the girl froze in terror.

Havant frowned. *What* had happened?

"Here," Hark said. He passed Havant a knife. "You will have to kill her, then open your heart to Our Lord."

Havant hesitated, despite himself. Sacrificing animals was frowned upon ... and sacrificing humans was completely beyond the pale. The intensity of the feeling surprised him. The girl was a commoner, his to use as he pleased ... and yet, he didn't *want* to sacrifice her. It was all he could do to hold the knife.

"Kill her," Hark said. "Or be nothing."

The girl stared up at him, trembling in fear. He knew, all too well, what she'd assumed was going to happen to her when she was dragged into the house. Her father was probably already dead, her mother given to the troops ... she'd assumed, no doubt, that she was being spared for Havant's personal pleasure. But being sacrificed was far worse. She couldn't move, but her eyes were terrified ...

What is she to you? A voice asked. He wasn't sure if it was something inside his mind or something else. *Kill her and claim the kingdom.*

Bitter resentment flourished inside him. His brother was dead. The family was doomed, unless he did something. And what did one commoner girl matter? She would be lucky to survive the next decade; even if he let her go, even if she survived the war. There were too many things that could take a young girl's life. This way, at least, her death would serve a greater purpose.

He stabbed down, hard. The knife sliced into the girl and ...

... Power flared around him, a surge of power so far beyond him that it swept him up and out of his body. Thoughts – great and terrible thoughts, each one utterly beyond his comprehension – echoed in the power, flashes of images that made no sense to him at all. He thought he saw Rufus, just for a second, followed by someone who could easily have been a younger Emetine. Hark was there, greater and more terrible than Havant had ever known, and then he was gone too. His father's voice rumbled in his head ...

"Open your heart," a voice said. He looked for the speaker, but saw nothing. "Open your heart and let me in."

Havant could feel the presence now, something so vast that it terrified and comforted him in equal measure. So much was clear now, so much that had once been hidden ... he was floating above the world, staring down at a multitude of ... options. And the presence wanted *in*. It was waiting, outside his mind, for Havant to open the door.

He reached for the presence and the presence *came*. Power flowed into him, following a presence so vast that ... that he could no longer control himself. He was dimly aware, as his awareness started to fade, that something was speaking through him, that something was moving his body, but it seemed unimportant. All that mattered was surrendering to the darkness ...

His eyes snapped open. He was lying in a bed, a strange bed. He reached for his sword, instinctively, but he couldn't find it. Had he been drunk? He swung his legs over the side of the bed and stood. He didn't *feel* as though he'd been drunk. And yet ... he looked out the window and blinked in surprise. It had been late evening when he'd ...

The memories snapped back. There had been a girl, hadn't there? He'd killed a girl. It was hardly the first time he'd killed, but ... some of the memories had faded, as if they'd been blotted out or overwritten by something else. Outside, he could hear the sound of chanting. Someone was saying a prayer. Whatever language it was, and he knew priests preferred to use tongues of their own, he didn't recognise it. More and more voices were joining in, echoing together in ways that ... that should have chilled him. But the sound felt almost welcoming.

He glanced up, sharply, as the door opened. A young manservant stepped into the room, looking nervous. Havant recognised him as one of Rufus's pages ... one of *his* pages now, he supposed. Rufus was dead ... oddly, the thought hurt less than he'd expected. Rufus had gone to a better place. And yet, the page was staring at Havant as if he'd never *seen* him before.

"Your Majesty," the page said, holding out a mug. His eyes were twitching oddly, as if he couldn't quite *look* at Havant. "The messengers from Allenstown have returned."

Havant blinked. "The messengers from Allenstown?"

"Yes, Your Majesty," the page said, carefully. He sounded terrified. Havant didn't really blame him. "You sent them out last night."

"Ah," Havant said, as he took the mug. He didn't remember sending any messengers, although he knew it was something he'd needed to do. Apparently, he had. "What ... what *else* did I do last night?"

Hark walked into the room. "Our Lord spoke through you," he said, as the page leaned away from him. "Our ultimate victory is assured."

Chapter Twenty

"Is there anything to this country," Big Richard demanded, "apart from wind, rain, mist, mud, and abandoned farms?"

Isabella concealed her amusement as the mist grew thicker. As much as she detested Big Richard, she had to admit that he had a point. The army had resumed the march the day after the battle, but the mists had slowed their advance. It was growing harder and harder to see what was in front of them. The remainder of the enemy army might be lurking in the mists and there was no way to tell.

"I'm sure there's *something* more to the country," Lord Robin said, easily. They'd taken point, riding at the head of the army. "We *did* pass a couple of decent-looking farms."

Isabella shrugged. She hadn't seen anything to suggest that the Summer Isle was particularly wealthy. Racal's Bay had been small, for a city that served as the gateway to the mainland; the towns and villages they'd passed, on the march, had all been depressingly poor. Lord Robin could talk of potential, if he wished, but Isabella suspected it would take years to turn the island into a jewel in Prince Reginald's crown. The handful of peasants they'd seen – the ones too old or too weak to run and hide from the army – had all looked too beaten down to take advantage of the conquest.

Not that things will change much, for the people at the bottom, she thought, as her horse shivered in dismay. *Their lives will be the same no matter who's on top.*

She reached out with her senses as the mists, improbably, grew thicker. It was easy to believe that they were lost, even though they were following the road. There were supposed to be pickets and flankers out there, watching for signs of enemy activity, but she was starting to think that they wouldn't have any warning until they literally stumbled into the enemy position. If, of course, the enemy army had regrouped. The only upside of the mists, as far as she could tell, was that the enemy would be equally disadvantaged.

Lord Robin glanced at her. "Can you sense anything out there?"

Isabella shook her head. Her spells *appeared* to be working properly, but she knew she couldn't take them for granted. She no longer disbelieved the stories about strange magics on the Summer Isle. The Red Monks had certainly shown powers she didn't recognise, let alone understand. And besides, they wouldn't need something new to block her senses. There was no shortage of concealment spells that would allow someone to hide from her.

If they have magic, she thought. *There's no proof that the usurper had a trained magician working for him.*

She shook her head, again. The usurper hadn't *needed* a trained magician. He had the Red Monks. And yet ... she shivered, remembering the power she'd sensed in the temple. The Red Monks were messing with ... *something*. They had to be stopped. What were they? And what were they doing?

A shiver ran down her spine as the wind blew colder. The mists were rolling towards them, twisting and turning like living things. Water droplets brushed against her, soaking her leathers. She shifted, uncomfortably, as water dripped down her front. *Anything* could be hidden in the gloom. The thought nagged at her mind as she quietly cast spell after spell, probing the darkness. But the spells revealed nothing ...

"We may have to stop," Lord Robin said. He glanced behind them. "At this rate, we're going to find the city by crashing into the walls."

Isabella followed his gaze. The entire army was supposed to be behind them, but ... there was no sign of the lead elements in the gloom. She couldn't even *hear* the men marching westwards, not any longer. The sergeants had started a cadence, but even the most enthusiastic soldiers had dropped the chant as the mists grew stronger. It was easy to believe that they were all alone in the fog.

"At least we'd find the city," Big Richard said.

Isabella looked at Lord Robin. He wasn't there.

She stared in astonishment. He'd been there, a moment ago. Hadn't he? It was suddenly very hard to swear to anything. She was sure he'd been there. And yet ... she looked at Big Richard, riding in front of her. He didn't seem to have noticed anything amiss ...

"Richard," she said. "Can you ..."

The mists rolled forward. Big Richard vanished in the gloom.

Isabella felt a twinge of panic as she reached out, desperately, with her senses. She was the only formally-trained magician in the army, but she should have been able to sense the hedge-witches ... surely. But there was nothing. She was all alone. The horse started, neighing loudly. And yet, the sound seemed to fade to nothingness within the mists.

She bit her lip, hard enough to draw blood. Cold logic told her that her comrades were nearby, but somehow it wasn't reassuring. Perhaps it *shouldn't* be reassuring. There were spells that could meddle with someone's perceptions, after all. If the Red Monks could mess with her memories – to the point where she'd had problems remembering what had happened inside the temple – why couldn't they fiddle with her perceptions too ...

"Isabella!"

Her father was standing in front of her. She stared at him. They were ... *somewhere*. The horse was gone, yet ... she bit her lip, again. This was an illusion. A spell of some kind. And yet, it felt real.

"You're a disgrace," her father said. "What were you thinking?"

Isabella looked down at herself. She was wearing her training outfit – grey trousers, grey shirt, grey gloves – but the rank insignia were missing, the bare patches all too visible to prying eyes. They'd been torn away after she'd been kicked out of the Watchtower, after she'd been caught in bed with another trainee. She'd been lucky not to be stripped completely and forced to walk out naked.

"What were you thinking?" Her father leaned forward. "Tell me, *what* were you thinking?"

This is an illusion, Isabella thought. And yet, it felt terrifyingly real. Time itself seemed to have rolled back, right to the moment her father had disowned her. She could *smell* the cigar smoke on his breath as he glared at her. They were the same height, yet he'd always made her feel small. *This is not real.*

Her father's face seemed to flicker, just for a second. She thought she saw something *else* there, a hint of something *else* buried below the facade. Gritting her teeth, she concentrated on reminding herself that the illusion wasn't real. She couldn't sense any magic interfering with her perceptions, but that was utterly meaningless. Her perceptions could no longer be trusted. She was a prisoner inside her own mind.

"I can no longer tolerate your reckless behaviour," her father said. His words crashed into her head with a sudden, terrible finality. "You put your petty pleasures ahead of the good of the family."

Shame washed over her, shame ... she hadn't been so ashamed last time, had she? She'd allowed herself to be caught deliberately, rather than finding a place where they could make love without any risk of discovery. She'd *wanted* to be kicked out. Now ... she wanted to sink into despair and die. She was the lowest of the low. And yet ...

"Shameful rutting like an animal in heat," her father snapped. "You're a disgrace!"

Isabella looked up sharply, despite the bleak despondency that was threatening to overwhelm her. He hadn't said *that*, had he? He'd told her off, sharply, yet ... he'd never said that. But he had, in her nightmares. She hadn't slept comfortably for weeks after she'd been ordered to leave the Golden City.

"You are no longer my daughter," her father said. He clicked his fingers. "You will never see this place again."

This is an illusion, Isabella told herself, again. The memories were wrong. And yet, it was so hard to escape. *This is not real ...*

It was growing harder and harder to *believe* it. She'd been on a horse ... hadn't she? She certainly hadn't regressed six years ... she looked down at herself again and frowned. Her body was *tiny*, so small she could easily have passed for a toddler. It wasn't real. It couldn't be real. And the memories didn't match. It was her nightmare, not bitter reality.

She forced herself to close her eyes and concentrated,

feeling for her power. It had always been with her – she couldn't remember the first time her magic had manifested – but now it was gone. No, it couldn't be gone. She worked her way through a spell, choosing to believe that the power was there. It should work ... it had to work ... something cut loose inside her, something powerful. The world turned white ...

***

"Your father killed me."

Reginald shook his head. His mother stood in front of him, wearing the long white robe she'd worn the last time he'd laid eyes on her. Queen Carline had been on the verge of going into confinement, where she would remain until she gave birth. But she'd died giving birth to his youngest sister. In his darker moments, he thought that Silverdale was a poor replacement for his mother.

"You died in childbirth," he said, through dry lips. His mother looked heavily pregnant. "I ..."

"Your father wanted a second son," his mother told him. "He insisted that I carry another child to term, despite everything that happened after Ruby was born. He wanted another son, you see. And yet ... I died after giving birth. You never saw me again, did you?"

"... No," Reginald said. "Mother ..."

He stumbled forward, desperately. King Romulus had mourned ... they'd *all* mourned. Ruby had been too young to comprehend that her mother wouldn't be coming back, but Reginald and Sofia had understood all too well. Queen Carline was gone. There had been hints that their father would remarry, over the years, but none of them had ever resulted in a betrothal, let alone a wedding. King Romulus would go to his grave mourning his long-lost wife.

"Your father knew the dangers," Queen Carline said. Her voice was cold and hard. "And yet, he insisted that I became pregnant again. He even had my ladies take away the herbs I used to ensure I wouldn't conceive. He killed me so he could get a replacement for you."

She laughed. "And he didn't even get another son, did he?"

"You're not real," Reginald said. His mother had been a strong woman. She might not have had any formal authority, but she'd had power and influence. Her husband had trusted her judgement, to the point of leaving her in charge when he had to leave the capital. There was no higher praise that could be offered to a queen. This ... this *spectre* was not her. "You're not real."

Queen Carline leaned forward. "Oh, my son," she said. "What has he *done* to you?"

Reginald glared at her. "What are you?"

"I'm your mother," Queen Carline said. Her voice dripped honey and poison. "Your father killed me. Did you not think that, when you were awake in the darkness? Your father sentenced me to death."

"You died in childbirth," Reginald said. It was hard to escape the feeling that he *was* talking to his mother. And yet, this cruel woman was a stranger. "You were not executed ..."

"I was sentenced to death because your father was desperate for another heir," Queen Carline told him. "What will happen to the kingdom, Reggie, if you die here?"

Reginald felt as though he'd been stabbed through the heart. No one, absolutely no one, called him Reggie. No one ... save his mother. He wanted her to hold him, once again; he wanted her to kiss his forehead and tell him that everything was going to be fine. But ... he looked down at himself and froze. He was a young man ... no, a boy on the verge of becoming a man. He hadn't worn that outfit since he'd been twelve ...

"I was so proud of you, the day you first wore those clothes," his mother said. "It was proof that you'd live into adulthood, despite everything. I watched as you won your spurs, days before I went into confinement. I never came out ..."

Reginald glared. His mother would never have talked to him like that, not even when she was angry. She'd always been kind and gentle and loving and ... it tore at his heart to turn away, but he knew she was not his mother. Whatever she was, she was not his mother. It felt as though he was wading through water as he turned, but he turned. The world seemed to go white ...

***

Isabella crashed back into reality. She was on a horse ... she'd *been* on a horse. She had to grab the reins, a second before she slid out of the saddle and fell to the ground. It wouldn't be the first time she had fallen off a horse, but it would have been humiliating to take a pratfall in front of Big Richard. She looked up, remembering that he was missing ... no, he was in front of her. He seemed to have been completely unaffected by the mists.

She tasted blood in her mouth. She spat it out, then looked from side to side as the mists faded away into nothingness. Lord Robin looked badly shaken, his face pale; Dolman was holding a dagger in one hand, as if he'd been on the verge of plunging it into his chest. No one, save for Big Richard, seemed to have been unaffected. She looked back at the army and saw an incoherent mess. The formation had come apart at the seams. Hundreds of men were on the ground or looking around with haunted eyes, tears dripping down their cheeks. A handful were even weeping helplessly. Normally, a man who showed weakness in public like that would be mocked relentlessly, but now ... now, she suspected no one would say a word. They'd all been tormented by the mists.

And if I saw my father – or a warped version of my father – what did they see? She doubted anyone would answer her, if she asked. *We all saw nightmarish visions of the dead.*

She shook her head, slowly, as Lord Robin began to bark orders, giving the squad something to do. Her father was dead ... it was odd, she supposed, that the thought had never crossed her mind while she'd been trapped in the illusion. She *knew* he was dead ... somehow, that had never occurred to her while she'd seen his ghost. Unless Alden had lied to her ... she dismissed the thought with all the contempt it deserved. Her elder brother had never had the imagination to lie.

"There's something up ahead," Big Richard called. He dug in his spurs, racing ahead of them. "Come on!"

Isabella followed him, even though she was still perplexed by his apparent immunity to the mists ... and whatever power had been woven into the mists. Surely, he would have seen Little Jim ... perhaps one of his amulets had protected him. She made a mental note to inspect them, just to see if one of them was more than it seemed. It was hard to believe, but Big Richard *had* been immune. She couldn't believe that he could hide his feelings when Lord Robin and the others had been shaken so badly.

Big Richard stopped and peered down at a body lying on the ground. Isabella came up beside him and followed his gaze. The body was young, naked, female ... Isabella slipped off the horse and knelt down beside the corpse. Someone had drawn runes on the body in blood, then stabbed the victim in the heart. She was sure she'd seen similar runes in the temple, back at Racal's Bay. They still meant nothing to her.

"Waste of a good body," Big Richard sneered.

Isabella ignored him. The girl looked to have been in her late teens, although it was impossible to be sure. Commoners and peasants aged quickly. Her hands bore the telltale signs of someone who'd grown up on a farm, although the marks weren't as extensive as Isabella would have expected. And it didn't look as if she'd struggled ... Isabella wasn't sure what *that* meant. Human sacrifice was banned, with good reason. It was amongst the darkest of dark arts.

And if the poor girl was a virgin, she thought, *they could have gained more power from the sacrifice.*

"Well?" Big Richard asked, as Lord Robin turned away. "What do you make of it?"

"I think they used her as a power source," Isabella said, slowly. She stood and looked around. The mists were almost completely gone, but there was no one in sight apart from the army. Whoever had sacrificed the girl had retreated as soon as they'd cast the spell. Or done whatever they'd done to enchant the mist. "And I think she might have been a volunteer."

"Silly bitch," Big Richard said. "I could think of other uses for her."

"I'm sure you could," Isabella said, darkly.

Lord Robin jumped down beside her. "What do those runes mean?"

Isabella shook her head, helplessly. She didn't want to confess ignorance, but ... she had no choice. Shouting echoed in the distance. Prince Reginald and his men were reforming the army. It wouldn't be long before the prince started demanding answers too.

"I don't know," she said. She took her notebook out of her bag and started to sketch the runes. She'd send copies to Alden. Her brother could check to see if there were any relevant records in the Golden City. "But I think we'd better find out."

Chapter Twenty-One

Reginald didn't want to admit it, even to his closest friends and comrades, but he'd been starting to have doubts about the whole venture by the time the army entered the Allenstown valley. Racal's Bay had promise, he supposed, but the rest of the countryside had seemed poor and worthless, inhabited by snivelling wretches and infested by strange and dangerous magics. It was a relief to discover, as his advance elements closed in on Allenstown, that the capital city was surrounded by a number of farms that clearly produced most of the region's food. The farmers might have hidden themselves, but he doubted they'd hide for long. He'd make sure to send heralds round to inform them that it was safe to come out, once he'd taken the throne.

Allenstown itself was larger than he'd expected from the description. It was a big city, built of grey stone, surrounding a trio of castles. The river ran through the city, allowing boats to sail down to Racal and the Summer Bay. It would be a tricky city to defend, Reginald noted wryly. Indeed, it was clear that the defences were more impressive than substantial. The walls became bridges – complete with gatehouses – where the river flowed in and out of the city. But then, Allenstown had changed hands several times over the last few years. The defences were designed to stand off a raid, rather than protect the city from an army. He suspected he could take the walls even *without* a siege engine.

Caen rode up and saluted, smartly. "Your Highness, the forward pickets have just encountered a welcoming committee," he said. "They request permission to approach."

"Search them, then invite them forward," Reginald said. He expected the locals to try to negotiate. The usurper was dead and his army scattered. Someone would try to pick up the pieces, sooner or later, but by then Reginald would be firmly in control. "And make sure the army continues to flank the city."

"Yes, Your Highness."

Reginald sat back on his horse and waited, nodding politely to Isabella and Lord Robin as they came up to join him. It was nearly twenty minutes before the welcoming committee arrived, escorted by a number of guardsmen. The committee members looked a little ruffled, but less affronted than he would have expected. None of them looked like professional military men. He guessed they were the city fathers, rather than the remnants of whatever administration the usurper had left in place when he'd ridden out to do battle. The latter wouldn't want to face Reginald unless they had something very important to trade for their lives.

The leader stepped forward. He was a fat man, wearing a plain shirt and trousers that suggested he was of low birth. Reginald wondered, as the man stumbled through a bow, if he was the leader by right or if he'd simply been pushed into being the spokesman. But it didn't really matter.

"Your Highness," the man said. He couldn't keep a quiver out of his voice. "I welcome you to Allenstown ..."

"Here are my terms," Reginald said, cutting the man off. "First, you will open the gates to my men and allow them to occupy all defensive and administrative points within the city. All weapons stockpiles are to be handed over; all men with military or magical experience are to report to my people within the week. Second, you will warn your people to behave themselves as I establish my authority. I will not tolerate defiance or rebellion. Third, and finally, you escort me to the Gathering, where I will be proclaimed king of the Summer Isle."

He paused, just long enough to allow his words to sink in. "The rights and properties of all inhabitants of this city will be respected, as long as they behave themselves. Those who fail to show me the proper respect – or try to impede my operations – will be severely punished. I trust I make myself clear?"

The leader bowed, so deeply that he almost fell over. "Perfectly, Your Highness."

"My troops will occupy the city now," Reginald said. He allowed himself a moment of relief. Fighting his way into the city would have been costly, particularly with some of his men still recovering from the nightmares in the mist. "And then you will escort me to the Gathering."

He forced himself to wait as Gars led the infantry down into the city. There was no resistance, according to the messengers, but many stockpiles of weapons seemed to have been removed. Reginald interrogated the city fathers, yet none of them seemed to know anything about the weapons. The only thing they could say was that Lord Francis – who'd vanished a few hours before the army came into view – had ordered a number of weapons destroyed. They didn't know why.

They could have tried to sneak them out of the city, Reginald thought. *Or even tried to turn them against us later on.*

It was nearly two hours before Gars felt confident enough to proclaim that the city was under control. Reginald glanced at Isabella, then started to ride down towards the main gates. The rest of the party followed, watching carefully for archers hidden on the roofs. It would be the height of irony, Reginald thought, if he were killed by an arrow. The usurper had been hit by an arrow too. He looked around with interest as he rode through the gates, noting that Allenstown was definitely richer than Racal's Bay. But the streets were just as deserted. A handful of men glanced at him as he passed, their blank faces revealing nothing of their feelings. There were no women on the streets at all.

Isabella rode up beside him. "There's no magic at all, as far as I can sense," she muttered, so quietly that no one else could hear. "But there *are* odd sensations near the temples."

"We can investigate later," Reginald said, as they approached the Gathering. "Stay with me."

The Gathering was a smaller building, built of wood rather than stone. Reginald wondered, as he slipped off his horse, if the building was *meant* to be impermanent. His father had never liked calling parliaments and done it as infrequently as possible, even though it was a long-standing way of raising money. The MPs seemed to believe they deserved a say in how the kingdom was run. And as long as they refused to grant money, they *got* that say.

The Summer Isle isn't as rich as Andalusia, Reginald

reminded himself. *And most of the men gathered here are nobles.*

He slipped off his horse and landed neatly on the cobbled pavement, handing the reins to one of his bodyguards. Isabella stayed close to him as the city fathers led him into a large chamber, lined with row upon row of wooden seats. Each of them was marked with a single name; two-thirds of them were empty. He forced himself to recall what he'd learnt about the local aristocracy, then frowned as he realised what the absences meant. The missing noblemen were largely from the north.

Goldenrod must be biding his time, Reginald told himself. Their clients wouldn't show themselves without permission from their master. *And Hereford is in retreat.*

He ignored the babbling from the city father and walked right to the throne at one end of the chamber. It was the only thing in the room that was *not* made of wood. Instead, it was made of cold stone. A genealogical chart hung from the wall behind the throne, showing countless candidates who'd taken the throne and been hailed as king. He was no expert – and the chart was more complex than any he'd seen back home – but it was clear that far too many of the candidates had taken the throne by force. The Gathering acclaimed whoever held them by the balls.

Assuming they have any balls, he thought. *And, with my troops surrounding the building, anyone with balls would be wise to keep them hidden.*

He turned, standing in front of the throne. The Gathering looked back at him, their nervousness hanging in the air like a cloud. They understood *usurpers* – men who took the throne by force – but *he* was something different. He was to be their king, yet he was son of another king across the waters. The balance of power had shifted sharply. They'd need time to grow accustomed to the new reality.

"I am Reginald of Andalusia, son of King Romulus of Andalusia," he said. His voice echoed through the silent chamber. "By rights, my father is the lawful heir to the Summer Isle, a right he has passed down to me. Will you acclaim me as your monarch?"

"YES," the crowd shouted.

Reginald kept his face expressionless. He'd never really doubted that he'd be acclaimed – if nothing else, he had an army to enforce his will – but it was always possible that *something* would put a spanner in the works. Technically, King Edwin's legacy might not be legal; practically, anyone who stood in Reginald's way would be taking his life in his hands. The only law that mattered, in the end, was the law of naked force. It was the strong who ruled – Reginald had learned that during the wars that followed the collapse of the Empire – and the weak who served. And he would always be the strongest ...

"I thank you," he said. He sat on the stone throne. It felt cold and hard, utterly uncomfortable. "Let it be known that, from this moment forth, I am King of the Summer Isle."

He paused. His father would now be able to claim the title of 'King of Kings' as well as his other titles – and it would actually be *meaningful*. But Reginald had no intention of allowing his father *too* much say in how the Summer Isle was run. It was *Reginald's* conquest.

"We will hold a proper coronation as soon as possible," he said, into the silence. The Summer Crown had vanished after the usurper's death. He'd assumed one of his men had robbed the corpse, but an offered reward – and a search – hadn't turned up the missing crown. Perhaps one of the usurper's men had grabbed the crown before running for his life ... it didn't matter. He'd simply have a new crown made before the ceremony. "Even so, I became your ruler as soon as King Edwin died. Those of you who serve me faithfully – who pledge themselves and their families to me – will have nothing to fear. Those of you who choose to take arms against me will be stripped of everything."

He gave them a thin smile. He'd be astonished if most of the Gathering *didn't* hurry to pledge its allegiance. Those who didn't would have their lands confiscated to pay Reginald's mercenaries. They'd bend the knee, at least as long as Reginald was the strongest man on the island. And he'd make sure they were so tightly bound to him that they couldn't escape.

"I see many empty seats," he said, hardening his voice. "Their occupants have two weeks to come and pledge their allegiance. Those who don't will forfeit their ranks and titles, their land and possessions, and will have to work hard to earn them back. Let word be sent to every earldom and holding, every patchwork of entailed land. Those who do not stand beside me will not stand at all."

Silence fell. Reginald took one last look around the room, then rose and walked towards the door. The Gathering looked stunned, as if he'd ordered their immediate execution. They weren't used to such treatment, not from their weakling kings. Even the usurper – damn the man – had had to move gently. The massed resistance of the Gathering would have been enough to bring him to heel. But Reginald had a large and experienced army – and his father a bigger one, on the far side of the channel. He was far more powerful than any of his predecessors and the Gathering knew it.

His bodyguards fell in around him as he walked back into the cold air. "We'll go straight to the castle," he said. Gars and his men would have taken possession already, rounding up the servants and anyone else who'd served the usurper. The staff wouldn't be in any real danger, but they would be interrogated before they were allowed to go back to work. "And then we'll plan our next step."

The city felt different, somehow, as he rode up to the castle. It was *his* city now. He had lands back on the mainland, of course, but they were gifts from his father. He certainly hadn't taken them by force. Allenstown ... was his, captured in war. Whatever happened, he wasn't going to let go of the jewel in his new crown. And everyone who lived in the city was his too.

"There are no wards surrounding the castle," Isabella said, slowly. They cantered over the drawbridge and into a large courtyard. "I can't sense any magical protections at all."

Reginald frowned. *That* was odd. There was no shortage of people willing to use magic to hex their opponents from a safe distance. The court wizard *should* have set up some basic protections before he'd been called to the Golden City, protections that should have remained in place until they were dismantled. Surely, the usurper wouldn't have taken them *down*. That was utter madness, even on an island where there were few – if any – magicians. But he supposed it didn't matter. Isabella could set up some wards before anyone had a chance to use magic against him.

Gars met him at the main entrance. "Your Highness," he said. "Queen Emetine is waiting in the throne room."

Reginald made a face. *Queen* Emetine? Technically, he supposed she still had the right to that title. The usurper had been unmarried. No one, not even Reginald, questioned King Edwin's claim to the throne, nor Emetine's right to call herself his wife. But she was no longer *queen.*

"I will speak with her," he said. "Did you find any trace of Lord Francis?"

"He left, apparently," Gars said. "We don't know where he went."

Reginald shrugged. Lord Francis had had plenty of time to flee north, if he wished. Or hide somewhere in the city ... he'd show himself sooner or later, if that was the case. Or someone would betray him. Reginald would offer a hefty reward, if Lord Francis didn't come forward and bend the knee soon. *Someone* would want a half-share of Lord Francis's former lands.

He allowed Gars to lead him through the castle, looking from side to side with interest. It looked as though the former occupants hadn't been sure if they wanted to make a fight of it or not. Some parts of the castle had been prepared for a bitter defence, while other parts had been left completely alone. Perhaps the defenders had expected the army to win, rather than break. Or maybe they'd assumed their magic – whatever it was – would be enough to stop Reginald in his tracks. He clenched his jaw with anger as he remembered, again, his mother's ghost. Whoever was behind the magic in the mists was going to pay.

The throne room was grander than he'd expected, although he supposed it really shouldn't have been a surprise. King Edwin had been forbidden to raise more than a few regiments of troops, so he'd clearly plunged his resources into constructing the appearance of regal power instead of the reality. Gold lined the walls, leading one's eye to the throne itself. It was gold, something that Reginald couldn't help finding mildly striking. The Golden City's throne was also gold ...

Queen Emetine knelt in front of the throne, her head bowed. She looked up as he entered, then rose to her feet. Emetine was a striking woman, Reginald thought; her long black hair framed a pale face and fell down her back. She wore a black dress – a widow's gown – that matched her hair, open at the front to expose the tops of her breasts. And she looked as though she was going to cry.

She threw herself at Reginald's feet. "My Lord," she said. "Spare me!"

Reginald looked down at her for a long moment. She was the usurper's sister, but ... she was a woman. She wouldn't have had any control over her own life, even after her father met an unpleasant end. Her guardianship would have reverted to her brother as soon as her husband died. And she was of noble blood. He couldn't help feeling a flicker of pity.

"Rise," he said. He bent down and helped her to her feet. "You are safe."

Emetine looked up at him, then down. "Really?"

"I swear," Reginald said. "I will assume your guardianship personally."

He nodded to one of his guards. "Take Queen Emetine to her chambers. I will speak with her later."

"She might be the last of her family," Gars observed, artfully. "Whoever marries her will have a claim on her lands."

Reginald shrugged. In truth, he hadn't even considered the possibilities. Gars was right, of course. Rufus Hereford was dead. If Havant was also dead, Emetine would have the sole claim to their lands. But she couldn't hold them in her own right.

Which means she's a bargaining chip, he thought. He'd been raised to protect women, particularly those of noble blood. Emetine couldn't do anything to hurt *him. But she's also worth protecting.*

He sat on the golden throne. "Prepare camps outside the city for the mercenaries," he said. It was a shame there was no time to enjoy the throne. "And then send messengers ..."

Caen entered. "Your Highness, Earl Oxley requests the pleasure of an audience," he said. "Will you see him?"

Reginald smiled. *That* was quick. That was *very* quick.

"I will see him," he said. Oxley had to have been near the city, watching events from a safe distance. "Give him safe conduct, then escort him here."

Chapter Twenty-Two

"Tell me," Lord Robin said. "What do you make of it?"

Isabella shrugged. The castle was big, but she'd seen bigger. Cleaner, too. The castle staff were slowly returning to work, but half of them had apparently fled or been drafted into the army that had marched to Alcidine. Most of the servants were constantly glancing around, as if they expected to be jumped at any moment. Lord Robin had already had to speak sharply to Big Richard for harassing a maid while she performed her duties.

"There definitely aren't any protective wards," she said. Either the Court Wizard had been an imbecile – which was possible, this far from the Golden City – or someone had undone his work in his absence. And yet, she couldn't even pick up any *traces* of magic. His quarters hadn't even been protected. She'd expected to have to unpick a dozen protective wards, each one nastier than the last, but instead the door had opened at her touch. "I'll have to build them myself, from scratch."

"You can do that later," Lord Robin said. "I have something more important for you to do."

Isabella lifted her eyebrows. She couldn't think of anything more important than protecting the castle. The gods alone knew how many secret passages were threaded through the stone walls. But Lord Robin *was* her boss ...

"I was checking the cells," Lord Robin said. "Most of the people imprisoned were locked up for daring to suggest that the usurper should try to negotiate before the battle, rather than afterwards. But one of them was locked up for telling stories."

"Telling stories," Isabella repeated, as she followed him down a flight of stairs. The air grew cooler as they reached the lower levels. "What *sort* of stories?"

"The guards insisted that he'd been talking about odd

events in the countryside," Lord Robin said. "But they weren't allowed to talk to him personally."

"Odd events," Isabella mused. Robin was right. The storyteller *should* be investigated. And yet, she knew there were too many other problems. "I'll do what I can."

Lord Robin grinned at her. "I never doubted it," he said. He jabbed a finger at the castle. "Do you know what we found up there? A fishpond!"

"A fishpond?"

"Oh, yes," Lord Robin said. "A fishpond, under the castle. It's *teeming* with fish."

Isabella rolled her eyes. She'd known aristocrats in the Golden City who'd bred fish for their tables, but the Golden City was nearly two hundred miles from the nearest coastline. Fresh fish was expensive, even with preservation spells. But here, anyone who wanted fish could just walk down to the Racal and start fishing. She found it hard to believe that the castle's staff didn't know how to fish. Maybe the fish were a special breed.

"We'd better try some," she said. "Just out of curiosity, you understand."

"A couple of other weird things too," Lord Robin said. "They were throwing out dozens of swords. I think they were going to melt them down."

Isabella frowned. "Why?"

"Buggered if I know," Lord Robin said. "There's nothing actually *wrong* with the swords, I think. They're just really old iron blades. None of the newfangled alloys."

"I see," Isabella said. It made little sense. Iron blades might not be particularly elegant, but they were serviceable. It was true that iron neutralised some forms of magic, yet any sorcerer worth his salt could get around iron weapons and armour with ease. "Perhaps they wanted to keep them out of our hands."

"Perhaps," Lord Robin said. They reached the dungeons and stopped. "You talk to him, Isabella. I'll see to the outer defences."

Isabella nodded and stepped through the door. The stench – piss, shit, bitter despair – struck her nostrils as she looked around, forcing her to cast a hasty filtering charm. A handful of cells, illuminated only by torchlight ... she felt a flicker of sympathy for the former inhabitants. No one wanted to spend a night in the cells, let alone weeks. Thankfully, only one cell was occupied now. The others had been emptied.

She stepped up to the bars and peered inside. The cell was bare, save for a tiny patch of straw she supposed was meant to be a makeshift bed. There wasn't even a slop bucket, although she understood the logic. Prisoners who had nothing to lose might turn a bucket of shit into a weapon. The prisoner himself was sitting on the floor, half-asleep. Isabella hoped he wasn't mad. She'd seen too many prisoners go mad after a few weeks in the cells.

Opening the door, she stepped inside. The prisoner looked up at her, his face hidden in shadow. Isabella cast a spell, summoning light. The prisoner bit out a curse as he covered his eyes, shrinking back from her. He might not have realised she was a woman, but he'd definitely realised she was a sorceress. It might well be the first real magic he'd seen.

She knelt down and removed the water gourd from her belt, then held it out to him. "Take a sip," she said. It was possible the prisoner needed a good meal too, but that would take longer to arrange. "I need to talk to you."

The prisoner sipped the water, warily. "No one needs to talk to me," he said. His accent was odd, as if the common tongue wasn't his first language. "That was made clear when they threw me in here."

"I need to talk to you," Isabella repeated.

She wove a charm into the air, one that would induce the man to talk freely. He gave her a long look, as if he suspected what she was doing, then looked away. Isabella frowned, casting an analysis charm. The man had a latent talent for magic, she noted, one that had never passed the threshold for proper training. Perhaps he could do nothing more than sense magic.

"I was supposed to report back here," he said. He laughed. His sanity might well be more impaired than she thought. "And they threw me in the cells!"

"I'm going to listen to you," Isabella said. She sat back on her haunches. "What's your name?"

"Kingsley," the man said. "I'm ... I'm a bard. And a quaestor. I don't know if I am any longer."

"A bard *and* a quaestor?" Isabella asked. A spy, in other words. Probably one who'd worked directly for the usurper. "What happened, precisely?"

Kingsley sat up. "I want a wash, clean clothes and something to eat that doesn't look like it's passed through the digestive system of a cow," he said. "And then I'll tell you everything."

Isabella eyed him for a long moment. "I'll make the arrangements," she said. She walked to the door, shouted for the gaoler and issued instructions, then walked back to Kingsley. "But start talking now."

There was a pause. "The king – the former king – had me going from village to village, keeping an eye on his clients," he said. "I spent the last seven years singing for my supper, listening to stories and ... generally trying to keep my finger on what was going on."

"You worked for King Edwin?" Isabella asked. "Or ... or King Rufus?"

"Edwin," Kingsley said.

He shook his head, slowly. "There were odd reports, you see," he said. "Sightings of strange creatures. Weird encounters. Lights in the sky, strange sounds in the ground, roads that went places no human should ever go. And people ... even entire *villages* ... that just vanished."

Isabella remembered what she'd seen in Andalusia and shivered. "So ... what happened?"

"King Edwin sent me out to compile a complete list," Kingsley said. "He wanted to do something, but ... Earl Hereford was marching on Allenstown to dispose the king. He'd put aside the earl's daughter, you see. I went from place to place, collecting stories and reports and putting them together ..."

He reached out and grabbed her hand, too quickly for her to jump back. "It's all changed out there," he hissed. "Everyone knows. There were always places where no one dares go, but now ... they're spreading. You walk near the woods or through empty fields and you feel watched, even when there's no one in sight. Anyone who goes out after dark is not going to come home. And ... and ...

"I saw things." His voice lowered until he was almost whispering. "I saw ..."

He let go of her hand and sat back, shivering. Isabella quietly checked her spell. It was working, she thought. But he could lie to her ... perhaps. In his state, a truth-spell might break his mind completely.

"I heard a child whispering words that would tear the skin from your bones," Kingsley said, "and another who spoke prophecy. I saw men become animals, women become ... *things*. I saw witches dancing in the night and shadows moving in the day and *things* that were *things* and ..."

He stopped himself, just for a moment. "I saw ..."

"It's alright," Isabella said. "Tell me in your own time."

"I don't remember," Kingsley said. "There was something in the woods and ..."

He threw back his head and *keened*. Isabella covered her ears, wishing she knew what Kingsley had seen. Whatever it was, it had left him in a terrible state. She considered possible options, but came up with nothing. His mind was too fragile to be pushed.

"I got out, somehow," Kingsley said. He giggled. "Earl Hereford was dead ... long live Earl Hereford! And he was the king. I travelled to the city and ... and no one listened to me. I told them everything and ... and ... and they threw me in the dungeons for telling stories. I was thrown in the dungeons! Didn't they stop to think I might be telling the truth?"

Isabella considered it for a long moment. If Kingsley had confronted the usurper with such a story, it was quite possible that he'd simply be beheaded. Madmen weren't usually tolerated unless they were from powerful families, whereupon the truth might be simply covered up with a combination of threats and bribes. But if half of Kingsley's story was true ...

If I hadn't seen that thing in the village, she thought, *I wouldn't have believed him either.*

She leaned back, thoughtfully. Alden had reported stories too. She wondered, suddenly, if Kingsley was one of the Golden City's spies. He was certainly in a strong position to serve the Golden City, without being prominent enough to attract unwelcome attention from the local rulers. But without the right codewords, she knew she'd never get any answers out of him. The truth would be hidden away in his mind and sealed with powerful spells.

And yet, there were some odd problems with Kingsley's story. The timing was odd, to say the least. When had King Edwin sent him out? Before or after the king had been forced to take refuge in Andalusia and build up his forces to retake the throne? And when had Kingsley returned?

He's on the brink of madness, she told herself. *I should expect some gaps in the story.*

The gaoler returned. "My Lady," he said. "I have prepared a comfortable and secure suite for our guest."

"My Lady?" Kingsley looked Isabella up and down. "You are no lady!"

"My father would agree with you," Isabella said. She helped Kingsley to her feet. "Come."

The gaoler led them down the corridor, up a flight of stairs and into what was clearly a guest suite for noble hostages. A comfortable bed, a washroom with a large tub of cold water, a chamberpot ... compared to Kingsley's former cell, it was paradise. A small tray of bread and cheese – and a jug of wine – rested on the dresser, waiting for him. The gaoler had done good work, Isabella decided, after she'd checked to make sure there was only one way in or out of the suite. Gaolers were normally a sadistic breed, but this one ... was probably trying to curry favour. There was rarely any shortage of eager young sadists willing to man the gaol and supervise prisoners. In the right hands, the post could be quite rewarding.

She walked into the washroom and cast a spell over the tub. The water warmed, just enough to allow Kingsley to take a comfortable bath. There was soap on the sideboard, along with a handful of expensive perfumes. Isabella was surprised they hadn't gone walking in all the excitement. It wasn't as if the castle's new owners knew to look for them. They'd fetch quite a bit of money on the black market.

"Have a wash, then get some rest," she ordered, firmly. "I'll visit tomorrow and we'll ... we'll discuss what you saw."

Kingsley looked at her. "You believe me, don't you?"

"Yes," Isabella said. She didn't know how many of the *specifics* she believed, but she knew that *something* was deeply wrong on the Summer Isle. The nightmare mist alone had unsettled the army. She was surprised the enemy hadn't attacked while the soldiers were recovering from the shock. "I believe you."

She nodded to him, then walked through the door, closing it behind her. The suite was very secure. The door was made of wood-plated iron, with no less than two locks and five bars. It struck her as overkill, but she supposed anyone who was put in the suite absolutely *had* to stay in the suite. There were no magical protections, as far as she could determine, yet unlocking spells would have problems with so many bolts and locks.

I could just blast the door down, she thought, as she headed off to find Lord Robin. *And so could every other magician with a year of formal training.*

A passing maid directed her to Lord Robin's quarters, on the same floor as Prince Reginald's new rooms. Someone had hastily removed all traces of the former occupant, probably someone very close to the usurper or his family. Queen Emetine was presumably still occupying her chambers, Isabella thought. She couldn't help feeling a little out of sorts at how the prince had shown her mercy. It spoke well of Reginald, Isabella thought, yet ... there was something about Emetine – a hint of cold calculation – that bothered her. Throwing herself to the ground in complete surrender might have been calculated to make her appear both helpless and desperate.

"Isabella," Lord Robin said. He was seated at a wooden table, munching his way through a plate of chicken and potatoes. "Care to join me?"

Isabella nodded and pulled out a seat. A maid appeared from nowhere, took the order for more food and vanished again. Isabella scowled, reminding herself – again – that servants saw everything. Hopefully, they'd keep their mouths shut too.

"Kingsley – the storyteller – had quite a tale to tell," Isabella said. "There are ... *things* ... in the countryside."

Lord Robin shot her a sharp look. "Could you be any less specific if you tried?"

"Things like the ... *creature* ... we encountered in Andalusia," Isabella said. "I'll be talking about it with him tomorrow, jotting down everything he says. But ... it's clear that *something* has been changing here."

"There have always been places humans dare not venture," Lord Robin said.

Isabella nodded as the maid returned, carrying a steaming plate of food. There were places the Empire had deemed forbidden, for one reason or another, and places that had bad reputations that echoed down the ages. She'd heard whispers about some of the forbidden zones, but talking about them openly was not encouraged. The Inquisitors had always moved rapidly to suppress such talk and no one, absolutely no one, wanted their attention.

Perhaps I would have been told more, if I'd taken the oaths, she thought. *Or perhaps I would have been killed with the others ...*

"I think it should be investigated," she said, firmly. She'd have to write a full report to Alden, if nothing else. "If there's any truth to the stories, we have to find out."

"We saw the creature that took a village," Lord Robin said. "There is definitely *some* truth to the stories."

Isabella took a bite of her food. It was a little bland, but it was filling. "Yeah," she said, through a mouthful of potato. "There's some truth. But what?"

She sighed as she splashed gravy over the meat. It was unusual for supernatural vermin to come out into the open ... although, she supposed, the ... events ... had remained well away from the towns and cities. The village they'd visited had been a day's hard ride from the nearest town. And yet ... normally, most supernatural creatures would stay well away from humanity. Even werewolves preferred to remain in their packs than travel too close to human settlements.

But things have changed, she thought. *The Empire is gone.*

"We'll find out," Lord Robin said. He nodded towards the wall. "The Prince is still in discussions with Earl Oxley."

"That's good, I suppose," Isabella said. "Do you think Goldenrod will bend the knee?"

"I have no idea," Lord Robin said. "But I hope he tries to fight."

Isabella nodded. Prince Reginald would accept Earl Goldenrod's submission, if the man offered it. But if the man chose to fight, his lands could be taken and parcelled out to Prince Reginald's supporters. Lord Robin wasn't the only one who wanted a share. It could get awkward, very quickly, if pretty much every aristocrat on the island bent the knee.

Prince Reginald will have no lands to share out, Isabella thought. Her lips twitched. *That would be very inconvenient.*

It would be, she knew. And it might lead to civil war. But she couldn't help feeling that a worse problem was brewing, out in the countryside. The world had changed, yet everyone was pretending that everything was normal ...

She couldn't help thinking that it was a terrible mistake.

Chapter Twenty-Three

"I was sorry to hear about the death of your brother," Earl Goldenrod said, once he'd entered the tent and the formalities had been concluded. He was in his late fifties, old for a nobleman still in full possession of his faculties. His hair might be white, but his body was fit and healthy. "I believe he had the makings of a fine king."

That's not what you thought when he was on the throne, Havant thought. He controlled his expression with an effort. Earl Goldenrod was old enough to understand *precisely* how to manipulate a young and prideful man. He was easily old enough to be Havant's father. *You have always seen our family as potential enemies.*

"I too sorrow for his loss," Havant said. He'd mourned his brother, briefly. There hadn't been time for more than a quick ceremony before the remnants of the army had resumed the march. "But the island has worse problems than merely the loss of a king."

"Indeed it does," Earl Goldenrod said. "And I assumed that was what you asked me here to discuss."

Havant nodded, curtly. Earl Goldenrod had been marching southwards, either to fight the invaders or bend the knee to them. Havant hadn't really been surprised when his scouts encountered Earl Goldenrod's army on the march. Earl Goldenrod would want to be in position to either make himself the kingmaker – or the king – or bend the knee to the invader in exchange for being confirmed in his lands. Prince Reginald hadn't given the northern lords much time to pledge themselves to him. Havant suspected the invader was secretly hoping that some of the lords wouldn't reach Allenstown in time.

Which suggests he has every intention of replacing our noblemen with his own, Havant thought. *He'll have to reward his followers somehow.*

"My father could happily spend hours discussing the meaning of a single clause in a treaty, even though everyone knew the answer already," Havant said. "I prefer to be blunt. Do you mind?"

"Of course not," Earl Goldenrod said. "Youth is always refreshingly honest."

And open, Havant thought.

He felt a flash of pure frustration, mixed with shame. He *hated* being so weak. If he hadn't been so desperate, he would have sent ambassadors to conduct the negotiations on his behalf. Earl Goldenrod held the whip hand and the bastard knew it. But it was also clear that he knew better than to dismiss Havant out of hand. The mere fact he'd brought his *daughter* with him – if the spies were to be believed – suggested he was looking for more than merely paying homage to the island's new king. And perhaps, just perhaps, that gave Havant an opening.

"The invader holds Allenstown," Havant said. "I have heard that Earl Oxley has already travelled north to pledge himself to Prince Reginald. Given a week, most of the south will be in Prince Reginald's hands."

"So it would seem," Earl Goldenrod agreed.

"Prince Reginald *isn't* an islander king," Havant continued. "He is the son of another king, one who possesses far greater resources than ourselves. The age-old balance of power between the monarchy and the nobility has been shattered. Prince Reginald can simply bring in enough forces to crush us utterly, if we don't bend the knee. But if we do bend the knee, like the noblemen of Andalusia, we will be weakened to the point where we will be little more than slaves."

He ground his teeth at the thought. The nobility had always been powerful. And they'd been effectively all-powerful in their lands. But now ... King Romulus had weakened *his* noblemen to the point where none of them could offer resistance, if the king wanted to crush them. King Romulus might *claim* that his streamlining of the kingdom's laws was intended to simplify the courts, but Havant doubted that any of his nobles were fooled. More and more power was slipping out of their hands ...

... And they'd already lost the ability to resist.

"That might be true," Earl Goldenrod said, calmly. "But we could also come to terms with him."

"There are two problems with that," Havant said, equally calmly. "First, he will possess enough power to destroy us – utterly – if we displease him in any way. The balance of power will be shattered, once and for all. It won't be long before he starts putting limits on the number of soldiers we're allowed to raise, limits we will not be able to subvert."

"There are always ways to get around such limits," Earl Goldenrod pointed out.

"But he will be watching for signs we *are* trying to raise more troops," Havant said. "The *second* problem is that Prince Reginald will need lands to pay off his supporters. I expect he will insist that you – and I – surrender some of our family lands, at the very least. It's quite possible that he'll start looking for ways to push us into rebellion, just to give him an excuse to confiscate the remainder of our lands. You know as well as I do that many of our supporters will edge away if Prince Reginald turns on us."

"Well, *quite*," Earl Goldenrod said.

He smiled, rather coldly. "And yet, what do you offer instead?"

Havant took a breath. "An alliance," he said. "I will marry your daughter. My child – your grandchild – will combine our lands."

Earl Goldenrod didn't look surprised by the offer. Havant understood. His family might have been weakened, but they still possessed vast power. Combining the Hereford and Goldenrod lands would create a power bloc that even Prince Reginald would have to fear. Indeed, it might put Havant's child on the throne. Earl Goldenrod might well have been angling for a marriage alliance – in which he would be the senior partner – all along.

"An interesting thought," Earl Goldenrod said, finally. "But *can* you win? Can you even delay the invaders long enough for your child to be born?"

Havant reached for a map and laid it out on the table. "The invaders will have problems following us northwards, at least immediately," he said. "They will need time to regroup, time to bring in reinforcements before the autumn storms. I don't intend to give them that time. We cannot seek a pitched battle, not now, but we can and we will devastate the farms Prince Reginald is planning to use to feed his army. His men will start starving soon enough."

Earl Goldenrod cocked his head. "You do realise you'll be devastating more than just their army?"

"Yes," Havant said, bluntly. Vast numbers of peasants and commoners would starve. He didn't care. Prince Reginald could not be allowed to make use of them. "And we'll be targeting the Oxley lands too. Let Earl Oxley try to push Prince Reginald to hunt us down. It will prove unsuccessful."

"Proving that Prince Reginald cannot protect his vassals," Earl Goldenrod finished.

Havant nodded. Oxley had clients of his own to protect. If bending the knee to the invader wasn't enough to protect Oxley's lands, he'd start to slip away. It wouldn't be long, Havant suspected, before Oxley opened communications with the north. But it wouldn't be enough to save him, once the two earldoms were combined. Earl Oxley would pay a steep price for deserting his countrymen.

Earl Goldenrod drew out a line on the map. "He might also march north," he said. "And try to take the war to us."

"In that case, he'd be exposed," Havant countered. "You and your army can take up defensive positions here, joined by the majority of my troops. He can challenge us on prepared ground, if he wishes."

There was a long pause. "Very well," Earl Goldenrod said. "You will marry my daughter tonight."

Havant wasn't surprised. No agreement was sacred, save one held together by blood. Blood ... his thoughts swam suddenly, as if something had disturbed them. He didn't remember much, if anything, of what had happened the night his brother died, but ... he shook his head, grimly. The blackouts had become more and more frequent, yet he found it hard to care. It wasn't important.

He collected himself. Earl Goldenrod would style himself the senior partner, of course, but he *was* in his late fifties. *And* he didn't have a son. *Havant* would take his place, after he died ... after, perhaps, he was helped to shuffle off the mortal coil. By the time Havant's son was old enough to claim his inheritance, Havant would have established himself as the elder statesman of the combined earldom. There would be plenty of time to train his son properly before Havant himself died.

And I may yet be king, he thought. He'd been careful not to claim the kingship in front of Earl Goldenrod, knowing that it would put the old man's dander up. *Once the invader is defeated – starved and then beaten in battle – we will be in a position to claim everything for ourselves.*

"Make the arrangements," he said. His father would be rolling in his grave – the Goldenrod and Herefords linked by blood – but there was no choice. "I'll need to head south again soon."

"Of course," Earl Goldenrod said.

He rose, bowed, and headed for the flap. Havant leaned back in his chair, forcing himself to relax. The tricky part of the negotiations was already over. Now ... once the marriage was solemnised, he had to go back to war. The invader could not be allowed to rest easy ...

It was getting dark, when he walked out of the tent. The soldiers were bustling around, running through training exercises as the sergeants prepared them for war. Dozens of Red Monks were clearly visible, speaking to the soldiers and encouraging them to give their lives for the cause. Havant hadn't issued any orders, but hundreds of soldiers were already praying around the plain stone altars. *That* was odd, yet it didn't bother him. Instead, it felt natural and right.

It won't be long before the faith is established everywhere, he thought. It felt strange, as if it wasn't entirely *his* thought. *And then the world will change.*

He wished, suddenly, that his sister had escaped Allenstown before the city surrendered itself to Prince Reginald. It would have been nice to have *someone* from his family beside him, even though she wouldn't have been able to stand beside him when he was bound to Roxanne Goldenrod. Havant had known he'd have to marry one day, but he'd never imagined being married to Earl Goldenrod's daughter. Rufus had been the only person who *could* have married her ...

... And now Rufus was dead.

He will be avenged, Havant promised himself, as he walked towards the fire. *And those who killed him will suffer.*

A space had been cleared in the centre of the camp, surrounded by the Hereford and Goldenrod banners. Havant felt his blood boil as he realised the Goldenrod banners had been placed in a position of superiority over the Hereford banners, although he knew it didn't really matter. He'd just have to endure the snide dismissal until the old man died ... perhaps with a little encouragement. Or, for that matter, a child was born. Their joint heir would inherit both sets of land. He could endure a ceremony conducted by one of their priests for *that*.

He sucked in his breath as he saw Roxanne Goldenrod, standing beside her father. She was taller than he'd expected, even for a noblewoman. Long red hair flowed down, framing a strikingly pretty face and flowing to her waist. The long dress she wore hinted at her curves, rather than following them. Her expression showed nothing of her innermost thoughts. She would have known, of course, that her father would arrange her marriage – and that her consent was nothing more than a formality. If she'd said no, her father would have beaten her for disobedience. No one would have batted an eyelid.

"Come forward," the priest ordered.

Havant strode up to the fire, watching as Earl Goldenrod and his daughter walked forward. It didn't *look* as though he was dragging her to the flames, thankfully. It was considered to be bad luck if the bride struggled, even though she was being traded as casually as a pig or a cow. Emetine had gone through the same ceremony, Havant recalled. And *she* hadn't struggled at all.

But she was going to be queen, Havant reminded himself. *That made putting up with a tiresome milksop worthwhile.*

He looked at Roxanne, aware that she was studying him too. She had good reason to be pleased, he thought. Her new husband wasn't *that* much older than her, after all. It wasn't uncommon for a young girl to be married off to a much older man, if the dictates of policy demanded it. King Edwin had been a good thirty years older than Emetine. Havant smiled, despite himself. He'd probably been too old to have any interest in taking his wife to bed, let alone conceiving children.

"Roxanne, Daughter of Goldenrod," the priest said. He wasn't a Red Monk. Havant couldn't help finding that annoying. "Do you swear, before all the gods, that you have never known man?"

"I swear," Roxanne said.

Havant nodded, curtly. It would be a terrible disgrace if it turned out that the bride wasn't a virgin. Roxanne would have been protected from birth, chaperoned by her mother and then by her serving maids. And if she'd somehow managed to lose her virginity despite that ... well, it wasn't uncommon for such girls to be quietly murdered for bringing disgrace upon the family. There could *not* be any question marks over the paternity of a woman's child.

"Join hands," the priest ordered.

Havant reached out and took Roxanne's hand. It felt warm and smooth against his skin. She would have spent her childhood learning to sew and spin, rather than preparing herself to run an estate or fight a war. Havant had no doubt that there were hundreds of young men in the Goldenrod lands who'd be unhappy, when they heard that Roxanne had finally married. No doubt some of them had been angling to marry her and eventually succeed her father as earl.

Which may be a problem, after the war, he thought. *But for the moment, it doesn't matter.*

He felt oddly disconnected from the world as the priest babbled his way through the marriage ceremony, reminding the young couple that they would now be united together for the rest of their lives and then calling on the gods to bless the match. The words didn't feel quite *right*, somehow, as if the priest was lying. But what was he lying *about*?

The ceremony finally came to an end. Havant kissed Roxanne gently, then led her to the table. A small feast had already been laid out for the handful of guests. It probably wasn't the kind of ceremony Roxanne had wanted – if she'd wanted anything at all – but there wasn't time to go all the way back to the Goldenrod Lands and hold a proper feast.

Later, perhaps, they'd be able to hold a more formal ceremony. But that would come after the war.

"Take good care of her," Earl Goldenrod said, as the wine began to flow. Havant had ordered wine distributed to the soldiers, just to give them an excuse to celebrate too. "And you" – he pointed a jovial finger at his daughter – "remember who and what you are."

Roxanne's face showed no expression. Havant wondered, idly, if she had anything resembling a personality. It would be boring to spend the rest of his life – or her father's life – with a girl who said nothing. Maybe she just didn't trust herself to speak. It would have been a terrible shock to be engaged and married in less than a day, even though she'd presumably known that her wedding day was fast approaching. She had to be nervous. It was quite possible that no one had bothered to tell her about the facts of life.

He ate and drank sparingly, careful not to make himself sleepy. Roxanne sat beside him, nibbling at food. She *was* nervous, he decided. The combination of sharp remarks from her father and bawdy romance ballads from the soldiers couldn't be making her feel any better about the wedding. Havant wished, again, that his sister had been able to join them. *She* would have been able to keep Roxanne company.

Finally, they rose and headed to the tent. Hark stood outside it, his face hidden behind his cowl.

"My congratulations on your wedding, Your Majesty," he said.

Roxanne shrank back against Havant. For the first time, her face showed real emotion. Fear.

"Thank you," Havant said, to Hark. He pushed Roxanne gently towards the flap. "I'll join you in a moment."

Hark waited until the flap was closed, then leaned forward. "I am sure she will be a good bride."

"She comes with a significant dowry," Havant said, bluntly. He might have pledged himself to the faith, but he didn't have to listen to sarcastic remarks. The Red Monks were his agents and advisors, not his masters. "What do you want?"

"Her father will inevitably betray you," Hark said. His voice was toneless. "You must take some of her blood."

The world seemed to blur, again. For a moment, Havant thought he saw the future. A hundred events, a hundred moments where things could go either way ... all centred on Earl Goldenrod. And a betrayal at the worst possible moment would be the end. He'd been so focused on combining the two earldoms that it hadn't occurred to him that the marriage made Earl Goldenrod heir to the Hereford Lands. No *wonder* he'd agreed so quickly.

"I will," he promised. He had a wife. He didn't need her father. Once he had a son, he could quietly dispose of the older man before he was assassinated himself. "And you can use it."

And then he turned and walked into the tent.

Chapter Twenty-Four

"That was ... an interesting set of discussions," Caen said.

Reginald nodded, tightly. Earl Oxley was terrifyingly fond of his own voice. He'd debated *everything*, from the precise level of homage he should pay to Reginald for his lands to the exact number of troops he should supply to the army. And he'd dropped dozens of little hints about a marriage between Reginald and his oldest daughter, or a betrothal between Reginald and one of his younger daughters. Reginald didn't really blame him for wanting to establish himself high up the food chain, but it was annoying. Oxley was already too powerful – and too well established – for Reginald's peace of mind.

And everyone else's too, Reginald thought. He'd hoped to carve up Oxley's lands and parcel them out, but Oxley's swift submission had made that impossible. *I'll have to go north, sooner rather than later.*

He looked up at Caen. "Have the terms of the submission written out, then checked," he said, through a yawn. It had been a very long day. "And then get some sleep yourself."

"Of course, Your Highness," Caen said. "I'll see you in the morning."

He hurried out of the door, leaving Reginald alone. Reginald rose and glanced around the chambers, shaking his head in amusement. King Edwin might have ruled a poor kingdom, but he hadn't skimped on his comforts. The bed was large enough for five or six people; the closet was full of fancy clothes; the bathroom housing a gold-edged bathtub that could easily hold two or three bathers. But there was no running water, of course, and the chamberpot was distressingly primitive. No one had bothered to give the castle piped water, let alone drains.

And now it's mine, he thought, as he slowly undid his leathers. He'd discarded the armour as a show of good faith, but he hadn't been entirely defenceless. *It's just a shame I won't have time to enjoy it.*

He shook his head, slowly. There were too many things to do. He had to accept homage from his new vassals, he had to sort out trade between Allenstown, Racal's Bay and Humber, he had to decide on a policy towards noblemen who were reluctant to bend the knee ... that, at least, was simple. They had a week to submit and then their lands would be forfeit. He wasn't sure what he'd do if they *all* submitted. He'd be unable to pay his mercenaries and reward his followers if he couldn't confiscate lands from short-sighted noblemen.

Perhaps I'll just have to push them into rebellion, he thought. He yawned again. *It might solve one of my problems.*

Something moved, behind him. He snatched the dagger from his belt and spun around, bracing himself for attack. If someone had managed to get into his chambers and catch him with his pants down ... he stared in disbelief. Emetine stood there, raising her hands in surrender. Her silken nightgown made it absolutely clear that she wasn't concealing any weapons. Reginald couldn't help staring. Even *whores* didn't wear such translucent garments. He could see every curve of her body, from the swell of her breasts to the patch of dark hair between her legs. It was hard, so hard, to raise his eyes and look at her face.

"I thought we should talk, privately," Emetine said. Her voice was light and breathy. It was hard to catch her words. "And perhaps reach a better understanding."

Reginald's mouth was suddenly dry. He couldn't think clearly. He'd never seen anything like her, not even when he'd seduced a pair of noblewomen in his teens. There had been brief conquests and long affairs, moments of pleasure and long relationships that he'd known wouldn't go anywhere, but ... but he'd always been in charge. Now ... he felt weak, helpless to resist. His heart was pounding like the beat of a drum, so loudly that he thought he could hear it.

"How ...?" Reginald swallowed and started again. "How did you get in here?"

Emetine smiled at him. It transformed her face. He'd never thought of her as particularly pretty, but ... her smile made her light up like the sun. She *was* pretty. He found it hard to believe that King Edwin had never touched her. They'd been man and wife. Surely, he'd found her impossible to resist.

His eyes dipped. He could see the outline of her breasts – and her hard nipples, pressing against the silk. He was suddenly achingly hard. He wanted her, desperately. She stepped forward and it was all he could do to keep from reaching for her. It would be easy, so easy, to grab her and throw her onto the bed, to tear away the nightgown and feast his eyes on her naked body. And yet ... it was hard, so hard, to think clearly. He couldn't look away.

"My brothers are dead," Emetine said. "I'm all that's left of the Herefords."

That might not be true, Reginald thought. He'd hoped to find the body of the *third* Hereford sibling, but an extensive search of the battlefield had turned up nothing. Reginald wanted to believe that Havant Hereford was dead, yet common sense forced him to doubt it. Havant had had plenty of time to make his escape before it was too late. *He might be out there somewhere.*

"And I can't hold land in my own right," Emetine said. She took another step closer. "I need a protector."

"I am your new guardian," Reginald reminded her. He managed to lift his gaze. Her lips were suddenly very tempting. He could kiss her. He *wanted* to kiss her. "I ... I'll see that you are protected."

"Marry me," Emetine said. She was almost touching him now. "Marry me and you get the lands ..."

Reginald tried to force himself to think. Cold logic warned that it would be a very bad idea. He *would* get the lands, if Emetine was truly the last of her family, but they'd come with a price. He wanted her – by all the gods, he wanted her – yet he knew she hadn't had children with her previous husband. What if she was barren? What if ... what if he married her and they couldn't have children? He would be deprived of a legitimate heir. His father would not be pleased if he committed himself to a woman who might be barren.

And yet, cold logic felt as insubstantial as a puff of wind.

She was standing right in front of him, her breasts almost touching his shirt. He felt nervous, as nervous as a virgin who was about to have sex for the very first time. His hand crept upwards, almost against his will, and brushed against her breast. She let out a moan and leaned closer, prolonging the contact. Sparks seemed to dance between them as she pressed herself against him, drawing him onwards. He was no longer aware of anything, but her.

His hands moved to the clasp and undid it. Her nightgown fell to the ground, pooling around her feet. She smelt ... she smelt wonderful. He tried to take a step back, but his legs refused to move. She was suddenly stronger, looming over him ... he felt a flicker of panic, which vanished almost as soon as it appeared. Something was wrong ...

Emetine was speaking. But he couldn't make out the words.

***

Isabella sat bolt upright in bed, an instant before her mind caught up with her. She grabbed for the dagger she kept under the pillow, half-expecting an intruder intent on forcing himself on her. It had happened several times, during her stint as a mercenary. Some drunken idiot would become convinced that she wanted him and stumble into her sleeping quarters ... But there was no one lurking in the darkness. She muttered a spell, illuminating the chamber with pearly white light. She was alone.

Something is wrong, she thought, as she swung her legs over the bed and stood. *But what?*

She clutched her dagger in one hand as she reached for her leathers. Thankfully, she'd slept in her shirt and trousers rather than risk sleeping naked. She'd known there was a chance she might be forced to wake in a hurry. And her instincts wouldn't have yanked her out of deep sleep for nothing. But ... she reached out with her senses, testing the wards. They were intact ... *no,* one of them *wasn't* intact. The ward hadn't snapped, it hadn't even been subverted. It was just *gone*.

"Shit," she muttered. "That's Prince Reginald's chamber!"

She grabbed her sword and wand, then ran for the door.

Prince Reginald was guarded heavily, but anyone who could take out a ward could presumably take out a handful of guards too. She ran up the corridor, slowing as she approached the chamber. The guards seemed alert, but they were completely unresponsive when she called out to them. They were entranced. Isabella bit off a curse, then tested the door. Unsurprisingly, it was locked.

Summoning her magic, she blasted the door as hard as she could. It disintegrated. Isabella ran inside, looking around for the threat. Prince Reginald was lying on the floor, staring up at nothing; Emetine was standing over him, surrounded by a haze of *something*. He was naked, his manhood clearly visible. Isabella wasn't sure if Emetine was trying to seduce the prince or kill him. There was something fundamentally *wrong* about the whole scene.

"Get away from him," she snapped.

Emetine turned. Her face ... her face looked *different*. It flickered, as if she was casting and recasting glamours over herself. Isabella could see *things* moving under Emetine's skin, as if ... as if they were on the verge of exploding out of her. And the haze ... Isabella took a breath and regretted it, instantly, as she felt a hot flush of pure arousal. A love potion ... no, not quite a love potion, but something that worked along the same lines. It was a rapist's dream.

Rage boiled through her. How *dare* she? Isabella reached for her magic and lashed out, hoping to stun the older woman. It was clear that Emetine was *far* from helpless ... whatever she was, she was far from helpless. And yet, what *was* she? The magic struck ... and splintered, fading into nothingness. Emetine smirked at her, the haze surrounding them growing stronger. Isabella tried to cast a filtering spell, but the magic seemed to vanish almost as soon as she summoned it.

Damn it, she thought.

She hurled herself forward. Emetine's eyes – so human and yet so ... inhuman – widened with surprise, an instant before Isabella crashed her fist into Emetine's jaw. The woman gasped in pain and stumbled, falling to the ground. Isabella bent down and hit her again, harder this time. Emetine stared at her for a moment, her face completely

uncomprehending, then blacked out. Isabella frowned –
Emetine hadn't looked *that* tough – then looked up. The
haze was already fading away.

Reginald groaned. Isabella hurried to his side. His eyes
were dazed, as if he'd been drugged. He *had* been drugged.
There was a *reason* love potions were banned. But then, it
wasn't that hard to find a love potion or a recipe on the black
market. Perhaps Emetine had had enough magic to brew one
for herself. It was vaguely possible that she might have
managed to brew a potion with just a *hint* of magic.

Or something else happened, she thought, as she half-
dragged Reginald towards the bathroom. *My spells didn't
work on her either.*

The guards, snapping out of their trances and belatedly
realising that something was wrong, came storming into the
chamber. Isabella gritted her teeth. If they caught a whiff of
whatever was left of the potion – or whatever it had been –
she was going to be in real trouble if her spells were no
longer reliable. And Emetine would be in trouble too ...

"I have the situation under control," she snapped. "Get out,
then seal off the corridor at both ends."

Thankfully, the guards obeyed without question. Isabella
breathed a sigh of relief, then finished hauling Prince
Reginald into the bathroom. A large tub of water sat in one
corner. She took a bucket, filled it to the brim and then
splashed water over the prince. He gasped and coughed,
shivering frantically as his eyes slowly returned to normal.
Isabella wondered, vaguely, just what had happened before
she'd arrived. Emetine ... had been on the verge of
controlling him. Or worse.

"I ..." Prince Reginald coughed, loudly. "I ... what
happened?"

"Emetine tried to enchant you," Isabella said. She patted
his naked shoulder. "Stay here a moment, please. I'll deal
with her."

The prince didn't argue. That worried her more than she
cared to admit. Love potions could have nasty long-term
effects, even if the original compulsion was overridden or
retargeted on something harmless. And he'd been rendered
helpless by a woman ... that would probably grate on him too.

She shook her head in annoyance – too many women had been rendered helpless by men – and then stepped back into the bedroom. Emetine was still unconscious, but Isabella took no chances. She searched the woman roughly, inspected her face – it was normal now – and bound her hand and feet. And, just to be sure, she shoved a gag in Emetine's mouth.

I'll have to take her to the cells, she thought, grimly. She knew what the guards would do, if presented with something that looked young, female and helpless. And she had a nasty feeling that Emetine would take full advantage of it. *If she has the same powers as the Red Monks, she might be able to escape with ease.*

She dumped Emetine in a corner, then walked back to the washroom. Prince Reginald was trying to stand, even though his legs were too wobbly to support him. He brushed aside her hand when she offered it, concentrating on standing under his own power. She didn't really blame him for trying. He couldn't afford to show weakness now he'd won the first round of the war. It would convince his enemies that further resistance *wasn't* futile.

"Ouch," he said, followed by a string of curses. "What happened?"

"I was hoping you'd tell me," Isabella said. She tried to ignore the prince's nakedness. He hadn't set out to expose himself to her, after all. "What did she do?"

Prince Reginald flinched. "I ..."

He closed his eyes, then told her the entire story. Isabella listened, nodding to herself. It hadn't just been a seduction, then. She'd been right. Emetine had been trying to *control* him, using her body – and her strange powers – to plant hooks in his mind. If Isabella hadn't come to the rescue ...

"You should have her executed, after we interrogate her," Isabella said, when the prince had finished. "She should not be left alive."

"We'll keep her in jail," Prince Reginald said. "I don't want to shed female blood."

Isabella fought down a hot flash of pure anger. It was late, she was tired ... she didn't have *time* for aristocratic stupidity. And she was too tired to care about the consequences of telling the prince the truth.

"How many women do you think have died in your father's wars?" Her voice was bitingly cold. "How many women and girls do you think have been raped? How many are going to starve to death or be forced into unhappy marriages because your armies killed their husbands and fathers and brothers? How many women have suffered because you decided you wanted the Summer Isle for yourself?"

Prince Reginald flinched, again. "I ..."

"She tried to *rape* you," Isabella snapped. "And she used ... she used strange powers to *do* it. And you're trying to forgive her because you think she's a woman? How helpless do you think she is? How helpless do you think *I* am?"

She took a long breath, calming herself. Prince Reginald was hardly the only offender. He'd even done everything in his power to ensure that the locals were treated decently, although his ability to keep his troops from committing atrocities was limited. She'd met mercenary captains who'd gloried in atrocity and noblemen who'd liked to spend their days hunting peasants for sport. Prince Reginald was better than most ... not perfect, but better. She didn't really want to walk away.

"I'll take you back to my room," she decided. She could hide the prince from passing eyes, at least for a few hours. "That'll give this room time to vent."

And time for him to recover himself, she added, privately. *He's in no state to talk to anyone right now.*

She found him a robe, then cast a concealment spell around him. The guards didn't see him as Isabella led him out of the chamber and down the corridor. They were too busy milling around, speculating on what had happened and trying to decide how best to avoid blame for the whole affair. Isabella didn't blame them for being worried. No one would believe that Emetine had managed to walk past them and into the prince's chambers without being seen.

They'll assume the guards were bribed, she thought, as she entered her room. *And if I hadn't seen them entranced, I would believe it too.*

She helped Prince Reginald to the bed and went back to the prince's chambers. The guards were eager to help her move Emetine to a cell, then seal off the royal bedchamber for a few hours. The maids would clean up the mess in the morning, once the remnants of the potion had faded away. They'd have to wash the chamber from top to bottom.

And I have to pray the prince doesn't suffer any ill-effects, she thought, as she spread a blanket on the floor. *If he does, we may be in some trouble.*

Chapter Twenty-Five

"Here's how it's going to be," Isabella said, as she stepped into the cell and glared at Emetine. The older woman was lying on the stone floor, bound and gagged, but her eyes were alight with anger and malice. And, perhaps, a hint of madness. "If you cooperate, you'll be unharmed; if you make a fuss, I'll hurt you. Do you understand me?"

Emetine nodded, curtly. Isabella would have felt pity for her – sleeping on the stone floor, bound, gagged and naked, couldn't have been any fun – if she hadn't known what Emetine had tried to do. Seducing someone was one thing, but using a love potion and dark magic to do it was quite another. She hadn't forgotten – or forgiven – what she'd felt when she'd sniffed the haze herself. Emetine was going to answer Isabella's questions, one way or the other.

Isabella knelt down and carefully removed the gag, half-expecting ... *something* to snap at her. The Red Monks had magic, but it didn't work like any magic *she'd* ever studied. She found it hard to believe that it was that far beyond her comprehension, yet without a chance to study it she was as blind as a magic-less mundane. It was a droll reflection of how mundanes – even powerful kings and princes – might feel when facing magic. It was a force beyond their understanding, let alone their control.

"Water," Emetine gasped. "Please."

Isabella took the water gourd from her belt and allowed Emetine to take a gulp. "Don't take too much," she warned. No one had fed or watered the prisoner. Emetine had been left strictly alone in her cell. Isabella had threatened the guards with unspeakable fates if they dared enter the chamber without permission. "You haven't drunk anything for hours."

"I know," Emetine said. She shifted, slightly. "Can you untie me?"

"Not yet," Isabella said. She sat down on the wooden bench, trying not to sniff. The air smelt foul. "I want some answers."

Emetine glowered at her. "To what?"

Isabella felt her temper snap. "Don't take me for an idiot," she said, coldly. "You used magic to break into the prince's chambers and ..."

She broke off. Emetine was starting to giggle, hysterically.

"Magic? You think I used *magic*?" Emetine smirked at her. "What makes you think I used *magic*?"

"You entranced the guards," Isabella reminded her. "And you seduced the prince ..."

"I waved my breasts under his eyes," Emetine said, sardonically. "Most men can't think when they see a pair of breasts. All the blood drains out of their big heads and pools in their little heads."

"It was more than that," Isabella said. She held up a hand and summoned a flame, allowing the fire to dance on her palm. "What did you do?"

"You're a man," Emetine said. She sniffed, disdainfully. "You wouldn't understand."

Isabella blinked, surprised by the abrupt *non sequitur*. She'd been called a man before – or a man in a woman's body – but almost always from men who'd made passes at her and been turned down flat. It was the first time she'd been called a man by another woman. Most women had little difficulty in seeing through her male garb, even though men rarely noticed her gender until it was pointed out to them. And yet, it didn't *sound* like she was being complimented. It sounded more like a blunt insult.

"I was a woman, the last time I checked," she said, dryly. "Why do you think I wouldn't understand?"

Emetine shot her a sly look. "Ah, but you're a woman who dresses like a man. Do you even have a dress? Have you ever worn one in your life?"

"Yes," Isabella said, shortly. She'd never been fond of formal dresses, but she'd worn them before she'd been kicked out of the family and ordered to leave the Golden City. "Do you want me to pull down my pants?"

"You misunderstand," Emetine said. "You *are* a man in

every way that matters."

"I know men who would disagree with that," Isabella said. She'd met hundreds of men who'd doubted her competence until she'd rubbed their noses in it. "Why do you think differently?"

Emetine smiled. "You see, you've been taught man-magic. You *think* like a man."

Isabella frowned. "Man-magic?"

"Magic as studied and practiced by men," Emetine said. "Physically, you are a woman; mentally, you're a man."

"I see," Isabella lied. Magic worked the same, more or less, for men and women. There were a handful of spells that could only be cast by men and others that could only be cast by women, but it wasn't hard to rewrite them so the opposite gender could use them. Man-magic? She'd never even *heard* of such a concept. "What do you mean?"

Emetine smiled, again. "Men are all about imposing themselves on the world," she said, seriously. "They think in terms of control, of controlling everything from their lands and their animals to their women. Deep inside, every man wants to control women, control *everything*. Man-magic is about taking those desires and making them real."

"If that was true," Isabella said slowly, "surely every woman in the Golden City would have been enchanted to obey men."

"I wondered where your accent came from," Emetine said. She sounded as if she thought she'd scored a point. "How did you end up here?"

"None of your business," Isabella said. She doubted the information would do Emetine – or anyone – any good. "But do carry on."

"Men build houses and bridges and plant fields and ... and generally impose themselves on the land," Emetine said. "Man-magic is nothing more than an expansion of that, really. It is a form of control over one's surroundings."

"Really," Isabella said. She rather doubted Emetine understood what she was saying. "And is that a bad thing?"

"It can be," Emetine said. "They've taught us to do the same thing, you see. Women can build homes and plant fields and ... and cast spells, just like the men. They don't see their own power because they're too busy pretending to be men."

She gave Isabella an odd little smile. "Female-magic is different, don't you know?"

Isabella said nothing for a long moment. She'd never heard of completely separate fields of magic ... indeed, she could see a number of oddities in Emetine's words, a number of points that didn't quite make sense. And yet, there was something about the quiet confidence with which Emetine spoke that made it impossible for Isabella to dismiss Emetine's words out of hand. Emetine *believed* what she was saying ...

"Men impose their will on the land," Emetine said. "*We* live in harmony with it. Men control the forces of nature; we allow them to guide and shelter us. Men write their own songs and sing them; women find the tune and sing along. It's a bit of a mixed metaphor, but ... I'm sure you get the idea."

"I don't," Isabella said, shortly. "What did you do to Prince Reginald?"

"He wanted me," Emetine said. "And the magic swept him along."

"*Really,*" Isabella said.

"Yes," Emetine said.

She paused, dramatically. "We *appeal* to the universe, to the forces beyond human ken," she added. "And they grant us their blessings."

Isabella's eyes narrowed. "*What* forces?"

"The forces that guide the universe itself," Emetine said. "We call and they answer."

Isabella met her eyes. "If this is true," she said, "why haven't I heard anything about it before?"

Emetine snorted. "What do men fear? Powerful women. How many men fear *you*?"

She shrugged, struggling against her bonds. "Think about it," she said. "The Grand Sorcerers taught a specific kind of magic to magicians, while systematically destroying any hints of *other* kinds of magic. They destroyed cults and misfit groups that refused to toe the line, wiping them out and concealing all evidence of their existence. The Empire even propagated false religions to give the people something to worship, rather than reaching out to what lies beyond. And now the Empire is gone."

And now all sorts of things are going to come out of the shadows, Isabella thought. She remembered Kingsley's story – and Alden's reports – and shivered. *Who knows what's going to happen while we're battling for the throne?*

She took a breath. "Who taught you this?"

Emetine smiled. "You don't think I could learn on my own?"

Isabella shook her head. She'd heard enough about how the Summer Isle treated women – even noblewomen – to doubt that Emetine had been taught more than the basic womanly skills by her family. It was quite possible she didn't even know how to read and write, even though the lowest serving girl in the Golden City was taught as a matter of course. A girl whose prime function was to marry well and bear the next generation didn't *need* to be taught anything else. It was a chilling thought. If she'd been born without magic, so far from civilisation, it would have been her fate too.

"Very true," Emetine said. "The Red Monks taught me."

"Ah," Isabella said. "And what *are* they?"

"They are the servants of Dusk," Emetine said. "And they are here to herald a new era."

"And they have magic," Isabella said.

Emetine showed a flash of anger. "Haven't you been listening? They draw their power from their lord!"

Isabella took a moment to compose herself. "What did they teach you?"

"A few rites, a handful of prayers," Emetine said. "And a few offerings ..."

Understanding clicked, suddenly. Isabella leaned forward. "You murdered your husband."

"He was going to put me aside again, soon," Emetine said. The bitterness in her voice was almost palpable. "Why should I *not* have killed him?"

Isabella scowled. On one hand, she knew the consequences of King Edwin's death had been horrific. On the other, she understood *precisely* how helpless Emetine must have felt. She'd been little more than a pawn in her family's power play, battered between her father, her brothers and her husband. Isabella had hated being *her* father's pawn and *she'd* had far more options to resist than the powerless Emetine. Her disownment hadn't been the end of the world.

Poor bitch, she thought. *And yet ...*

"I would have felt sorry for you, if you hadn't tried to seduce Prince Reginald," she said, tartly. She doubted *Reginald* would complain about King Edwin's murder. As long as the king had been alive – and as long as there was a faint prospect of producing a male heir – King Romulus's claim to the Summer Isle would remain inactive. "You would have broken him."

Emetine met her eyes, defiantly. "And men don't break women?"

"That isn't an excuse," Isabella said. "Now tell me ... what exactly did you do?"

She listened, carefully, as Emetine stumbled through an explanation, but very little of it seemed to make sense. She'd taken some of her husband's blood, then ... simply given it to a messenger, who'd taken it out of the city. And then, she'd waited for her husband to die. It made no sense. *Something* must have been done, but by whom? The Red Monks? They were the only logical suspects. What *were* they?

"Prince Reginald wants to keep you alive," she said, when she'd finished picking Emetine's brains. She needed to sit down and think about what she'd been told, then ... then what? "If you ..."

Emetine laughed, bitterly. "I'm not a *person* to him, am I?"

"If you were a man, you would have been beheaded by now," Isabella pointed out, sharply. It was churlish to complain about someone deciding to keep one alive, although she understood Emetine's point. Even now, even after a blatant attempt to subvert the Crown Prince, she wasn't being treated seriously. "And if it was up to me, you *would* be beheaded."

"And yet, it *isn't* up to you," Emetine said. "Tell me, do you think one of his male counsellors would have his opinion dismissed so quickly?"

Isabella shrugged. As far as she knew, *she* was the only person – apart from Reginald himself – who knew what had happened. Reginald would definitely want to keep it that way. The mere rumour that he might have had his head turned by magic would be destructive, even if it wasn't entirely true. It would suggest weakness, a failure of masculinity ... it would turn him into a laughing stock. The cold truth – that anyone who'd caught a sniff of the haze would have been affected – would be meaningless, compared to the chance to weaken the prince's grip on power.

"I don't know," she said. "But he does have good reason to keep you alive."

"To *use* me," Emetine said, bitterly. "If he marries me – and kills my brother – he gets the lands."

"Probably," Isabella said. The confirmation that Havant Hereford was alive was useful, if annoying. "But if he kills both of you, wouldn't he get the lands anyway?"

"It would depend, I suppose," Emetine said. She looked away. "Dear old Dad killed most of the people who *might* have had a claim."

Isabella felt another flicker of sympathy. She and Emetine weren't *that* different, she supposed. They'd both had fathers who'd sought to use them, although Isabella's father had been more interested in pushing her into a powerful position, rather than using her for breeding stock. And Isabella had been able to get away. She dreaded to think what would have happened to Emetine if *she'd* been caught *in flagrante delicto.* She would have been lucky if she had *merely* been kicked out to starve.

"Listen to me," she said. She reached out and forced Emetine to look at her. "I'll be back soon. You'll be moved to more suitable quarters, but kept under heavy guard. If you do *anything*, and I mean *anything*, to excite suspicion, you will be chained to the wall and *kept* chained up until we decide how to dispose of you. Or I'll simply turn you into granite."

"It must be nice to have power," Emetine said. She looked oddly wistful. "Is it good to be able to defend yourself?"

"It has its moments," Isabella said. "Is it good never to

have to fear punishment for your misdeeds?"

She rose and walked out of the cell, closing it behind her. Emetine would have an uncomfortable time of it – Isabella hadn't bothered to untie her – but there was no way she could be allowed to roam free. If it had been *entirely* up to Isabella, Emetine would never have been allowed to wake up. The Red Monks had changed the rules. There was just no way to be *sure* she was harmless.

And yet, the Red Monks are men, she thought. *Or are they?*

The thought startled her. Yet, once it had passed through her mind, it refused to leave. The Red Monks wore cowls, if the witnesses were to be believed. There was no *reason* it had to be a man under the red cloth, was there? A woman could easily pass for a man if her face and body were hidden. *Isabella* had passed for a man without bothering to cover herself so completely. The assumption that the Red Monks were all male would be more than enough to keep anyone from looking too closely.

She walked up the stairs slowly, mulling over what she'd been told. Emetine had spoken the truth, Isabella thought, but it was only what she *believed* to be true. It was possible that everything she'd said was true, yet it was also possible that the Red Monks had told her flattering lies. Emetine would *want* to believe there was a particularly feminine power that she could use, a power her father or husband couldn't claim for themselves. And Isabella knew from bitter experience that conmen depended on their targets wanting to believe the lies.

And yet, Emetine did have power, Isabella reminded herself, as she stepped into her bedroom. *There was some truth in what she was saying.*

Prince Reginald looked up from a sheaf of reports. "Welcome back," he said. "I was getting bored."

"You had plenty of reports to read," Isabella said, dryly. The prince had clearly *called* for the reports. By now, everyone would know he'd been in her bedroom. Hopefully, most of them thought she was a man. There was nothing strange about two men sharing a bedroom, if one of them had to vacate his own at short notice. "How are you feeling?"

"I've felt better," Reginald said. He gave her a rueful smile. "I can't believe I was such a fool!"

"You were drugged," Isabella said. She didn't waste her time being sorry for men who got drunk and then ran into trouble, but it wasn't fair to blame a drugged man for what he did while under the influence. Besides, Emetine had been in control. "Did you make sure to drink plenty of water?"

"Yeah," Reginald said. "I ..."

"Don't worry about it," Isabella said. "She had some quite interesting things to say."

She sat down and went through everything, scribbling down notes to herself as she spoke. She'd have to make sure to send Alden a full report – and a request that he dig through the archives for anything that might corroborate Emetine's story. Isabella had never heard of anything like it, but she *did* know that cults and small religious groups were regularly hunted down and destroyed. The official reason was that they practiced human sacrifice – and other crimes against the natural order – yet she couldn't help wondering if there was another reason.

"The Red Monks were destroying temples and killing priests," Reginald said. "I've had quite a few complaints."

"Then we should investigate," Isabella said. She smiled, faintly. "But I'll put Emetine somewhere safe, first."

If I can find such a place, she thought, sourly. *There might not be anywhere safe now.*

Chapter Twenty-Six

"This isn't what I signed up for," someone muttered.

Big Richard nodded in agreement as the queue slowly advanced towards the alleyway. The handful of whores they'd been able to find, when they'd been allowed to leave the camp and enter the city, didn't look very appetising. Their pimps didn't look very decent either, although they'd been smart enough not to start overcharging the mercenaries. A horde of horny – and heavily armed – men weren't going to tolerate being told that prices had doubled or tripled since Prince Reginald had taken the city.

"I haven't been paid in four days," someone else muttered. "When are we going home?"

"And this city is boring," Big Richard muttered himself. Allenstown wasn't Havelock or even Humber. There was very little to do, after dark. "When *are* we getting paid?"

He looked towards the castle, feeling a hot flash of anger. He'd been a mercenary long enough to know that whoever paid for his services called the shots, but what happened when the money wasn't paid? Lord Robin might be willing to wait for his promised lands – and Big Richard had to admit that the mere prospect of owning lands was better than payment in hand – yet there were limits. How long was Lord Robin prepared to wait?

"We have to go home soon or we'll be stuck on this shitty island until spring," another person said. The muttering ran up and down the line of men. "The storms will block our escape."

"We signed up to take the kingdom," a fifth person said. "We *have* taken the kingdom!"

"There's still people who don't acknowledge their new king," someone countered. "They have to be beaten into a bloody pulp before he's secure on his throne."

"Then he should bloody *pay* us to beat them to a pulp," Big

Richard said. "Are we going to hang around here, doing nothing?"

He felt a surge of resentment, frighteningly powerful. He had no qualms about slaughtering peasants or even burning down noble estates, as long as he got paid. And yet, he hadn't even been given the deeds to his lands! Worse, it was starting to look as though most of the southern noblemen were bending the knee to Prince Reginald. They'd get to keep their lands if they switched sides quickly enough. He didn't have to be a beancounter to know what *that* meant. Prince Reginald wouldn't have enough lands and money to parcel out to his supporters.

And the island is piss-poor, he thought. The prospect of an ongoing conflict would have been tempting, if he'd thought the rebels could pay for his services. *There's nothing here worth taking.*

"I wouldn't mind, if there were *women*," someone snapped. "But all we have are ..."

He waved a hand down the line, which was inching slowly forwards. Big Richard nodded in agreement. A woman would be something, at least. But the city's womenfolk were all locked up in their homes, guarded by their men. Prince Reginald had made it clear that anyone who molested any of the women would be hanged. Big Richard appreciated a strong leader – there was nothing worse than a milksop in a position of power – but a smart leader knew to reward the fighters *first*. It wasn't as if the mercenaries were *soldiers*. They could simply walk away ...

No, we can't, he thought. *We can't even get back across the channel without a ship.*

It was a sobering thought. Normally, a mercenary could simply walk away. It was easy to cross the border and take up service with another mercenary band. There was never any shortage of work for mercenaries to do. But here ... they couldn't go anywhere without a ship and crew. Unless, of course, they walked to the Northern Realm. But the North was even poorer than the Summer Isle. There was little prospect of money or women if they offered their services to the Cold King.

The line inched forward again, gradually. Big Richard

ground his teeth in frustration. They were meant to be back at the castle in time for dinner. At this rate he wasn't going to get his shot at the whore before he had to hurry back. He knew better than to be late, even though Lord Robin was spending most of his time with Prince Reginald rather than supervising his men. Alexis or Dolman would turn a blind eye if Big Richard was late, but Mandan would report him. The fool thought he was officer material. He certainly had the asshole act down pat.

He looked down the line, peering into the alleyway. A whore could be seen within the darkness, kneeling in front of one of the men. It looked as though she was working hard ... not that she'd see most of the cash, of course. Big Richard had pimped a few girls in his younger days. The pimp kept most of the money in exchange for protecting the girl from other pimps and the occasional aggressive customer. And there was rarely any shortage of women so desperate that they had no choice but to sell themselves to a pimp.

The sound of cantering hooves echoed through the air. He glanced up, just in time to see Prince Reginald riding past ... escorted by five bodyguards, Lord Robin and Isabella. Big Richard felt a surge of pure hatred as he saw the sorceress, a hatred that almost overwhelmed him. His dagger was halfway out of his belt before he realised what he was doing. Stabbing the wretched sorceress would be satisfying, but Lord Robin would kill him. The poor bastard didn't know he was enchanted ...

Grumbling echoed up and down the line. Big Richard listened, adding his own comments and savouring the discontent. Soldiers and mercenaries always grumbled – and smart leaders knew better than to crack down on it too hard – but this was different. Too many men felt that they'd risked their lives for ... for what? They had neither been paid nor given land.

And if we don't get paid soon, he thought, as he reached the end of the line, *we'll start taking matters into our own hands.*

***

Reginald felt ... he didn't know how he felt. There was no sign of actual danger – no mobs in the streets, no armed men save for his bodyguards – but he felt on edge. He was used to women trying to seduce him, yet ... Emetine had used magic. He'd been putty in her hands and he knew it. She could have done anything to him. He knew that too.

It had been a disconcerting experience, he thought, as the small group cantered into Temple Row. His father hadn't hesitated to remind him, time and time again, that there was always someone better; his trainers had knocked him on his ass, time and time again, just to make it clear that merely being a good swordsman wasn't enough to guarantee victory. He *knew* he wasn't the strongest or the most capable. And yet, Emetine had reached into his head and *twisted*. He'd been at her mercy.

And she could have done that to her husband, he thought, grimly. *Why didn't she?*

The memories tormented him. There was a part of him that had wanted her – that *still* wanted her, despite what she'd tried to do. He told that part of himself, firmly, to shut up, but it refused to listen. Isabella had assured him that he wasn't enchanted, yet it was impossible to be *sure*. The Red Monks had magic, but it wasn't *her* magic. Reginald *wanted* to believe that Isabella had missed something. It was better than believing he was too weak to throw off Emetine's influence.

He swung himself off the horse and dropped to the ground. Temple Row had once been a thriving street, lined with a dozen temples. Now, all but one of the buildings were nothing more than piles of debris. Knocking down temples was blasphemy – all the gods were real, including the ones he didn't worship – yet the Red Monks hadn't hesitated. Their building – a brooding grey monstrosity at the edge of the street – was all that remained. Even the statues had been torn down and destroyed.

"They tore it all down," Isabella said, jumping down beside him. "All of it. They even killed the priests."

Reginald sucked in his breath, genuinely shocked. Priests weren't *entirely* immune to the fortunes of war – he'd known some priests who'd donned armour and fought in wars – but killing them deliberately was frowned upon. The gods they'd served would take a dim view of their priests being slaughtered. And yet, the Red Monks had killed every last priest in the city. They'd imposed themselves on an entire community.

"And then what?" His eyes flicked to the grey building, waiting for him. "What happened to them?"

"They vanished," Isabella said. Her voice was icy cold. "They ... just left."

Lord Robin stayed on his horse. "When did they leave?"

"If the reports are to be believed, they left a few hours before the army reached Allenstown," Isabella said. "But it might have been earlier."

Reginald nodded, shortly. Commoners rarely needed to tell the time precisely. Even when they did, they normally depended on sundials rather than mechanical watches. It was extremely rare for a commoner – even a wealthy merchant – to wear a watch. And that meant there was no way to be sure *precisely* when the Red Monks had left.

He turned to gaze upon the city. The Red Monks might not have gone very far. Allenstown was smaller than Havelock, but there were still plenty of hiding places. A careful man could easily find a place to hide, a place that wouldn't be uncovered unless the searchers got very lucky. Methodically searching the entire city would take months. It was possible, he supposed, that he could make the population's lives so uncomfortable that they'd reveal any known hiding places, but that might also push them into open rebellion. Too many weapons were unaccounted for ...

And the Red Monks have strange powers, he reminded himself. *A magician can hide himself in plain sight. Why can't they?*

"We need to figure out what they are," he said. Emetine had talked freely, but he had no way to tell how much of what she'd said was true and how much was utter nonsense. He would have believed it was *all* nonsense if he hadn't tasted her power. "After they knocked down the temples, what did they do?"

"Nothing, apparently," Isabella said. "They didn't even force people to worship at their altars."

Reginald stroked his chin. It made no sense. He could understand why fanatics would want people to worship their god – and their god alone – even though it was forbidden. The Golden City had always insisted on religious toleration, permitting any religion as long as the religion's leaders and followers behaved themselves. And yet, free of the Golden City's power, the Red Monks *hadn't* imposed themselves on the population. They hadn't ordered people into their temples on pain of death. They'd merely smashed every other temple in the city.

He looked up at the darkening sky. It looked like rain, again. He'd been warned about the rain, but ... but he hadn't believed what he'd been told. It was summer, yet it felt as though they were heading straight into autumn. And there was something prickly in the wind, as if a thunderstorm was about to form. The roiling grey skies promised a deluge.

"They could be anywhere," he mused. He held the capital – and dozens of noblemen had bent the knee to him – but he knew he had yet to stamp his authority on the island. "Did you manage to get any idea of where they came from?"

"Nothing specific," Isabella said. "The Red Monks made contact with Emetine, somehow. I think they must have a base somewhere in the Hereford Lands."

Reginald wasn't so sure. The Summer Isle's women might be restricted, and only allowed to move under heavy escort, but the Red Monks had no such limits. It would be easy for one of them to make his way into Emetine's boudoir and preach to her ... or, perhaps, convert one of her ladies-in-waiting and rely on *her* to preach. Reginald had already ordered Emetine's women sent out of the city, just in case they were dangerous. They'd be held at Racal's Bay until matters had been settled.

And I want to believe she is nothing more than a pawn, he thought, grimly. *I want to believe that she's blameless ...*

He could feel the thought nagging at him, the cool suggestion that Emetine wasn't responsible for her own actions. How *could* she be blamed for following her brother's orders? If, of course, her brother *had* given the orders. Reginald found it hard to believe that *any* brother would issue such orders – *he* certainly wouldn't – but Havant Hereford had to be desperate. His army had been smashed and he'd been driven north. It wouldn't be long before his enemies started to circle, like vultures surrounding a dead body. Reginald privately hoped that Earl Goldenrod would take advantage of the chance to rid himself of the Herefords once and for all. It would certainly make Reginald's march north a great deal easier.

Isabella cleared her throat. "I'll take a look inside the temple," she said. "You stay here."

Reginald frowned, but nodded slowly. He wasn't *used* to sending women into danger. And yet ... Isabella's words ran through his mind. He *had* put women – countless women – in dreadful danger, no matter what orders he gave. A girl who'd been raped by one of his men might be too frightened to file a complaint. Why should she expect him to take her side? She didn't *know* him.

He watched, one hand resting on his sword, as Isabella walked slowly up to the temple, checking everything before stepping through the door. Sweat dripped down his back as he waited, wondering just how long they should wait before going after her. Lord Robin didn't seem *quite* so worried about his sorceress, but even *he* started to look concerned as the minutes slowly ticked by. It felt like hours had passed before Isabella finally re-emerged from the temple. Her face was very pale.

"It's like the other one," she said, studying a notebook in her hand. "I could feel it trying to pluck at my memories as I left."

Reginald cursed as the implications sank in. "Someone could have gone into the temple and done ... done *something*, then forgotten it as they left."

"I think so," Isabella agreed. "And if I hadn't taken notes, I would have forgotten everything too."

"Post a guard," Reginald ordered, looking at Lord Robin. "The temple is to be completely sealed off, at least until we can figure out how to destroy it safely. If worse comes to worst, we'll build a wall around it permanently."

He clambered back onto his horse, then cantered off down the street. Isabella followed, her horse neighing as it caught up with his. She rode like a man, he noted; she didn't seem to care to ride side-saddle. But then, she wasn't wearing a dress either. There was no reason she *had* to ride like a woman at court. He couldn't help being reminded of his sister. Ruby had flatly refused to wear dresses when riding, despite blandishments from her governess and threats from her father. There had been something about her determination that had been almost admirable.

"We cleaned out your room," Isabella said, as they rode onwards. "You can sleep there again, I think."

Reginald shrugged. It would be a long time before he felt safe in that room, even if he had a sword by his bed, a dagger under the pillow and a couple of guards sleeping at the foot of the bed. Emetine had enchanted his bodyguards, somehow. None of them remembered anything from the moment they'd taken up their posts to the moment they'd discovered that the door had been smashed to splinters. Isabella had cast dozens of wards, tying them all together into a complicated spider-web, but she'd been brutally honest. There was no longer any way to guarantee his safety.

Not that there ever was, Reginald thought. When he'd been a child, the Court Wizard had been a brooding presence in the background, the true power behind the throne. His magic tricks could easily have turned nasty, if the king had defied the Grand Sorcerer. And he hadn't been the only threat. There were no shortages of factions that had wanted – that still wanted – to kidnap or kill the king's son. *All I can do is watch my back.*

Thunder rolled, high overhead. A moment later, rain started to splatter down. Reginald glanced up, then spurred the horse onwards as the streets rapidly emptied. The rainfall grew stronger, water dripping down his helmet and pouring into his armour. He looked up at the clouds, tasting the water as it fell. It tasted pure. And yet ...

His eyes narrowed. Was that a *face* in the clouds?

Reginald blinked. The face was gone.

He shook his head. It couldn't have been real. He was imagining things. It was hardly the first time he'd seen shapes in the clouds. And yet, there had been something about the face that lingered in his mind. It was hard to believe, no matter how hard he tried, that it was truly imaginary.

The sooner we resume the war, the better, he thought, as

they cantered through the gatehouse and into the castle. A page took the reins of his horse, allowing Reginald to hurry into the building itself. The thunder followed him, shaking the building. *We're going to go mad here.*

Chapter Twenty-Seven

Isabella opened her eyes as the last of the wards dropped into place, surrounding the council chamber. King Edwin hadn't seemed to be too concerned about protecting his discussions from magical surveillance, let alone attacks, but there had been nothing he could do to keep magicians from spying on him anyway. Even basic protections had been neglected since the Court Wizard had been summoned to the Golden City. The man had never returned.

And we'll just have to hope the protections actually work, she thought, as Prince Reginald's council of war started to file into the chamber. *Who knows if they'll keep the Red Monks out?*

She gritted her teeth. A number of councillors had made snide remarks, questioning her value as a magician if she couldn't fight the Red Monks. Prince Reginald and Lord Robin had defended her, but the hell of it was that the doubters had a point. She knew how to analyse spells and devise countermeasures, yet whatever the Red Monks used was beyond her understanding. She'd hoped they'd somehow found a way to deceive her spells – there was no shortage of tricks devised to conceal how a spell actually worked – but none of her attempts to break their magic down to bedrock had produced anything. It was something completely outside her experience.

Female magic, she said, Isabella thought, as she took a seat next to Lord Robin. *But what does that mean?*

She leaned back in her chair and forced herself to relax. She'd sent letters – detailed letters – to Alden, but she was grimly aware that it would take months for them to reach the Golden City. She wasn't even sure if her brother was still in Havelock. Alden probably wouldn't have stuck around, not with so many other problems demanding his attention. And there was no way to guarantee he'd even *get* the letters. The days when the mail coach was inviolate were long gone.

The council rose as Prince Reginald stepped into the chamber. He looked more confident, Isabella noted, but there was something oddly brittle about his demeanour. It wasn't entirely unexpected, yet ... she winced, inwardly. There were quite a few men who needed to be taken down a peg or two – she'd done it herself, simply by showing them what magic could do – but Prince Reginald wasn't one of them. He was a decent sort, for a prince. He'd grow into a fine king.

She wondered, grimly, just how many of his councillors had noticed. Men were generally less emotionally perceptive than women, but most of the councillors depended on Prince Reginald for their power and positions. Reading his emotions would be a survival skill for many of them, even the ones who were reliant on the king instead. Prince Reginald could easily kill one of his father's spies and swear blind it was an accident, with his household backing him up. The king probably wouldn't ask too many questions. He certainly wouldn't be *that* concerned about someone he'd already deemed expendable.

He'll just have to assert himself, she thought. Prince Reginald was mature enough to realise that some people were just stronger, physically or magically, than others. Being overwhelmed by a woman had been humiliating – men were less sore about losing to other men – but he'd just have to get over it. *And besides, hardly anyone knows the truth.*

Prince Reginald sat. "Be seated," he said. "We have much to discuss."

He nodded to Caen, who unfurled a map and placed it on the table. Isabella studied it carefully, reminding herself – once again – that the local mapmakers hadn't bothered to aim for accuracy. They had the shape of the island correct, she thought, but the land looked oddly stretched. It looked as though one could walk from Racal's Bay to Allenstown, while the distance between Allenstown and Georgetown was incomprehensibly vast. *And* a number of mountain ranges were missing.

At least we have a rough idea where everyone is, she told herself. A number of noble estates had been marked in green ink. *And we know better than to take the map for granted.*

"Before we begin," Prince Reginald said, "is there anything we need to consider?"

Gars leaned forward. "Your Highness," he said. "There has been grumbling amongst the troops."

"Indeed there has," Lord Robin agreed. "I've heard a number of complaints about payment."

Prince Reginald scowled. "The majority of the payment is due upon discharge," he said, stiffly. "The campaign is not yet over."

Isabella winced. She understood the prince's reasoning – it was better to owe money, knowing the mercenaries would stick around long enough to collect their pay – but she also understood how her comrades felt. They'd want solid proof that the prince intended to pay them, sooner or later. And if they were starting to think that the campaign was already over ...

"It isn't just payment," Gars said. "It's the shortage of entertainment. And the weather."

"There isn't much we can do about the weather," Prince Reginald said. "And what sort of entertainment are they expecting?"

"Wine, women and song," Lord Robin said. "Right now, a good four-fifths of our men are in the camps. That isn't conductive to morale."

Isabella winced. She'd never liked the camps either. Normally, war leaders were smart enough to put on entertainment for the troops – alcohol and brothels, in particular – but Allenstown didn't have much in the way of either. The alcohol had been poured away when the city was occupied. Prince Reginald hadn't wanted his troops to get drunk and ransack the place. And there was nothing to be gained, anyway, by sacking Allenstown.

Prince Reginald lifted his eyebrows. "Would you advise me to hand out some of the captured gold? Or tell the troops that they can loot, rape and kill at will?"

"No," Lord Robin said. "I would advise you to pay them an advance on their wages."

The two men stared at each other for a long moment. Isabella felt a flicker of sympathy for both of them. A down payment wouldn't satisfy everyone, but it might put a curb on the grumbling for a few weeks. More money meant more entertainment ... at least until the money was spent or simply gambled away. She had no doubt that the army's card sharps were already licking their lips in anticipation. She'd once lost half a month's pay because she'd been too stubborn to realise that her opponent had slanted the odds in his favour.

"It will be done," Prince Reginald said, finally. His eyes swept the table. "Are there any other issues of importance?"

There was a pause. No one spoke.

"Very well." Prince Reginald pointed to the map. "As you can see, I have received submission and homage from nearly all of the southern lords, including Earl Oxley. A handful have refused to submit. Accordingly, their lands will be confiscated and parcelled out."

Isabella kept her thoughts to herself. The owners – the *former* owners – would be driven into rebellion, but there would be little hope of recovering their lands even if Prince Reginald was driven out of the Summer Isle. Their peasants would hardly fight for the masters, not when there was nothing to gain by risking their lives. It wasn't as if anything would change for *them*. And the *new* owners would have every incentive to support the prince until they put down roots.

"It isn't enough," Caen said. "Your Highness ..."

"I know," Prince Reginald said, cutting him off. His hand drew a line on the map. "We have received fewer submissions from the midlands – and none whatsoever from the north. Earl Goldenrod has ignored my summons, as has Earl Hereford ... the *new* Earl Hereford. *He* has good reason not to show his face" – he smiled, rather cruelly – "but Earl Goldenrod has no excuse. And nor do any of the northern noblemen. *Their* lands will be confiscated too."

You didn't give them much time, Isabella thought. *He's not going to give up his lands without a fight.*

She winced, inwardly. It was an old trick, one that the Golden City had banned centuries ago. A man could be punished for refusing a summons from his overlord, but he had to be given a reasonable chance to make the deadline. Earl Goldenrod might not even have *heard* the summons before time ran out. She scowled as she remembered one of her father's nastier tricks. Ban or no ban, he'd done the same to some of his clients. No one had dared report him to the Grand Sorcerer. He had been too powerful to challenge openly.

"Accordingly, we will be marching north within the week," Prince Reginald continued, calmly. "We'll mass our supplies here, then advance north to Rupert. There are a number of noblemen who haven't submitted there, so we'll deal with them while preparing to leapfrog forward again. We don't know what happened to the remainder of the usurper's army, so we'll be sure to leave strong garrisons here and at Racal's Bay. It would be very embarrassing if we were to lose either of the cities while we were on the march."

A chuckle ran around the room. It *would* be embarrassing. It was difficult, perhaps impossible, to force a confrontation in open countryside unless both sides chose to offer battle. The side that wanted to evade could almost always find options, unless they were trapped against a river or otherwise pinned in place. But Allenstown would be sure to lure the enemy like a magnet. And so would Racal's Bay.

Racal's Bay might even be more *important*, she thought, as she studied the map. *It's the place we land our supplies. We'd have to live off the land if we lost access to the sea.*

She wondered, sourly, just what the previous kings had been *thinking*. Racal's Bay and Georgetown were the only two cities with access to the sea, even though there were plenty of towns and villages that could have been upgraded into full-scale ports. Hell, there were hundreds of fishing communities along the coastline. But easier access to international trade would have brought problems as well as opportunities, she supposed. Serfs might hear radical ideas such as fair wages, free trade and an end to the nobility, and grow restless. The Summer Isle apparently had a long history of brutal peasant rebellions, often put down with even greater brutality. Contact with the outside world might make matters worse.

But only for the former rulers, she thought. *Prince Reginald will have to change that if he wants to turn the island into a prosperous colony.*

"Obviously, we will have to adapt our tactics to the situation," Prince Reginald informed the council. "Does anyone have any comments?"

Lord William raised a hand. "Your Highness ... is it truly wise to push the earls into open revolt?"

Prince Reginald tilted his head. "I'm not going to allow them to defy me," he said, curtly. "I will *not* become another King Edwin."

"Yes, Your Highness," Lord William said. "But they did not have time to respond to your message."

"They had enough time," Prince Reginald growled.

It was a lie, Isabella knew. And the others knew it too. How could they not?

"We could also offer decent terms to the Herefords," Lord William persisted. He tapped the map. "Your Highness, a long campaign into their lands risks everything."

He had a point, Isabella conceded. But she could also see Prince Reginald's point. On the one hand, he needed to punish the Herefords for ignoring King Romulus's claim to the Summer Isle; on the other, he needed confiscated lands to reward his followers. Setting an impossible deadline for Earl Goldenrod was little more than a transparent attempt to forge an excuse to confiscate his lands. And, oddly enough, it might even convince people outside the Summer Isle. *They* wouldn't understand how bad the roads were between Allenstown and the Goldenrod Lands.

"There are no terms that can be offered to usurpers," Prince Reginald said. "Havant Hereford has been declared outlaw. The man who brings me his head will be richly rewarded."

And you can marry his sister off to a man of your choice, Isabella thought, coldly. She doubted it was a good idea, but she could see the logic. The only problem would be keeping the wretched woman under control. She didn't think that was possible. The Red Monks might be able to interfere with a slave collar or a compulsion spell. *Or you could execute her and then divide up the lands between your supporters.*

"He could be sent into exile," Lord William said.

"As long as he is alive, he is a threat," Prince Reginald snapped. "Or do you think that my father's enemies won't hesitate to use him against us?"

Just like your father armed King Edwin and sent him back to cause trouble, Isabella thought, wryly. *You're afraid of someone else doing it to you.*

"And there is an unknown magic here," Lord William said. "Surely, we should be careful."

"We also cannot afford to sit here and *wait*," Prince Reginald said. His voice dripped contempt. "Or do you think we can campaign in winter?"

He looked around the table. "I want the supplies brought up from Racal's Bay as fast as possible, followed by a redeployment for a hasty march north to Rupert. The troops will be given a down payment, which they can try and spend in the next two days. After that ... we'll be on our way."

Isabella nodded slowly to herself. She understood the prince's logic – *and* his need to keep the army occupied. Grumbling could easily turn into mutiny, if the officers failed to keep it under control. An army of mercenaries that didn't have an obvious threat to fight – or an objective to reach – was one that could turn sour very quickly. And yet, with an unknown threat in the countryside, she wasn't sure that going forward was the right idea.

And I listened to everything Kingsley had to say, she thought. Even after some proper food – and rest in a proper bed – Kingsley's stories had ranged from odd to unbelievable. *I just don't know how much of it was real.*

"Lady Isabella, please remain behind," Reginald said. "Everyone else ... dismissed."

Isabella studied the prince as the room rapidly emptied, leaving them alone. He looked ... tired, but enthused. The prospect of action was doing him good, even if it was likely to turn into a brutal slog into Earl Goldenrod's lands. He was right about moving quickly, no matter what Lord William said. The autumn rains – not to be confused with the summer rains – and winter snows would put an end to campaigning before spring. And the gods alone knew how much mischief the Red Monks could produce if they were left alone.

"You'll be accompanying the army," Reginald said. "We'll do everything in our power to capture one of the Red Monks."

"Understood," Isabella said. "I'd also like to question the

villagers as we head north."

"And see what they have to tell us," Reginald said. "Will they tell us anything?"

Isabella shrugged. Villagers rarely talked to strangers, particularly strangers in the vanguard of an invading army. But she had ways of making people talk. A couple of spells could loosen lips ... and if the villagers proved resistant, she'd know she was on the right track. She just wished she had another sorcerer to back her up. Even her *father* would have been more than welcome.

He'd probably be trying to take over the army, she thought, wryly. *Or bossing everyone around.*

She pushed the thought to one side. "We'll get to the bottom of this, somehow," she said, although she was starting to feel more than a little frustrated. She understood the laws of magic, but the Red Monks seemed to defy them. The idea that there might be things out there that were beyond her comprehension was irritating as hell. "I trust you slept well over the last few days?"

Reginald looked ... haunted, just for a moment. "Well enough," he said. "Thank you for your help."

"You're more than welcome," Isabella said. Keeping the prince alive was important. The army would shatter without him. "Just remember what I said about Emetine."

The prince sighed. "You understand the logic," he said. "I need to keep her alive."

"Perhaps." Isabella rolled her eyes in a manner that she knew was strikingly childish. "Or perhaps there's more to gain by simply executing her."

"She's a bargaining chip, right now," Reginald countered. His voice was firm. "We cannot simply throw her away, not as long as her brother is alive."

Isabella snorted. "I feel sorry for whoever you marry her off to."

"Me too," Reginald said. "But I do have a use for her."

"As long as she doesn't put a knife in your back," Isabella said. She wasn't sure why she was surprised. Noblemen had always been reluctant to kill other noblemen – and noblewomen were almost always spared the noose. It simply wasn't done. But it was also hypocritical as hell. She had no idea how many men and women had been killed in the wars, over the last five years, but she was sure it was in the millions. "Watch yourself."

"You too," Reginald said. "You too."

He gave her an odd little smile. It made her wonder, suddenly, if he might be attracted to her. It was an odd thought – it wasn't as if she was the picture of a noblewoman – but ... she shook her head, dismissing the thought. Reginald was nice to look at, she supposed, yet ... they were from very different worlds. He wouldn't like the idea of a wife who had more power than him. Emetine had shaken him badly ...

And you're too tired for your own good, she told herself, as she headed for the door. *You're thinking nonsense.*

Chapter Twenty-Eight

"I'm surprised you joined us, Your Majesty," Captain Floras said. His white teeth gleamed in the darkness. "I thought you'd be busy with your wife."

Havant shrugged. The risks of joining the raid were immense, particularly as his brother was dead and Emetine was a prisoner. There were no successors waiting in the wings – except, perhaps, Earl Goldenrod – if Havant was felled by a lucky blow. But it was important, now more than ever, that he proved himself willing to share the risks. His men knew he'd been weakened. He couldn't let them think he'd lost his nerve.

"It has to be done," he said. Riding cross-country had been dangerous, but it had also been exhilarating. He'd enjoyed it even though he knew that danger lurked at the end of the ride. "Are we ready?"

Floras waved to the small collection of horsemen waiting in the clearing, a short distance from the road. "We're ready," he said, once he'd handed out the flamers. "We can go on your command."

Havant smiled. "Go."

He spurred his horse down towards the roadside, cursing the enemy army under his breath as the beast picked its way through the mud. The enemy probably hadn't *intended* to tear the road to shreds, but the passage of ten thousand men – or thereabouts – had done a *lot* of damage. Paving stones, already weakened by years of neglect, had been pushed out of place, allowing the rain to soak into the foundations. Men might be able to move down the road at a healthy clip, but parts of it were almost impassable to carts and horses. Given time, it might slow the enemy reinforcements down to a trickle *without* his troops ...

Too much to hope for, he thought, as the small force picked up speed. *And besides, we have to show that we can still fight back.*

He glanced upwards, hoping and praying for fog. The enemy would outnumber them, probably. Speed and surprise were their only advantages and neither one was likely to last very long. Nor was the road, he supposed. But then, it wouldn't be long before Prince Reginald started forcing the local peasants to leave their fields and start repairing the road. The peasants – worthless bastards to a man – would do as little as possible, but their work might last long enough to let Reginald bring his supplies to Allenstown.

The enemy camp came into view in the moonlight, pitched by the side of the road. It was larger than Havant had expected: several dozen carts, a handful of tents and a number of horses tied to wooden stakes, either grazing or sleeping. Havant clutched his flamer in one hand as the force picked up speed, charging right towards the enemy camp. A pair of sentinels shouted the alarm, but it was already too late. Havant and his men were upon them.

"Fire," Flores shouted.

Havant picked a target – a cluster of carts – and threw the flamer as hard as he could. It struck the nearest cart and burst into flames, which spread rapidly from cart to cart. Night turned to day as more flamers were hurled into tents, one even striking the horses. Havant felt a flicker of regret – horses were valuable in a way peasants were not – which was lost in the exultation of a successful attack. The presence within him thrilled with excitement and glee as the unbelievers ran in all directions, some screaming helplessly as they burned to death. Hark had delivered more than he'd promised, Havant thought, as he ducked a wild sword-swing from one of the handful of survivors. It looked as though every cart – and the supplies they carried – was burning brightly.

"Move," Flores shouted. "Move now!"

Havant wanted to rebel. He *wanted* to turn around and slaughter the remaining enemy soldiers, even though he knew it was pointless. There was nothing to be gained by giving the enemy the chance to turn defeat into victory. The enemy commander – or whoever had assumed command – would be in deep shit, when he reported to Prince Reginald. He'd do everything in his power to score a victory he could use to save himself from a well-deserved execution.

Should have had more pickets out, you idiot, Havant thought. The enemy army was supposed to be experienced, but whoever had been in command behind him was an ignorant fool. *Did you think the island was under your boot?*

He laughed, despite himself, as they hurtled into the darkness. The light behind him was growing brighter, driving the darkness away. Hark had promised that the flamers would burn until every last drop of blessed oil was gone, no matter what the enemy did. As long as a mere splash had landed on a wooden cart, that cart was doomed. It was just a shame they could only produce a little of the oil.

The horses ran faster as they went off the road, climbing up the embankment and slowing as they plunged into the dark forest. Havant glanced behind him, listening for the sound of pursuit, but there was nothing. It was tempting to believe that the enemy had all been consumed by the flames, although he knew it was unlikely. They were probably trying to put out the fires before it was too late – an impossible goal – or simply trying to think of a story they could tell Prince Reginald. Havant wondered, idly, how many men the enemy commander would claim to have killed. He'd need to have killed a small army to save his neck from the block.

"We did it," Flores said, as he brought his horse up beside Havant. "We did it!"

Havant nodded. Flores was the closest thing he had to a friend. He hadn't been encouraged to get close to anyone – his father had snapped and snarled at anyone who spoke to his sons – but Flores had somehow ignored the older man's bloodcurdling threats. It was almost a shame that there was a new barrier between them, one that no amount of comradeship could dispel. Havant ... was king or nothing. Flores was just a common nobleman.

"Excellent work," he said, allowing his voice to carry through the gloom. He *had* to show that Flores had his trust. The men needed to understand that their leader was held high in their king's esteem. "Your plan worked perfectly."

Flores bowed his head. "I thank you," he said. "And we're heading straight for the rendezvous point now. After that, we'll start looking for more targets."

Havant nodded. Prince Reginald would find out about the attack within two days, perhaps less. It was impossible to be sure. Havant had taken care to scatter a handful of pickets on both sides of the enemy camp, hoping to intercept a fleeing horseman, but he was too experienced a soldier to be *certain* they'd keep word from reaching Allenstown. Prince Reginald *would* find out. And then ... he'd have no choice, but to double and redouble the escorts. *That* alone would make it harder for him to push northwards.

And they're planning to head straight for us, he thought, grimly. *We have to keep them off-balance until winter arrives.*

Silence fell as they moved further and further into the forest. The men stopped talking and glanced around nervously, hands falling to their weapons as they saw *things* moving in the shadows. Havant felt nothing, not even a hint of concern. The forest was sinister – almost alien – but he knew, on some level, that it wouldn't hurt him. It was almost *part* of him.

The camp loomed out of nowhere, a small collection of tents buried deep within the forest. A Red Monk stood at the end, bowing deeply to Havant as he passed. Some of the soldiers stared at the monk in awe, others looked away in fear. Havant felt a flicker of disgust for the latter, a flicker that seemed to come from somewhere far outside his mind. There would be no room in the new world for those who refused to open their hearts to him ...

Hark was standing in front of him. Havant blinked in surprise, realising – slowly – that he'd blanked out again. It was hard, so hard, to remember anything after they'd entered the forest ... where was his horse? When had he dismounted? What had happened? But it didn't bother him, either. Slowly, he forgot that it had even happened.

"Your Majesty," Hark said. "All is prepared."

Havant glanced around the campsite, making sure that the pickets were in place and a handful of soldiers were ready to defend the camp while their comrades slept, then followed Hark out of the campsite and down a grassy path. It felt eerie, almost as if he were in a dream. Strange shapes moved overhead, gliding through the night; he looked up, but his eyes refused to focus on them. The moon was larger, somehow. Its pale radiance seemed to belong to another world.

It was quiet, so quiet. Havant could hear nothing, not even his own breathing. *Things* flickered through the trees, then vanished again; he welcomed their presence, even as he feared them. *They are part of the natural order*, something seemed to whisper. This was how the world was meant to be. The moonlight grew brighter, driving back the shadows and illuminating a giant clearing. Strange ruins stood at the edges, remnants of a building long since lost to the ages. A single altar stood in the exact centre, glowing with a faint unearthly light. It called to Havant, welcoming him ...

His limbs moved forward, practically of their own accord. He was a passenger in his own body, watching helplessly as someone else took control. It should have panicked him, but it felt ... it felt normal. He strode up to the altar and stood, waiting. The world seemed to grow even quieter, as if it were holding its breath. It was waiting for something to happen.

A girl stepped out of the forest and walked towards him, removing her white dress as she moved. Another followed, and another ... they were young and old, their bodies shining white under the moonlight. A faint sound echoed through the air ... it took him a moment to realise that they were singing, singing so softly that he could barely make out the words. He certainly couldn't *understand* them. But the presence within him understood. He could feel anticipation flowing through his mind as the girls climbed onto the altar and lay down.

Havant felt his body move forward and touch the altar. Power rose up – or down – into him, directed by ... by something. His mind expanded, as if his body was suddenly too small to contain his thoughts. He was suddenly very – very – aware of the young women, aware of every last cell in their bodies, aware ... aware of the power flowing through them. They were connected, connected to the land, connected to the sky ... great thoughts sang through the air, welcoming him. It was suddenly so easy to just reach out and touch the world ...

His eyes snapped open. He was kneeling in front of the altar, tired and drained. He'd blanked out, again. And yet ... he fought to recover his memories. Something had happened, but what? He forced himself to his feet and looked at the altar. It was covered in dust and ashes. The girls ... the girls were gone. His instincts warned him not to even *think* of touching the altar.

He turned, slowly. Hark was standing behind him, his face hidden behind his cowl. And yet ... Havant could *see* him. Hark was ... Hark was ... he looked away, quickly. There was something about him that was very far from human. It was ... it was ...

"It is done," Hark said. "The first Great Working in centuries."

Havant forced himself to remain standing. The world ... the world had changed. It was dark, yet he could see ... *things*. Flashes of light darted through the trees, blurring together into something else. It wasn't magic, he knew, although he wasn't sure *how* he knew. It was something else, something more fundamental ... something more *right*. The presence within him seemed to grow stronger, the more he looked around with his new awareness. He carried a seed within him ...

The thought should have worried him. But it didn't.

He managed, somehow, to speak. "What happened?"

"You performed a Great Working," Hark said, calmly. He turned and walked back towards the path. "And now the land itself will serve Our Lord."

Havant followed him, somehow. His legs felt odd, as if they weren't really *his*. He had to look down to convince himself that he still *had* his legs. The dream had faded, but ... but it had been replaced by something else. Everywhere he looked, he could see ... *things* ... *creatures* ... right at the edge of his awareness. It felt as though he'd been blind all his life, yet now he could see. A whole new world was opening up in front of him.

The path was straight. The path was twisted. It made no sense, yet ... it was natural and right. They were outside the camp. They were inside the camp ... he found himself entering his tent with no clear memory of how he'd passed through the perimeter. The guards would have to be whipped for letting him through ... no, somehow he knew the guards hadn't had a hope of seeing him. He'd been walking the path.

A great tiredness overcame him. He lay down on the blanket – even for a king, there was no bed – and closed his eyes. And he dreamed ... storms were moving, spreading over the waters. He could *hear* the winds howling, *feel* the waves as they lashed against the shores, forcing fishermen to flee to the nearest harbour. The storms were growing stronger and stronger, driven by ... driven by the forces he'd awakened. There were *faces* moving within the storm ...

He jerked awake again, one hand grabbing for his dagger. Flores was standing by the side of his bed, looking down at him worriedly. Havant felt a hot flash of rage, mingled with an odd unconcern that puzzled him. Flores could have cut his throat ... no, somehow he was sure that Flores could *not* have cut his throat. Death wouldn't touch him as long as he opened himself to his lord.

"You were crying out, Your Majesty," Flores said. "Are you alright?"

Havant glanced at the flap. It was light outside ... midmorning, by his estimate. He rubbed his forehead as he sat upright, realising – grimly – that his body was caked in sweat. He'd been dreaming ... everything had a lucid dreamlike quality, leaving him wondering – helplessly – how much of it had been real. The presence was sleeping. And yet ...

"It was just too much cheese," he said, slowly. Something told him not to tell Flores the truth – or anything resembling the truth. "I ate too much before we set out on the raid."

He stood on wobbly legs. "Did they try to find us?"

"Not as far as we can tell," Flores said. He still looked worried. "We *are* pretty deep within the forest."

No one will find us here, Havant thought. He wasn't sure if it was *his* thought or something from the presence. *The forest itself will protect us.*

He stripped off his shirt. There was no way he could have a proper bath, but he could wash himself. And yet ...

Flores lifted an eyebrow. "When did you get tattooed?"

Havant looked down at himself. His chest was covered in blue tattoos. They were a strange series of circles and lines, drawn together into a cat's cradle that made no sense, yet felt natural and right. He had no memory of getting them ...

"It's something my brother and I devised," he lied. He walked over to the bucket and splashed cold water on his face. "Are you ready to take the offensive?"

"We'll start heading out again at nightfall," Flores said. "How about yourself?"

"I'll head back to the main camp," Havant said. Flores could handle the raiding, at least until Prince Reginald brought in enough troops to shut the whole operation down. "I have a feeling I'm going to be needed there."

"Very good, Your Majesty," Flores said. "We'll keep in touch through the Red Monks."

"Make sure you snipe at Racal's Bay," Havant added. "And feel free to snipe at any passing troops too."

He'd be surprised if Flores actually managed to *take* the city, but riding past and harassing the defenders would remind Prince Reginald that he actually had to *defend* it. Forcing him to tie down a thousand or so men several days from Allenstown would be worth it, even if it meant there was no hope of recapturing Racal's Bay. But then, the city could be recovered after Prince Reginald had been forced to surrender. There was no point in wasting men and time taking a city when it wouldn't need anything like as much effort to neutralise it.

"Of course," Flores said. They shared a vicious grin. "We can't have them getting too comfortable."

Havant finished washing, pulled on a new shirt and strode out of the tent. A dozen men were kneeling in front of a Red Monk, muttering prayers in a strange language; others were sharpening their weapons or patrolling the edge of the campsite. Flores followed him, noting the names of a handful of men who'd performed well. Havant felt almost normal again. In the bright sunlight, everything that had happened felt like a dream ...

But he could still see *things* in the shadows ...

And, in the distance, he could *sense* the thunder.

Chapter Twenty-Nine

"What the hell happened?"

Reginald glared down at the report, then up at the hapless messenger. "What the hell happened?"

The messenger looked as though he was about to faint. Reginald would have felt sorry for him, if the army hadn't been heading north for the last two days. Five thousand men – on foot and on horseback – spread out over a wide area, flanked by pickets watching for signs of enemy activity. Everything had been going so well, too. A handful of towns had surrendered, the moment his forces had arrived; a number of local dignitaries had bent the knee as soon as they realised their former patrons could no longer protect them. Reginald had been on the verge of breaking camp and heading further north when the messenger caught up with him.

"A convoy was attacked, Your Highness," the messenger whispered. "Did you not get word?"

Reginald shook his head, impatiently. "Details?"

"I was sent back to Racal's Bay," the messenger said. "And then I was ordered to ride to Allenstown and find you. Didn't you hear from the other messenger?"

"No," Reginald said. He gritted his teeth. If the messenger had had to go the long way around, his report was at least six days out of date. Perhaps longer. "What happened to the convoy?"

"It was destroyed, Your Highness," the messenger told him. "And ... and ... Your Highness ..."

"Spit it out," Reginald snapped. He was *not* about to kill the messenger. "What happened?"

"Storms in the channel," the messenger said. "Shipping has been curtailed."

Reginald swore. The weather was dangerously unpredictable, but he'd been assured it would be at least a month before the autumn storms *really* began. If they'd started now ... he forced himself to think, hard. He'd brought a vast amount of supplies with him, when he'd landed on the Summer Isle, and more had been shipped over since, but if they could no longer sail between the island and Andalusia ...

"I see," he said, finally.

He cursed under his breath. The absence of the *other* messenger was telling too, in its own way. The man must have met a violent end somewhere between Racal's Bay and Allenstown. It was possible, he supposed, that some of the villagers had killed him, but he doubted they could be that lucky. No, there was an enemy force operating somewhere in his rear. And that meant that all of his plans had been based on a false premise.

They can't fight us directly, so they hit our supply lines, he thought. If nothing else, future convoys would have to be given heavier escorts, sapping his deployable forces. *And that will make it harder for us to stay on the offensive.*

The messenger cleared his throat. "Would you like me to take a message back to Allenstown, Your Highness?"

"Not yet," Reginald said. He pointed to the mess tent. "Grab yourself something to eat, then wait. I'll have a message for you later."

He watched the messenger scurry off, then waved to Gars and Jones. The two men hurried over to join him. Neither of them looked very confident, he noted sourly. By now, rumours were probably already starting to spread through the camp. The messenger would keep his mouth shut, Reginald was sure, but it wouldn't matter. An announcement would have to be made before the army came to believe that the enemy had moved in behind them and recaptured Allenstown.

"We have a problem," he said, stiffly. He ran through the details, such as they were. "What does this mean for us?"

"In the short run, nothing," Gars said. "We weren't planning to resupply the army any time soon."

"Yes, but we do need supplies," Jones countered. "The Summer Isle is short on food."

Reginald nodded, curtly. The serfs weren't very efficient farmers. He'd bet half his estates that the peasants hid at least *some* of their produce, just to keep their lords and masters from starving them, but finding the caches would be difficult. And if they couldn't find the food ... he cursed, again. Keeping his men from slaughtering sheep, cows and goats for food – or eating the seed corn – would be impossible.

And that will ensure famine next year, he thought. *We won't even be able to replace what we take.*

Jones was counting on his fingers. "Assuming we don't lose any other convoys, we should be able to keep the army fed throughout the winter," he said. "But it will be very tight."

"Too tight," Gars said.

"I know," Reginald said. Jones was a good man – he'd been on campaign, unlike his father's beancounters – but his estimates of how much the troops would need were still too low. Any serving officer knew that armies consumed more supplies than predicted. And even if Jones was correct, there was no way to guarantee that they *wouldn't* lose any other convoys. The estimates might have to be revised if new reports reached the army. "And we still have a war to fight."

He looked down at his map, grimly. The scouts had made it clear that Earl Goldenrod had joined forces with Lord Havant, bringing his forces south to block Reginald's march to the north. It made a certain kind of sense, Reginald acknowledged, particularly in light of the reports that Lord Havant had married Roxanne Goldenrod, but it was frustrating. He'd hoped to crush Havant and intimidate Earl Goldenrod into submission. The upside was that Goldenrod's lands could be seized and parcelled out to Reginald's supporters, he supposed, but the downside was that those lands would have to be taken first.

Some of his clients will try to defect, he told himself, firmly. *But we have to prove we can win first.*

"They're preparing to challenge us, Your Highness," Gars told him. "We can crush their armies quickly, then dig in for the winter."

"Yes," Reginald said. His finger traced out a line on the map. "We will continue the advance, pushing forward as hard as possible. Ideally, we will force them to face us before they have a chance to retreat."

"Yes, Your Highness," Gars said.

Jones frowned. "The longer our supply lines become, Your Highness, the harder it will be to keep the army fed. We can't live off the land."

Particularly as the enemy will be doing everything in their power to remove or destroy anything we might use, Reginald thought. *The longer we delay, the more time they'll have to strip the country bare.*

"We cannot afford to show weakness," Reginald said. He smiled, despite himself. Lord Havant and Earl Goldenrod would doubtless have made the same calculation. A display of weakness – or irresolution – would be enough to have their clients looking for ways to make contact with their enemies. "We'll keep moving north until we encounter the enemy."

"The snows might come early too," Jones said. His expression darkened. "Your Highness ... what if the Red Monks *made* the storms come early?"

Reginald shrugged. He'd studied a *little* magic when he'd been a child – the Court Wizard had taught him the basics, concentrating more on what magic could do rather than teaching him how to *use* magic – and he'd never heard of spells powerful enough to shape the weather itself. It was hard to believe that the Red Monks *could* change the weather ... although he did have to admit that their powers didn't seem to follow the usual rules. And if rumours about their abilities started to spread, it wouldn't be long before the army was convinced that the Red Monks could destroy them all with a wave of their hands.

It's the unknown that bothers us, he thought, sourly. *We know what regular magic can do.*

"If they're that powerful," he said, "why don't they already rule the world?"

He looked up as Lord William walked over. "Your Highness," he said. "Is it true that our supply lines have been cut?"

"We lost *one* convoy," Reginald said. The messenger clearly *hadn't* kept his wretched mouth shut. Reginald *hoped* that meant Lord William had bullied the messenger into talking. He'd hate to execute the man for talking out of turn *without* a great deal of pressure. "We will continue the offensive."

"It would be unwise, Your Highness," Lord William said. He glanced from side to side, as if he expected the entire enemy army to be charging towards them. "We are already in unknown lands ..."

Reginald felt a hot flash of anger. He had no problems with his boon companions disagreeing with him, at least as long as they did it in private, but Lord William was nothing more than his father's lapdog. It would be easy, so easy, to draw his sword and cut the man down where he stood. Reginald's father would not be pleased, of course, but he'd understand. No one, not even his father's watchdog, could be allowed to get away with contradicting the Crown Prince in public.

"There is no need to panic *just* yet," he said, instead. "An *experienced* soldier would know that such things happen."

Lord William flushed. His military experience was practically non-existent. Reginald didn't *know* if Lord William genuinely *had* been ill when King Romulus was fighting to keep his crown, or if he'd merely been hiding in his tent, but Reginald had no qualms about turning the rumours into weapons. Lord William just got on his nerves.

"We will continue with the offensive," he said, again. He considered, briefly, sending Lord William back to Allenstown. But the advantages of getting rid of the asshole were outweighed by the disadvantages of letting him out of Reginald's sight. "And when we find the enemy, we will destroy them."

He turned to Gars. "Ready the army," he added. "We break camp in one hour."

Gars tapped his chest in salute. "Yes, Your Highness."

***

The forest felt ... *creepy*.

Isabella fought to resist the urge to look in all directions at once as the small force picked its way down the muddy road. It wasn't really a road at all, she thought, more of a muddy track designed to make life difficult for tax collectors, recruiting sergeants and other plagues on the land. The trees were so close to the road that it was all too easy to imagine a team of bandits lying in wait, hiding within the shadows as they awaited their chance to strike. There was nothing under the trees, as far as she could tell, but the sense of being watched was almost overpowering. She wasn't the only one to find the forest unnerving.

She reached out with her senses again, but sensed nothing. There was no magic in the air, nothing like the tainted hotspots she'd visited during her training or the Blight in the Golden City. There was no movement at all, not even birds or small animals. And yet, the sense of being watched by unseen eyes was impossible to dismiss. She couldn't help wondering if they were walking into a trap.

"I told you everything had changed," Kingsley said. The former spy sounded as though he was on the verge of panic. "We shouldn't be here."

Isabella glanced at Lord Robin, who shrugged. It had been difficult to convince Prince Reginald to allow them to travel through the forest, even though there was a solid reason to take a detour as the army headed north. Who knew *what* might be lurking in the endless forest? A skilled team of soldiers – or even someone *born* in the forest – would be able to hide for years, before emerging to strike at their foes. The forest was wild land, utterly untamed. There were no reliable maps of the interior at all.

"We'll be fine," she said, as reassuringly as she could. She turned her head towards Kingsley. "There's nothing to fear."

"Shows how much you know," Kingsley said. "I should never have let you bring me out here."

Isabella winced, feeling a pang of guilt. She'd both bribed and threatened Kingsley to get him to accompany them, making all sorts of promises she knew she'd have a hard time keeping. There had been no choice. She *needed* to know what was going on, even if it meant walking straight into danger. And yet, *now*, she found herself wondering if it wouldn't be wiser to turn around and rejoin the army. The sense that she was walking into something she couldn't handle was too strong for her peace of mind.

She glanced back at the others, grimly. They all looked spooked, even Big Richard. He was holding his axe in one hand, his eyes flicking from side to side as he watched for potential threats. Isabella had a nasty feeling that he was about to lash out with his axe, even though there were no enemies in sight. None of the others were any better. They were all jumpy, all ready to fight. She found her hand dropping to her sword, time and time again. The unseen eyes *felt* close ...

"Aha," Lord Robin said.

The muddy road widened suddenly, leading down to a village. It was larger than Isabella had expected, from Kingsley's description: twenty or so hovels, a handful of larger buildings, a pigpen and a couple of barns. Chickens and pigs wandered freely, watched by children in rags; their mothers, washing clothes or planting seeds in small gardens, eyed the mercenaries warily and waved their daughters inside. A couple of young girls shot almost *challenging* glances at the mercenaries before they slipped into their hovels. Isabella felt her eyes narrow in suspicion. *That* was odd.

Unless they want to leave, she thought. As much as she'd disliked the Golden City, she had to admit that it had offered far more opportunity than a muddy village in the middle of nowhere. *They might hope for one of us to take them away.*

A man came forward, wearing slightly better rags. The headman, Isabella assumed, although there was little to separate him from the other villagers. He looked old enough to be her grandfather, even though she knew that could be deceiving. Life in a village was hard, very hard. The women washing clothes looked older than her, but it was quite possible they were younger. She studied the villagers while Lord Robin spoke to the headsman, informing him that the country was under new management and demanding a place for the mercenaries to sleep. She'd seen villagers who were nervous and villagers who were resentful, but these villagers were scared. And she didn't think they were scared of the mercenaries.

The headman bowed low, then led the way to one of the larger buildings. A handful of villagers scurried out as they approached, carrying a handful of possessions. Isabella felt a twinge of guilt at turning the family out of their home for the night, mingled with the grim awareness that there was nowhere else to stay. An iron horseshoe hung over the door, puzzling her. It would have been cheap, in the Golden City, but here ... the villagers couldn't *afford* to waste iron.

"You'll have to ask Mother Lembu," the headman said, when she asked. He pointed a finger towards a small hovel at the edge of the village. "She insisted that we mark our doors with horseshoes."

"You go see her," Lord Robin said, as they stepped into the house. "We'll get set up here."

Isabella nodded, concealing her disgust as she looked around the hovel. The floor was muddy and the air thick with flies. She wondered, unpleasantly, if the villagers kept their animals in the house at night. There were certainly animal marks on the walls. She told herself, firmly, that she'd slept in worse places, and hurried to the door. Normally, she would have suggested sleeping in the open air, but she had a sense that being outside after dark would be very dangerous.

Mother Lembu's hovel was little different from the other buildings, apart from a tiny herbal garden outside. It looked like a hedge witch's hut, save for the complete lack of magic ... or, at least, magic that Isabella could *sense*. She tapped on the door and waited for the invitation to enter, then pushed the door open. Inside, the building was surprisingly light. Someone had cut skylights in the thatched roof, allowing light to beam down into the chamber. It was an odd design, she thought. What advantages were gained by letting the light in would be negated by the rain *also* coming in ...

Maybe the rain doesn't come in, she thought.

"Ah, young woman," Mother Lembu said. "Welcome."

Isabella's eyes narrowed. Mother Lembu was sitting by the fire, her body wrapped in a grey blanket that had been patched and patched again until there was nothing left of the original garment. She was tall and thin, grey hair covering a sharp face and sharper eyes ... Isabella still couldn't sense any magic on the ancient woman, but she found it easy to see why she'd been left alone in her hut. Hedge witch or herbalist, Mother Lembu was clearly formidable.

And she pegged you as a woman straight away, Isabella

thought. Judging by the way the village girls had eyed her –
and shied away – Mother Lembu was the *only* villager to see
through Isabella's male guise. *What is she?*

"Greetings," she said. "I ..."

"Have come for answers," Mother Lembu said. There was
a power in her voice, a power that could not be denied. "I
can't give them to you, not yet."

Isabella frowned. "Not yet?"

"Tonight, you will follow the girls out of the village,"
Mother Lembu said. Her voice was certain, very certain.
"And you will have your answers."

"Oh," Isabella said. She found herself unsure how to
proceed. Her training demanded that she force answers out
of the old woman; her instincts told her that *trying* would be
very dangerous. "Are you sure?"

Mother Lembu smiled. "If you don't go, you won't have
your answers," she said. "Of *course* you're going to go."

Chapter Thirty

Big Richard couldn't sleep.

The building – the hovel – wasn't the worst place he'd slept, but it was easily the most unfriendly. It was hard to believe that it was the best accommodation in the village, even though he suspected it was true. The villagers had nothing, beyond a handful of tools and animals they couldn't afford to replace. The slop they'd fed the mercenaries before nightfall – before everyone had hurried back to their homes – had been thoroughly unpleasant. It would have been better to force them to slaughter a hog or a chicken for their guests.

He frowned as he watched the sorceress slip towards the door and out into the night. The woman *had* discussed the matter with Lord Robin, but Richard was sure she'd been lying about *something*. Why *hadn't* she forced the old woman – the *wise* woman, everyone called her – to talk? It wasn't as if it would be hard. Richard had plenty of experience in finding ways to make people spill their guts, either through torturing them directly or forcing them to watch while their friends and family were made to suffer. He would have been glad to offer his services if Lord Robin had asked. Instead ...

Something was wrong, he thought. The sorceress had betrayed them. Or something. Richard hadn't missed how friendly she was with the prince, particularly now the army had completed the first part of the war. Isabella was looking to jump ship, he was sure. He had no doubt she'd use her body to snare the prince, then ... then make herself queen. And then she'd kill her former comrades, just to be sure her past never came to light. He *had* to know what she was doing. The power that rested within the Summer Isle was dangerous. It could not be allowed to fall into her hands.

It was hard to move quietly in the suffocating atmosphere, but he had plenty of experience in sneaking around too.

Besides, if anyone asked, he was going to the privy. But no one moved as he stealthily opened the door and went out into the night. The moon shone brightly, casting an eerie light over the village. It looked like something from a dream – or a nightmare. No one moved, not even the farm animals. They'd been taken inside for the night. The iron horseshoes on the doors seemed to gleam under the light. He shivered when he saw them and looked away.

He spotted the sorceress at the edge of the village, walking down a dark path into the forest. She had her back to him, but he was careful to clutch one of his protective amulets to his chest and remain in the shadows as he walked after her. The enchanter who'd sold them to him had warned him not to take their protections for granted, particularly against someone more dangerous than the average hedge witch. Isabella was a sorceress – and therefore untrustworthy on principle – but Richard knew she was a capable magician. The last hedge witch he'd killed had been so surprised that her attempt to turn him into a slug had failed that he'd cut her down before she could muster another spell. Isabella was faster ... and a capable swordswoman too.

Nothing seemed to move in the gloom as he slipped forward, flitting from tree to tree. He would have lost her altogether, he suspected, if she hadn't been taking as much care to remain hidden as himself. She was using trees for cover, rather than relying on her magic ... it was a smart move, he grudgingly admitted. If her magic was unreliable, it was better to rely on the tried and true methods of remaining hidden. And yet ... the air was so quiet and still that he rather suspected a single sound would be enough to draw attention.

She's following someone too, he reminded himself. The wise woman hadn't been particularly clear, apparently. *And any sound she makes might draw their attention to me too.*

He paused as he caught sight of a light, up ahead. It looked like a bonfire, burning brightly in the middle of a clearing. Shapes were clearly visible, people moving around the bonfire in a complicated dance. Others – including the person Isabella was following – were appearing out of the shadows and walking into the light. He could hear whispering – no, *chanting* – echoing through the air as he started to slip closer. The wind brushed against him, sending cold shivers down his spine. Something felt ... *off*.

Isabella stopped, dead ahead of him, and knelt down in the undergrowth. It was hard, even knowing *precisely* where she was, to spot her in the darkness. The bonfire light made the shadows darker, somehow. And yet ... there was something *wrong* about the fire. It was a little *too* bright to be real.

He inched to one side, getting closer to the clearing without exposing himself too much to Isabella. If she thought to look ... she'd be watching for others heading to the bonfire, even if she didn't realise she'd been followed. Richard knelt down himself, then leaned forward. It was easier to pick out details, now. A dozen women were dancing around the bonfire, chanting words in a strange language. Others were pouring drinks into mugs and handing them round. And a couple were walking around the edge of the clearing, waving wooden sticks in the air. Wooden sticks ... or wands?

Richard tensed, clutching his amulets, as the women walked around the clearing. Nothing happened, nothing at all. And yet, he couldn't shake the feeling that he'd had a very lucky escape. There was magic in the clearing, dangerous magic. The old hatred welled up within him, reminding him – once again – of how his parents had died. And how Isabella had left his brother to die.

The women rejoined their sisters once they'd completed their circuit, then started to remove their clothes. Richard stared, hypnotised. There were young women and old women, all as naked as the day they were born. It wasn't something he'd seen before, not outside an expensive brothel. A well brought up young woman simply did *not* remove her clothes, certainly not outside the marital bed. And yet, the women were naked ...

His heart started to pound as he watched them resume their dance, ducking and weaving around the bonfire. It wasn't like any dance he'd ever seen before, a strange combination of free movements that somehow managed to look like part of a pattern. There was something erotic about their movements, yet the power thrumming on the air scared him almost as much as it excited him. The more he stared, the more his feelings became jumbled. The women were calling to him, but they were also warning him to run.

He tried to look away, but his head refused to move. His entire body was transfixed. He couldn't help staring, he couldn't help ... he couldn't help slowly standing and walking towards the circle. His body moved of its own accord. He knew, deep inside, that something was terribly wrong, but he just couldn't stop himself.

And then one of the women looked around and saw him.

And screamed.

***

Isabella hadn't found it too hard to follow the village women – one elderly woman and three younger girls – down the muddy path to the clearing. It had been harder to find a hiding place that wouldn't be exposed, the moment the meeting – whatever it was – came to an end. Old memories flickered through her mind, vague statements from some of her instructors about forbidden rites performed by banned cults. She was no expert – only full-fledged Inquisitors were told everything – but the dancing reminded her of some of the warning signs. There were quite a few spells that could only be performed naked, yet almost all of them were frowned upon even when they weren't banned.

She had to call on all of her discipline to keep from walking forward, stripping off her clothes and joining the dance. It called to her, called to her in a manner too strong to ignore. And yet, she knew she *had* to ignore it. It was a siren, luring her to her doom. Whatever they were doing was strong, dangerous ... and *unknown*. Spells that should have revealed any compulsions in the area were detecting nothing, nothing at all. She kept one eye closed as she watched the dancers, trying to determine the patterns in their movements ...

... And then she heard someone stumbling through the undergrowth.

Isabella stared, stumbling to her feet. Big Richard was there, staggering haphazardly towards the clearing. Her mind raced. Was he drunk? What was he *doing* in the forest at night? Had he been called by the dancers? Had they reached out and lured him to the bonfire? She glanced behind him, trying to see if the others had followed him. But she couldn't see anyone. The forest seemed deserted.

The dancers screamed. A handful fell out of the pattern, but the remainder kept moving, their chanting taking on a more ominous tone. Isabella couldn't understand it, yet the general intent was clear enough – and unfriendly. She could feel its power brushing against her lightly, as if she were being touched by an invisible man. Or an invisible insect ... she shaped a spell in her mind as the chanting grew louder, then snapped off a stinging hex at Big Richard's behind. He yelped, startled out of the trance. Isabella allowed herself a smirk at his surprise, then leaned forward.

"Come on," she shouted. She could hear *things* moving through the undergrowth, coming closer. "This way."

Big Richard stared at her for a long second, then started to run towards her. His face was dazed, as if he were still feeling the after-effects of the call. She didn't really blame him for falling prey to it. The call had been so intense that she knew she would have fallen too, if she hadn't been trained to resist mental influence. Even so, it had been a very close run thing.

She heard someone shouting behind them as they turned to run. It didn't sound friendly in the slightest. They'd be chased, of course. The women would be in real trouble if they were caught walking around naked, let alone performing midnight rites. Unless ... she remembered, grimly, the odd expressions on the faces of the villagers. Could it be that the changes in the world had already cowed most of the locals? Very few people dared to go out after dark these days.

Big Richard stumbled along beside her, weaving unsteadily as he moved. She kept a wary eye on him, noting just how close his hand was to the axe on his belt. He couldn't be trusted, not if the call had affected him that badly. Her lips twitched with wry amusement. No doubt seeing so many bare chests had affected him too. And ... she stopped herself as she heard something crashing through the undergrowth. It was right on top of them ...

She turned, just in time to see a small fox spring out of the bushes and hurl itself at them. Big Richard drew his axe in one smooth motion and cut the beast in half, sending blood and guts flying in all directions. Another followed, teeth bared as it leapt through the air; Isabella tried to summon a spell, but the magic refused to gel properly. Big Richard killed it an instant before it could snap at her. She drew her sword and stood at the ready, slicing through a hare as it appeared out of nowhere. Whatever the women had done, it was clear they'd summoned every creature for miles. She could hear more and more wild animals moving towards them.

"We have to run," she said.

"There's nowhere *to* run," Big Richard said. He killed two more foxes, then bit off a curse as a small rabbit sank its teeth into his boot. "We have to fight here!"

Isabella killed the rabbit, then a snake that made a lunge at her leg. Big Richard was right, she realised as she lashed out again and again. They couldn't hope to outrun the wild animals. She glanced at the trees, wondering if they could climb to safety. But there were so many animals lunging at them now that she knew it was impossible. She couldn't even dig the firelighter out of her pocket and start a fire without exposing herself. And she couldn't think of any other options. A handful of bites would be enough to bring them down.

"Use some magic," Big Richard urged. "Do *something*!"

"It isn't working," Isabella said. Perhaps if she clambered up a tree ... no, that would mean abandoning him to a very unpleasant death. Maybe if they headed back to the clearing ... she shook her head, dismissing the thought. The women – whoever they were, whatever they were – were unlikely to welcome their uninvited guests. Surrender would just get them killed quickly – or worse. "Is there any way back to the village?"

The attack seemed to pause, just for a second, as light flared behind them. Isabella turned carefully, keeping one eye on the watching animals, and saw Mother Lembu holding up a lamp. It glowed with an eerie yellow light, driving the animals back. The light felt welcoming and yet ... cold ... at the same time.

"Come with me," Mother Lembu ordered. "Quickly."

Isabella glanced at Big Richard, then hurried after Mother Lembu. The animals followed, keeping their distance from the lamp. Isabella kept looking behind her, just to make sure they *were* staying back. It crossed her mind that they might be walking into a trap, but they didn't seem to have any choice. Besides, it was hard to believe that Mother Lembu meant them any harm. She had to fight to resist the temptation to return her sword to the scabbard.

"They won't come within the circle," Mother Lembu said, as they reached a small hut, half-hidden within the foliage. A circle of burnt grass had been drawn around the hut, lined with ashes. "The hex sign will keep them away."

Isabella allowed herself a moment of relief, but kept her sword at the ready anyway. Beside her, Big Richard held his axe in one hand, ready to strike.

"Put your weapons away," Mother Lembu said, as they reached the door. "You must not come into this place bearing weapons."

"Oh, I must not?" Big Richard demanded. He shot her a challenging look. "And why should I not?"

"I could tell you that how you enter this place will determine how you are treated," Mother Lembu said coolly, "but you will not listen, will you?"

She reached out, as quick as a snake, and tapped Big Richard on the forehead. He staggered, then fell to the ground and began to snore. Isabella jumped back, torn between taking a stab at the ancient woman and doing as she was told. Her natural caution told her to keep her hand on the blade, but ... she didn't *think* Mother Lembu meant her any real harm. Slowly, carefully, she returned her sword to the scabbard, silently praying she'd done the right thing.

She has powers I don't understand, Isabella told herself, as she followed Mother Lembu into the hut. *I may already be at her mercy.*

Mother Lembu gave her a tight smile. "Your friend will be safe enough out there," she said, dryly. "I just couldn't allow him to bring a weapon into this place."

Isabella looked around, carefully. The hut looked like a typical hedge witch's establishment, complete with worktable, herbal potions, cauldron and a roaring fire, but ... but it was strange, as if there were parts of it that remained forever at the corner of her eye. It was bright, yet she couldn't see where the light came from. There were no lanterns, no candles ... not even any magic lamps. The light seemed to come from everywhere and nowhere.

"I apologise for his conduct," she managed, finally. It felt hard to talk, as if the words were catching in her throat. "I beg your pardon."

"I have a feeling that if you start apologising for him, you'll never stop," Mother Lembu said, curtly. "Please, take a seat. I'll have something for us both to drink in a minute."

"I don't need something to drink," Isabella said. The words seemed to come easier now. "I need answers."

Mother Lembu smiled. "Do you expect me to give you *all* the answers?"

"You promised me answers," Isabella said, as she sat on a stool by the worktable. "Didn't you?"

"I told you you'd get some answers," Mother Lembu agreed. "What did you make of the sabbat?"

Isabella hesitated. "The dancing? What *is* it?"

"An invocation," Mother Lembu said. She took a kettle from the stove and poured something purple into two earthen mugs. "A summoning. A calling. A ... a prayer to forces higher than ourselves."

She passed Isabella one of the mugs, then sat down on the workbench. "I see Kingsley made it back to the city," she added, after a moment. "The dice said he'd make it home, but the dice often mislead. They don't *lie*, you see, yet it's easy to see patterns that aren't there."

"Foretelling the future is illegal," Isabella said, automatically. She frowned as a thought struck her. She'd always been told that foretelling the future was impossible, but ... why forbid something *impossible*? It had never been questioned, as far as she knew. "Why ... can you foretell the future?"

"Anyone can," Mother Lembu said. She took a sip from her mug. "Drink up, young lady. I have quite a bit to show you."

Isabella looked at her. "Answers?"

"As many as you can handle right now," Mother Lembu assured her. "And maybe a few hints too."

Chapter Thirty-One

"You've been taught to look at the world in a specific way," Mother Lembu said, putting her mug to one side. "I'll show you a different way of looking at it."

Isabella took a sip of her drink. It tasted of blackberries. Alcoholic? She tested it with a spell, but the results were inconclusive. Part of her knew she should be careful, yet her instincts were insisting that she was in no real danger. But Mother Lembu clearly had power, even if it wasn't a power Isabella understood. She forced herself to listen, hoping for answers that actually made sense. Perhaps, just perhaps, she was on the verge of solving the mystery.

"The world has changed in the last five years," Mother Lembu said. "You do understand that, don't you?"

"I've seen signs of change," Isabella said, neutrally. "What is happening?"

"The rules are changing too," Mother Lembu said, dryly. "You need to put aside your preconceptions and *listen*."

She rose and walked around the workbench, stopping in front of the collection of herbs and bark. "Dandelion. Nettles. Elm Bark. All smashed up" – she carried the collection over to the bench – "and boiled in water. What does that tell you?"

Isabella frowned. It wasn't any alchemical concoction *she* recognised. Indeed, all of the listed ingredients were alchemically inert. A magician might be able to infuse *some* magic into the brew, but it wouldn't *do* very much. Perhaps an energy potion? Or a simple way to store magic for later use?

"It isn't a potion recipe," she said, finally. "A base liquid?"

Mother Lembu pointed a finger at her. "You're still thinking like a sorcerer," she said. "You need to think like a wise woman."

Isabella snorted. "No one has ever considered me *wise*."

"You're young," Mother Lembu said. "An aged woman is wise."

Perhaps here, Isabella thought.

Her lips twitched. She'd met a number of elderly women in the Golden City who'd been unable to comprehend that their day was long gone. They'd controlled High Society with a ruthlessness that daunted even the Grand Sorcerer, crushing any younger upstarts who dared to challenge their rules. It had meant social death to go against them, Isabella recalled. She would probably have been driven out if her father hadn't been so powerful. The silly biddies had long since forgotten what was *important*.

But that might not be true of a wise woman in a forest village, where there was no way to hide from reality. Someone who survived long enough to have grandchildren – perhaps even *great*-grandchildren – in a world where men and women rarely lived past fifty could reasonably be assumed to know a thing or two. Mother Lembu's age would give her words credence, particularly as she was too old to marry or bear children. Although ... Isabella reminded herself, once again, that she had no idea how old Mother Lembu actually *was*. She might well be a great deal younger than she looked.

"You think in terms of commanding the world," Mother Lembu said. "But if you went to the lord's manor and commanded him, what do you think it would get you?"

Isabella shivered. Her father had a fishpond he'd filled with people who'd annoyed him, once upon a time. A peasant who tried to *command* a lord on the Summer Isle would be lucky if he was *merely* beaten to within an inch of his life. One approached the powerful with politeness and tact, knowing that the courtesy would not be returned. It seemed that one of the rules that *wasn't* going to change was the assertion that shit always rolled downhill.

"Nothing good," she said, finally. "What are you doing instead?"

"Making an offering," Mother Lembu said. She started to smash the plants together, crushing them in a pestle. "Showing due respect to the powers that be."

"I see," Isabella said, slowly. It reminded her of what

Emetine had said, after she'd tried to kill Reginald. "And this would be *female* magic?"

"Of a sort, although there's no reason *men* can't use it," Mother Lembu said. "It's more of a way to *bargain* with the world, rather than forcing it to obey."

Isabella frowned. "And if you're bargaining with the world," she said, "what are you offering it?"

"It depends," Mother Lembu said. She finished grinding the ingredients and reached for a pot. "Respect, at times."

She glanced at Isabella and winked. "Think of it as a bribe, if you like," she said. "Or simply a way of doing things. You wouldn't try to get across a ravine by jumping off the cliff, would you? Or play cards on a chessboard?"

"I suppose not," Isabella said. "But why are the rules changing?"

Mother Lembu hung the pot over the fire, then reached for a long iron spoon. "The Empire is gone," she said. "And now there is no one hunting those who practice the old ways."

Isabella felt cold. The Empire had endured for over a thousand years, perhaps longer. She'd always been told that history records dating back more than five hundred years or so simply weren't reliable, that there was no way to be entirely *sure* what had happened so long ago. A series of wars – and population relocations – had obliterated whatever traces remained of the pre-empire world, save for a handful of forbidden zones, which the Inquisitors had prevented anyone from visiting until recently. Now ...

She took a breath. "How old?"

"Thousands of years old," Mother Lembu said, seriously. "And, over those years, a handful of the old folk survived to wait for their time to come again."

Isabella leaned forward. "And now?"

"And now word is spreading," Mother Lembu said. "The rules are changing. Those girls you saw are learning to harness their power. Some will do good, some will do evil ... some will lose themselves completely, surrendering to the forces they unleashed. And others will be so terrified of the changes that they will bend the knee to anyone who offers protection."

She looked up. "Your young man is fighting the wrong battle," she added. "And he doesn't see the war."

"The prince isn't *my* young man," Isabella said, hotly.

"You like him," Mother Lembu said. "Is there something *wrong* with liking him?"

Isabella felt her cheeks heat. "Yeah," she said, reluctantly. She wasn't sure where the sudden change in topic had come from. "I ... I cannot afford to let myself like him."

"You *do* like him," Mother Lembu said. "Why don't you want to admit it?"

Isabella gritted her teeth. Reginald *was* attractive. And smart. And better than most of the princes and sorcerers she'd met in her life. He wasn't scared of her, nor did he treat her as a freak. Honesty compelled her to admit she could do a great deal worse. But ...

"My comrades would think less of me if I was openly feminine," she said, finally. It was true, unfortunately. She could no more court the prince – or be courted by him – than she could wear a dress on a battlefield. She couldn't *afford* to let them see her as a woman first, rather than a swordswoman and sorceress. "Does that answer your question?"

"Perhaps it answers one of yours," Mother Lembu said. "You're hiding your true nature."

Isabella felt a hot flash of anger. "Do you think I should walk around naked?"

"I think you should know yourself, first and foremost," Mother Lembu said. She took the pot off the fire and poured the contents into a sieve, straining the liquid. "The rules are changing."

"Into what?"

"You'll see," Mother Lembu said. "I'm not going to give you all the answers."

Isabella felt her hand drop to her sword. "Then give me something I can use!"

"That is what I am going to do," Mother Lembu said, patiently. Her voice hardened, suddenly. "And I *strongly* advise you not to draw your weapon in here."

Isabella looked around. The light had dimmed. The shadows seemed to have grown darker, somehow. She could swear she could see *things* hiding within the darkness, teeth and claws and ... and ... she forced her hand to let go of the sword, feeling shivers running down her spine. Whatever protections surrounded the hut were incredibly dangerous. She doubted she'd survive if they lashed out at her.

"In temples, people worship false gods," Mother Lembu said, very quietly. "And now, the *real* gods are coming back."

Isabella stared. "False gods?"

"False gods," Mother Lembu confirmed, curtly. She picked up the jar and held it in one hand. "Come. Let us go out into the night."

"I don't understand," Isabella said, as Mother Lembu opened the door. "*What* gods?"

"A very long time ago, they were banished," Mother Lembu said. She walked into the darkness. "And now they are returning, granting powers to those who embrace them ... who *appeal* to them."

Isabella stared. "In exchange for *what*?"

Mother Lembu said nothing. Instead, she glanced down at Big Richard and then turned to peer into the darkened forest. There was no sign of anyone in the gloom, not even watchful animals or owls gliding through the night. But the sense of being watched was growing stronger by the second.

"I'm going to put some of this ointment on your eyes," Mother Lembu said, holding up the jar. "Open them and stay still."

Isabella hesitated. Cold logic told her that the ointment would do her no harm, but she wasn't sure cold logic *meant* anything any longer. Mother Lembu let out a sigh and waved a hand at Isabella. She couldn't move, no matter what she did. Her mind felt disconnected from her body. Mother Lembu dipped her fingers in the ointment, touched them to Isabella's eyes and then stepped back, out of Isabella's line of sight. A moment later, Isabella could move again.

"Look into the forest," Mother Lembu ordered.

Isabella gritted her teeth, but did as she was told. Her eyes weren't stinging. They were ... she wasn't sure *how* to describe the sensation. It was as if they were slowly opening, even though they *were* open. Flashes of light darted through the trees, as if they'd always been there; *things* sat on branches, peering at her through unblinking eyes. She couldn't make out the details – it was as if her eyes refused to see more than a blur – but they were there. Larger things moved silently through the trees, pulses of energy moved through the ground ... tendrils of ... *something* ... slid in directions beyond her comprehension. The forest was so much *bigger* than she'd realised.

She looked down at the hex sign and saw ... an impassable barrier. It was just a line of ashes on the ground, yet it was also a solid wall ... her head swam as she tried to comprehend what she was seeing. They couldn't *both* be true, could they? But ... she thought she understood, just for a moment. There was nothing stopping a chess piece from making an illegal move, save for a shared understanding that doing so would ruin the game. The newcomers – whatever they were – followed rules that no human understood, yet.

The horseshoes keep them out, she thought. No *wonder* the villagers were being so wasteful. The horseshoes – the cold iron – was the only thing keeping their homes safe. *And the Red Monks were trying to get rid of pure iron blades ...*

Isabella turned, slightly. "The Red Monks," she said. "What *are* they?"

"I can't answer that question," Mother Lembu said. "Not yet."

"I need an answer," Isabella said. She turned to look at the old woman. "I ..."

The world went white. Mother Lembu blazed with light, light so bright that it burned through Isabella's eyelids even though she'd squeezed them closed. She could *feel* the light burning into her mind, slicing through her thoughts ...

"You made one mistake," Mother Lembu said. Her voice echoed through the air. "And your time to recover is short."

The light seemed to grow brighter, just for a second. And then it was gone. Isabella found herself on her knees, staring down at the muddy ground. She looked up, expecting to see the hut, but there was nothing. The hut was gone. Mother Lembu was gone. Big Richard was lying on the ground, groaning. And, in the distance, she could see the first glimmers of dawn breaking over the horizon.

She slumped, nearly landing in the mud before she caught herself. Dawn? It couldn't be dawn. It had been midnight, only an hour or so ago. Her head spun as she tried to understand what she was seeing. She'd been in the hut, hadn't she? If her eyes hadn't been dripping with ointment, she would have wondered if she'd dreamt it all. The world no longer seemed to make sense.

The rules are different now, she thought, grimly. Mother Lembu had been ... what? It was hard to believe that the old woman was human, not after the light ... she rubbed her eyes, feeling the remnants of the ointment drying rapidly. *Maybe, just maybe ...*

She forced herself to stand upright. She needed time to sit down and think, then ... then what? She had no idea how to proceed. Go back to Reginald and tell him ... tell him what? Or write to Alden? Alden wouldn't know any more about the distant past than Isabella herself, unless there were long-forgotten truths buried in the Black Library. The old gods were coming back? Isabella wouldn't have believed it if she hadn't seen the new world for herself. *Something* had definitely changed.

It started here, she told herself. *But it won't stop here.*

Big Richard groaned, again. "What happened?"

Isabella frowned. "How much do you remember?"

"Girls," Big Richard managed. "There were girls. And they were ..."

His voice trailed off. "What happened?"

"I'm not sure," Isabella said. If *all* Big Richard remembered were girls ... she shook her head in annoyance. "We have to get back to the village."

She glanced up at the lightening sky, then glanced around. Were they lost? No ... a pathway led down towards the village. She nodded to Big Richard, then started to walk. The world felt eerie the moment they stepped over the hex sign, even though the ointment was no longer affecting her eyes. She made a resolution to brew more ointment for herself – there wasn't much to the recipe – and see if she could get it to work. Perhaps, just perhaps, it would allow her to understand how the new rules actually *worked*.

There was no one moving in the village as they walked

down the path, not even a chicken or a pig. She was sure that people were watching them from hidden slits – the huts didn't have windows, let alone glass – but she saw nothing. A chill ran down her spine as she realised that the villagers were afraid to walk out at night, save for the girls who'd joined the sabbat. They might well be safe in the darkness ...

Lord Robin met them at the door, his face anxious. "What happened? Where have you been?"

Isabella and Big Richard exchanged glances. "It's a long story," she said, finally. She still wasn't sure why Big Richard had followed her. If the call had reached all the way to the village, why had Big Richard been the only one affected? "We have to leave, sir, and catch up with the army."

"I see," Lord Robin said. He whistled loudly, waking the other mercenaries. "What happened?"

"This place isn't safe," Isabella said. She made a mental note to gather ingredients for the ointment before they left. "And we have to warn the prince about the Red Monks."

"He *knows* about the Red Monks," Big Richard sneered.

"How nice to see you back to normal," Isabella snapped. "Why did you follow me?"

Big Richard leered. "They were calling me," he said. "And I could not deny their call."

Isabella felt her temper snap. "If someone wanted to capture you, all they'd have to do is parade a naked whore around with her tits thrust out so far ..."

Lord Robin cleared his throat, loudly. "We'll discuss the matter later," he said. "Right now, grab your bags and some hardtack. We'll eat on the way."

"Yes, sir," Isabella said. Her body felt weird. Her internal clock kept insisting that it was midnight, even though she could *see* the sun in the distance and hear the sounds of the village waking up. A thought struck her and she turned to the door. "I'll be back in two minutes."

She hurried out and down towards Mother Lembu's hovel. It was gone. There wasn't even any sign it had *been* there, only yesterday. Even the herbal garden was gone. She stared for a long moment, then turned and started to walk back to the hut. The villagers didn't seem surprised that the hovel was gone, even though one of them had pointed her there. She shivered, helplessly. She'd heard of mass compulsion spells, but this ... this was different.

And terrifying, she thought. *What* was *she?*

It wasn't a reassuring thought. She'd assumed Mother Lembu couldn't possibly have taught Emetine – they'd lived hundreds of miles apart – but if Mother Lembu wasn't human ... could she have visited the Hereford Lands? What *was* she? A god? Or merely someone very skilled in the new-old ways? Isabella could imagine ways to create the illusion of a hut, yet she couldn't see a way to do it without tipping off anyone with even a *hint* of magical sensitivity. The hut should have been drenched in magic.

And she gave me some of the answers, she thought, as she hurried towards the nearest garden to collect some supplies. *And maybe she gave me enough to allow me to figure out the rest.*

Chapter Thirty-Two

Lord Havant snapped awake.

He was sitting in his chair, looking at the map on the table. Someone had covered the map with notations in a language he didn't recognise, indicating the enemy's path northwards from Allenstown and suggesting possible countermeasures. He rubbed his forehead, cursing under his breath. Intellectually, he knew he should be worried about the blackouts; emotionally, it was hard to feel much of anything. They were becoming as natural as breathing.

A faint light was starting to glimmer through the open flap, suggesting that the sun was starting to rise in the distance. How long had he been out? He rubbed his forehead, trying to remember ... he couldn't remember anything, beyond a brief discussion with Hark and a marathon drinking session with several of his most trusted followers. They'd had questions, he recalled vaguely ... he'd answered them, hadn't he? He wasn't sure of anything any longer.

The enemy is coming and we will beat them, he told himself firmly. *And that is all that matters.*

He glanced at the bed as he heard a faint rustling sound. Roxanne Goldenrod was waking up, looking around blearily. No doubt she was surprised he hadn't paid much attention to her, even when they'd shared a bed. She'd been raised to believe that she would be expected to conceive a child as soon as possible – a child would bind the alliance together permanently – but Havant had barely touched her. Hark had warned him, several times, that getting Roxanne pregnant would offend their lord and have all sorts of repercussions. Havant believed him.

And besides, her father is not long for this world, he thought, as he nodded to the young woman. *There will be time to sire a child later if she survives.*

He held her eyes until she looked down, her face barely

showing any trace of emotion. He'd told her, firmly, to stay in the tent and, somewhat to his disappointment, she'd obeyed. Aristocratic wives were meant to be obedient, but that just made them boring. His lips quirked at the thought. King Edwin's ghost, wherever his soul had gone after death, was probably rueing his wife's *lack* of obedience. But then, Emetine had certainly *pretended* to be obedient. The act just hadn't fooled anyone, least of all her husband. He'd tried hard to put her aside before his untimely death.

Reaching into his pocket, he took a scrap of bloodstained cloth and closed his eyes. It was suddenly easy, very easy, to see the links between Roxanne and her father, just waiting for him to put them to use. Hark had barely scratched the surface of the possible, Havant thought. The presence within him was pushing further forward than the Red Monks appeared to believe possible. Or maybe they were trying to limit him. There might come a time when he and Hark would find it necessary to part ways.

He pulled on a robe, then strode out of the tent. The chilly morning breeze greeted him, but he ignored it. He'd grown up further to the north, where snow lay on the ground even in autumn, and summer was a rumour no one believed. Prince Reginald and his men were likely to have problems continuing their campaign in the winter, he told himself as he headed for the command tent. If worse came to worst, he had every intention of melting into the hills and carrying out an insurgency until the invaders became tired of fighting and went back home.

A servant greeted him as he entered the tent, holding out a jug of mulled wine. Earl Goldenrod stood at one end of the table, drinking and talking with two of his trusted retainers; Hark and a handful of other senior officers stood against the wall, waiting for their superior. Havant took a mug of wine – it warmed his heart in the cold air – and paced over to the table. The latest reports from the scouts – and the Red Monks – were prominently displayed on the map.

"Three new scouts came in this morning," Earl Goldenrod said. He'd insisted on taking command of the conventional side of the war, an insistence to which Havant had offered no more than token resistance. It wouldn't have done to accidentally talk the earl *out* of taking command. "The enemy army will be on Rupert in two days."

Havant nodded, tartly. Unless Prince Reginald thought a mere show of force would be enough to bring the north to heel, he wouldn't *stop* at Rupert. He'd keep moving northwards until he reached the Hereford Lands. It was possible, he supposed, that they'd try to invade the Goldenrod Lands instead, but there was no way to know how much *Reginald* knew. Did he know that Hereford and Goldenrod were now allies? Or did he still believe he could convince Earl Goldenrod to remain neutral?

"We'll meet them just past the town," Havant said. He looked at one of his generals. "The region has been stripped?"

"We have driven everyone out of the area," the general confirmed. "And anything that might have been used to support the army has been removed."

Havant nodded. The locals were going to suffer – they'd be lucky if they survived the winter – but it was a minor price to pay for stopping the invaders. Besides, there was nothing stopping them from heading north or south in search of succour. *Someone* would take them for serfs, if nothing else. Prince Reginald might even take them as porters.

Until he runs out of food for them, Havant reminded himself. *His army isn't going to be able to live off the land.*

"Very good," he said. He looked at his father-in-law. "You are ready to meet them?"

"Most of the combined army is already in position," Earl Goldenrod said. "We'll advance forward once the enemy scouts have been turned back and meet them on the moor."

"Be careful," Havant advised. "Prince Reginald is known to be devious."

"He also will have to charge our positions or leave us in his rear," Earl Goldenrod assured him. "Either way, we win."

Havant nodded, shortly. Prince Reginald *couldn't* get anything larger than a raiding party up north without moving across the moors, not when the road network was an absolute nightmare. Havant silently blessed his father as he studied the map, even though the old bastard had cursed the roads himself when *he'd* been trying to move armies south. His delaying tactics, when King Edwin had wanted to construct new roads, might well save his son's lands from invasion.

"Very good," Havant said. "And you are ready to depart?"

"I'll head south this afternoon," Earl Goldenrod said. "And yourself?"

"I'll be going south too," Havant told him. He'd be staying in the rear, again. It was an unsubtle insult – and a snide reminder that Havant's brother had lost the only pitched battle of his career – but he didn't mind. It played right into his hands. "Once the enemy has been defeated, we can go to Allenstown and settle accounts with Oxley."

"Of course," Earl Goldenrod agreed. "He has always been too big for his boots."

And now you're measuring my back for the knife, Havant thought, as he turned back to the map. *And once your daughter is pregnant, you intend to kill me.*

He listened as the assembled officers ran through the details once again, making sure that everyone was caterwauling off the same song sheet. Earl Goldenrod seemed to take an inhuman delight in the details – he insisted on discussing each and every single detail – but Havant supposed it made a certain kind of sense. The north hadn't really gone to war in decades, save for raids and brief charges southwards when the earls had made bids for the throne. Prince Reginald, by contrast, commanded a well-oiled battlefield machine. The north needed to make sure it was ready for anything.

But Prince Reginald doesn't know what he's facing, Havant told himself. The presence within him thrummed with anticipation. *Or just how bad things are about to become.*

"We will win," Earl Goldenrod said, when the long and exhaustive list of details was finally concluded. "And then we will have our island back."

"Of course," Havant agreed. He knew perfectly well Earl Goldenrod had no intention of sharing ... not that *Havant* did, of course. One way or the other, Earl Goldenrod wouldn't leave the coming battlefield alive. And then, with his daughter married to another earl, his lands would be absorbed into the new kingdom. "The gods will be with us."

The meeting broke up as the officers headed for lunch. Earl Goldenrod had given orders to slaughter vast numbers of requisitioned cows, pigs and sheep, just to make sure that every man had a good repast before setting out to march to the battlefield. Havant privately admired the man's determination to be a *good* commander, even though Earl Goldenrod had learned his trade from books. The man hadn't commanded anything larger than a raiding force heading into the Northern Realm. And experience was often a hard teacher.

Hark fell in beside him as they walked around the camp. "I have received word from my brethren," he said. "The storms have cut all contact between the island and the mainland."

Havant let out a long breath. He hadn't quite believed it possible. Magic on such a scale was beyond anything he'd ever dreamed of, outside fantasies and fairy stories. The Grand Sorcerer, for all his power, had never been able to control the weather. But the Red Monks had somehow brought the autumn storms early. Prince Reginald would neither be able to bring in supplies nor retreat. There was no way home unless he wanted to court death.

"Very good," he said. "How long will the storms last?"

"There's no way to say," Hark said. "We pleaded for them to last for a long time, but ..."

"Prince Reginald will be having problems," Havant finished. "I wonder just how many of his transport convoys have been attacked."

He allowed himself a tight smile. Prince Reginald *had* to attack northwards, if he didn't want to lose his momentum, but he could no longer trust that his rear would remain secure. Worse, if he *did* lose his momentum, his new allies and clients would no longer see him as the certain victor in the ongoing conflict and start to edge away. Prince Reginald needed time to consolidate his gains, yet he didn't *have* time ...

"He'll push right into our trap," Havant said. Everything he'd heard about Prince Reginald made it clear that the prince was a man of action. The idea of shifting his forces onto the defensive would be unthinkable. "And then we'll best him."

"The sacrifice is ready," Hark assured him. "We can

perform the ritual at any time."

"We'll wait until the main body of the camp has departed," Havant said. "We don't want too many questions."

"There is no shame in serving Our Lord," Hark said, reprovingly. "They will all come to us in time."

Havant shrugged. He felt no shame himself – now – but he was all too aware that not *everyone* liked the Red Monks. His men were becoming believers, but not all of them were prepared to put the false gods aside and worship Dusk. And destroying temples and shrines – even personal icons – was something most soldiers regarded as bad luck, even if they didn't worship the gods in question themselves. The presence in his mind shifted in disapproval, sending sparks of anger through his thoughts. The heretics had to be removed before the army went into battle.

"Once we win the war, we can impose worship right across the kingdom," Havant promised, seriously. "And then the false gods can be removed."

He wasn't sure if he intended to keep the promise or not. On one hand, he knew the Red Monks had access to *power*. The presence inhabiting his mind was proof that they could do remarkable things. And yet, on the other hand, he was aware of the dangers in allowing a single religious faction to become too powerful. The Red Monks might find themselves in a position to influence policy, even – perhaps – to dictate to him. It could not be allowed.

They joined Earl Goldenrod and his men for lunch, enduring a succession of bawdy jokes about sowing one's seed from the earl's loyalists. Havant kept his annoyance from showing as best he could, knowing that he'd made the same jokes himself when he'd dined with newly-wed men. There wasn't any time to waste, normally, in siring children. Earl Goldenrod would certainly be insulted if he knew that Havant wasn't doing his best to impregnate the earl's daughter. The gods knew the Herefords had seen King Edwin's apparent lack of interest in Emetine as a cause for war.

"We'll see you on the battlefield," Earl Goldenrod said, when the last carcass had been picked clean and the last bawdy joke told to howls of drunken laughter. "And the gods will be with us!"

Havant watched the earl and his men ride out of the camp – the men singing a song about the north rising again – and then followed Hark back towards his compound. The Red Monks had established a camp within the camp, walled by a wooden stockade and heavily guarded by their followers. It wasn't uncommon for soldiers to set up small shrines while they were in camp, but the Red Monks had taken the concept to a whole new level. He couldn't help shivering as he passed the two cowled figures guarding the gate. It looked as if there were more and more Red Monks every time he entered their compound.

"The prisoners are ready," Hark said, as they paused outside a large tent. "Are *you*?"

Havant looked at him. "What do you mean?"

"The time has come for you to make a sacrifice," Hark said.

"Another one?"

"Oh, yes," Hark told him. "Perhaps the most *important* sacrifice. You must make an *offering* to Our Lord."

He pushed the tent flap open. "Come."

Havant noticed the smell, first, as his eyes slowly grew accustomed to the darkness. The stench of piss and shit ... and quiet, helpless desperation. He could *hear* men moaning in pain ... he peered into the gloom, trying to see through the haze. Hark snapped his fingers and the tent was illuminated, suddenly, by an eerie white light. Twenty-one naked men knelt on the solid earthen floor; their mouths gagged, their hands and feet bound so tightly that their extremities were turning purple. They weren't common villagers, Havant realised in dull surprise. They were soldiers.

"These men contradicted the teachings of Our Lord," Hark said. "And so they were removed and held until the time came for their lives to be offered to Him."

Havant stared at them for a long moment. The men looked back at him, desperately. It wasn't *common* to kill someone for refusing to worship a particular god, but he knew – now – that Dusk was real. He wanted – he *needed* – the power to win the coming battle. And he couldn't sacrifice volunteers any longer. Dusk demanded blood. The presence in his mind thrummed with impatience, pushing him forward. It *wanted* him to make the choice to kill his own men.

Traitors and heretics, something whispered inside his head. His thought? Or something else? *They are worthless. They will betray you if you give them a chance.*

Hark passed him a ritual blade, gleaming silver. Havant looked down at it, then up at the helpless men. He liked to think he was a good lord, in his way. Loyalty should always be rewarded, just as disloyalty should always be punished. And yet ... he remembered the power he'd touched, the power that – just for a few minutes – he'd bent to his will. He *needed* that power to win. He *had* to offer their lives to Dusk.

His lips moved soundlessly as he advanced forward. It was his decision, he knew on some level. The presence in his mind wasn't trying to *force* him to take it. It was his decision. It *had* to be his decision. He weighed it up, carefully. Their deaths would strengthen his army, guaranteeing victory. It was worth it. And yet, part of him recoiled in horror from what he had become ...

There's no choice, he told himself, firmly. He couldn't tolerate religious dissent, not any longer. Not when it might cost him victory. And religious dissent could easily become mutiny, given time. He couldn't tolerate a mutiny at the best of times. Now, when his army was held together by spit and baling wire, he couldn't tolerate even the slightest hint of mutiny. *There's no choice at all.*

He slit the first throat with practiced ease, watching through calm eyes as blood spilled onto the ground. Power flared through the air, building up slowly as he slit neck after neck. It was intoxicating, burning away all his doubts and fears. He could *feel* the presence welcoming it, greeting the power as if it were an old friend. *Something* was going to happen, when Prince Reginald began the battle. The invader had no idea what he was about to face.

The last prisoner slumped to the ground, dead. Havant stood alone in the midst of the power, feeling it ebbing and flowing around him. It was his power, all his ...

"It is done," Hark said. "Welcome, My Lord."

The world went black, just for an instant. And then he was

outside the tent.

"Our victory is now assured," Hark told him. "Our Lord has promised it."

"Very good," Havant said. He felt dazed. He'd done something wrong, yet ... he felt no guilt. No, that wasn't right. He hadn't done anything wrong at all. "I look forward to our victory."

Chapter Thirty-Three

"Witches," Reginald said, slowly. He didn't *disbelieve* Isabella, not really, but ... he wasn't sure what to make of her report. "Witches and ... and gods?"

"Yes, Your Highness," Isabella said. She had the air of someone who knew, all too well, that she wouldn't be believed. Reginald had seen it before, too many times. "The world is changing."

"I already knew *that*," Reginald muttered. "But changing like *this* ...?"

He shook his head as he looked around the commandeered office. His men had secured Rupert without a fight, if only because the entire population had seemingly vanished into thin air. The enemy had done an excellent job of stripping the wretched town bare, he conceded ruefully. Everything that might have been even *remotely* useful, from food to tools and supplies, had been removed. The scouts hadn't even been able to find traces of the townspeople, although he hadn't had the time to search the vast forests. If Isabella was correct, even *trying* might be dangerous.

"If this is true," he said slowly, "what do we do about it?"

"I don't know," Isabella said. He could tell the admission cost her. "But the Red Monks are clearly unfriendly."

"You don't say," Reginald said. He wanted time to think. Fighting an unknown force of great power and potency was dangerous, all the more so because its power was *unknown*. He could devise plans to counter an enemy army two or three times the size of his own, but *gods?* How did one handle *gods*? "And what happens if we pull back?"

He shook his head in annoyance. He *had* to press forward, now the autumn storms had come early ... Was that a coincidence? Or was it the first sign of godly intervention? He cursed the enemy under his breath, savagely. There was no way to *know* what he was facing. He'd understand an enemy force appearing in his rear, even though it would have bottled his army up and forced him to try to break out before the noose tightened, but gods? He was going to be spending the rest of his life second-guessing himself if *gods* were involved. How was he supposed to evaluate the threat when it steadfastly refused to obey known laws?

"We can't pull back," he said. Quite apart from the dangers of abandoning the campaign – and allowing Hereford and Goldenrod time to build up their forces for a march south – there was no way to withdraw the army. "And even if we do, what happens when the threat jumps the channel?"

He met her eyes, silently willing her to say something reassuring. The Summer Isle had never been a threat to Andalusia. None of its kings had ever managed to master the island to the point where they could muster the force for a little overseas expansion. There had been no reason to think the now-dead usurper would have been any different. King Rufus wouldn't have been able to solidify his control over the island either. But now ... with strange gods and creatures and magics ... who knew what sort of threat his homeland would eventually face? He didn't think the *gods* would choose to remain confined to a single small island.

"They have to be stopped, Your Highness," Isabella said. "But the problem may *already* have jumped the channel."

Reginald scowled. "How so?"

"We encountered a strange creature before we joined your invasion force," Isabella reminded him. "And there were reports of other strange encounters too."

"And rumours of more," Reginald said.

He looked down at his hands. His scouts *had* reported odd things, from an ever-present sensation of being watched by unseen eyes to weird creatures that had flickered in and out of existence. The further one went from civilisation, such as it was on the Summer Isle, the stranger the reports. And some of his scouts had never reported back. He'd assumed the enemy had caught and killed them, but now ...? He wasn't sure what to make of it.

"The Red Monks have to be stopped," he said, flatly. "And we cannot allow our enemies time to build up their forces."

"And master their new powers," Isabella added.

Reginald frowned. "But ... but that old woman taught you some of *hers*?"

"She wasn't human," Isabella said, flatly. "Whatever she was, she wasn't human."

She took a long breath. Just for a second, she looked *vulnerable*. It stirred Reginald's protective instincts, even though he knew that *trying* to protect her was a very bad idea. She didn't *need* his protection. And yet, the urge to take her in his arms was suddenly overpowering. He pushed it down, hard. It had been a long march along bad roads and through muddy fields and he was tired. Too tired.

"The recipe she gave me should be useless," Isabella said flatly. She looked down at the earthen floor, her face unreadable. "I was never a Potions Mistress – I never had the patience to master brewing, still less alchemy – but I know enough to tell you that the recipe is completely useless, alchemically speaking. It's more of a folk cure than anything more ... more useful. And yet, it worked! I watched her brew it!"

"Have you tried brewing it yourself?" Reginald leaned forward. "Or perhaps asking someone else to brew it?"

"I have the ingredients," Isabella said. She looked doubtful. "I *know* the recipe shouldn't work. And yet, it *did*."

Reginald gave her a smile. "I know that pointing your finger at someone shouldn't turn them into a frog," he said. "And yet, it *did*."

Isabella looked up at him. "Point taken."

"Try and brew it yourself," Reginald said. "And ask Kingsley to track down other folk cures."

Isabella gave him an odd look. "That's ..."

She broke off. Reginald understood. Folk cures were technically forbidden, but commoners – who couldn't afford to go to a druid for healing – used them whenever their betters weren't looking. He'd never seen the point of folk cures, but he'd never been particularly interested in hunting down the people who turned herbs into makeshift potions. If they helped, they helped ... it wasn't as if they were practicing magic. His soldiers used them all the time. But if

Isabella was right, the commoners might have been playing with magic – or something worse – without ever knowing it.

"I might have to go myself, or find another woman," Isabella said. "I doubt most of the practitioners will talk to a man."

"See if you can find someone," Reginald commanded. "I'm going to need you here."

There was a sharp knock on the door. Reginald raised his voice. "Come!"

Gars stepped into the room, followed by Lord Robin. "Your Highness," he said, as Lord Robin and Isabella greeted one another. "The scouts have returned. They have located the enemy army."

"They're dug in along the moors," Lord Robin added grimly, as Gars held out an annotated map. "We apparently outnumber them, but they have a tough position."

Reginald looked at Isabella. "Try and brew the ointment now," he ordered. "We may need it for the battle."

"Understood," Isabella said. She nodded to Lord Robin, then saluted Reginald. "I'll do it now."

Reginald watched her go, then looked down at the map. "A tricky position," he said, thoughtfully. "Are we facing both of the earls?"

"Both sets of banners have been reported," Lord Robin said. "Earl Goldenrod's are apparently in the superior position."

"I see," Reginald said.

He contemplated the problem for a long moment. Had Havant conceded command to Earl Goldenrod? Or had Goldenrod insisted on taking it? Or ... he shook his head in annoyance. The absence of actionable intelligence from the enemy's inner circle was quite frustrating. He'd assumed that *someone* would defect, but so far no enemy nobleman had taken advantage of the chance to better himself by switching sides. It spoke volumes about *something*. He just wasn't sure what.

Of course, being in the van isn't always a good place to be, he thought. His father had always cautioned him *against* putting himself out in front, even though it was a good way to command loyalty. Men followed leaders who put themselves at risk too. *Earl Goldenrod might be exposed deliberately.*

He looked up. "Do we have any idea how many men they have?"

"Roughly five thousand, if we go by what we've seen," Lord Robin said. His finger traced out a line on the map. "We've sent scouts past here, Your Highness, but none of them have returned. The enemy flankers are apparently very good."

"Or the land itself got them," Gars said, pessimistically. "The moors are supposed to be boggy."

And we don't have a native guide, Reginald thought. He'd planned to take a local from the town, but the enemy had made that impossible. *We'll be marching forward blind.*

"Not *that* boggy," Gars said. "It's apparently stable all the way to the enemy lines."

Reginald tuned them out as they argued, choosing – instead – to concentrate on the map. The enemy position was simplistic – suggesting that their commander had studied books rather than fighting actual wars – but good. There was no apparent way to turn their position, let alone force them to withdraw in disarray. He wasn't even sure he could slip cavalry through the forest to take them in the rear. Whatever had killed his scouts might still be lying in wait.

"We can't delay," he said, more to himself than to either of the men. "There's no way we can stay here."

"No, Your Highness," Gars agreed.

Reginald gritted his teeth in frustration. The thought of leaving a force to hold Rupert and pulling back was tempting, but the enemy wouldn't have any trouble bypassing the town and striking south. He *could* try to lure them onto a battleground of his choosing, yet the enemy presumably knew the land better than him. They could keep marching and evading combat until he ran out of supplies. And they'd have plenty of time to build up their own forces ...

He scowled as he studied the map. The earls had worked hard to build up their forces over the past few years, if the reports were to be believed, but they had to be careful. Too many men trained in arms was an open invitation to revolt, particularly if their lords and masters looked weak. The chance to smash most of their trained men in one battle was almost impossible to resist, which worried him. They could be bait in a trap.

And with strange powers involved, he thought, *the trap could be anything.*

"We prepare to attack," he said, savagely.

It wasn't a good option, he conceded, as his subordinates hurried to obey. But it was the only one that made sense. He couldn't stay where he was – he'd run out of supplies – and he couldn't withdraw without risking the southern nobility changing sides. And besides, he *needed* the northern lands. They were the only way he could pay his mercenaries. It wouldn't be long, he knew all too well, before the demands for payment grew too strong to resist.

He buckled his sword to his belt, then headed for the door. The enemy would see his men forming up, of course, but they wouldn't know *precisely* when he intended to attack. He'd use his cavalry to make feints at the enemy position, keeping them on alert constantly. They'd be worn to a nub before the *real* attack began.

And if we smash their force, we win, he thought. It didn't matter if the earls survived the battle or not. They wouldn't have a hope of regaining their power if their armies were destroyed. Their clients would switch sides or risk being wiped out along with their former masters. *We win.*

***

Isabella looked down at the workbench, feeling a deep sense of ... dissatisfaction. She knew – she knew all too well – that the ointment was alchemically inert, yet ... she'd watched the useless ingredients being turned into something *useful*. It bothered her more than she cared to admit. The sense of doing something forbidden – something fundamentally *wrong* – nagged at her mind as she slowly cleaned and chopped the ingredients. She hadn't felt so ... so ... *naughty* since the day she'd crept into her father's library and read his collection of restricted and banned tomes. The old man had been furious when he'd caught her ...

She glanced up, suddenly convinced that her father was right behind her. It was impossible – her father was dead – and yet, the conviction was so strong that she found herself looking around the bare room. There was nothing, save for the crackling of the fire and a faint breeze blowing through the window. She could hear men shouting outside as they prepared for war, but ... she was alone.

This is wrong, she told herself. She felt sick at heart, as if she *knew* she was about to do something wrong ... and she was about to do it anyway. *This is ...*

The sense of being watched grew stronger. Her hand dropped to her sword, her eyes flicking from side to side. The door was locked, the window too small for anything larger than a toddler ... yet there was no way to escape the sense that she was not alone. Ice trickled down her spine as she put the ingredients into the mortar and started to crush them, one by one. Tiny droplets of juice formed on the china pestle, mocking her. It felt more like cooking than brewing. The thought wasn't very reassuring. She'd never been a good cook.

And Big Richard wanted me to cook for the band, she thought, feeling a flicker of droll amusement. *What an idiot.*

She snorted at the thought. Aristocratic – and magical – girls were not taught to cook. A commoner girl *would* know how to cook, of course, but not a magician. She'd had far too many other things to learn. And besides, the servants had done all the cooking. And yet ... she looked down at the ground ingredients, waiting to be put in the pot. There was an odd sense of *satisfaction* from grinding the ingredients that she'd never felt when brewing potions.

Shaking her head, she poured the ground ingredients into the pot and waited for the water to boil. Mother Lembu had put the ingredients into boiling water ... she wondered, absently, if that made any difference. Her old potions teacher would have exploded with rage if she'd dared to ask such a stupid question in class – of *course* it made a difference – but now she wasn't so sure. Perhaps, just perhaps, intent was more important than anything else.

It was unsettling, more than she cared to admit. She'd been raised to understand how spells were put together, how casting a spell – even when one didn't know what the spell *did* – actually worked. Spells were built up, piece by piece; the ointment, it seemed, was something different. It made her wonder, despite herself, what would happen if she used different ingredients – or no ingredients at all. Logic told her the results would be different each time – if indeed there *were* results – but emotion suggested otherwise. It made no sense.

I'll have to ask Emetine, she thought. She had a feeling the former queen would be more than happy to answer her questions. *And who knows what will happen then?*

The liquid boiled. She poured it into another basin and waited for it to cool. It smelt right, thankfully. She wasn't sure what she would have done if it hadn't. And yet ... she felt a breath on the back of her neck and spun around, drawing her sword instinctively. There was nothing there ...

... But she still felt as though she was being watched.

The sensation faded rapidly as the ointment cooled. Isabella poured a tiny amount onto a plate, then dipped her finger in the liquid and pressed it against her left eye. The room seemed to shimmer, just for a second. Blue lights danced through the walls, then faded into nothingness. She turned slowly, keeping her right eye closed. The room seemed familiar, yet strange. Her head hurt when she tried to make sense of it. But the sense that she was being watched was gone.

There was a tap at the door. "Isabella," Lord Robin said. "Are you in there?"

"Yeah," Isabella said.

She rubbed the ointment out of her eye, then opened the door. Lord Robin stood outside, looking concerned. She felt an odd pang of guilt as she motioned him inside, even though she knew she was following the prince's orders. Lord Robin *had* hired her, after all. She was technically *his* subordinate.

"I think it worked," she said, as she bottled the ointment. There wasn't much, but she thought it would last for a day or two. She'd have to go source more of the ingredients at some point, then start looking into other folk cures. "What can I do for you?"

Lord Robin glanced at the pot, then shrugged. "The guards spotted a Red Monk near the temples," he said. "The Prince wants you to find the bastard and take him prisoner."

"Alive rather than dead," Isabella noted. She didn't fault

the prince for sending her. She probably had the best chance of surviving an encounter with the Red Monks. And a Red Monk might actually be able to give them answers. "Are you coming with me?"

"I'm needed with the scouts," Lord Robin said. "Big Richard will go with you."

Isabella sighed. She didn't *like* Big Richard. But then, he might be useful.

"Very well," she said. Who knew what the Red Monk was doing? "Do we know *exactly* where he is?"

"No," Lord Robin said. "The report said he was near the temples, nothing else."

"Understood," Isabella said. She pocketed the ointment and checked her sword. "I'm on my way."

Chapter Thirty-Four

"This is a boring town," Big Richard grumbled.

Isabella couldn't help agreeing with him. Neither Allenstown nor Racal's Bay had been particularly lively – certainly when compared to Havelock or the Golden City – but Rupert was little more than a large collection of grey houses and warehouses. There was no manor, no castle ... there didn't even seem to be any shops. She had no idea how the population had survived before being herded out of their town and into the surrounding forest. The drab grey town would have driven her mad years ago.

You can get used to anything, provided you accept it as normal, she reminded herself. It had been a shock to discover how people lived outside the Golden City, people who had no magic or wealth or anything else going for them. She'd thought she'd known everything until she'd come face-to-face with a very different reality. *The people here probably think Allenstown is a wild party town.*

She dismissed the thought as they made their way down the cobbled street. It was a surprisingly decent road, despite the damage caused by hundreds of horses and thousands of men marching through the town. The prince would have to find whoever built the road and put them to work, linking the different towns and cities together with a proper road network ... perhaps even iron dragons, if the craftsmen could build them for themselves. It would unite the Summer Isle and, hopefully, make it harder for the nobility to act as independent agents. Andalusia's network of roads allowed the king to move troops anywhere he liked within a matter of days.

And I can hear troops moving northwards now, she thought, as the sound of a moving army echoed over the town. Prince Reginald was preparing to attack ... and she was hunting for a Red Monk. *I have to find the bastard and get back to the prince.*

They turned onto Temple Row and studied the piles of debris. It was hard to be sure, but it looked as though there had been three or four temples in the town before the Red Monks had smashed them into ruins. Isabella wasn't sure *what* means they'd used to tear down the temples. It looked as if the buildings had just collapsed into rubble. The remains weren't even scorched. Magic? Or something truly weird?

Big Richard snorted, rudely. "Where *is* the bastard?"

"Good question," Isabella said, tartly. She looked from side to side, trying to spot the Red Monk. Nothing moved, not even a bird. The Red Monk might be hiding, protected by his powers, or ... he might be gone. He'd certainly had more than enough time to hide. Or maybe someone had sent them out on a wild goose chase. "Do they even *have* a temple here?"

"I don't know," Big Richard said. He sounded more angry than usual, as if she was distracting him from a greater thought. His piggish eyes flicked from side to side nervously. "Aren't *you* meant to be finding him?"

Isabella swallowed several nasty responses to that question and reached for the tiny bottle of ointment. If the Red Monk was hidden, the ointment *should* be able to help find him. Or her. Containing the monk afterwards would be harder, but she was sure they could do it. If nothing else, they could give the bastard a fright. She took a last look around, wondering if they should search the nearby houses, then dismissed the thought. There were only two of them and they had to stay together. They couldn't seal off the area and search it methodically.

And the prince can't give us any more men, she thought. She'd known there was no point in asking. *He needs everyone he has for the coming battle.*

She braced herself, then dabbed the ointment against her left eye. The world seemed to shift, shadows growing darker – and longer – as she looked around. Entire buildings seemed to shift out of place, moving in directions she couldn't even begin to comprehend; *things* moved in the shadows, barely touching the human world. She felt herself cringing back as she saw a ghostly spider – except it wasn't a spider – looking at her. Her skin began to itch, as if invisible creatures were crawling under her shirt. It was all she could do not to slap at herself.

Big Richard grunted. "Careful," he said, mockingly. "This is hardly the time or place."

Isabella flushed, angrily. She *had* been backing away, then; she'd backed away until she'd bumped into Big Richard. No doubt the bastard had *enjoyed* the brief contact, damn him. He'd been one of the loudest grumblers about the lack of wine and women in Rupert, she knew; he'd spent most of the night moaning and whining about Prince Reginald's decision not to allow camp followers to accompany the army. She clenched her fist, then unclenched it slowly. Turning Big Richard into something small and slimy would be satisfying, but it would also be a distraction.

She kept her right eye closed as she looked at the remains of the temples. Unlike the other buildings, the piles of debris looked almost *normal* ... a little *too* normal. She frowned as she tried to understand what she was seeing. The temples looked exactly the same, no matter which eye she looked through. It was almost as if they had no presence in the other world at all. They were just piles of dead stone. There was no ghostly light, no translucent glow ... no strange creatures hidden in the shadows. They were just ...

The temples and prayers were laid down by the Golden City, she thought. The Inquisitors had never tolerated unauthorised prayers and rituals. *What if they were designed to cut us off from the other world?*

She frowned. It was hard to believe that something so important could have been *forgotten*, but ... if the secret had been limited to the Grand Sorcerers and the Inquisitors alone, she could understand why it might have been lost. There had been too many secrets she'd been warned she would never know until she took the final oaths, oaths she'd never had the chance to take. Now, with the Inquisitors a spent force, there was no way to keep the kingdoms from devising religions of their own. Or, perhaps, from making contact with gods.

The implications stunned her. She'd worshipped back home, of course; she'd left offerings in front of the family shrine and attended temple services every week ... had she been wasting her time? Did those gods even exist? Or ... were the temples designed to *prevent* them from making contact with the gods? Were their prayers falling on deaf ears? Or ...

She turned slowly, peering through her left eye. The world was so much bigger than she'd thought. Lines of blue light hung in the air, moving so faintly that she wasn't sure they were moving at all. She looked down at her hand and saw blue light, as if her hand was slowly turning translucent. No ... she could see her bones, glowing with light. It looked as if she was dissolving ... she blinked hard, looking away. The world was changing, slowly shifting back to normal. The ointment was wearing off.

Big Richard grunted. "Anything?"

"No," Isabella lied. He didn't need to know anything, save for the fact she hadn't spotted the monk. "I ..."

She looked at him – and past him. The Red Monk was right *behind* him. And ...

Mother Lembu's voice echoed in her mind. "You made one mistake," Mother Lembu had said. "And your time to recover is short."

She could *see* it. A spider-web of corrupt light, draped over Big Richard. The Red Monks had *got* to him, somehow. Perhaps they'd got to him weeks ago. She could *see* the light burning into his soul, driving him mad. And she'd had a chance to spot the corruption when she'd been with Mother Lembu, a chance to *do something* about it before it was too late, a chance she'd missed ...

Big Richard growled and drew his axe.

"Think," Isabella said, reaching for her magic. She doubted it would work – his collection of protective amulets would make enchanting him difficult, even without the Red Monk – but she had to try. "You're not in your right mind ..."

She jumped backwards as he came at her, swinging his axe wildly. Isabella drew her sword, glancing from side to side as the mundane world and the other world started to blur together into a single universe. Big Richard was normal ... no, he *wasn't* normal. She knew she should close one of her eyes, but she didn't dare. The Red Monk had been lurking in the other world, almost completely invisible. If she closed her eye, the monk might attack her from the shadows.

Big Richard kept coming, growling with rage. His face was twisted into pure hatred ... she'd known he disliked her, but ... the Red Monk had clearly had ample time to work on Big Richard's feelings, stroking his dislike into a murderous rage. She dismissed the thought as she ducked one of his swings, casting a spell that should have punched through his defences and left him flat on his back. Not entirely to her surprise, the magic splintered out of existence before the spell even left her fingertips. She could *see* the magic fade away as it fell into the other world.

"You killed my brother," Big Richard growled. "Die!"

He swung at her again. Isabella jumped back, glancing from side to side. The Red Monk was still behind Big Richard, watching the fight from behind a red cowl. And yet, there was an undeniable sense of satisfaction surrounding the creature. Isabella didn't dare look too closely, even through her left eye. There was something about the Red Monk that warned her that looking too closely would be dangerous.

Damn it, she thought.

She tried to think of an option as a second spell flickered and died. She could turn and run, but she knew Big Richard could bury the axe in her back before she got more than a few paces away. Getting close enough to stab him would be difficult ... even trying to *parry* would be dangerous. He could knock her sword out of her hand, if the blade didn't shatter on impact. And then ... she forced herself to think. If she didn't have magic, how could she beat him?

The Red Monk, she thought. She could *see* the creature, keeping its distance from the two fighters. Faint traces of light darted between the monk and Big Richard. *That's the key.*

She dodged another swing, trying hard to think. There *had* to be a solution, but what? Big Richard was too consumed by hatred to listen to reason ... she couldn't even call for help or attack the monk without leaving herself exposed. And there wasn't any help within shouting distance ...

Big Richard feinted, then kicked out. The movement caught her by surprise, the kick slamming into her chest and throwing her backwards. Her rump hit the cobbled streets, hard; her sword clattered down next to her, narrowly missing her arm. She reached for it, a second too late. Big Richard landed on top of her with enough force to knock the breath out of her body. It felt as though she'd cracked a rib or two.

He drew back a fist, ready to smash her lights out. His face was completely shrouded now, the corruption clearly visible through her left eye. And he was driven by rage ... he wanted her dead. Nothing would distract him, not now. She fumbled for the knife in her sleeve, twisting her head as his fist slammed down, narrowly missing her nose. If he'd hit her ... she slipped the dagger out as he drew back for another punch, then drove it up and into his eye as hard as she could. Big Richard shuddered violently, then tumbled. The force of the impact nearly stunned her ...

Get out, she told herself. Big Richard might do more harm to her in death than he ever had in life. It was hard, so hard, to crawl out from under his corpse. *Move, you stupid idiot.*

The Red Monk was still there, standing within the other world. Isabella wondered, as she staggered to her feet, if the bastard *knew* she could see him. She'd certainly seen her fair share of peeping toms who'd assumed their invisibility cloaks or notice-me-not spells would allow them to slip into the girls changing rooms without being spotted and *they* had known the girls studied the same spells. The Red Monk might assume she was grasping in the dark ...

He saw me use the ointment, she reminded herself. The Red Monk was ... he was standing still. But he was also moving. Her brain hurt as she tried to process what she was seeing. He was going away, but in a direction she couldn't comprehend. *He knows I can see him.*

She turned and picked up Big Richard's axe. It was heavier than she'd expected, even for a swordswoman with fourteen years of experience. Big Richard had boasted, once, that he'd been given it by a young woman in exchange for services rendered, although Isabella hadn't believed a word of it. The axe was crude, yet functional. And it was made of cold iron.

Gritting her teeth, she drew on her magic and thrust the axe at the Red Monk. The spell started to splinter at once, of course, but the axe was already flying through the air. It buried itself in the Red Monk's side, sending him crashing into the real world. Blue light flared around the axe, shining brightly for a long moment before it flickered and died. There was no visible wound, as far as Isabella could make out, but she knew – on some level – that the Red Monk was dead.

No blood, she thought numbly. A human who'd been struck like that would be bleeding helplessly, if their guts weren't spilling out of the wound. The shock of the impact alone would prove fatal. *What are they?*

She walked forward, carefully. The body was pinned down by the axe ... she couldn't escape the feeling that *removing* the axe would be very dangerous. Up close, the Red Monk looked ... odd, as if there was something about him that didn't belong in the mundane world. A fish out of water couldn't have looked stranger. She no longer needed the ointment to see the creature.

He's not human, she told herself. She was sure of that, even if she wasn't sure of anything else. *Whatever he is, he's not human.*

She slowly walked around the corpse, drinking in the details. But there was very little to see. The Red Monk's cowl covered him from head to toe, somehow managing to flow around the axe to make it harder for her to see what the cold iron had actually *struck*. The cowl was covered with sewn runic patterns that meant nothing to her, patterns that matched the ones she'd seen in their temples. And it seemed to be repairing itself ... She remembered the swords that had been marked for destruction in Allenstown and shivered. If cold iron was the only thing that could kill the monks ...

And most of our swords are made from forged steel, she thought, as she knelt beside the body. Iron swords were relatively rare, although she could understand why they might have been redeveloped on the Summer Isle. Steelmaking wasn't *easy*, particularly now international trade had collapsed. *Those iron blades might be the only weapon we have.*

She looked up as she heard the sound of battle being joined. Prince Reginald was fighting the enemy then, under a darkening sky. She peered at the clouds for a long moment, then turned her attention back to the Red Monk. There was no way she *wanted* to know what was under the cowl, but she had a feeling she *had* to know. Wishing there was a witness, she touched the cowl – it felt almost *liquid* under her hands – and pulled it back to expose the head. The Red Monk looked human ...

... And then the face changed.

Isabella stared, unable to look away, unable even to *blink* as the Red Monk became something else, something utterly inhuman. Her thoughts juddered to a stop as she tried to comprehend what she was seeing, but it was impossible. She had to look away ... yet her eyes refused to let her go. Pain flashed through her head, a sudden wave of nausea assailing her ... she had to swallow hard to keep from throwing up everything she'd eaten over the past week. The universe seemed to be spinning around her ...

... A series of impressions slammed into her mind, jagged edges ripping through her thoughts and tearing them apart. She'd been praying ... no, *he'd* been praying. He'd called on a god by name. And ... the world had opened up around him and ... he'd gone into the light and ... he'd changed, somehow. He'd become something different, something better ... he'd become a servant of his god and ... he'd been moulded like clay, turned into something new. He'd been human once, but he was different now ...

... *Things* scuttled along the outer edge of reality, wanting in. He'd seen them ... she could see them. The universe was so much bigger than she could comprehend. Her mind kept trying to bind it to something she *could* understand, but it was defying her. It was a web ... no, it was a house ... no, it was a village, a town, a city ... She opened her mouth to scream ...

... And then the world plunged into darkness.

Chapter Thirty-Five

"The enemy is on the move," Captain James reported. "They're moving precisely as you predicted."

"Excellent," Earl Goldenrod said. "Order the troops to stand fast. We'll greet them in the trenches."

He smiled to himself as he peered through the telescope. There was a risk in getting too close to the battle, but it was one that had to be endured. He *needed* to show the men – his men and Lord Havant's men – that he was willing to share the danger with them, if only for a single battle. It would do wonders for morale and, more importantly, make them more inclined to support him when Havant had an unfortunate accident or two. As soon as the younger man had sired a son, he'd die ... leaving Goldenrod in command of the joint earldom, perhaps even the kingdom itself.

And Roxanne might already be pregnant, Goldenrod thought. He'd made it clear to his daughter that she *had* to keep her husband in her bed, at least until her monthly courses stopped. And that she had to behave herself in all ways. There could not be the *slightest* doubt over his grandson's paternity. *Once she gives birth, her husband can be pushed down the stairs at will.*

He smiled again, then turned his attention to the oncoming troops. Prince Reginald was starting to mount a frontal assault, instead of picking his way through the boggy moor or trying to outflank the defenders by sneaking through the forest. It wasn't a good move, Goldenrod noted, but it was pretty much the *only* move open to the invaders. He could no more outflank the defenders than he could withdraw and leave the northern earldoms alone.

And he cannot show weakness, Goldenrod noted. The mainland might *claim* to be more civilised than the Summer Isle, but at base all men were the same. *He dares not show weakness or his allies will desert him.*

"Order the archers to open fire when the enemy troops cross the line," he said. "And then prepare the reserves to move forward and seal any gaps in the trenches."

"Yes, Your Excellency."

Goldenrod nodded, curtly. The enemy would charge into the teeth of his archers ... they had no choice. They *had* to charge. It would cost them badly ... and then they'd hit the trenches, where his infantry were waiting for them. Prince Reginald's men were good, but they'd never faced northerners on their own soil. Goldenrod's men wouldn't break, not when they *knew* they held the cards. Prince Reginald's men, on the other hand ...

And then the future opens up before me, Goldenrod thought. Joining Havant instead of betraying him immediately had been a calculated gamble, but it looked as though it had paid off. The invaders would be broken, there would be a joint heir ... and Goldenrod, as the sole survivor, would be poised to rule the kingdom in his grandson's name. *The world awaits me.*

He felt dizzy, just for a second. The world seemed to fade ...

He shook his head, dismissing the sensation. He was old, by the standards of the Summer Isle, but he wasn't *that* old. He'd live long enough to see his grandson become a man, ready to take the throne. And then ... who knew? The Summer Isle wouldn't be enough for a boy who shared two of the noblest bloodlines in the world. Perhaps his grandson would take an army to Andalusia ...

The world faded, again. He gritted his teeth, biting his lip until he tasted blood. He didn't have time for weakness, not now. He had too much else to do.

"And pass the word to the men," he added. "No quarter."

***

Havant sat in the middle of a runic diagram, drawn with blood, and *concentrated*.

It wasn't easy, even with the presence gently pointing him in the right direction. Even now, it was hard to push his thoughts down the bloody link. He could feel his wife ... and, beyond her, her father. The Red Monks already had Roxanne in their custody, ready to kill her if matters spiralled out of control. Whatever her father thought, she wasn't pregnant.

He felt Earl Goldenrod's thoughts as he pushed through the link. The Earl didn't seem to be aware of the mental intrusion, but he did know that *something* was wrong. Havant caught a flicker of concern about age, of all things ... Earl Goldenrod was old, he supposed. The man was actually ten years older than Havant's father, if he recalled correctly. Earl Goldenrod was technically old enough to be Havant's grandfather.

Not that it matters, he thought, as he peered through the Earl's eyes. No doubt the earl had anticipated treachery – it was practically a tradition – but he couldn't imagine the power Havant had learned to master. He'd surrounded himself with loyal bodyguards, a precaution that was completely useless. *It won't be long now.*

The presence inside Havant thrummed with anticipation. He could *see* the battlefield, as if he were peering down from a vast height. The skies were darkening, forces gathering for the great working that was soon to take place ... he could feel it, great powers returning to the world that had banished them long ago. Prince Reginald and his men had no idea what was waiting for them ...

... And they would merely be the first to die.

***

"The archers are in position," Gars said. "Your Highness?"

Reginald nodded, curtly. He'd sent men into danger before – he'd even sent men to their deaths before – but this felt different. It felt ... *wrong*. His instincts were telling him to pull back and find another way to march north, but he knew there was *no* other way to reach the northern earldoms. His last attempt to send a message to the Northern Realm had apparently failed. The messenger had certainly not returned.

He gritted his teeth. Withdrawal was not an option. And yet ... losing too many men in battle might be disastrous too, even if he emerged the winner. There would be no reinforcements from Andalusia as long as the storms raged in the channel ... there wouldn't even be the chance to abandon the invasion and sail home. He was caught in a trap. He knew he *had* to attack and yet ... he also knew that attacking could be disastrous.

"Order the archers to open fire," he said. The enemy archers would be forced to duck, if nothing else. "And tell the first line to advance on my command."

"Yes, Your Highness," Gars said. "With your permission, I'll take command of the first companies myself."

"Granted," Reginald said, reluctantly. He knew he'd need *someone* he trusted in the thick of it, particularly when it became impossible to direct the battle from a distance. But he didn't want to lose his friend. "Be careful."

"They have to be careful, Your Highness," Gars assured him. "They're standing in our way."

***

Lord Robin had no illusions about the coming battle. He would never admit it to anyone, but part of him had been tempted to quietly desert the prince and make his own way back to the mainland. Only loyalty to his band – and the prospect of getting a *real* lordship – had kept him close to the prince. The first kings had just been lucky warlords, after all. Robin wasn't aiming *that* high, but he wanted enough power and prestige to ensure that he would never be poor or hungry again.

He knelt in the trench as enemy arrows started hissing over their heads. The enemy seemed to be shooting at random, although – with so many men assembled nearby – the odds of hitting *someone* were actually quite good. He winced – hiding the reaction quickly – as an arrowhead cracked into the makeshift shield and shattered, pieces of wood falling to the ground. The enemy had designed their arrows to break apart on impact, making it harder for them to be removed from the wound. Worse, perhaps, it prevented the archers from reusing them.

And Isabella isn't here to help, he thought, grimly. He'd grown used to having a personal druid, someone who could use magic to help her comrades heal. *If we get hit, we're fucked.*

He felt a thrill of anticipation, despite himself, as the first whistle blew. *This* was war. *This* was what he loved. No supernatural creatures, no magic ... nothing, but the clash of cold steel on cold steel. Maybe he would never be able to walk away from it, even after winning his lands and title. Maybe he'd start attacking his neighbours, just for the thrill of it ...

"Keep your shields raised," he ordered, raising his voice. Most of the men were hardened mercenaries, but a handful were raw recruits. They'd learn by doing – or soak up arrows and blades that would otherwise kill good men. "And keep moving. Don't let their archers get a clear shot at you!"

His eyes swept over the group as they took their places, ready to advance. The hardened men were bracing themselves, the newcomers were terrified ... Robin moved from man to man, offering words of reassurance and diplomatically ignoring the evidence that some of them had lost control of their bowels. They hadn't understood what a battle was like when they'd joined ... they still didn't, really. None of their comrades would make fun of them, if they survived. They'd all wet themselves in terror when they'd started too.

The second whistle blew. "Go!"

There was no longer any time for thinking. He ran up the ramp and onto the moor, cursing under his breath as his feet threatened to slip. The damp land was hardly *ideal* battlefield terrain. He kept moving, holding the shield out in front of him as he ran towards the enemy lines. His men followed him, howling their defiance at the universe. Arrows flashed over their heads, smashing into shields and disintegrating. He heard a man cry out in horror as an arrow struck him, screaming that he was unmanned. The thought was enough to make Robin wince. He'd sooner die.

"Move, move," he bellowed, as more and more men joined the charge. "Get into their trenches."

The ground turned muddy under his feet, an instant before he reached the trench and plunged down. An enemy soldier had no time to react before Robin slammed his shield into his face, then beheaded him with a swift blow from his sword. Two more stumbled out of their hiding positions and lunged at him, lashing out with their blades. It was laughably obvious that they were raw recruits, waving the swords around as if they were on the practice field rather than in a real battle. Robin felt a moment of pity for their sergeants as he sliced both men down, then turned to look for other targets. The untrained men hadn't thought they needed to defend as well as attack.

More men jumped into the trench, ducking low into the mud as enemy arrows started to hiss towards them. The enemy commander had ordered his men to fire *into* the captured trench, despite the possibility that some of his men were still alive and fighting. But then, the untrained troops were probably considered expendable. *Robin* certainly wouldn't have put his *best* troops to meet and greet the enemy's frontal assault. Better to have them break against men who were easy to replace.

A body crashed down next to him, an arrow sticking out of his gut. Robin glanced down, noted that the poor bastard was already dead, then dismissed the matter. There would be time to cremate the bodies and mourn later. Instead, he had to focus on the charge.

"Get reinforcements up here," he bellowed. They'd overrun the first trench, but there were five more. The enemy archers, damn them, didn't appear to be on the verge of running out of arrows anytime soon. "We need to press onwards!"

***

The messenger barely had time to salute before he started to gabble out his message. "Your Highness, Captain-General Gars has overrun the first line of defences," he said. "He requests reinforcements!"

Reginald nodded, doubtfully. He'd expected to take the first trench, but it had been suspiciously easy. Hundreds of dead bodies lay on the field, yet ... he'd expected a harder fight, somehow. But then, it was just the first line. The enemy wasn't foolish enough to put all their soldiers in *one* trench.

"Order the second line to advance," he said. The enemy archers were concentrating on the captured trenches now, thankfully. It would be hell for the men under their fire, but it would give him time to get reinforcements into position. "And send in the caterpillars."

"Yes, Your Highness."

***

"That's clever," Earl Goldenrod admitted. He could see why Prince Reginald had such an impressive reputation. "Do you think he carried the turtles north or had his engineers make them here?"

"I don't know, sir," Captain James said. "But they are a serious threat."

Goldenrod nodded. The turtles were really nothing more than giant, inverted wooden boxes, but they would each protect a platoon or two of men as they moved towards the occupied trenches. Worse, with the enemy already assaulting the second set of trenches, the archers didn't have time to do anything about the turtles. Prince Reginald could move his defences forward in relative safety.

"Order the archers to light their flaming arrows and try to set the turtles on fire," he said, curtly. "And then ..."

He frowned as he heard a Red Monk haranguing the reserves as they formed up, ready to go into battle. Havant had insisted on the Red Monks accompanying his men, even though they gave Goldenrod the creeps. There was something about the cowled figures that bothered him on a very basic level. But he hadn't seen it as being worth an argument, when they'd been planning the battle. Now, watching the Red Monks slowly converting more and more of his men to their cause, he wondered if that had been a good idea. He'd seen them as harmless, just another religious sect willing to take advantage of soldiers who wanted to believe that the gods were looking out for them. Now ...

Captain James cleared his throat. "Sir?"

"Never mind," Goldenrod said. "And prepare the horsemen to charge."

***

"They're shooting flaming arrows at the caterpillars," the messenger said. "Two of them have caught fire."

"I can see that," Reginald snapped. "Order the archers to provide covering fire."

He frowned. His men were overrunning the second trench now and making preparations to take the third. It wouldn't be long until it fell ... and yet, it felt too easy. Something felt wrong. But what? The battle seemed to be going his way.

"Order the reserves to stand at the ready," he added, after a moment. "I want them to be ready for anything."

***

Havant allowed himself a tight smile as he surveyed the battlefield from his strange vantage point. The invaders were doing well, but ... but they had no idea that they were forcing their way into a trap. Earl Goldenrod's plan was on the verge of failing – he hadn't really understood just how experienced the invaders were – but *Havant's* plan, the *real* plan, was about to work. The trap was about to snap shut.

He gathered himself, then forced his way down the link. Earl Goldenrod's mind let out a yelp – a startlingly apt reaction – a second before Havant took complete control. The man struggled, but he had no experience at all in mental combat. Havant forced him down, locking him away in his own mind, then spoke through Goldenrod's mouth.

"Saddle my horse," he ordered. It felt strange – as if he were in two places at once – but he held the thread together through grim determination. "I'll lead the charge personally."

Goldenrod screamed, deep within his mental prison. Havant ignored him as he moved the body forward, allowing its instincts to take control. It was hard to remember how to breathe, let alone how to move. Everything felt wrong ... Goldenrod was old, very old. The presence in Havant's mind leaned forward, studying Goldenrod with interest. Havant smiled coldly as he heard Goldenrod scream again.

He scrambled onto the horse, smiling coldly as he heard the men – Goldenrod's men – cheering him. They thought their earl was going to lead the charge personally and, in a sense, they were right. Goldenrod would be remembered as a hero, a martyr ... it would be easy, in the aftermath, to take control of his earldom. Everyone would bow to Goldenrod's son-in-law, his chosen heir. Havant wouldn't even dissuade them from hailing their former leader as a hero. It was the least he could do for a man who'd done him such a wonderful service.

You're mad, Goldenrod said. Or thought. *What are you? What have you done?*

Havant blinked in surprise. He'd thought he'd locked Goldenrod away for good. And yet ... he could *feel* the man's horror at what had happened. And, perhaps, at just how foolish he'd been. He'd played a game without knowing anything about it, even the rules. Now ... now he could see too much, too late. Goldenrod had thrown his earldom into his enemy's hands.

Shut up, old man, he thought, savagely. He *hated* old men. His father had been a nightmare and Goldenrod, for all that he'd made a show of treating Havant like an equal, had talked down to him time and time again. And he'd planned a betrayal too. *Your time is over.*

He reached out, drawing on the power of the ritual, and pressed down hard. Goldenrod's thoughts winked out of existence, leaving his body empty ...

Now, Havant thought. It was growing harder to control Goldenrod's body, now the man's soul was gone. *Let us lead the charge.*

Chapter Thirty-Six

For a long moment, Reginald refused to believe what he was seeing.

The enemy horsemen were leaping across their trenches and charging his men. He could *hear* them hooting and howling, strange words echoing through the air as they converged on their targets; he could *see* them waving swords in the air, daring his men to stop them. It was *insane*. They'd all be killed. Cavalry *might* be able to take infantry if their targets panicked, but *his* men knew what to do. They were already taking up defensive positions as the horsemen charged towards them.

"Move up the reserves," he ordered, shortly. "And get the archers targeting those fools."

"Yes, Your Highness."

The messenger hurried away. Reginald barely noticed as he pressed his eye against the telescope, determined not to miss a moment of the spectacle. His archers had *already* switched targets, dropping hundreds of arrows over the advancing cavalry. Reginald felt a flicker of pity — cavalrymen were almost always drawn from the upper classes — as the horses began to fall, their riders slamming into the boggy ground with terrifying force. And yet, he couldn't help cursing the enemy commander under his breath. What terrible sin had his men committed to deserve to be under *his* command?

He sucked in his breath as the cavalry kept coming, even though more and more were falling to the ground. They were amongst his men now, lashing out with their swords; a handful of Reginald's men fell, instants before their comrades could bring the horsemen down and hack them to bits. Reginald opened his mouth to issue orders for prisoners to be taken, then closed it as he realised there was no point. Their blood was up now. They wouldn't listen to orders to take prisoners, even though *Reginald* was good at making sure the ransoms were fairly distributed. And issuing orders he knew wouldn't be followed was dangerously unwise.

A messenger appeared, holding a metal hat in one hand. "Your Highness, the cavalry would like to charge."

"Certainly not," Reginald snapped. He'd hoped to use *his* horsemen to chase the enemy, once their lines broke. He was certainly *not* going to send them into that meatgrinder, just because his cavalrymen wanted to show that they too could be suicidally brave. "Tell them to hold position and *wait*."

He turned his attention back to the trenches, frowning in displeasure as the enemy charge finally came to an end. They hadn't broken, not even at the last. But they'd died ... it would have impressed him, a little, if it hadn't been so pointless. His troops were already ransacking the saddlebags and stripping the dead men of their armour and anything else they might be carrying. There wouldn't even be any ransoms to collect afterwards ...

Maybe the heirs will want the bodies, he thought, wryly. It wouldn't be the first time someone had refused to accept that their father or brother was dead, either through sentiment or more calculative motives. A wife couldn't be dispossessed from her husband's castle if there was no clear proof that the poor bastard was dead. *But they won't pay so much for a corpse.*

He scanned the battlefield as the wind changed, cold air blowing towards him. The skies were growing darker, promising rain, but he doubted it would start before the battle was fairly won. Perhaps they'd overestimated the enemy's strength. It wouldn't be the first time a scout had counted the same man multiple times and returned with a grossly exaggerated estimate. Maybe the enemy had decided to mount a charge rather than retreat to inglorious disaster.

And maybe we can end this sooner than I'd thought, he told himself. *A push through now might just win the battle.*

Turning to the messengers, he began to issue orders. It was time to put an end to the affair.

***

Havant closed his eyes for a long moment as he fell back into his own body. Earl Goldenrod was dead, his body lost somewhere in the trenches. The last set of impressions – before the pain had become unbearable and he'd lost contact – had spoken of multiple stab wounds, knives and swords digging into the dead man's flesh. And Goldenrod's men had followed him on a charge they'd *known* was suicidal ...

"The sacrifice is complete," Hark said. "We may begin."

He lowered his voice. "Our Lord comes ..."

Havant felt the presence rising up within him, power surging through his mind and up and out into the world beyond. Someone was singing ... a song that pressed against his thoughts, forcing him back into his own mind. He'd had problems coping with having his mind expanded, but it was as natural as breathing to the presence. Power rose – the power from the sacrifice – and reached out, sliding into the land. And then it started to rise again.

IT BEGINS, a voice said. Havant wasn't sure if it was speaking to him directly or something else. *OUR TIME IS NIGH.*

The power surged forth. A series of impressions roared through Havant's mind – voices speaking, worlds unfurling, power walking upon the land – an instant before the pressure got too much for him. He was dimly aware that the presence was speaking through him – that it had done it before, when he'd blacked out – but this was different. The pressure was rising ...

... And he finally, mercifully, blacked out.

***

"This one was carrying a bag of gold coins," a mercenary shouted. "Mine!"

"Mine," another snapped. "I brought the bastard down!"

"I knifed his horse," the first shouted. He drew his dagger. "Mine!"

Lord Robin raised his voice. "Shut up," he ordered. Perhaps the enemy had sent the horsemen on their suicidal charge in the hopes of starting a civil war within Prince Reginald's ranks. A dispute over who got to loot the corpses could easily turn violent, simply because the men were feeling underpaid. "We'll divide the money later!"

"It's mine," the first man snapped. He clutched the pouch to his chest with one hand, while holding his dagger in the other. "I found it first!"

"Later," Robin snapped. More and more men were running up to the third trench, forming up for an attack on the fourth and last. He didn't have *time* to let his troops start an argument over money. "It will be fairly distributed!"

"Hah," the second man said. "Officers will take half of it ..."

Someone screamed. Robin blinked in surprise, then swung around, blade in hand. The cry hadn't *sounded* like a man who'd been hit. It had sounded more womanish ... a young man, so young that he hadn't even started to grow a beard, was stumbling away from one of the dead horsemen. Robin stared, unsure what to make of it. Peasants, even *female* peasants, were rarely squeamish about dead bodies. Only aristocratic women could afford such luxuries.

"It moved," the youth said.

Robin bit down several nasty remarks. The trench was muddy, water splashing down and pooling at the bottom. Of *course* the body had moved. It was so poorly balanced that it was lucky it hadn't already slid down and landed in the mud. The horse looked to have died in agony, unsurprisingly. It went against the grain to eat the beasts, but what *else* were they going to do with the remains? Horsemeat would improve their rations beyond belief ...

The corpse moved. Again. Robin stared as the dead body lumbered to its feet, staring at them through beady yellow eyes. Dead silence fell. There was no doubt that the body was dead – no human could possibly have survived a broken neck, not without very strong magic – but it was moving. Somehow, impossibly, it was moving. He looked back at the other body and cursed in disbelief. It was moving too, its skin slowly turning grey. They were *all* moving.

"Get back," he snapped. He remembered, all too well, stories about necromantic plagues, about zombies that had been trapped in the ice for centuries until some idiot had come along and accidentally unleashed them once again. "I ..."

The corpse lunged forward, its hands becoming ... *things*. It stabbed right at the young man, stabbing deep into his neck. The man's skin slowly turned grey, his eyes turning yellow as he turned to face his comrades. His *former* comrades, Robin realised. Whatever foul sorcery had been unleashed was converting the victims into new enemies. It had to be stopped.

He lashed out with his sword. The young man's head flew off as Robin cut through his neck, but the rest of his body kept coming. Robin heard the sounds of panic behind him as he sliced the poor bastard's body apart, then did the same to the dead horseman. It wasn't enough, he realised grimly. *Every* corpse on the field was coming back to life. Eerie yellow eyes followed him as he jumped out of the trench and looked around. A dull grey fog was rolling southwards, right towards him. The ground was shuddering below his feet.

"Move south," he snapped, as another dead man came at him. He wished, suddenly, that Big Richard had accompanied him. An axe would have been ideal for fighting the dead men. "And ..."

The ground shook, again. He turned, just in time to see the forest slowly moving towards them. The trees were uprooting themselves, marching forwards inch by inch ... he thought he saw, just for a moment, wooden faces within the branches. They didn't look happy, he thought as the ground continued to move: they looked angry, as if they were marching to a ruthless war of extermination. And there were *things* in the ground under his feet ...

He shook his head, grimly. He was a brave man, but he knew he couldn't fight magic on such a scale. He didn't even know where to begin. What would happen if he hacked at the trees with his sword? He didn't know ... he didn't think *anyone* knew. The battle had turned into a catastrophe. They had to fall back and rethink their tactics.

"Run," he ordered. "Get back to the city and ..."

Wooden tendrils erupted around Robin's feet, wrapping around his ankles and holding him down. Robin stumbled, then fell to the muddy ground. The water felt different – alive, somehow – as he splashed down, faint flickers of energy dancing around him as the tendrils grew stronger and stronger. He drew his dagger from his belt in the hopes of cutting himself free, but no matter how many tendrils he cut there were always more and more, choking the life out of him. It was suddenly very hard to breathe ...

The ground shook, time and time again, as the walking trees approached. They were blurring into the land, he thought numbly, their roots crawling underground and spreading rapidly through the trenches. He remembered his mother complaining about tree roots attacking the foundations of her house and shivered, helplessly. If a slow-growing tree could do so much damage, what could a mobile tree do?

A tree loomed over him, branches lashing down. It was impossible to avoid seeing the wooden face blurring into the trunk, twisted with madness and a sheer hateful rage he hadn't seen outside slave revolts. The tree hated him. It wanted him dead.

The branches slammed down. There was a moment of pain, a moment when it felt as though his body was being ripped apart, then ...

Darkness.

***

"*Gods*," Reginald breathed.

The scene before him was nightmarish. He pinched himself, just to make sure it *wasn't* a dream. But his body refused to wake up. The dead bodies were coming to life, the trees were coming to life ... he looked up as droplets of rain started to fall and saw watery *faces* within the dark clouds. He wished, suddenly, that he'd paid more attention to Isabella. But who could have predicted *this*?

"Tell the archers to start launching fire arrows into the trenches," he ordered. "Now!"

It was all he could do to keep his voice steady. Fire. Fire was a standard countermeasure against walking corpses, right? But there were *gods* arrayed against him. Fear trickled down his spine as the ground shook, the trees completing the destruction of the trenches and then turning to face Rupert. Reginald cursed as he saw his men breaking and running, their officers and sergeants too scared themselves to restore order. He'd seen men panic before, but not like this. None of them had anticipated gods ...

The men streamed into Rupert, looking for a safety

Reginald suspected was largely illusory. He couldn't believe the town would last long, even if his men regained their nerve. The trees could simply press against the walls, such as they were, and break them down. Or maybe they could launch seeds into the city, seeds which would grow into more trees ... he cursed himself, once again. The entire army was on the verge of being destroyed.

We can't stay here, he thought, grimly. Whatever the enemy had unleashed was too powerful to stop, at least for the moment. *Maybe we can outrun it.*

He waved to the messengers. "Sound the retreat," he ordered. "And then order the town to be abandoned."

The messengers hurried off, leaving Reginald alone with his thoughts. Sounding the retreat was an empty formality at this point, but it might restore a *little* order. He wouldn't complain if the men kept retreating until they reached the formal regrouping point. Reginald's father had hammered into his head, time and time again, that he had to prepare for defeat as well as victory. Reginald silently blessed the old man as he turned, silently promising himself that he *would* be back. The war wasn't over *yet*.

And we'd better hope that Isabella makes it out of the city, he thought. In hindsight, sending her after the Red Monk had been a dangerous mistake. *She might be the only one who can tell us how to fight back.*

***

"Wake up," a voice said.

Isabella jerked awake, half-expecting to find someone kneeling next to her. Long experience on the campaign trail had taught her that it could be *dangerous* to be unconscious during the aftermath of a battle, but ... she was alone. She kept one hand on her sword as she rose, glancing from side to side. The Red Monk's body was just a pile of dust in an empty robe, the axe pinning what remained of it to the ground: Big Richard's body hadn't moved, but ... the ground was shaking. Something was very wrong.

She looked around, then realised her own mistake and dabbed some more of the ointment on her left eye. The world seemed to come alive, *things* running south like animals fleeing mounted hunters. She turned slowly, feeling *power* thrumming through the air as she peered north. An entire *world* seemed to be touching the ground, something so *large* that her mind refused to grasp it. It seemed to be infinitely large and infinitesimally small, so vast it contained the universe and so small it was just a single point ...

"You have to move," the voice said, firmly. It sounded as though the speaker was right behind her. "You're not safe here."

Isabella spun around, but saw nothing. The hidden world was shifting ... the physical world was changing too, a building crashing to the ground as the two worlds started to interact. She could feel the ground shaking under her feet, *hear* a terrible voice echoing through the air. Men were screaming, crying out in horror ... she could *feel* them being crushed by something immensely greater than themselves. Prince Reginald hadn't just *lost* the battle, she realised numbly; his forces had been decisively defeated.

"Go," the voice ordered.

The earthquakes grew stronger. She looked north and saw ... the hidden world rolling towards her, a sphere of light and power and energy, directed by something so vast she could barely make it out. The world was changing, warping ... she heard more buildings crashing to the ground as their time ran out. Gritting her teeth, she turned and looked at Big Richard's body. She knew she should try to take it home, but she doubted she could carry it. A levitation spell failed to work ...

She gave him one last look, then turned and ran. The ground shook, time and time again, as she fled towards the south gates. A handful of men were already passing through them, running so quickly that it was clear they were terrified. This was no retreat, she realised in horror. This was a rout. Behind her, she heard the remaining buildings shatter as the world warped around them. It was hard to escape the sense that doom was following her, right on her heels. How could one fight against such forces? How could one ...?

If we give up, we've lost already, she told herself, firmly. She'd faced opponents stronger that her in the past. But they'd also been *understandable* opponents. She understood muscles or magic or simple cunning. Godly power? She didn't understand *that*. *I don't even know where to begin?*

The remains of Prince Reginald's army were streaming past as she ran through the gates; some crying out to their gods, others concentrating on putting as much distance as they could between themselves and the forces that the enemy had unleashed. Tears ran down their cheeks, tears that bore mute witness to just how badly the army had been routed. Strong men didn't cry ...

We will find a solution, Isabella thought. *Somehow ...*

She turned and looked behind her. Rupert was collapsing, the entire town crashing down into a sinkhole. Trees – walking trees – were tearing up the ground, destroying the fields that had once kept the population alive. And behind them, looming over the battlefield, was a giant humanoid figure that chilled her to the bone. She hoped she was the only one who could see it ...

... But she knew, all too well, that that might not be true.

Chapter Thirty-Seven

It was a battered, dispirited army – a mob of men, in so many ways – that slowly made its way back into Allenstown.

Reginald cursed under his breath, again, as he watched his men return to the city. He'd failed them. A defeat was one thing, even a defeat that threatened to undo everything he'd achieved, but *gods* ...? He'd heard the rumours spreading through the ranks, despite everything the officers could do to keep them under control. The soldiers were wondering if they were on the right side after all. And the mere fact that they'd lost a battle ...

He rubbed his forehead as he turned to look around the war room. His senior officers – his remaining senior officers – had gathered, as he'd ordered, but he was damned if he knew what to tell them. Gars had survived, thankfully, but Lord Robin had died in the trenches and Captain-General Stuart had died ... no one was quite sure *where* he'd died. They certainly hadn't found a body. It bothered Reginald, more than he cared to admit, that he hadn't seen his trusted friend die. Too many others had died, but Stuart's loss nagged at his mind. In hindsight, trying to scout the forest had been a mistake.

"We will impose strict discipline on the city, of course," he said. When in doubt, fall back on the basics. Allenstown *might* rise up against the occupiers if its population knew what had happened up north. "And we will also impose it on our men."

"Distribute iron swords," Isabella said. She sat at one end of the table, her face haunted. She'd made a very brief report, when they'd met after the retreat, but since then she'd kept herself to herself. She was, as far as Reginald could tell, the last survivor of her mercenary band. "It might give them a fighting chance."

"See to it," Reginald ordered Gars. "And get the

blacksmiths forging more."

"Yes, Your Highness," Gars said.

"I think we should reconsider our approach," Lord William said. "Our army has been broken."

Reginald gritted his teeth. Captain-General Stuart was dead, Lord Robin was dead, countless men he didn't know were dead ... and Lord William had survived? The man had been at the rear, of course. He'd probably fled the battlefield the moment the dead had started to rise. It just seemed terribly unfair. Lord William deserved *nothing* from him.

"The men have had a shock," Gars said. "They ..."

"A shock," Lord William repeated. He looked at Reginald, his eyes conveying an unspoken challenge. "They saw *magic*, Your Highness. Magic on a vaster scale than *any* of them – any of us – have ever seen before. And they don't know how to fight back against such power."

He paused, waiting for Reginald to say something. But Reginald said nothing.

"We should withdraw immediately, Your Highness," Lord William added. "The invasion has failed. Your father's investment ..."

"My father's future is at stake here," Reginald growled. "We cannot be seen to withdraw!"

"And we cannot be seen to throw good men after bad," Lord William said. His tone was achingly reasonable. "How do you propose to defeat *gods*, Your Highness? How do you propose to capture the land you need to pay the men? How do you propose to *keep* this island ...?"

Reginald met his eyes. "So you're suggesting we run away?"

Lord William's eyes flashed angrily at the unsubtle accusation of cowardice. But, somehow, he managed to keep his voice calm.

"There is nothing on this wretched island worth taking," he said, calmly. "It rains all the time and the women ... they are ugly." He laughed, unpleasantly. "We have encountered an enemy we cannot defeat, Your Highness. It is time to withdraw to the mainland and ..."

"And what?" Reginald felt his anger start to flare. "I don't know *what's* been unleashed here, but I *do* know we cannot allow it to spread to the mainland."

"And how do we stop it, Your Highness?"

Reginald met the older man's dark eyes. "And even if we *do* decide to run, have you forgotten the storms? There is no way we can get a single boat across the channel, let alone an entire fleet!"

"They summoned the storms," Lord William said. "Perhaps we can come to an arrangement ..."

"So you're suggesting we surrender," Reginald said, flatly. "Do you really *think* we can bargain with them?"

He drew his sword in one smooth motion. "I cannot abide spinelessness," he said, as Lord William stumbled backwards. "And we cannot surrender."

His blade flashed, once. Lord William's body tumbled to the stone floor.

Reginald drew in a long breath. He'd wanted to do *that* for a long time, but now ... Lord William would have worked to undermine Reginald's position, if he'd been allowed to live. Most of the senior officers were all loyal to Reginald personally, but the ones who weren't might have sided with the older man ... and even the loyalists might well have doubts, after the rout. Killing Lord William would make it harder for the bastards to challenge him.

He wiped the blade and returned it to its scabbard, then looked around the room. "We will find a way to fight back," he said, firmly. "Until then, we will prepare the men to fight to hold the city."

His voice hardened. "Or do any of you see a way to escape?"

There was no answer. He hadn't expected one. They couldn't move the army to Racal's Bay, let alone cross the channel and get home. The combination of enemy attacks and storms – storms directed by the enemy – would see to that. And they all knew it too.

He allowed himself a cold smile. "Isabella, remain behind," he ordered. "The rest of you, dismissed."

The room emptied rapidly. Reginald took one last look at the dead body, then made a mental note to have the servants take the corpse and burn it before it reanimated. He had no idea if the ... *power* ... could reach so far south, but there was no point in taking chances. Too many reports of dead men walking had reached his ears.

"We need a solution," he said, once they were alone. "Can you think of anything?"

Isabella said nothing for a long moment. Her face was pale and worn. Reginald guessed she hadn't been sleeping properly over the last two days, just like the rest of them. And she'd lost her friends ...

"I have to speak to Emetine," Isabella said. "She might have a few answers for me."

"Do whatever you have to do to get answers out of her," Reginald said. He'd never ordered a woman tortured before, certainly not a woman of noble blood, but he was prepared to do whatever it took to keep the army alive. "Did your ... ointment ... help?"

Isabella shrugged. She looked smaller, somehow ... she was sitting upright, but he had the impression that she was hugging her legs against her chest, like a little girl who'd been given some very bad news. He felt a surge of protectiveness that surprised him with its intensity, all the more so as part of the reason he'd been attracted to her was that she *didn't* need his protection. But she'd had her worldview torn apart as much as his own.

"It was useful," she said. "I saw ... things ... that I might understand, one day. But right now we're just fumbling through the dark."

"Then perhaps you should take some rest," Reginald said. He glanced at the window. The sun was already starting to drop below the horizon. "You can interrogate Emetine tomorrow."

He wondered, suddenly, what she'd say if he invited her to share his bed. A courtly woman would have been honoured, if the Crown Prince had made the offer. Becoming his mistress would have given her high status, particularly if she bore a natural-born son ... even after he tired of her. And no one would have questioned her, afterwards ...

... But he had the feeling it would be different for Isabella.

"Get some rest," he ordered, gently. He knew he should take some himself, but he was too keyed up to sleep. Down below, his men would be trying to rest themselves. "I'll see you in the morning."

"Of course, Your Highness," Isabella said. "Good night."

"Hah," Reginald muttered.

***

"But what is *happening*?"

Roxanne Goldenrod looked terrified, Havant noted, as he stepped into the temple. Being guarded by the Red Monks – and tied down, when Havant had been using her blood to control her father – would have been terrifying, but being stripped naked and marched into the temple had to be worse. The Red Monks had tied her hands, then drawn blood runes on her bare skin. The whole experience had to have scared the girl to death.

"You will serve a greater cause," Hark informed her. His face was hidden completely now, his form starting to shift in ways human minds couldn't comprehend. "The Ascension is at hand."

Roxanne stared at Havant. "What are you doing?"

Havant ignored her. He was aware, on some level, that her treatment should have bothered him – she was his wife, whatever else she was – but it was hard to feel anything beyond anticipation. The presence within his mind was growing stronger, far stronger, feeding on the power he'd channelled through the sacrifice. He felt almost as though he was dreaming, seeing things that couldn't be there, yet there was a hard edge to the dream which made it impossible to let go of the world. The presence wouldn't *let* him let go.

"Let go of me," Roxanne said. "Please ..."

"Be silent," Hark ordered. He looked towards the moon, casting an eerie light over the temple. "We begin."

He snapped his fingers. Two Red Monks appeared behind Roxanne and frog-marched her towards the altar. She began to scream and fight, struggling desperately to get free, but it was futile. The Red Monks hoisted her up, placed her on the altar and pressed her down. Hark pressed a knife into Havant's hand, then nodded curtly. It was time.

Roxanne screamed louder as she saw Havant walking towards her, crying and pleading with him not to hurt her. Havant ignored her, even after she offered to help him overthrow her father and take the Goldenrod Lands for himself. She didn't know that her father was dead, nor that her husband already owned the Goldenrod Lands ... or, after the battle, that the remainder of her father's troops had pledged themselves to him. The Red Monks had seen to that!

He stared down at her naked body for a long moment, feeling as though he was seeing double. In one view, Roxanne was naked and lovely and very *human*; in the other, she was a glowing ball of energy, just waiting to be tapped. He stepped forward, feeling the energy reaching up towards him as he brought the knife down. Roxanne's screams cut off abruptly as the energy surged forward, dancing up the blade and into his body. The power rose ...

NOW, a voice said.

The presence grew stronger with terrifying speed, drawing on the power and reaching out in a direction Havant couldn't quite comprehend. Everything seemed to *twist* around him for a second, as if he were straining to accomplish a herculean task, then ... then power surged back in the opposite direction. The presence grew stronger and stronger, taking on shape and form in his mind. And ...

Havant recoiled in shock as he jerked awake, the scales falling from his eyes. The presence ... the presence wasn't what he'd *thought* it was. He could see it clearly now, a vast implacable force, so far beyond him that even the least of its thoughts was meaningless to him. He was a gnat in a storm, an insect crawling over a dragon's back, and ... he'd made a terrible mistake. They'd *all* made a terrible mistake. Hark and his comrades had merely been the first to lose themselves to forces beyond their comprehension. They'd been puppets. They'd *all* been puppets. And now they were no longer necessary.

The power kept growing stronger and stronger. There was no longer any *need* for sacrifice, not now; there was no longer any need to make offerings or pledges or ... the power just kept building, pressing down on his mind. He wanted to scream, but even *that* was denied him as the presence pushed down on him. Dusk was all around him, imprinting himself on the universe, reaching through the blood link to touch Emetine ... Havant could see, all too clearly, just what the Red Monks had brought into the world.

We were fools, he thought, numbly. *What have we done?*

He could see it now, in hindsight. They'd been offered what they wanted, in exchange for allowing the Red Monks to flourish. And they'd *got* what they'd wanted too. But it had never occurred to them to worry about the price ... perhaps they'd been manipulated ... no, he knew now they hadn't been controlled or influenced. They'd merely made the mistake of believing what they wanted to believe. The pressure grew stronger ...

... And then his thoughts just ... went away.

***

Isabella couldn't sleep.

She lay in her comfortable bed – too comfortable, if the truth be told – and tried to meditate, but her thoughts were too uneasy for her to concentrate properly. The sense of unease just kept growing stronger, no matter what she did. Guilt and shame and fear boiled through her mind, numbed by tiredness and the grim awareness that none of her training had prepared her for *gods*. She didn't have the slightest idea how to proceed ...

... And Lord Robin was dead.

The thought gnawed at her as she lay in the darkness. Lord Robin had trusted her, believed in her ... he'd kept her in the company, even after Big Richard and Little Jim had challenged her right to join them. Part of that, she'd been sure, had been him asserting himself over his men – no mercenary captain could tolerate his men trying to boss him around – but he'd also had faith in her. It had felt ... *good*. She'd never loved Robin, no matter what snide comments Big Richard had made, but she'd liked and respected him. It had felt nice to know that there was a place for her.

And now the entire company is gone, she thought, morosely. Big Richard had been warped by the Red Monks, then killed in self-defence. Lord Robin and the others had died on the moor outside Rupert. *I'm the last of the company*.

She sighed. Normally, enlistment and service monies – and bonuses – would be doled out to the survivors, but she had a feeling that both would be lacking. Reginald hadn't *quite* given up on conquering the entire island, she thought, yet they both knew that even keeping control of the south would be difficult. Earl Oxley might not believe the stories from the north – she had trouble accepting that *anyone* would believe them without question – but he'd known that Reginald had suffered a dreadful defeat. He'd have to start thinking about switching sides again, if only to keep himself alive.

Bastard, she thought.

She rolled over, closing her eyes. Perhaps, if she concentrated, she could sleep. But her thoughts were so jumbled ...

... Her eyes snap open. She is standing in the middle of a clearing, beside a glowing pool of light. Mother Lembu stands on the other side of the pool, a pair of black ravens perched on her shoulder. She is looking down at the water; her face grim, her eyes pooled in shadow ...

... Isabella knows that she is dreaming, somehow. The dream feels real, yet unreal. Mother Lembu is changing, her face growing older and younger ... it is hard to believe that the three faces are the same person, but Isabella knows it to be true. Mother Lembu's hands and feet are bound by chains, iron chains. She cannot move ...

... The chains weren't there before, Isabella thinks. But in the dream, it seems perfectly logical that Mother Lembu should be chained up without warning. The strange woman – the entity – keeps shape-shifting, her face moving from a young girl to a motherly figure to a terrifying old crone and back again time and time again. She tries to speak, but a gag rests over her mouth. Isabella wants to walk around the pool to remove the gag, to free the entity, but her body cannot move. Her arms and legs are frozen, yet she is unbothered ...

... She looks into the pool. A monster is moving below, deep within the water. It is immense and free and ...

Isabella jerked awake, sweat running down her brow. A dream. It had been a dream. And yet, it had been so real. She sat upright, feeling a conflicting series of emotions. She was angry, she was sad, she was horny ... she took a long juddering breath, trying to calm herself before she could act on any of her feelings. How long had she been asleep? She glanced at the window and made a face. The sun was glimmering into existence on the horizon.

Dawn, she thought, as she stood.

Her legs felt unsteady. She hadn't had such a powerful dream since she'd experimented with pleasure-potions, back in her final year at the Peerless School. It wasn't a pleasant memory. Her father had threatened her with a fate worse than death if she even *thought* about drinking the brew again, and he'd given her such a beating that she'd been bruised for weeks afterwards, but she'd already learnt her lesson. Giving her thoughts to someone else to control – even indirectly – could be very dangerous.

She pushed the thought aside with an effort. It was hard to escape the sense that the dream had been a warning, in some way. But a warning of what?

Get something to eat, she told herself, as her stomach growled. *And then you can start the interrogation.*

Chapter Thirty-Eight

The guard looked scared, Isabella noted, as he escorted her into Emetine's chambers. It didn't bode well.

She scowled at the thought. Outside the Watchtower – now gone – she'd never known guards to be *afraid* of their prisoners, even prisoners who might be restored to their former positions in the very near future. There was certainly no reason to believe that Emetine would be freed any time soon, not after she'd tried to kill the prince. Isabella didn't intend to allow Emetine to go free, even if the city was recaptured by her wretched brother. But the guards might reason that it was time to treat the former queen better ...

It didn't seem right, somehow. The guards would have been obsequious if they'd expected Emetine to become queen again, or even merely to be in a position to insist on having them punished for mistreating her. But instead ... the guard looked scared, as if he expected *something* to jump out of the shadows at any moment. Isabella gritted her teeth as she glanced around the chamber, half-expecting to see traces of magic or ... or whatever Emetine used to contact her gods. She'd given explicit orders that Emetine was *not* to be allowed to perform any rites. And yet, there was nothing.

Emetine sat on the bed, looking surprisingly calm and composed for someone wearing an undershirt in the presence of a strange man. It wasn't the nightclothes she was accustomed to wearing, Isabella was sure, but she'd been extremely paranoid when it came to fitting out the cell. Reginald would probably have objected if he'd known the full details – it wasn't as if Emetine was a commoner – yet Isabella found it hard to care. The prince might have problems wrapping his head around the idea of a dangerous woman, but Isabella knew – all too well – that the female could often be deadlier than the male.

"Lady Sorcerer," Emetine said, pleasantly. "How *lovely* to

see you again."

Isabella glanced at the guard. "Leave us."

The man scurried away, looking relieved. Isabella didn't like that, even though she didn't want witnesses. She'd given signed orders for Emetine's treatment, orders that should have absolved the guards of all responsibility ... although she knew, as well as anyone else, that a sufficiently angry former prisoner might choose to ignore the fact that the guards had only been following orders. And besides ... why would the guard be scared of an imprisoned woman? Emetine didn't *look* formidable ...

"My brother gave you quite a thrashing," Emetine said, as soon as the man was out of the chamber. "Did he not?"

Isabella's eyes narrowed. "How do you know what happened?"

Emetine smirked. "Do you expect me to tell you *all* my secrets?"

"I could have you killed right now," Isabella said, sharply. It was hard, so hard, to contain her anger. "The prince wouldn't complain if I told him you *accidentally* fell down a flight of stairs."

"And destroy your only chance of getting answers?" Emetine gave her another smirk. "I don't think you'd do *that*, Lady Sorcerer."

Her eyes seemed to grow brighter, just for a second. "You met *her*, didn't you?"

Isabella frowned. "Mother Lembu?"

"Is that what she told you she was called?" Emetine shrugged. "She has many names."

"What is she?" Isabella demanded. "And what did she teach you?"

"She's a teacher," Emetine told her. "And she taught me to see the world in a whole different light."

Isabella took a moment to gather herself. "How did you know about the defeat?"

"I heard it whispered on the winds," Emetine said, cheerfully. "I heard it humming through the air and echoing through the ground. Words sang to me as I lay on my bed ..."

"The truth," Isabella interrupted.

"It's all true," Emetine assured her. "You just don't

understand what I'm telling you."

"Then explain it to me," Isabella said. "Now."

Emetine smirked, once again. Isabella had the feeling she'd lost control of the conversation.

"I told you," she said. "Magic. *Female* magic."

"Explain."

"Women are naturally *better* at this sort of magic," Emetine said. She smiled, as if she was thinking of a joke. "But you, Lady Sorcerer, are practically a *man*. You have yet to grasp how the magic truly functions."

She stood, her undershirt flowing down to her knees. It would have been considered indecent practically everywhere outside the Golden City – Isabella had protected women who would have screamed blue murder if they'd been forced to show their ankles to a man – but Emetine moved as if she didn't care. Perhaps she didn't, Isabella reflected. Emetine had been a king's wife, whatever else she'd been. Lesser people were nothing to her. The guards were so far below her that she probably didn't consider them human.

"You can explain it to me," Isabella said, tensing. The sense of danger was suddenly overwhelming. "I'm sure ..."

Emetine pressed herself against the stone wall ... and stepped right through, as if the stone was somehow as insubstantial as air. Isabella stared in disbelief, then ran forward – and right into a solid wall. Cursing her own mistake, she scrabbled for the ointment and splashed some into her left eye, peering at the place where Emetine had been. She was walking down a long corridor ...

She didn't go through the wall, Isabella thought, numbly. The other world was growing brighter, pressing against the castle. Emetine's chambers were growing larger, the walls parting to allow the other world to step inside. *She went around the wall.*

Gritting her teeth, she ran for the door. Emetine would have to return to the real world at some point, wouldn't she? It was hard to escape the sensation that Emetine could just keep walking, picking her way through the other world until she could find a safe place to return home. She could practically *fly*, able to simply pass over walls and defences while Isabella was stuck on the ground. Isabella could see ghostly corridors and passageways opening up around her, intersecting with her world, but she couldn't see any way to *enter* them. Some instinct told her that *trying* would be a very bad idea.

The guard gaped at her as she ran out of the cell. "Go to the prince, go directly to the prince," Isabella snapped. "Tell him that the prisoner has escaped and tell him ... tell him to make sure the iron swords are passed out!"

"Yes, My Lady," the guard said.

He hurried off. Isabella glared after him, then looked around with her left eye. Emetine was clearly visible, walking down a long corridor that wasn't *really* a corridor ... Isabella reminded herself, once again, not to look too closely. There were *things* lurking at the corner of her eye, terrifying things. She split her attention, silently blessing her father for drilling mental disciplines into her head as she hurried down the *real* corridor. She wanted – she needed – to be close when Emetine returned to the real world.

This must be how she got out of her chambers, back when she tried to kill the prince, Isabella thought grimly. Teleporting was rare, so rare that even the most powerful sorcerers often didn't bother to ward against it, but this ... she wasn't sure where to *begin* blocking the other world. *How the hell do we defend against someone stepping through the other dimension?*

She ran past a trio of tired-looking maids, who gaped at her. Isabella barely noticed them. It was growing harder to see Emetine, as if she was moving further and further away from the real world. And yet ... she was also coming closer. Isabella's head started to hurt as she ran through a pair of doors and into a large room. The pool of water she'd noted weeks ago – back when the castle had been occupied – was still there. She could see *things* moving in the water.

Emetine materialised in the middle of the pool, water splashing against her undershirt. It clung to her skin, revealing every last inch of her curves, but there was nothing *vulnerable* in her. She looked ... transfigured, as if she'd changed while she'd been in the other world. Isabella remembered the impressions she'd taken from the Red Monks and shivered, helplessly, as Emetine looked at her through bright eyes. Anyone who walked the other world was vulnerable to its denizens ...

"It is time," Emetine said. "Farewell, Lady Sorcerer."

Isabella *saw* something unbearably vast moving through the other world, heading right towards the pool. Emetine *changed*, growing larger and larger, her body expanding in directions Isabella couldn't comprehend. She was a doorway, Isabella realised as she backed away hastily, a doorway allowing something far larger than herself entrance to the real world. The water started to steam as *things* splashed through the gateway, things Isabella's mind refused to comprehend. They were humanoid, but ... they weren't humanoid. Some of them wore recognisable livery ...

Lord Havant forced his men through the other world, she realised. The floor shook below her feet. In the distance, she heard something crashing to the ground. *He turned them into monsters*.

She felt sick. She'd grown used to aristocrats who treated commoners as if they were nothing, but this ... this was a level of horror that passed understanding. The soldiers were no longer human. Teeth, claws and inhuman arms were the least of it. Warped forms rushed towards her, just as their master emerged from the gateway. Isabella couldn't even *look* at him directly. Lord Havant hadn't just warped his men, twisting them into nightmares given flesh; he'd warped himself too. No ... he'd been overshadowed ...

Something is riding him, she thought. Her back bumped against the far wall. *He's become something else.*

A creature that – might – have once been a man lunged at her. She tried to cast a spell, but nothing happened. Of course ... her defences had already failed. The drain had been so bad that she hadn't even felt them go. She drew her sword – an iron sword she'd taken from the collection that had been marked for disposal – and stabbed the creature through the heart. It seemed to wilt, then collapse into dust. She had the strangest feeling of *gratitude* a moment before it died.

"Run," a voice said. The gateway was growing larger, tearing through the stone walls. The castle was the sturdiest building in the city, but it was already starting to crumble. "Move or die!"

Isabella swung the sword at the next creature – it flinched back – then turned and ran for the door. The world seemed to shift and change around her, the distance growing longer and longer, but the ointment let her pick out a viable route to the door. Behind her, she could hear growling as the enemy bridgehead continued to expand, more and more monsters flowing into the castle. She threw herself up the stairs as fast as she could, hoping that she'd find help and knowing that it wouldn't be enough. Secret passages were hardly unknown in castles – they'd found and blocked two when they'd searched the building – but no one had anticipated someone managing to bring such a large force into the castle. Prince Reginald's men were on the battlements or manning the walls, not patrolling the lower levels.

A scream echoed behind her. One of the maids, perhaps. Or a guard ... she wanted to turn back, but she knew there was nothing she could do. The lower levels were infested now, infested with so many monsters that it was only a matter of time before they surged upwards and blocked all lines of retreat. Once they held the ground floor, the end was just a matter of time.

She turned the corridor and practically ran into a small force of guards. They looked terrified. Isabella didn't blame them. The castle was shaking so badly that it felt as if the entire building was on the verge of collapse. She was impressed they'd actually stood their ground after the rout. Morale had been in the pits ever since Prince Reginald and his men had been forced to retreat from Rupert.

"Set up a chokepoint here," she snapped. The castle *had* been designed to cope with a prisoner revolt, although it would require an *extremely* careless guard to let the prisoners break free and grab enough weapons to be dangerous. Normally, prisoners were chained up at all times. "Use the iron swords, nothing else. They'll kill those monsters!"

The guards didn't even *try* to argue. Isabella glanced at them, silently gauging their ability to actually slow the enemy down for a few minutes. She doubted they'd last long, even *with* iron swords. The chokepoints hadn't been designed to defeat foes who could simply walk *around* the stone walls. She had a feeling that it wouldn't be long before

Havant – or the creature that had overshadowed him – would start doing just *that*.

She reached out with her mind, feeling for the wards, as she ran up the stairs. The wards were gone, unsurprisingly. Her magical senses seemed useless ... she felt blind, so utterly blind that she might run straight into a magical trap of her own making. It was a grim reminder that magic was feared, outside the Golden City. And why not ...?

A second group of guards was standing at the top of the stairs, aiming their swords at her. She barked orders, hoping and praying they'd listen to her. Thankfully, their commander didn't seem inclined to object to taking orders from a woman. But then, he'd probably been grateful that *someone* knew what to do. The bodyguards knew how to handle assassins and attacks on the castle walls, but monsters coming up from below the ground? Or slipping through the walls ...?

Prince Reginald was standing by his door, holding a longsword in one hand and a shield in the other. He looked relieved to see her, even though the building was shaking again and again. His senior officers were glancing around nervously, torn between loyalty to their prince and an overwhelming urge to run. Isabella didn't blame them. They might not know *precisely* what was happening, but they knew it was bad.

"Emetine allowed them access to the castle," she said, shortly. "The lower levels have been infested with monsters!"

A week ago, they wouldn't have believed her. Monsters? But now, after the rout, they believed her. They'd *seen* the dead come back to life, they'd seen trees grow legs and march upon their foes ... why *not* monsters?

Reginald raised his voice. "I want everyone armed," he said. He sounded surprisingly calm, despite the situation. "We'll make our way down to the ground floor and seal off the lower levels."

Isabella was impressed, almost despite herself. And yet ...

"We have to get out of here," she said. "They'll overrun the castle soon."

"Better to keep them penned up until we can call in the

reserves," Reginald said. A row of armed soldiers clattered up, swords at the ready. "And ..."

"You *can't* keep them penned up," Isabella said. "They can walk through the walls!"

A thought struck her. "I'll give some of the ointment to the men," she said. "Whoever has it should be able to see attackers approaching, if nothing else."

"Good thinking," Reginald said. "Now, *hurry*."

Isabella followed him down the stairs, careful not to trip and fall as the building shuddered again and again. It struck her, suddenly, that the ointment might not *work* for the men, that perhaps she should summon the remaining maids and give *them* the ointment, but she doubted Reginald would be happy at allowing the maids to join the battleline. He'd object to putting them in danger ...

They're in danger already, she thought, sourly. They were *all* in danger. *We have to get out of the castle.*

"I've got two companies rushing in from the walls," Gars reported, as they reached the bottom of the stairs. "We *should* be able to hold the line."

Isabella gritted her teeth. They didn't understand. Lord Havant could funnel as many men – as many monsters – as he wanted into the castle, simply by making them walk through the other world. They'd keep advancing over the bodies of their own dead, even if they *couldn't* simply walk around the chokepoints and appear in the rear. The castle was untenable. And yet, she could see the prince's logic. Out on the streets, it would be a great deal harder to contain the situation.

Except it can't be contained, she thought. She dabbed more ointment on her eye and looked down. Something immeasurably vast was rising up beneath her. She could *see* it. She could see the power flaring down the link to the other world, the presence imprinting itself on the real world. *Everyone in the city, soldier or mercenary or civilian, is doomed.*

"Here they come," a voice shouted.

"Stand your ground," Prince Reginald ordered. He moved from man to man, speaking words of encouragement. "They shall not pass!"

Isabella grinned, feeling a flicker of admiration. There were worse commanding officers, she supposed. And worse people to die beside. And ...

She reached for her magic, feeling it flickering and failing. Perhaps, just perhaps, she could do something. But any spell she used would fail before it reached its target. Even her reserves were failing ... *she'd* failed. Whatever forces Havant and the Red Monks had unleashed wouldn't remain confined to the Summer Isle. Alden and his allies wouldn't have any warning before it was far too late. They certainly wouldn't realise that their enemies could walk *around* the channel, or raise storms to shield themselves from view.

A thought struck her. It was dangerous, it was risky, but ... it might just work.

And we're dead anyway, she thought, as she reached for a sword. *We might as well go out with a bang.*

Chapter Thirty-Nine

Reginald blanched as he saw the monster.

It had been human once, he was sure. And yet, now, it was so inhuman that it was hard to see it clearly. He could see snapping teeth and weirdly-elongated arms and legs, but his mind refused to pull the impressions together into a clear picture. The only *human* thing about it was the eyes, which were silently screaming in agony. Reginald slashed out at the creature, the iron blade slicing through its head. It collapsed to the ground and turned to dust.

Sweat ran down his back as two more creatures burst up through the chokepoint, claws lashing out at his men. They'd already discovered, the hard way, that armour didn't provide any protection against the creatures. Reginald had kept his armour, but most of his men had ditched theirs as soon as they realised it was useless. Being hit, even once, was often enough to kill. He didn't want to *think* about the prospect of the bodies being reanimated and turned against their former comrades. He'd given orders to make sure that no dead body could walk again, afterwards, but his men had been reluctant to carry them out. It felt too much like turning on their own.

He cut the first creature down instinctively, then blocked a blow from the second. Gars killed it a moment later, covering his prince's back. Reginald glanced around for Isabella, seeing her muttering charms over a blade. He shifted slightly, moving into position to protect her if the creatures mounted a charge. The chokepoints hadn't lasted long, no matter how hard his men had fought to hold them. The creatures could appear out of nowhere.

Something – it looked like a flying brain – flew right towards him. He sliced it out of the air instinctively, then swore in horror as he saw a similar creature land on top of one of his bodyguards. The man's body twisted, his head bulging in unfamiliar directions; his skull exploded a second later, blood and bone fragments flying in all directions. Reginald had to swallow hard to keep from vomiting. He'd thrown up after his first battle, after he'd come face to face with the bloody reality that war was not all honour and glory, but this was different. Nothing in his life had prepared him for *this*.

The ground shuddered, once again, as a guard shouted out a warning. Reginald turned to face the wall, bracing himself. A creature materialised a second later, claws already extended towards its target. Reginald stabbed it instinctively and watched the creature die, then cursed again as blood splashed in all directions. As much as he hated to admit it, the castle was rapidly becoming undefendable. But retreat was likely to be equally dangerous.

And we have no way of knowing how the civilians will react, he thought. He'd seen retreating armies savaged by peasants and commoners who'd been keen to ingratiate themselves with their new masters. Or, perhaps, to extract a little revenge. Reginald had hanged rapists and thieves, but he wasn't naive enough to believe he'd managed to prevent *all* abuses. *They might side with us or they might attack us.*

He swore as he saw a line of tiny spider-like creatures making their way through the former chokepoint, scuttling along the stone floor in a manner that made him feel physically uneasy. They were moving faster, attacking his men from below ... he brought his sword down on one, but the others kept coming. They were tough too, tougher than they looked. He had the feeling that anything less than smashing them to a pulp would be completely ineffective.

"Get back," Caen shouted.

Reginald saw what Caen was holding and jumped back, an instant before his old friend splashed lantern oil over the spiders. The creatures seemed shocked, scuttling around in confusion; the oil appeared to disorientate them in some way. And then Caen lit a firelighter and dropped it on the spiders. The oil caught fire, burning the creatures alive. Reginald could have sworn he heard screaming before they died.

"Good work," he said. "Did you get everyone out of the upper levels?"

"Yes, Your Highness," Caen said. The building shuddered

once again, underlining his words. "The castle is empty, save for the defenders and ... and them."

Reginald made a face. There was no way to *keep* the enemy from materialising in the outside world – or from bringing an army to Allenstown and storming the walls while the defenders were distracted. Even if they didn't, he was too experienced a soldier to believe they could keep the invaders back indefinitely. They seemed to have limitless manpower, throwing creature after creature at his men ... he was all too aware that it was only a matter of time before his forces were worn down to a nub. His arms and legs were already aching. It had been far too long since he'd fought such an extended battle.

He looked around the chamber as another row of creatures appeared out of nowhere. His orderly lines were long-since gone. Men fought with whatever partners they found, watching each other's backs as they struggled to survive. The defensive position was steadily coming apart at the seams ... one good push would be enough, he suspected, to crush the defenders completely. He thought rapidly, trying to think of a way out, but nothing came to mind. If he'd been fighting a regular opponent, he would have run up the white flag by now. There was nothing to be gained by throwing away lives on a pointless last stand.

But we can't even surrender, he thought, grimly. He'd seen one of his men throw away his weapon and hold up his empty hands, only to be eviscerated by one of the nastier-looking monsters. Surrenders were not accepted, it seemed. He supposed it made a certain kind of sense. Why bother taking prisoners when you could reanimate their dead bodies and turn them into slaves. *All we can do is fight.*

He glanced at Isabella. She was holding a silver sword in one hand, a sword that glimmered brightly under the light. It didn't look dangerous, not really. He'd seen his men attack the creatures with steel or wooden weapons, but neither had had any visible effect. Cold iron was the only thing that seemed to hurt them and even *that* had its limits. He'd watched one creature keep moving even after losing most of its limbs.

The ground shook, once again. This time, pieces of dust

and debris started to fall from the ceiling.

"Sound the retreat," he ordered. "We'll take this fight to the courtyard."

***

Isabella wondered, as she held the silver sword in one hand and the iron sword in the other, if it was possible to overuse the ointment. The two worlds seemed to be blurring into one, confusing her senses until she felt dizzy. The walls were solid; no, the walls were translucent, completely insubstantial. The creatures were human, or had been human; no, they were monsters through and through. And the floor was both solid and starting to crack open as *something* forced its way upwards. She *hoped* she was overusing the ointment. The alternative – that the two worlds were actually blurring together – was far worse.

And the iron sword only seems to belong to one, she thought, as she followed the others through the entrance and into the courtyard. It was weird. She could see the iron with her right eye, but her left eye couldn't see the sword at all. It was as if her hand was empty, even though she could *feel* the sword. *I wonder what that means.*

Reginald barked orders as they emerged into the grey half-light. Allenstown was wreathed in fog, blowing down from the north ... it felt profoundly unnatural, even when viewed through her right eye. Her *left* eye saw faces within the gloom, little entities that controlled the fog ... or were part of it. It was hard to be sure. Water droplets stung her eyes, mocking her. They could win the battle, but not the war.

She felt the world *screaming* as the castle started to collapse, walls buckling inwards as if they were being twisted and warped by a powerful force. She'd never seen anything like it, not even when she and the other trainees had been taught how to cast immensely powerful destructive spells in their second year. Properly warded, a castle should have stood up to those spells, but now ... the entire building was collapsing in on itself. She wanted to pray that the debris would crush the creatures, burying the gateway Emetine had opened under a mountain of rock and stone, but she had a feeling that it wouldn't. The ground shook, one final time, as the castle disintegrated. Something *big* was moving in the ruins.

Someone caught her arm. She pulled herself free, spinning around ... she almost bisected Reginald before she realised who he was. The prince looked determined, but she thought she saw hopelessness in his eyes. There was no way to retreat, not now. They were trapped on the Summer Isle.

"You have to go," Reginald said. "You've got the best chance of hiding somewhere until the storms fade. You have to warn my father ..."

Isabella shook her head. She was damned if she was going to run, not now. And besides, it was pointless. By the time the storms faded – if the storms faded – the Red Monks and their master might have already walked through the other world and invaded Andalusia. King Romulus wouldn't know what was coming his way until it was far too late. She lifted the sword, bracing herself. Havant – and the creature imprinting itself on him – had to be stopped now. There wouldn't be any chance to stop him in the future.

"Take this sword," she said, as the debris began to move. "Stab him with it."

Reginald stared at her. "It's silver!"

"*Trust* me," Isabella said. "And give me your iron blade."

The prince stared at her for a long moment. She knew he wouldn't be *happy* about handing his blade over to anyone, particularly as it was the only effective weapon he had. And she didn't dare tell him the truth, not when she had no idea who – or what – might be listening. If he hadn't been a better swordsman than she was a swordswoman, she would have wielded the weapon herself.

Reginald reversed his blade and held it out to her. Isabella took it, feeling touched. He trusted her enough to surrender his blade, to allow her to watch his back ... she wanted to kiss him, all of a sudden. Very few people had ever shown her *that* level of trust, not even her long-dead mother. She wondered what would happen if she did lean forward and kiss him ...

The debris exploded. Brilliant white light flared up in front of them. A ... *creature* ... was standing within the light, a creature so strange that it was beyond her comprehension.

Her spine crawled as she looked at it, trying not to peer too closely. The creature was so fundamentally *wrong* that she thought she'd go mad if she stared for too long. Energy flared over its form, rushing backwards and forwards as it grew stronger. She could see the creature through both eyes, but the energy was only visible through the ointment ...

I'm right, she told herself. *I have to be right.*

"*KNEEL*," the entity said.

Isabella's legs wobbled. It took all of her determination to keep from falling to her knees and begging for mercy. There was power in the entity's voice ... no, more than just power, an unbearable *rightness* that tore at her mind. She didn't just *want* to fall to her knees, she *should* fall to her knees. The compelling voice her rivals at school had used when they'd wanted to make her do things, for a joke, was a pale shadow of the entity's voice. She supposed she should be grateful to those little bitches. They'd stiffened her defences against mental manipulation long before she'd left the city for good.

She forced herself to look away. Reginald was standing – she'd expected no less, even though he didn't have a magic bone in his body – but the others were either on their knees or looking as though they were on the verge of surrendering. She could *see* tendrils of energy moving from the kneeling men to the entity, as if it was feeding on their worship. It wanted them ... no, it *needed* them. She looked back at the creature and shuddered, trying to parse out its secrets without getting too close. It was wrapped around a human soul, a trapped and helpless human soul ...

Havant, she guessed. The Herefords had played with fire. Eventually, inevitably, they'd been burnt. She couldn't help a flicker of sympathy, despite their crimes. There were some powers that were never meant to be touched. She'd had that lesson drilled into her, time and time again, at the Peerless School. *Poor bastard.*

She touched the iron blade. The compulsion vanished, as if it had never been. The entity seemed diminished somehow, although it hardly seemed to matter. She gritted her teeth and raised the swords, ready to distract the entity. Very few people dared try to wield two swords at once, certainly not in a *real* battle. But it might just distract the entity ...

Power shimmered around the entity as she moved closer. She could *see* it clearly now, although she still didn't want to look too closely. It was surrounded by a halo of light, a light that called to her even though her instincts screamed in protest. A trick ... she couldn't help thinking of it as a trick, although she knew all too well that it wasn't. The entity was powerful enough to bend reality to its will.

"KNEEL," the entity said. *"KNEEL AND I WILL GRANT YOU MY BLESSINGS."*

The words crashed into her head with terrifying force. It was telling the truth, she knew; its voice was so powerful that it was impossible to doubt it. The entity existed outside the rules of reality – and magic – as she understood them, rewriting them at will to make *anything* possible ... as long as it had the power. She shivered as she remembered the old stories about omnipotent genies that had the power to grant wishes, wishes that inevitably left the poor fool who'd tried to cast them worse off than ever before. Perhaps, just perhaps, there had been something in the stories after all, a warning about a threat from the distant past ...

... But magic didn't make a person all-powerful. They'd just been stories.

"No," she said. She moved forward, circling the entity. "I ..."

Power lashed out at her, slamming into her body with all the force of a tidal wave. She flew backwards ...

***

Reginald had always had a very high impression of himself. It was inevitable, really. Save for his father, who rarely seemed to have anything like enough time for his children, there was no one with the power to tell him no, let alone discipline him. Fear of his father's discipline – and a steady march towards adulthood and *real* power – had taught him maturity, but he'd still thought highly of himself. It was enough, just enough, to keep the entity from forcing him to kneel.

He stumbled forward, feeling naked. A silver blade didn't strike him as very effective at the best of times and *certainly* not when cold iron was the only thing they'd found that could harm the creatures and their master. He could *tell* the creature was laughing at him, even as it slapped Isabella away with effortless ease. It didn't see him as a threat. And yet ...

Reginald felt a flash of pure rage as Isabella's body hit the ground and lay still. How *dare* the creature hurt her? He lunged forward, stabbing the silver blade straight into the light. The creature laughed – he felt the sound, rather than heard it – as the blade stabbed into the halo, then turned to iron. Reginald stared. What? The blade had turned to iron? No ... it had *been* iron until Isabella had turned it to silver. And the creature had drained the magic, reverting the blade to its natural shape.

The creature screamed, a sound that echoed through the air and tore at Reginald's ears. Raw power flared over its body, but it couldn't remove the blade. Reginald let go of the handle as the creature buckled, then hit the ground hard enough to trigger an earthquake. The bright light was fading rapidly ...

... And then it was gone.

A body hit the ground. Havant's body. A moment later, it crumbled into dust. Reginald couldn't help thinking, just for a moment, that Havant was *glad* to die.

He turned and hurried over to Isabella as his men returned to life. The entity was gone. Its control over their minds was broken. They looked stunned and horrified, but at least they were alive. Reginald barely cared. Isabella was all that mattered.

She was alive, barely. He helped her to sit upright, holding her gently. Her body was bruised, but she didn't seem to have broken anything. The entity might have wanted to take her alive, he thought. Or maybe she'd just got lucky. There was no way to know.

"It's gone," he said. The remains of the castle were unmoving. Anything left under the debris had been crushed. Even the fog was rapidly blowing away. "We won."

"For the moment," Isabella said. She staggered to her feet, leaning on him just long enough to stand upright. "But there are more of those ... *things* ... out there."

"And we know how to beat them now," Reginald reassured her. "We can do it."

Isabella, somehow, didn't look convinced.

Chapter Forty

"The storms have yet to clear?"

"Yes, Your Highness," Caen said. He'd just returned from Racal's Bay. "The sailors said they'd *try* to get a ship across the waves, but they didn't think *you* should try to make the crossing."

Reginald nodded, shortly. It wasn't as if he had *time* to make the crossing – he had too much work to do on the Summer Isle – but it would have been nice to know he could go home for a brief spell. If nothing else, his father had to be updated on the status of their latest principality. With the death of two earls – and the third pledging his full support – the Summer Isle was *his*. No one could take it from him.

Unless the Red Monks get reorganised, he thought. No one had seen a Red Monk since Lord Havant's death, but Reginald was too seasoned a campaigner to think they'd got them all. No, the bastards had gone underground to bide their time. They'd be back when the thrill of being a principality wore off and his new vassals started chafing under the bit. *And then they'll start to regain their power.*

"If they get the letters across the channel," he said, "it will be sufficient."

"One would hope, Your Highness," Caen agreed. "Can I set out for my lands tomorrow?"

"I think so," Reginald said. "You'll be taking a strong force with you, of course."

He studied the map carefully, noting where he'd placed his garrisons. He'd parcelled out the forfeited lands to his survivors, making sure to put the core of the Hereford and Goldenrod Lands in the hands of his most loyal supporters. Hereford's clients might have renounced him – rumours about blood rites and human sacrifices had made their way northwards with a speed a mounted courier might envy – but it wouldn't be long before the north rose against the south once again. Caen had a hard job ahead of him, yet it would be worthwhile. His lands would put him among the highest of the nobility.

"Some of the mercenaries want to go home," Caen noted. "Others want to find local women and put down roots."

"It will be a while before they *can* go home," Reginald said. The weather would make the crossing suicidal until March, at least. "They may as well make themselves useful."

He shook his head. He'd watched his father administrate his kingdom, but he'd never really appreciated just how much work it actually *was* until he'd started to administer a kingdom of his own. The Summer Isle had never had much of a bureaucracy, nothing to enforce the king's will and help bind the different counties into one. It would take time to put one together, let alone start building the road networks he'd need to unite the island. He'd have plenty of work to do until a whole corps of administrators was trained and ready to take the reins.

And then there'll be problems with my new servants, Reginald thought, wryly. *And even some of the newcomers will have their doubts.*

"I'm sure they will, Your Highness," Caen said. "I'll be happy to take more of them up north, if you wish."

"If they'll go," Reginald said. There had been alarmingly few volunteers to go north, even though the roads were supposed to be clear now. "Offer them extra money, if they'll go."

Caen smiled. "They'll want to be paid, sooner or later."

"I know," Reginald said. There just wasn't much *money* in the Summer Isle. Not immediately, at least. Given a few years, he was sure he could make the Summer Isle very wealthy indeed. "Good luck."

He dismissed his friend, then turned to peer out the window. Allenstown was starting to come alive, now the war was over. It would be a long time before the invaders and the locals became more than uneasy allies, but Lord Havant's defeat – and his crimes – had turned the population against him. His friends within the city had been driven out or killed as soon as the truth leaked out. It wouldn't last, Reginald was sure, but it was a start. Allenstown stood to gain a great deal from the invasion, if it played its cards right. He'd make sure of it.

And we have no idea what's happening on the far side of the channel, he thought, grimly. It was hard to believe that *anything* could have happened to his father's kingdom, but he was starting to feel isolated. The chill in the air was a grim reminder of things to come. It wouldn't be long before the winter storms started, freezing the entire island. *Who knows what we'll find when we go back home.*

He shook his head, irritated. The Red Monks might be gone, but his intelligence officers were still hearing reports of strange creatures in isolated places. Whatever had changed, whatever had been unleashed, hadn't gone home after Havant's defeat. He couldn't escape the sense that the world had changed, that the rules were slowly being rewritten, that ... he sighed. He knew what he wanted to do, what he needed to do. He was putting it off.

Turning, he checked his sword and strode through the door. His guards fell in beside him, one of them turning his head from side to side to make sure there was nothing approaching from the other world. The others all carried iron swords; a couple even wore iron bands around their wrists or necks, trying to minimise the influence from the entities. Not *gods*, he told himself firmly. They were powerful, but they were not gods. And yet ...

He stopped outside Isabella's door and knocked, once. She'd been setting up her own intelligence network, talking to girls and young women who fancied an adventure outside the big city. Reginald wasn't sure what he made of that, but between Isabella and Emetine it was clear that women were more than just mothers, daughters and wives. Come to think of it, he reminded himself as the door opened, no one had found any trace of Roxanne Goldenrod. Havant's wife might still be a player in the game ...

Isabella was sitting at a table, reading a report from one of her agents. She looked up at him and smiled, motioning to the chair on the other side. Reginald closed the door, leaving the guards on the far side. Isabella was more capable of protecting him than any of them. It was an odd thought, but it was one he'd come to realise over the last few weeks. And besides, he had his iron sword. He could deal with a handful of creatures.

"Kingsley found a recipe for a healing salve," Isabella said, as Reginald sat down. "The woman who taught him said it had been passed down from mothers to daughters for centuries."

Reginald nodded. "And does it work?"

"Apparently so," Isabella said. Her lips twitched, humourlessly. "But it *shouldn't* work."

"Maybe you need a leap of faith," Reginald said.

"Maybe," Isabella said.

She rubbed the nasty-looking bruise on her cheek. "What can I do for you?"

Reginald found himself speechless. He knew how to talk to courtly women – and he knew how to deal with commoners – but Isabella was something different. His mouth was suddenly dry. He knew what he wanted to say, but how could he say it? The slightest mistake could ruin everything? And yet ...

"Marry me," he managed.

Isabella's blue eyes widened. "Marry me? Why me?"

Reginald took a long moment to gather his thoughts. Any courtly woman would accept at once, without thinking; her family wouldn't even *think* of challenging her decision. They'd be too busy considering the advantages of having their daughter married to the Crown Prince. But Isabella was an orphan, as far as he knew, and she was a sorceress. She might have different ideas about the world ...

"You're clever," he said, finally. He hadn't been so tongue-tied since he'd had to explain a particularly stupid mistake on the training field to his father. "You're strong in magic. And I like you."

Isabella cocked her head. "And you're not obliged to marry to support the dynasty?"

"I have to choose well," Reginald said. "As a sorceress, you rank as a high noblewoman, so no one could challenge you on *those* grounds. And while you don't have ties to other kingdoms, that's as much an advantage as a disadvantage. If I married the princess of Azeri, I might find my kingdom dragged into its border dispute with Wadena. Or ..."

He met her eyes. "I need to marry well," he said. "And I like you."

***

Isabella had known, when she was a child, that her marriage would be dictated by her parents. Not her lovers, thankfully, but her marital partner ... the man who'd father her children. She'd known she might hate him, although she'd hoped they'd find an accommodation if they really couldn't get along. Their marriage was more than just a union between two people. It would bind two entire *families* together. It had been a relief, in so many ways, to realise that she would no longer have to enter an arranged marriage when she'd been disowned. And Reginald was offering her ...

She felt conflicted. She *did* like him, although she wasn't sure if she could grow to love him. Every single one of her former lovers had started to grate on her, eventually. It would be harder to leave Reginald if he was father to her children, let alone king of an entire kingdom. He was practically king of the Summer Isle already. It certainly wasn't as if his vassals could complain to his father.

An affair would have been fun, particularly if she could leave at any moment. But a marriage ...

It would be a family of your own, her thoughts told her. *Reginald isn't going to turn the children into bargaining pieces.*

But that wasn't true, was it? Reginald was the Crown Prince! He could no more give up the crown than she could give up sorcery. And he'd *have* to treat his children with an eye to the kingdom's future, rather than their happiness. Isabella had seen hundreds of girls – and boys – married off to satisfy their families, rather than themselves. Some of the marriages had ended well, she supposed. Others had failed and failed badly.

"I'll think about it," she promised, carefully. What would Alden say if his baby sister became a queen? "It isn't something I can just ... just *leap* into."

A flicker of something – disappointment, perhaps – flashed across Reginald's face. Had he hoped she'd say yes at once? Perhaps he'd expected it ... the gods knew that most girls would have leapt at the chance to win a prince. Their lives would be perfect ... assuming, of course, they bore heirs. Isabella had no reason to think she *couldn't* have children, but it would put a strain on their marriage if it proved impossible. Reginald would be *expected* to give her up if she failed to give him a heir.

"I understand," Reginald said. He rose. "But ... I can't wait forever."

"I know," Isabella said. Men could marry later than women, if they wished, but Reginald *needed* a male heir. A bastard son wouldn't satisfy *everyone*. Did he even *have* any natural-born sons? She didn't know. "And I do understand."

She stood, feeling a flicker of sympathy. Reginald had taken a terrible risk by asking her to marry him, even though no one had overheard. He'd put his heart on his sleeve for her. No one would know, save for Reginald and Isabella herself. But it would overshadow their relationship for the rest of their lives.

Reginald started to walk towards the door. Isabella hesitated, then took his arm, pulled him to face her and kissed him as hard as she could. He tensed in surprise, just for a second, then kissed her back. She smiled, inwardly, as the kiss grew more passionate. Reginald probably wasn't used to the woman taking the lead.

And we'll see what he makes of it, she thought, wryly. *Wife or mistress or whatever, I will never belong to him.*

She smiled and reached up for another kiss.

***

Later that evening, she walked along the battlements and watched the sun slowly dropping behind the horizon. Reginald had asked her to keep an eye on the streets and watch for strange threats, even though she'd made sure there was plenty of ointment around for everyone. The Red Monks seemed to have vanished completely, although she knew that meant nothing. They could just have walked into the other world and come out somewhere deep in a northern forest.

Or travelled all the way to Andalusia, she told herself. Reginald hadn't said anything to her, but she'd picked up on his concern. Who knew *what* was happening on the mainland? *We really need to find out as soon as possible.*

Isabella stopped as she saw a young girl sitting on the battlements, swinging her bare legs over the walkway. She looked to be on the verge of bursting into womanhood, wearing a long white dress that shone in the half-light. And yet, there was something *ancient* and *knowing* about her smile as she turned to look at Isabella. None of the guards below seemed to have noticed her ... Isabella didn't think they *could* notice her. She was invisible to them.

"Well met," the girl said. Her voice was soft and warm. "You're quite an interesting person."

Isabella felt her eyes narrow. "What are you?"

The girl stood. "We've met," she said. "Don't you know me?"

"Mother Lembu," Isabella said, slowly.

"*Maiden* Lembu," the girl said. "Although it is really just *one* of my aspects."

Her lips twisted into a wry smile. "You *really* don't want to meet the *other* one of me," she added. "Once you see *her*, sanity becomes a more challenging proposition."

"Oh," Isabella said. "You and she are the same person?"

"In a manner of speaking," Maiden Lembu said. She climbed onto the battlements and stood, glowing pearly white against the darkening sky. "But that wasn't what I came to ask you."

Isabella studied her for a long moment. "What *did* you come to ask me?"

"A simple question," Maiden Lembu said. "Are you ready for your lessons to begin?"

Epilogue I

She was going to be married.

Princess Sofia of Andalusia stared down at the pool of water, unable to hide the bleak despondency that threatened to overcome her. She'd banished her ladies from her presence at once, then walked down to the tiny garden that was hers and hers alone. Once, she'd seen a god amidst the trees and flowers; now, the garden was deprived of all human and divine contact. She was alone.

The missive from her father was scrunched in her hand, but she didn't need to smooth it out to recall what it said. The Crown Prince had not returned from the Summer Isle. All *contact* with the Summer Isle had been lost, save for a single handwritten letter her father had refused to show her. Women were not supposed to take part in ruling, he'd said, and dismissed her without further ado. A day later, he'd told her that she was going to be married.

She shuddered at the thought. The man her father had chosen might have many good qualities, but – as far as she could tell – they were very well hidden. He was strong enough to rule the kingdom, yet too weak to be a challenger to the throne in his own right. Sofia understood her father's logic – if Reginald returned, his brother-in-law would be no threat – but she hated it. Her prospective husband was easily old enough to be her father. Surely, a match between herself and his *son* would be a far better offer.

But the son has nothing while the father is alive, she thought, numbly. *He'd be an even worse match for me.*

She watched the waters for a long moment, feeling cold. Her fiancée was a renowned soldier, a great leader of men ... not a patch on her father or brother, she told herself loyally, but nothing to sneer at either. And yet, he'd expect her to stay in her chambers and do needlework – and bear his squalling brats – while he ruled her kingdom. He'd probably make sure that his clients got all the best postings and landed heiresses, just to solidify his power base. Reginald might be in some trouble if he returned home too late ...

... And there was nothing she could do.

She'd prayed extensively for succour, but the gods had chosen not to respond. And yet, what *else* could she do? She didn't know *how* to survive outside the castle. Running away wasn't an option when her father's men would track her down and bring her home immediately ... besides, where did one get *food*, outside the castle? *Sofia* certainly didn't know. No, she was to be married to a man she barely knew ...

The waters moved. She peered down into the murky depths, distracted from her bitter contemplation. The pool was barely deep enough for fish or she would have considered throwing herself into the waters to drown. But really, it would have got her nothing more than a ruined gown and a sharp lecture on ladylike behaviour. Her father wouldn't want her to do something – anything – that would dissuade the bastard from marrying her.

I could have a humped back and a scarred face and he'd still want to marry me, she thought, as she studied the dark waters. Something was *moving* down there, something impossibly deep. *I'd bring him a kingdom as my dowry ...*

She saw, just for a second, *something* deep below, then the waters burst up and around her. Sofia stumbled back, feeling her head start to spin. A young woman, a few years older than Sofia herself, was standing in the muddy remains of the pond. She was naked, naked enough to make Sofia flush with embarrassment, yet there was nothing vulnerable about her. She was somehow more *real* than the world around her.

"Greetings," the woman said.

"Uh ... greetings," Sofia said. She wasn't sure *what* to make of it. Strange women normally *didn't* come out of ponds, not in *her* experience. "Who are you?"

The woman smiled. It was the sort of smile that promised the world.

"My name is Emetine," she said. "And I think we're going to be the very best of friends."

Epilogue II

The Golden City was a wasteland.

No, Alden Majuro told himself, it wasn't a wasteland. But it *was* a backwater when – only five short years ago – it had ruled the world. Any of the local kings, princes or warlords could have claimed it for their own, if they'd been inclined to bother. But they'd seen the Golden City as the past and their own cities as the future. It wouldn't be long before the uniformity enforced by the Peerless School vanished like a snowflake in the seventh hell.

He paced his office, troubled beyond words by Isabella's letter. Even *getting* it had been sheer luck. The courier had collected the letter from a crew who'd barely survived the crossing, then carried it through three disputed zones and an outright *war* zone. There wasn't enough money in the *world* to pay the man for what he'd done, although Alden had tried hard. He could no longer push couriers – and lesser family – around.

And yet, part of him wished he *hadn't* read the letter. Gods and witches, entities and ... and *things*? Magic useless? Cold iron the only thing that worked? He wanted to believe that Isabella was playing a particularly stupid joke, even though he knew better. Isabella had been a bratty little sister who'd grown up into a bratty trainee who'd finally got herself kicked out of the city, but she was no liar. She certainly wouldn't have lied about *gods*. Even a half-trained magician knew the dangers of crying wolf.

He glanced down at the last paragraph and sighed in frustration. Isabella had urged him to check the Black Vault, but that presented a problem. The Black Vault had been sealed, along with most of the Great Library, when the Last Empress had left the city. And while he *had* checked the family archives, all he'd found had been a collection of blackmail information that was no longer even remotely useful. The people his father had planned to blackmail were all dead.

No, he told himself. *I'll have to seek my answers elsewhere.*

It wasn't a pleasant thought. His father had taught him to take control of the family, but the old man had been careful not to share any power as long as he'd been alive. Alden knew, without false modesty, that he lacked the fire of his youngest sister, let alone the sheer drive to dominate that had led their father to the very highest levels of society. Alden was an *éminence grise*, not a man of action. If things had been normal – if the Golden City *hadn't* been so badly damaged and so many magicians hadn't been killed – he knew that he would have been displaced by one of his more ambitious siblings in short order. The hell of it was that it wouldn't really have bothered him.

And yet, he had to take action. There was no one else left.

Gritting his teeth, he called for his servants and started to issue orders. There was no point in delay, even though he'd hoped he could remain in the Golden City for the next few years. He'd have to walk through the tunnels to Knawel Haldane and catch an iron dragon north to Ida. He had no idea what sort of reception he'd get, when he reached the mountainous kingdom. It was quite possible he'd be told to depart at once. The Last Empress didn't welcome guests.

But he had to try.

What else could he do?

End of Book One

Elsewhen Press
an independent publisher specialising in Speculative Fiction

Visit the Elsewhen Press website at elsewhen.press for the latest
information on all of our titles, authors and events; to read our blog; find
out where to buy our books and ebooks; or to place an order.

Sign up for the Elsewhen Press InFlight Newsletter at
elsewhen.press/newsletter

Bookworm series by Christopher G. Nuttall

Bookworm

Elaine, an inexperienced witch in Golden City, has her life turned upside down when she triggers a magical trap to end up with all the knowledge in the Great Library stuffed inside her head. Avoiding the Inquisition she tries to understand what has happened to her. But she is a pawn in the dark plans of one who wants the Grand Sorcerer's power.

Bookworm won the Gold Award in the Adult Fiction category of the 2013 Wishing Shelf Independent Book Awards.

ISBN: 9781908168320 (epub, kindle) / 9781908168221 (368pp, paperback)

Visit bit.ly/Bookworm-Nuttall

Bookworm II – The Very Ugly Duckling

Not every ugly duckling becomes a swan ...

In the wake of the disastrous attack on the Golden City, Lady Light Spinner has become Grand Sorceress and Elaine, the Bookworm, has been settling into her positions as Head Librarian and Privy Councillor. But any hope of vanishing into her books is negated when a new magician of staggering power appears in the city, one whose abilities seem to defy the known laws of magic.

ISBN: 9781908168382 (epub, kindle) / 9781908168283 (432pp, paperback)

Visit bit.ly/Bookworm2-Nuttall

Bookworm III – The Best Laid Plans

Elaine and Johan prepare to leave Golden City, with Daria and Cass, to search for the Witch-King. But Elaine is arrested on the orders of a new Emperor, puppet of the Witch-King. She must escape and destroy him. Privy Councillors and Heads of the Great Houses have bowed to the Emperor. Only Elaine and her friends can prevent an all-out war.

ISBN: 9781908168764 (epub, kindle) / 9781908168665 (400pp, paperback)

Visit bit.ly/Bookworm3

Bookworm IV – Full Circle

Until now the Witch-King had remained hidden as a lich. But Elaine was intent on his destruction. Bonded to the unknowingly powerful Johan, she was the only other magician who understood the deeper layers of magic. As they slowly made their way towards the catacombs in Ida where his lich was hiding, he had to rely on the new Emperor to stop them.

ISBN: 9781908168948 (epub, kindle) / 9781908168849 (416pp, paperback)

Visit bit.ly/Bookworm4

Now available as audiobooks from Tantor

Christopher G. Nuttall's Royal Sorceress series
Book I: The Royal Sorceress

In an alternate history, the principles of magic, discovered in the 1770s, saw Britain win the American War of Independence. Master Thomas, the King's aged Royal Sorcerer, needs a successor with mastery of all magical powers. The only candidate, untrained & unacknowledged, is perfect in every way but one: the Royal College of Sorcerers has never admitted a girl before.

But even before Lady Gwendolyn Crichton can begin her training, London is plunged into chaos by a campaign of terrorist attacks co-ordinated by Jack, a powerful and rebellious magician.

ISBN: 9781908168184 (epub, kindle) / 9781908168085 (400pp, paperback)

Book II: The Great Game

After the uprising in London, Lady Gwendolyn Crichton is settling into her new position as Royal Sorceress and fighting the prejudice against her gender and age that seeks to prevent her from fulfilling her responsibilities. But when a senior magician is murdered in a locked room and Gwen is charged with finding the culprit, her inquiries lead her into a web of intrigue that combines international politics, widespread aristocratic blackmail, gambling dens and personal vendettas... and some of her discoveries hit dangerously close to home.

ISBN: 9781908168375 (epub, kindle) / 9781908168276 (400pp, paperback)

Book III: Necropolis

The British Empire is teetering on the brink of a war with France that may, for the first time, see magicians in the ranks on both sides. As Royal Sorceress, Gwen will be responsible for the Empire's magical resources when the time comes. But her adopted daughter Olivia, the only known living necromancer, has been kidnapped. Intelligence soon establishes that it was Russian agents who took Olivia, so an incognito Gwen joins a British diplomatic mission to St Petersburg.

ISBN: 9781908168726 (epub, kindle) / 9781908168627 (416pp, paperback)

Book IV: Sons of Liberty

War! South East England has been invaded, and Gwen and the Royal Sorcerers Corps are helping to fight off French magicians and drive the invaders back into the Channel. When an inexperienced major disobeys orders, sending two hundred hussars to their deaths, Gwen compels him to sit down and shut up but, in doing so, permanently damages his mind. Afterwards Lord Mycroft suggests she needs to be less prominent for a while. The colonies are also under attack, so he sends her to New York to train the few locals with any magical talent. She sets off on HMS Duke of India, along with Irene Adler and Irene's new apprentice Raechel Slater-Standish, accompanying a naval squadron and a regiment being sent to reinforce colonial defences. But even before they reach New York they meet armed opposition.

ISBN: 9781908168986 (epub, kindle) / 9781908168887 (416pp, paperback)

Visit bit.ly/RoyalSorceress

Don't Look Back
John Gribbin

"A real scientist writing science-fiction with real science — what more could one ask? John Gribbin is a visionary, and one heck of a good storyteller."
– Robert J. Sawyer
Hugo Award-winning author of QUANTUM NIGHT

Retrospective SF short story collection from the master science writer
John Gribbin, widely regarded as one of the best science writers of the 20th century, has also, unsurprisingly, been writing science fiction for many years. While his novels are well-known, his short stories are perhaps less so. He has also written under pseudonyms. Here, for the first time, is the definitive collection of John's short stories. Many were originally published in *Analog* and other magazines. Some were the seeds of subsequent novels. As well as 23 Science Fiction short stories, three of which John wrote with his son Ben, this collection includes two Science Fact essays on subjects beloved of science fiction authors and readers. In one essay, John provides scientifically accurate DIY instructions for creating a time machine; and in the other, he argues that the Moon is, in fact, a Babel Fish!

The stories, many written at a time when issues such as climate change were taken less seriously, now seem very relevant again in an age of dubious politicians. What underpins all of them, of course, is a grounding in solid science. But they are also laced with a dry and subtle wit, which will not come as a surprise to anyone who has ever met John at a science fiction convention or elsewhere. He is, however, not averse to a good pun, as evidenced by a song he co-wrote for the Bonzo Dog Doo Dah Band: *The Holey Cheeses of Nazareth*.

Despite the exhortation of this collection's title, this *is* a perfect opportunity to look back at John's short stories. If you've never read any of his fiction before, now you have the chance to acquaint yourself with a body of work that, while being very much of its time, is certainly not in any way out of date.

ISBN: 9781911409182 (epub, kindle) / 9781911409083 (272pp paperback)
Visit bit.ly/DontLookBackJohnGribbin

THE GHOST IN YOU BY KATRINA MOUNTFORT
A first-hand account from beyond the grave

What do you do if you're dead but haven't 'moved on'? You keep finding yourself back where you died, with very little control over when; sometimes you can be away for days, weeks or even months, and then you're back. Between times, when you're 'away', where do you go, what do you do? You've seen some other ghosts asleep at their graves, but you don't even know where your own grave is.

The Living shiver if they walk through you, but they can neither see nor hear you. With practice you can pass through walls and doors, but curiously you can sit on a park bench without falling through it, climb stairs, even lie on a bed. You're stuck in the clothes you were wearing when you died, at the age you died. Waiting.

Then, after years of this intermittent existence, you realise what you have been waiting for, what it is that you have to do in order to finally move on. Just as you have found the best reason to stay. That's what happened to Rowena...

A haunting ghost story as told by the ghost herself, *The Ghost in You* is a first-hand account, from beyond the grave, by an innocent girl who dies before her time and tries to make sense of what is happening to her and discover her purpose.

ISBN: 9781911409328 (epub, kindle) / 9781911409229 (184pp paperback)
Visit bit.ly/GhostInYou

About the author

Christopher G. Nuttall has been planning sci-fi books since he learnt to read. Born and raised in Edinburgh, Chris created an alternate history website and eventually graduated to writing full-sized novels. Studying history independently allowed him to develop worlds that hung together and provided a base for storytelling. After graduating from university, Chris started writing full-time. As an indie author he has self-published a number of novels, but this is his tenth fantasy to be published by Elsewhen Press. The first instalment in a new series, *The Promised Lie* introduces us to new characters and new kingdoms in the world of his bestselling *Bookworm* series. Chris is currently living in Edinburgh with his wife, muse, and critic Aisha and their two sons.